EARLY AMERICAN MAYHEM

In Puritan New Hampshire, young girls vanish in a whisper of witchcraft.

In the misty Carolinas, an island of monsters rises eerily from the waters.

In New York, a lavish Christmas ball erupts in a nightmare of blackmail and murder on Old Broad Way.

In revolutionary Philadelphia, Benjamin Franklin's dog is slain and a stunning forgery thrusts the fight for independence into dire peril!

All puzzles to overpower the most astute modern detective. But Jeremy Cork is not a modern detective. . . . Here then, are thirteen tales of mystery and adventure drawn from the pages of *Ellery Queen's Mystery Magazine* and featuring the incomparable Captain Cork and his ever-present sidekick, Wellman Oaks.

FATAL FLOURISHES

S.S. RAFFERTY

AVON
PUBLISHERS OF BARD, CAMELOT AND DISCUS BOOKS

"The Margrave of Virginia" August 1975, "The Rhode Island Lights" September 1975, "The Bright Silver of Maryland" October 1975, "The New Jersey Flying Machine" November 1975, "The Georgia Resurrection" February 1976, "The Witch of New Hampshire" May 1976, "The Pennsylvania Thimblerig" August 1976, and "The Christmas Masque" December 1976 were first published in ELLERY QUEEN'S MYSTERY MAGAZINE.

"The South Carolina Cicisbeos" August 1976 and "The North Carolina Corruption" May 1977 were first published in ALFRED HITCHCOCK'S MYSTERY MAGAZINE.

Indeed for Kit

AVON BOOKS
A division of
The Hearst Corporation
959 Eighth Avenue
New York, New York 10019

Copyright © 1975, 1976, 1977 by S. S. Rafferty
Published by arrangement with the author.
Library of Congress Catalog Card Number: 78-61899
ISBN: 0-380-41772-3

First Avon Printing, February, 1979

AVON TRADEMARK REG. U.S. PAT. OFF. AND IN
OTHER COUNTRIES, MARCA REGISTRADA, HECHO EN
U.S.A.

Printed in the U.S.A.

CONTENTS

ONE

The New Jersey Flying Machine

DESPITE ALL MY carping about Captain Jeremy Cork's pre-occupation with the solution of what he calls "social puzzles," I must give him good marks for the winter of 1750. We had come to Philadelphia in November, and he actually took part in some discussion of future contracts for his ship, *The Hawkers*, and even read a proposal I had written out for our participation in a chocklit mill in our home colony of Connecticut. Not much, you might say, but if you had known Cork and worked for him as long as I have, you would see that it was as close to exertion in affairs of commerce as he would ever come.

Of course, Philadelphia kept him in good humour, for it abounds in fine taverns, coffee houses, and intellectual fellowship. However, I was very much surprised when he elected to spend Christmas there, for he considers New York the only place on earth to keep the holidays. But spend it we did, in grand style, at dances and feasts of all descriptions. I, for one, was quite content, for I find New York a bawdy place teeming with rascals.

1

It was in the forenoon of December 27th that he sprang his surprise on me. I was going over the account books in our rooms at Morby's in Spring Garden Street when he stamped in bundled in his greatcoat.

"Pack up, Oaks," he said, knocking the frost from his barba, "we're off to spend the New Year's Eve in New York. To miss it would be criminal."

I put my quill down slowly and smiled, wondering if he had drunk too much of his own Apple Knock. He has a great capacity for liquor, but only a drunkard or a madman would talk that way.

"Well, of course, Captain," I smiled. "If some angel is going to carry us there, I will pack in a trice. But may I remind you that this is the twenty-seventh and New Year's Eve is just four days away. Have you grown wings, sir?"

"I have a Flying Machine, and we are chartered for two seats."

My throat grew tight with fear. I always knew that wild living would corrupt his mind to a point of insanity.

"Pray, Captain," I said, getting to my feet to help him, poor soul, "come rest a while, and I will fetch a doctor."

He glared at me and growled, "Damnation, man, pack, I tell you! We are off at the stroke of three to-morrow morning, and shall be in New York three days later. Here" —he tossed a penny paper at me. "If you read Ben Franklin's *Gazette*, you would know what is happening these days."

I took up the newspaper and saw exposed this paid notice:

PHILADELPHIA TO NEW YORK
In Three Days' Time
Via the Flying Machine

The rest of the report described a wondrous stage coach system which would convey the traveller from the Sign of the Dead Fox in Strawberry Alley on December 28 to the Inn of the Blazing Star on the New Jersey shore of the Hudson, and thence by boat to New York by December 30th evening. Cost was 30 shillings for inside accommodations, 20 for outside.

I could hardly believe my eyes, and quickly opened a copy of the vade mecum, which lists all the major roads and taverns, and checked the table of distances. I picked up my quill to make calculations. Cork, observing me, said, "Eighteen hours a day on the road, Oaks. If on schedule, we will reach Trenton's Ferry on the first night by ten or eleven o'clock, and rest till three a.m. or so, then be off again for Brunswick, and then on to the Hudson shore."

"It is truly a wonder." I shook my head in disbelief.

"Why? All you need are some good roads and proper planning. Well, man, pack. We will move to the Sign of the Dead Fox this afternoon, and rest until departure."

I did not relish being jostled in a stagecoach for 18 hours at a time, only to go back to the torture after a scant four or five hours' rest; but I could see that Cork was intent on spending New Year's Eve in New York and intrigued by this new method of rapid travel. So I packed.

We ensconced ourselves in a room at the Sign of the Dead Fox, but I found slumber hard to come by, since I had slept well the previous night. Cork, on the other hand, has trained himself to sleep at will. He can even do it, when he cares to, with his eyes open. Around ten in the evening a knock brought a man into our room. He said his name was Zeb Laine, and that he was an agent from the Flying Machine Line. For my part he brought us good news.

"You mean there is no room in this morning's coach for us then?" I said, after he had explained the situation. It seemed the inside of the coach sat only six people, and Cork had bought the last two tickets. However, unknown to the ticket seller, all six of the inside seats had already been sold.

"You see, sir," Laine explained, "the ticket man saw four names on the passenger list, and assumed there were two seats open. It's really my fault, for I contracted the entire inside to Mr. Lovelace and his party. There are only four people involved, but it seems that Mrs. Lovelace is ill, and requires one whole side of the coach to recline on. I can refund your money or put you on the next coach, which will leave on the thirtieth. It's most embarrassing, this mixup is, but what can I do?"

"You can keep sick women home where they belong." Cork, whom I had thought asleep, was rising to his feet. Mr. Laine stood in awe as the Captain's six-foot-six frame shot up like a tree.

"Beg pardon, Captain, sir," Laine said. "I would accommodate you if I could. But this is Mr. William Lovelace himself, the famous actor just in from England, and he must be in New York by the thirty-first."

"Mr. Laine," Cork roared, "I am Captain Jeremy Cork *himself*, and I own two tickets for to-morrow's ride. I will not be displaced by a pack of actors, even though I enjoy the theatre."

"Well, they are not all actors, sir. There is a young woman who must be in New York on the thirty-first for some legal purpose or other, and there is Mrs. Lovelace's personal physician, Dr. Pritchard. What can I do, sir?"

Cork paced about and then turned. "You admit all this is owing to your oversight," he said, pointing a finger at the quaking man. "And, of course, you give preference to an actor because you feel him more capable of publicizing your new service. Now, sir, I am not without a public platform. You will refund our money and we will ride outside, atop the coach, for free."

"Good Lord, Captain!" I was aghast. "It's twenty degrees out there, and will be near ten by midnight."

"There are ways to fight cold, Oaks," he said with that tone of determination I have heard so many times before. He was going to be in New York for the New Year or die of exposure. Laine meekly returned our coin and left, and I was about to appeal to Cork's sense of pity for me when he was up and gone.

It was close to midnight when he returned, accompanied by a spare young man who helped him with an enormous bundle. The bundle turned out to be three bearskins. The helper was Thaddeus Horton, law clerk of the firm of FitzMorris and Payne, of New York. Horton, unfortunately, would share the seats atop the coach with us.

"It was my good fortune to meet the Captain in the public rooms below, Mr. Oaks," he said, helping Cork to spread the bear skins. They were all complete pelts, with arms and legs still attached. "My firm was too frugal to spend the extra ten shillings for an inside seat, and I feared I would freeze to death atop the coach alone."

"You travel on legal business, then?" I asked.

"If it weren't for the cold weather, it would be pleasant business indeed." He had a likeable smile, and was good-natured about his plight. "I was sent to meet and escort Miss Alice Denby safely to New York. I've been in Philadelphia for three days, waiting for the *Golden Rooster* to bring her in from England, and none too soon, I can tell you. One more day, mind you, and she would have lost her inheritance."

He explained that her late uncle had extensive holdings in the upper Hudson Valley, and in his will had bequeathed the entire estate to any child of his brother, Amos. If none appeared to claim it in person by January 1, 1751, all monies would pass to a young lad named Charles Potter, who had worked for old Denby. The executor of the will was the firm of FitzMorris and Payne, of Maiden Lane.

"They had London agents at it for over three years now, and were about to give up, when one of the agents finds this Alice Denby tucked away working as a seamstress in a lodging house in Sussex. Pretty as a picture she is, too."

I could see this young fellow was smitten, but I did not know if it was coin or contours that had raised his blood. By now Cork had all three skins inverted so the fur side faced inward. He then ran leather thongs through holes he had made at the edges of the legs, arms, and torso.

"Some Indian trick, no doubt?" I asked him.

"Many an Iroquois has lived through a snowstorm by this method. We will lace ourselves into these skins with the fur side next to our bodies. The friction will build up our body heat, and we, sirs, will be warm as mulled wine. Which reminds me, Horton, you had best go below and make sure the barkeep has three flagons of buttered rum ready for us before departure."

After the law clerk had left, I could see that Cork was thoroughly enjoying himself.

"You are taking this as a challenge, aren't you? Just to see if you can survive the trip. Good heavens, Captain, is it worth it?" It was a useles question. I have seen him swim a river in mid-winter, just to prove it could be done.

It is one trait I do not like about these native-born Americans. They are always testing themselves against Nature to see if they can win. And Cork usually wins.

"Take heart, Oaks," he said, gleefully. "We have good company. An actor for entertainment, a doctor for emergencies, and an heiress to fall in love with. What more could you ask?"

He was a little too jovial for a man out to spend 50 or more hours riding in winter cold, and I was beginning to suspect that the challenge of the trip lay not only in the physical difficulties we would certainly face. With Captain Jeremy Cork, you never know.

"Best keep your eyes open, Oaks," he said. "This may prove to be a trip of great interest."

Our breakfast was served at 2:30 the next morning, and, although not hungry, I stoked my inner fires with eggs, pork slabs, and sack posset. Horton joined us at table and proved to have a healthy appetite. I was in the midst of my fourth egg when I noted the arrival in the public room of a group of people who, I assumed, were to be our travelling companions. Leading the way was a tall, handsome man, who was hardly dressed for a rough journey. His red brocade suit and green silk vest were more fit for a ball. With him was a comely lass with flaxen hair, and large brown eyes that looked for all the world like a pair of wild daisies.

The second man in the party was a portly fellow of middle years. He carried a small doctor's satchel. The innkeeper spoke a few words in the tall man's ear, and he approached our table while the others seated themselves across the room near the fireplace.

"Gentlemen, sirs," he said with a low sweeping bow, "I have just been informed that my party has displaced you from the coach. It gives me great pain to see another creature inconvenienced." He stood erect again and folded his hands as if in prayer. "Oh, let me in some small way repay the offense. I, sirs, am William Lovelace, late of the London stage, actor, poet, orator . . ."

As he went on, I felt there was no need to tell us what we could obviously discern for ourselves. Cork surprised me when he asked Lovelace to join us for a drink. The actor accepted and sat down with a flourish.

"So you are off to New York with us," Cork said when the drinks arrived. The "us" dismayed Lovelace.

"Good sir—er—I thought it had been explained that my party had prior claim to the coach. You see, my dear wife took ill aboard ship. Nothing debilitating, but the doctor insists she lie prone during the trip."

"We have been so informed, Mr. Lovelace. We ride atop with Mr. Horton."

"My word!" Lovelace cupped his mouth as if to block his amazement. "Ride outside in this weather? My word, you colonials are a hardy lot."

"Is Dr. Pritchard part of your troupe, sir?" Cork asked.

"Oh, no." Lovelace giggled at the thought of it. "He was fortunately aboard ship, and is also travelling to New York. Quite conveniently for us, I must say."

"You open your show on the first of January, I take it. I should enjoy seeing you. In which theatre will you perform?"

"Well, Captain, you realize I have my choice. We shall see."

"Are you a soliloquist or is your wife part of your troupe, Mr. Lovelace?"

"A pure jewel of the theatre, my poor lass. But she'll be to rights for our premiere American performance."

"Shakespeare?" Cork wanted to know.

"Yes, of course. *Macbeth* and *King Lear*. I do hope I can find competent actors to fill out the cast."

"Be advised, sir, that every person over the age of ten in New York is an actor."

Lovelace frowned and then broke into a giggle again. "Over the age of ten—very good—most amusing. You know, you would make a wonderful ghost on the battlements."

"Thank you, Mr. Lovelace, but I have tried to avoid that role all my life."

More giggles. Everything seemed to amuse this popinjay. "Of course, we have something new to offer this colonial public. *The Gamester* by Moore, and a delightfully naughty piece by Cibber called *The Careless Husband*. Well," he said, getting to his feet, "good morrow, gentlemen. I must be to breakfast, for I am not sure when we depart on the swift feet of time."

Cork looked up and smiled. " 'Time travels in divers paces with divers persons'."

Lovelace looked at him with a simper. "Clever man you are. *As You Like It*."

"Act Three, I believe," Cork said.

"Well, well, well. I am impressed. I was led to believe I was about to herd with savages. Anon, gentlemen, anon."

When he was out of earshot, I said to Cork, "I never thought I'd ever see you pay court to a fop."

"Yes," he said, his eyes squinting at Lovelace's back as he crossed the room, "an actor can play many roles. Did you know that Shakespeare was more right than he knew? We are all actors on a stage, but some are better in their parts than others. Come, lads, we must get ourselves bundled for the trip."

It must have been quite a shock to the early risers at the Sign of the Dead Fox to see what looked like three bears tromping out into the stableyard. I must admit that the bearskin was quite effective against the cold.

The Flying Machine was truly a marvellous thing to behold. It was a giant apparatus of solid wood sitting upon wheels as high as a man, and pulled by four huge Palatine horses that stamped their massive hooves fiercely into the frosty ground in anticipation. A driver and a coachman were packing baggage at the rear of the coach as we climbed up to take our cold seats on top.

The party for the inside arrived moments later, with Lovelace dressed in a scarlet cape leading the way. Miss Denby followed in a heavy-hooded cloak, and the doctor brought up the rear carrying Mrs. Lovelace in his arms. She appeared as a bundle of clothes swathed in several blankets. There was noise below of the inner party arranging themselves, and then all was quiet.

The driver, a brute of a man, and well matched to the snorting horses he controlled, swung in his seat. "All in, all in," he cried. "Last call for New York. All in!"

He was just about to signal the coachman when a figure darted out from the shadows and handed the driver a ticket. The new arrival was a young man, or possibly a boy, and he took a seat behind the driver, well away from our position at the rear. "All in!" the driver called anew, and nudged the coachman, who blew three blasts on his horn.

I thought at the time how dramatic it all was, but hardly worth waking the immediate neighbourhood for. The sound of the driver's whip cracked in the crispy air, and we lurched forward into the darkness of early morning.

Two hours later, the sun came up over the icy Delaware River as we rattled northeast towards the Trenton Ferry. When we were a few miles outside of Bristol, the sun was at ten o'clock, and the secret of the stage line's efficiency became apparent.

We pulled into a small farm, where fresh horses awaited us. We were offered the comfort of a small rude cabin, where hot porridge was served at three pence the bowl.

Lovelace and Dr. Pritchard ate their food at a separate table, as did the mysterious last-minute passenger at another. The doctor then took a bowl of the hot mush back to the carriage, and Miss Denby appeared for what seemed her relief from tending the ailing Mrs. Lovelace.

When she removed her cloak, her fine angel's hair fell in a cascade about her shoulders, and I told myself that such a beauty need not be an heiress to find good fortune on these shores. I half wished she were a penniless child in need of help. I confess I even considered what it would be like to leave the Captain for another kind of life, and was snapped out of my reverie by Cork's strange action of tearing a button from my coat.

"What the deuce—" I started.

"You've been ogling that piece of frippery since she came in. Now you have an excuse to hold her in conversation, since Lovelace is going out," he said, handing me the button.

"Ogling? Me? Sir, I can assure you that I am quite capable of sewing on my own buttons."

Horton looked up from his porridge. "You're a clever one, Captain. I wish I had asked for your aid, or ogled her more."

"I should think you have had ample opportunity for talk, since she is your client."

"Not mine, sir. FitzMorris and Payne's. I am but a clerk. I barely spoke five words with her at the docks before Lovelace whisked her away."

"Yes, he does seem quite protective. Tell me, Horton, are these employers of yours good at their trade?"

The young man shrugged. "As good as any. Why do you ask?"

"Well, I am no lawyer, but I do know there is no need for this January first deadline. Once the girl was located by the London agent, and properly identified, all Fitz-Morris and Payne had to do was file a writ of easement, delaying the exact demands of the Denby will."

"Oh, to be sure, but there was some complication or other, so that it could not be granted. But there is no need to worry, for we will certainly make it on time."

The Captain turned back to me. "Are you still here, Oaks? On your feet, fellow, and ask the lady to sew the button on for you."

I was about to protest anew when he shoved me off my chair, and I had to stand erect to avoid tumbling on my back. I was indeed embarrassed, and yet titillated, to make my way over to that fair morsel of womankind.

"Good morning, Miss Denby," I said, bowing from the waist. "I wonder if you have a needle and thread I might borrow. I seem to have torn off a button, and the wind is a bit cold atop the coach."

She looked up at me with eyes that spoke poetry. "Oh, you're one of the three bears." She laughed in a coquettish way. Charming. "I'm sorry, sir, but I don't carry needle and thread with me. Perhaps the farmer's wife?" She nodded her head at the slattern who had served us porridge and was now clearing the tables.

"No time for mendin' and sewin'," she said gruffly. "You'll find some needles and thread in that basket by the fireplace. Two pence to borrow."

Alice Denby hid a grin behind her hand and winked at me. "Come," she said. "It's the least I can do after displacing you from the inside of the carriage."

I paid the farm hag her money and followed Alice Denby to the fireplace, where I removed my coat, and watched her delicate hands sew on the button. It was not the glow of the fire that warmed me as we talked.

"I am Wellman Oaks, Miss Denby. My associate, Captain Jeremy Cork, and I are men of commerce in these parts."

"He's the tall one, isn't he?" she said and then leaned forward to whisper, "Does he have Indian blood? I've heard most of these natives do."

I didn't get a chance to answer, for she went right on talking.

"I am acquainted with your second friend. I don't like lawyers much. In fact, I don't know why he insists on riding outside. I told him he could take a later coach. There," she said, as she bit the thread and handed me my coat.

"A thousand thanks, Miss Denby. I must repay you in some way."

"Good sir, it is nothing but a Christian woman's duty."

"Still, if your party would be good enough to join us for dinner when we stop for the night, I would be most happy."

"My, my, Mr. Oaks, how much you colonists are maligned at home. Here we expected rude huts and savages, and instead we find gracious men and good food. One thing that surely amazes me is your road system. If only the outlands in England could boast such convenience."

My head felt as if I had drunk a pipe of madeira at that lovely picture—the beautiful girl, the fire, the sewing basket, and me. My serenity was shattered by a sharp voice behind me.

"Alice! We had better board the coach," William Lovelace said, with no masking of the irritation of his voice.

Outside, the driver's voice was calling, "All in, all in!" and I hurried to get into my bearskin. Cork helped me with the lacing.

"Well, my lad, you'll hardly need this mere skin to keep you warm." I felt sheepish, for he had noticed my flush. "Then again, I may have to tie you down atop the coach lest you float on to New York ahead of us."

"Now, Captain, I protest this—this—"

"Hold still, Oaks, my Romeo, or I shall never get you laced." He stopped and fingered my newly-sewn button, which I shall treasure all my life. "Try not to breathe deeply, Oaks," he said with that smirk-a-mouth of his. "I give that button its anchor till midnight." Even though Horton thought him funny, I did not.

As we continued northward along the river, I did not

need the warm thoughts of Alice Denby to heat my vitals.
I was now aboil with rage at Cork's jibing. I thought to
myself that possibly the time had come for me to settle
down. After all, I have trod across the face of these colonies in Cork's wake for a number of years. Now, perhaps,
was the time for fireside and comfort. I am a man of good
sense and careful record, and would be an asset to the
upper Hudson Valley.

We sped onward past small farms and villages, and
watched the sun grow as gray and dull as iron. Snow
clouds started churning in the eastern sky like ominous
waves. After sundown we stopped again for another change
of horses at a farm called Holly Dell, where we bought
hot mugs of cider and thick pasty buns called crullers.
Most of the party were too tired and wagon-sore to talk,
and we all ate and drank in silence.

When I went back outside into the stableyard, Cork
was talking to the driver, who was saying, "You read your
sunset clouds like an Injun, Captain. I just hope it holds
till we reach Trenton Ferry." His name was Augustus
Broeck, which explained his adept handling of the Palatine horses. He had offered Cork a crooked stick of tobacco which he called a seegar, and they were sending up
an abomination of acrid smoke. "Keeps the skeeters away
in summer and the frost off your beard in winter, and good
for all that ails you to boot."

"Perhaps we should recommend some to Dr. Pritchard
for his patient, eh, Gus?" Cork asked.

"Might do 'er good at that." The brute let out a roar of
laughter. "Don't know how much she can rest with all the
joggin', though. It's enough to break a body's back, it is.
I hope you gentlemen can't hear me cursing the horses
back there in the rear. Horses only understand the devil's
language, you know."

"We have heard worse, although I think the lad behind
you may come away from this trip with a new vocabulary."
Cork blew his fumes my way.

"Oh, he's a nice enough boy. But shy. He had cider with
Molloy and me—Molloy is the coachman. But poor Molloy
thinks he's before the walls of Jericho when he gets that
blasted horn in his mouth. The lad's named Sam, and he's

indentured, bound for somewhere called Long Island. Now, I could take a boy like that, put about forty or fifty pounds of muscle on him, and in two or three years have him handling four-in-hand like they was kinters."

Suddenly a blast of the coachman's horn split the night air, startling us all. "Gloriation, Molloy!" Gus screamed at him. "Stop blowing that foul thing! You'll wake up the birds."

If the horn didn't, Gus's "All in, all in" bellow certainly did.

We were not ten minutes out of Holly Dell when the first snowflake struck my face like the *avant-courrier* of an invading army in white. The first assault of snowflakes fell swiftly in flakes as wide as mushroom caps, serving as the storm's cavalry screening the assault of icy crystals carried by a barrage of rising wind. So blinding was the rage of Nature that we could not see in front of the coach, and Heaven knows how Gus kept to the slowly disappearing road. So complete was this falling invasion that, within an hour, the horses had been slowed to a clumsy trot, with Molloy perched out on the crossbrace of the traces, holding a lantern before him in an effort to stay on course.

It was well past midnight when we finally came to the Pennsylvania side of the Trenton Ferry. Our troubles were just beginning, however, for a truculent ferryman refused to take us across. This invoked great oaths from Gus, but to no avail. It was only after Lovelace bribed the scoundrel with £10 that he condescended to ferry us to the New Jersey side.

"That rascal should be hung," I said to Cork as we waited on shore while the horses were taken over first. "Ten pounds indeed! It's highway robbery."

Cork accepts dishonesty as a fact of life, and he shrugged. The carriage, now without horses, sat helplessly on the ferry landing, awaiting its turn on the rope-pulled barge. Suddenly, Cork walked to the front of the coach, took the lad named Sam by the arm, and then abruptly opened the coach door.

"What the devil are you doing?" I heard Lovelace say.

"This lad's near frozen to death, sir, so make room inside."

I expected to hear an argument, but strangely enough, Lovelace showed some humanity. "My dear child," he said, "you are shivering. Come in, come in."

The entire portage took over an hour, and the snow was still howling when we started off again. Gus had told us that the Blue Goose Inn lay ahead about a mile, but it might as well have been a league, so treacherous was the way. At one point the snow was so thick and deep around the wheels that Horton, Cork, and I alighted to help lead the horses, while Molloy furrowed ahead in the drifts, serving as a weak beacon. Finally, we heard Molloy's voice cry, "There she be, to the right, Gus, to the right."

Cork tugged at the lead horse's bridle and pulled the beast forward, and we emerged into the stableyard of a large two-storey building, or so it appeared to be in its vague outline. Our clatter aroused the sleepers within, and candlelights started to flicker at the windows. I followed Cork to the inn door and he banged at it. Seconds later, the bolt was thrown and the door opened to bathe us in warmth and light.

"My God," the man in the nightshirt cried out, "bears, bears!" Before he could close the door again, Cork had burst into the room.

"Only in the sense that we are as hungry as our bruin brothers. Are you the innkeeper?"

"Thomas Joust at your service," he bowed. "You startled me, sirs, with those costumes. Are you with the Flying Machine? I thought she had holed up at Holly Dell. That you, Gus? Come in, come in all."

"You'd best bestir your staff, mine host," Cork said, taking over as usual. There is some strange power he possesses which turns innkeepers into kittens. He once said it is a mutual respect between good guest and good host. That might be, but I often think they do his bidding for fear of the shambles he may create if they refuse.

"We'll need two rooms for the ladies. Best make Mrs. Lovelace's below stairs, perchance the doctor needs hot water. And the fire, man, stoke those fires. Ah, here is the goodwife of the house, and quite a charming woman indeed." He was truly being ingratiating, for she was as plump as a pullet, and had a face like a plate of sausages. But her eyes twinkled.

Dr. Pritchard carried his charge to a room at the end of the eating hall, Miss Denby accompanying them. The rest of us took off our outer clothing and drew up to the newly-logged fire. The appointments of the public room befitted an inn on a main road. Polished mahogany tables gleamed in the firelight, and behind the bar was a fine array of potables. The rugged fieldstone walls were freshly whitewashed, and decorated with old muskets and Indian trappings of bygone days.

While we were resting, Cork returned with the inn-keeper's wife, tittering over something he had undoubtedly told her in the larder. On his shoulder he had a haunch of hung venison which he deftly spitted, and appointed one of the stable boys to the task of basting. The tavern clock said three and a quarter, and I feared that Miss Denby was in peril of losing her fortune. It didn't seem the proper time for Cork to be having a party.

The Captain then proceeded to make Apple Knock for everyone, the law clerk Horton helping him. Two serving girls hastily set plates, and soon we were all at table except Mrs. Lovelace, who had been fed hot broth in her room by her husband.

"How is your patient, Doctor?" Cork asked between bites of the hot venison slabs on great slices of rye bread.

"As well as can be expected, Captain. I don't fear for her life, but the cold and damp, you know."

"Not cholera morbus, then. I feared it might be, you just coming off the sea."

"Heavens, no, that would be fatal. More an ague."

"Well, I'll tell you we can use some trained medical minds in these parts. All that our doctors seem to know is amputation. Take this malady of Mrs. Lovelace's. If she were in the hands of some local devil, he would lace her with whisky and boneset, and call it a day. I hope you are using the miracle mithridate we read so much about?"

"The very thing, Captain." The doctor smiled through his chubby jowls. "You are knowledgeable in the medical arts, sir."

"By observation only. I read everything I can get my hands on, especially the Royal Society tracts. We may appear to be rude colonials, but we try to keep up. Is everyone out of Apple Knock?"

Horton said he would do the honours since he had just learned the receipt. Thomas Joust brought a bowl of mutton stew to the table and Cork bid the innkeeper to have a drink with us.

"I was surprised to see Indian signs in the area, mine host. Have you had trouble?" Cork enquired.

"Indian signs! Ho, ho, you are jibing me, sir. There are no hostiles round hereabouts."

"Truly? Must have been boys then, having some sport."

"What actually is an Indian sign, Captain Cork?" Alice Denby asked. I was pleased to see that she ate daintily.

"Trail markings, or indications that a track has been covered. Things like that."

"And you saw something like that to-day or to-night?" She looked frightened.

"Come, come, Miss Denby," I said to comfort her. "These tales of Indian raids are ancient history. Captain, can't you see you are frightening the young lady?"

"I am sorry for that, my dear, but I could have sworn I saw Iroquois markings out there."

"Now I know you jest," the innkeeper said. "No Iroquois have been this far south."

"Well, I can't argue it. Now for bed, sir. How many rooms have you, Joust?"

"Well, the sick lady has one below stairs, and Miss Denby the other. Then three above stairs."

"Good. The doctor and I shall take a room downstairs, Oaks and the lad Sam shall have one of the upper rooms, and Lovelace and Horton can share another, while Miss Denby can take the third."

"Isn't this a little high-handed, Captain?" Lovelace asked. "I can well stay with the doctor."

"Indulge me, sir, and keep a clear head for to-morrow. If the doctor gets no sleep to-night, you will be needed to minister to your wife on the trip."

"Do you think we will be able to travel in this snow?" Horton asked, pouring more Apple Knock, which was really not as good as when made by the Captain's hand.

"To be sure. Tell them, Gus."

The driver, who had just come back from the stable, gave a broad toothless grin. "Right you are, Captain. Your idea of using the four fresh horses and the four from to-day in the rear traces will see us through."

"Good. Then let's abed with a call for six A.M., Joust. And you, Sam," he said to the indentured boy, "keep your eyes open to-morrow, for you will see a man handle eight-in-hand, a rare sight in these parts." Gus bid us all good-night and left for the stable, beaming at the compliment.

All of us got up and started for our beds, but I cornered Cork near the kitchenway.

"I don't understand," I said with some irritation. "Why quarter me with a stripling of a lad who will probably cough or sneeze all night?"

He grabbed me by the coat, pulled me into the shadow of the stairs, and spoke in a whisper.

"Be quiet, man, you've got the best of the lot. As I told you earlier, keep your eyes peeled, for something is awry here."

"But I don't—"

"Shhh. Consider our situation. We have a woman who will lose a fortune if she is not in New York by New Year's Day."

"Yes," I agreed, mystified at his behaviour.

"Let me tell you something. Miss Denby is purportedly a seamstress, yet that button on your coat is not sewn properly, not as a seamstress would do."

"Then you think she is an impostor?"

"Perhaps. But we have more raisins in the bun. We have a doctor who knows nothing of rudimentary medicine. Cholera morbus is not fatal, as any medical student could tell you. And our Dr. Pritchard agrees that mithridate is just the thing for ague. Come, man, think."

"Of course, Captain," I suddenly remembered. "Mithridate is an antidote for poison. My word, the man *is* a fake."

"And that's not the end of our cast of double players. Horton is no law clerk. There is no such thing as a writ of easement against a last will and testament. A will is sacrosanct."

"And this fop, this Lovelace? What of him?"

"That's a point of confusion. He overacts the fop, but I'm sure he's a man of the theatre. He seems to be the only one who is telling the truth."

"And his wife?"

"Yes, but unfortunately we have not met her. Well, I think to-night will tell the tale, Oaks, so be alert. Now off we go, and if you hear my call, come running."

"You can trust to that, Captain," I said, and went up-stairs, while Cork repaired to his room.

I lay down on my cot with a heavy heart, thinking of Alice Denby, or the woman who said she was Alice Denby. I tried to use Cork's eyes and view her without emotion. Why would she lie? Then it all came clear to me in a flash. The real Alice Denby was Mrs. Lovelace! Of course, she was an actress, and the fake doctor was probably one, too.

Now I had the entire plot in my hands. Lovelace, his wife, and the "doctor" meet Alice aboard ship and she tells them of her inheritance. Then those three conceive a plan to do her out of her claim by substituting the Love-lace woman for the real Alice.

But would they chance murder? Not in Philadelphia. So they drugged the poor heiress, bundled her up as a sick person, then reserved a coach all to themselves and would have "Mrs. Lovelace" conveniently die along the way, with plenty of witnesses and a "doctor" to swear she had been ill.

I knew I must get to Cork immediately. I realised now why he had insisted on arranging the sleeping accommodations so that he would be next to the sickroom. I had to get up to warn him—but I couldn't. My eyes were like lead, and I fell back to sleep, telling myself that Cork had the situation well in hand. Slumber came quickly, and I could hear only the gentle breathing of Sam on the ad-joining cot.

The next thing I knew, I was in a nightmare where gar-goyles were pouring molten metal down my throat. I gagged on the brew and opened my eyes to find Cork ministering hot rum to me. Nearby the innkeeper's wife was doing the same to the boy. My head was pounding as I sat up and took the mug into my own hands. I could see from the sun's shadow on the floor that we were well into the forenoon.

"Have we all overslept, Captain?" I asked.

"No, we have all been drugged. Get up, Oaks, we have work to do. How's the young fellow, Mrs. Joust?"

"He's coming around. These arc strange doings, sir. Folks being drugged and kidnapped. It's witchery, sir."

"Kidnapped! Who's been kidnapped?"

"The sick lady, Mr. Oaks," Mrs. Joust said wide-eyed. "The Captain was right about Injuns, surely."

I was on my feet, shaking the dullness from my brain. "Cork, I have the answer to this riddle. The sick woman is Alice Denby!"

"I see you have been detecting. Well, come downstairs. A local Justice of the Peace has been summoned, and we'll see what's what."

I splashed water on my face and looked out at the snow. I could see that it must have stopped soon after our arrival, because it was no deeper in daylight than it had appeared during the night.

Below stairs in the public room, there was much hub-bub. A big, redheaded Scotsman, almost as tall as Cork, was sitting at the largest table, with everyone involved facing him. Dr. Pritchard was nervously fingering his mug; Lovelace sat sternly silent, and Alice Denby hunched in her cloak, although the room was warm enough. Horton's eyes were closed, as if he were still drugged.

As I made the last stair, I could see the reason for Alice Denby's chill. The door to the sickroom was wide-open, and the bed was covered with snow, which had obviously come in through the window at its side. The window was now closed, but the chill of the room had set up a draft, explaining Alice Denby's cloak. I refer to these scoundrels by their plot names, for I had no others to give them.

"Ah, there you are again, Captain Cork," the Justice of the Peace, whose name was Fergus Dowd, said, raising a red eyebrow. "Ye bound aboot like a rabbit, ye do."

"Forgive me, your Honour, I was tending to the rest of the party. The lad will be down shortly."

"Very well. Now, this is a fine kettle of carp to dump on a man during Holiday, but that's the nature of the work and office. Now, you say this woman was stole away by Injuns?"

"The Captain saw signs last night," Joust the inkeeper put in.

"I'll thank ye, Thomas Joust, to let these folk speak for themselves. Now what did she look like?"

"Heavens, Magistrate," I said in astonishment, "how many women do you think are roaming around in the woods?"

Dowd curled the other red eyebrow. "An' who might ye be?"

"He's my friend and associate, Magistrate Dowd. I would say the missing woman is small-boned, about up to my second shirt button, brown-haired, and most pleasant to look at. Is that correct, Mr. Lovelace?"

Lovelace looked bewildered and fumbled for words. "Why—yes—that's accurate, I guess."

"Ye know, Mr. Lovelace, ye are a strange cut of mutton, ye are. Don't ye know what ye own wife looks like, mon?"

"I said the description was accurate."

"So ye did. Now, when did you see her last?"

"I saw her last, Magistrate," Dr. Pritchard volunteered. "Just before I retired. She was sleeping comfortably."

"I see. Now, according to Joust, you were all reeling drunk last night."

"Drugged, Fergus," Joust said with embarrassment. "I said drugged."

Both red eyebrows went up. "I'll thank ye, Thomas Joust, to refer to me by me title when I'm about me official duties. Drugged, is it? Drugged, indeed. Could be that some sort of orgy took place here last night and some damned fool left the poor woman's window open, could it? Then you hid the poor soul's body away and dreamed up this cock-and-bull story to cover ye tracks."

"If you'll excuse the intrusion, Your Honour," Cork said, "but that would be unnecessary with a doctor at hand. May I have a word with you in private?"

They retired to the kitchen and returned in ten minutes or so. Dowd was grinning from ear to ear.

"I don't know what this gentleman's going to spring on ye, but he has given me the background, and I'm willing to let him take hold. It's yours, Captain."

Cork strode to the fireplace and faced us all. I knew it was coming, only this time I was ahead of him, for I, too, had solved the mystery. Yet I couldn't help feeling remorseful about the death of the real Alice Denby, whose body was probably buried somewhere outside in the snow.

"We will have to start at the beginning of the affair to put it in perspective," Cork commenced. "We have a young heiress rushing to beat the clock for a vast fortune. She is prey to all type of vermin, is she not? Let us assume she confides her problem to people aboard ship, and they take advantage of her. A sleeping potion, someone to play her part in New York, a private coach, a sick woman unseen by all but the conspirators. It is the stuff that good theatre is built on." Cork paused. "But not life, I'm afraid."

"But it is, Captain!" I said. "You have it precisely."

"Really, Oaks? Well, let us carry it forward a few steps. Where, then, is the body of this drugged woman?"

"Buried in the snow," I replied.

"You may have observed that the snow must have stopped falling soon after we arrived. The Magistrate assures me that there are no footprints about the grounds, and none outside the death window."

"Here in the inn, then. In some closet."

"No, Oaks, we will have to look elsewhere. But we have to look not for a body, old friend, but for a plot. Now, let us reverse ourselves and say that Alice Denby confides in honourable people who agree to help her, possibly for a price from her inheritance. It is not an uncommon story where people coming from England have found themselves cheated out of an inheritance by some skulduggery. So let us assume that Alice has been forewarned, by the London agent, possibly, and she seeks help from a group of actors. Now how would an actor conceive a plan to foil an attempt on the life of Alice Denby? By disguise? Yes, it fits the profession."

"I see where you are going, Captain," Horton said, "but where is the body if Alice was posing as the sick Mrs. Lovelace?"

"A good point, young man. *If* she was posing as Mrs. Lovelace. There is no body, my friends, because *there never has been a sick Mrs. Lovelace.*"

Cork paused again, to give us time to digest this revelation.

"Yes, a playwright or actor would use that device,"

Cork continued. "Pin the audience's attention on one thing, while another slips by. Our so-called doctor here was ministering to just what lies on that snow-covered bed—a mere bundle of clothes. You tried to kill nothing more than a clever actor's illusion, Mr. Horton."

The clerk looked aghast. We all did. Then Horton sputtered, "What are you saying, Captain? I was as drugged as you were last night."

"Sir, and I call you that for the last time, I do not drink from a cup prepared by someone I do not trust. You were too anxious to make that second batch of Apple Knock last night. I assumed that you would make a move, and you did so quite cleverly.

"You observed that the woman who called herself Alice Denby was a fake when she so clumsily sewed on Oaks's button. I made sure that it would not escape your attention by saying that the button would not stay anchored till midnight. Once your suspicion was aroused, you had only one conclusion left: that the real Alice was posing as the sick woman.

"But you were doubly tricked, young man. When I observed you entering the sickroom after everyone else had drunk the drugged Knock, you were convinced that the form on the bed was Alice. What better way to get rid of her than to open the window and let the snow enter? She would seemingly die of exposure, and you could then unmask the fake Alice Denby in New York and claim the estate, Charles Potter."

"Potter?" I asked. "The person who would inherit if a relative failed to appear in time?"

"Correct, Oaks. I would take him into custody, Magistrate, although he doesn't look as if he has much fight left in him. I'm sure the firm of FitzMorris and Payne can identify him and give testimony that he knew of Alice Denby's impending arrival."

Potter-Horton let loose a stream of vile names at Cork, which were quickly stopped by a sound clump from Dowd's fist. He leaned over the unconscious man and then looked up at us. "Cold as a cod, Captain. Won't ye go on?"

"On? What else is there? We have our plot. We have our villain. What's the more?"

I could have strangled him. "*Alice Denby!* Where is

Alice Denby?" Then I stopped. I could see he was testing me. "Of course. Alice Denby is Alice Denby. The lady merely played herself. The real thing used as a decoy."

I was truly hurt when she tossed back her blonde head and laughed.

"My dear fellow," Cork said, "you would make a poor playwright. We had a clue in the very beginning, when Lovelace accurately noted my quotation from *As You Like It*."

"Aha, I have the last laugh, then," I crowed. "I called Lovelace a fop, did I not? So we have our Alice in man's garb. Lovelace is Alice!"

More laughter at my buffoonery.

"Let me put you out of your misery, Oaks. May I present the real Alice Denby? Your roommate."

I looked at what used to be Sam, the indentured boy, who was now a comely lass in girl's clothing. I was mortified, not at being made the clown, but by the sudden thought that I might have snored in my sleep.

Cork later explained to me that the road was truly blocked, but that he had contrived with Gus to assure Potter-Horton that we would reach New York in time, and thus to force Horton's hand.

"And when did you catch on to the fact that Sam was Alice?" I asked him.

"Sam was either an assassin or a friend. The mysterious way he boarded the coach at the last minute and then kept to himself roused my curiosity. So when we were at the ferry crossing, I suggested he be allowed into the coach. Lovelace agreed quickly and even called him a 'poor child.' Hardly the way to address a lad. But the main point was: Lovelace would not have allowed anyone in that coach who was not in on the secret."

"And so you were on to the whole affair from the beginning?"

"Not entirely, Oaks. When we were told there was no room for us because some poor creature had to lie prone, I knew that something was amiss. As Gus agreed, that would be a good way to break one's spine. Then there was Horton's story, which to say the least was hard to believe. Surely it semed odd that a lowly law clerk would be so dedicated that he would be willing to freeze atop a coach when the person he was sent to meet had absolved him of the duty."

Well, that shows how little I really know him. As it turned out, we spent New Year's at the Blue Goose. Since Potter-Horton was under arrest for conspiracy and intent to murder, he was nullified as the inheritor of the Denby estate. Fergus Dowd assured us that his statement to the law firm would guarantee Alice's succession.

And so we greeted the New Year with Cork at the helm. We had the kitchen staff work double time and Fergus Dowd and his clan were invited.

My final shock of the whole proceeding was to learn that Alice Denby had married William Lovelace before she left England. They had indeed had a warning from the wary London agent to be on the lookout for foul play once they set foot in Philadelphia. The blonde beauty who had first attracted my eye was Mary Lovelace, the actor's sister.

At the stroke of midnight Cork gave us a toast. "The secret of life, my lads and lassies, is that, if things do not seem what they should, then take care to make them be what they are." We were all too befuddled to figure that out.

We cavorted till dawn and Cork did not interfere once in my dancing with Mary Lovelace. Instead, he made a great deal of Mrs. Joust, guiding her fat jolly body around the dance floor, and paying court to her with drink. There is no understanding that man. But you must admit, whatever he does, he does with style.

TWO

The Rhode Island Lights

THE AUTUMN OF 1736 was kind indeed to the coast of the northern colonies. Normally expected foul winds and fouler weather turned out to be a cool, clear sky and a placid sea lapping gently like a puppy against the eddyrock from Boston to New York. For the first time in 18 months, Captain Jeremy Cork and I were once again ensconced in our natural surroundings at the Oar and Eagle at Sea Bluff on the Connecticut littoral.

"Well, by jing," I said, opening the letters that had come by the post rider early that evening, "it appears that your social puzzles have produced some coin at last."

He was sitting at what he euphemistically calls his "work" table, absorbed in a newly-arrived book from England. He looked up and grunted a slight note of interest.

"You remember Squire Delaney of the Rhode Island colony?"

"Of course, Oaks. We helped him in the Narragansett Pacer affair."

"Yes, well, he has seen fit to give your spermacite candle factory in Warwick a substantial contract. It's rather astounding, though. What could he possibly do with two-pound candles? My God, it says here, 'For delivery to the Pharos at Point Judith.' Could Delaney have fallen in with some pagan ritual?"

Cork closed the book and looked up at me with that smirk-a-mouth he uses when he is about to jape me. "Perhaps we ought to refuse the contract. We wouldn't want to be party to the Dark Arts, hey?"

Now there you have it. As Cork's financial yeoman, I am patiently building him an empire of holdings that may some day make him the richest man in the Americas. However, it is part of his sport to ignore my efforts and waste his time in the solution of crimes, which he calls "social puzzles." He has other unprofitable pastimes which are not mentionable in Christian company. This present piece of sarcasm about refusing the Delaney contract was a backhanded reminder that I once proposed the importation of shrunken heads from Spanish America. I said, give the public what it wants, but he was against it.

"I didn't say 'Dark Arts,' sir, you did. I was merely curious about the use of so large a candle, and in such quantity."

"Actually, Oaks, I am guilty of bad imagery. White Arts would have been a better choice."

I looked at him querulously, and he went on, "Even in the absence of all the information, we have the thread of the tapestry. Where does the good Squire live?"

"In the Rhode Island colony."

"More specifically, at Point Judith, does he not?"

"Yes, he owns his horse ranch, as he calls it, and everything in sight."

"And does not Point Judith's recent notoriety bring anything to mind?"

"Of course, the shipwrecks! Four, over the summer, I believe. Shifting sandbars and tricky shoals, the *Gazette* reported."

"And here we have a wealthy, public-spirited man ordering immense candles—"

"A lighthouse! He's building a lighthouse."

"Or Pharos, as mariners term it. But if he is now ordering his light source, I would guess that the Pharos is already built. Now that is something I want to see."

With *The Hawkers*, the ship he owns but never sails in, away to the Indies, we were forced to make the trip overland, and arrived at the Delaney ranch three days later.

I must point out here that our party also included Tunxis, a tame Quinnipiac, who serves as Cork's shadow and as my vexation. Although he speaks passable English, the Indian always talks to Cork in Injun jabber, and a three-day trip spent with two men laughing over incomprehensible jokes is not my recommendation for pleasant travel.

I once heard a back-stair rumour that Cork was related to the Quinnipiac by blood. I would have no truck with that notion. However, when observing Cork's demeanour once he entered the woods and wild, I admit to some doubts. He and Tunxis possess uncanny hearing, and I swear their sense of smell is even better than their eyesight. Perhaps it is these underlying animal instincts that give Cork his reputation as a detector.

In any case, I spent three days ahorse with two boys on a frolic with Nature.

In a previous visit to the Delancys, I marvelled at the luxury of their center-hall mansion. It had changed only for the better, now sprouting another wing. This annex, I assumed, was to accommodate the issue of the ever-fruitful Madame Delaney. As we were to learn later, the Delaneys, having produced seven brawny sons, were now one shy of matching that mark with females.

We arrived at dinnertime, but were not in peril of taking pot-luck. At the Delaney table it is always pot-wealth. There was the normal complement of cod chowder, steamed lobster and clams, and, of course, great hot bowls of succotash and pork. But, good wife that she was, Madame Delaney also served one of the original dishes for which she is justly famous. On this evening it was a platter of succulent squabs, which were as curious as they were delicious. Under Cork's prodding, she told us that they were spit-roasted and basted with a pungent, salty liquor used in China, called sauce of soy. I know little of the Chinese, but their bellies must be content. Since Tunxis refuses to eat or sleep under a roof, he took his repast outdoors.

Later we were sitting in the drawing room with clay bowls and mugs of Delaney's usquebaugh, a potent corn liquor of dark Scotch-Irish reputation, when I brought up a point that had bothered me since we arrived.

"When we turned into your property, Squire, I could see two towers far off on the Point. Yet your order said a Pharos."

"Technical terminology, Oaks," Cork cut in. "One or several lights in one place are considered a unit, and referred to in the singular. I assume, Squire, that you have gone to the expense of two towers to give sailors a seamark that is clearly different from others along the coast."

"That and more," the Irishman said.

"Is it worth doubling the investment, just to be different?" I asked.

Cork refilled his bowl and said, "You'll have to forgive Oaks, Squire. He is a businessman, not a navigator."

"Nor am I, Captain, but mariners tell me it is worth the investment. Perhaps if you will explain it to Oaks, it will further clarify my own mind."

"Surely. Well, Oaks, you have certainly been at sea at night. It is something like waking up in a pitch-black room."

"I leave that to the helmsman," I said.

"And whom does he leave it to? Like an awakened man in a dark room, he can bump into things, not having a bearing on a fixed point. However, when our man at sea bumps into something, it is not a chair or a footstool, producing but a stubbed toe. No, my friend, his obstacle can be a reef or shoal, which can tear the bottom from his craft and send her under."

"What about stars?"

"Helpful in deep water, but when near a landfall, you require well defined objects ashore. Most charts are not well defined. The sextant is only valuable in skilled hands, and then, of course, there are starless nights. But we are digressing into science. The Squire has put up two lights to tell all at sea who might be off course that the two lights are Point Judith and nowhere else, and I compliment him on his public spirit."

"Oh, that I could accept it, Captain," said the Squire, with a moan. "But I cannot. The Pharos was built to protect my own good name, as well as the men at sea."

"Go on, man," the Captain said, squinting his eyes in interest.

"You might have read of the shipwrecks off these shores over the past year."

"Yes," I said, "the *Boston Weekly Gazette* mentioned them."

"But what they didn't mention was the ugly rumour that spread in these parts and which implied that I had somehow contrived to cause these wrecks for salvage rights."

"Did you salvage them?"

"Yes, Captain, the first one. But after the rumours I stopped. God help me, my eldest son is at this moment apprenticed to the master of a coaster. Would I be so callous?"

"Indeed not. But tell me, why do you carry the financial load alone? Other townships have raised Pharos with lotteries. Why not here?"

"The townspeople, like those everywhere, resent the wealthy, and feel they can't afford it. Those lottery-built lighthouses are near ports where a lighthouse tax is collectable. Such is not the case here. I bear the load, but alas, not out of public spirit."

"Tell me, Squire," Cork asked, "is there any suspicion that the wrecks might have been caused by foul play?"

"It's a perplexing question. The shoals off our shore are treacherous, and the sandbars seem to have shifted, so accident is highly possible. I have personally surveyed the surrounding waters at low tide, and I had a young fellow from Yale draw up some charts. When word got out that I was going to erect a lighthouse, a single one, all hell broke loose from here to Narragansett."

"But why?" I asked. "You would be protecting shipping by warning them away from underwater hazards."

"And away from Narragansett Bay, or so the dockmen up there claim. As Cork said, night navigation is tricky at best, and if my lone light was a beacon of danger, there was fear that a ship's master would steer a northerly parallel course to the light and end up in Buzzard's Bay, which would enrich New Bedford."

"That's nonsense," Cork growled, "and can be proved so."

"Captain, did you ever try to explain logic and reason to a group of more than three or four men? Especially on a technical subject?"

"Touché," Cork said, with a smile.

"Well, how do two lighthouses solve the problem?" I asked.

"The Yale student suggested it. Our charts show that a deep channel cuts through the shoals. If a means could be found to guide a ship through it at night, a master could safely change from a northerly course to a westerly line, go through the channel, and then swing northeast towards Narragansett."

"Aha." Cork slapped his knee and tossed his head back. "I should have seen it at once when I noticed that the two towers are not in parallel line. The second tower is set back, is it not?"

"Twenty-five feet."

"So you have not only a distinctive seamark, but a unique navigation aid. You present the sailor with a simple light-in-one sighting."

"That's precisely the term John Knox, the student, used."

Following this discussion was becoming as difficult as listening to Cork and Tunxis talk Injun. "Forgive me, gentlemen," I said, "but this is all beyond me."

"Shall I explain, Squire?"

"Pray do. I barely understand it myself."

"Probably because the academician likes to cloak his knowledge in long words. Actually, a light-in-one sighting is simple, but it is more easily demonstrated than explained. May I conduct an experiment for Oaks here so that he might understand?"

The Squire seemed delighted with the entertainment, and Cork set to it. "First, Oaks, you will go into that closet on the far wall. When you emerge, the room will be in darkness except for these two candles, which will be burning on the table to represent the two towers on the Point.

"Now, when you emerge from the closet, you will be facing north, and the floor area in front of you will be cleared of all furniture. This will represent the safety of deep water. Now, as you walk due north, keep your eye on the candles. At a certain point, you will see the two lights start to merge into one. It is no illusion, Oaks. The lights really aren't moving, *you* are. Now the trick is to get you to change to a westerly course. That would be to your left, and bring you forward without breaking your neck on the stools I will have scattered there to represent the shoals."

"Captain," I said suspiciously, "I don't mind barked shins, but a broken neck?"

"Have faith in the system, Oaks, as must the mariner. When the lights merge into one, you will turn to your left and proceed so through the aisle I will have made between the stools, to represent the deep channel. Now I have a question, Squire. Are the lanterns designed to emit light on a 180-degree radius?"

"Yes, that's the reason for the immense candles."

"To be sure. So when Oaks is safely through the aisle, he will again see two lights."

"Correct."

"Then you have nothing to fear, Oaks. Now into the closet while I scale the mathematics to fit our simplified situation in this room. Well, come, my boy, you will be just as safe as in your own bed."

On Cork's guarantee I left my dark closet and entered the room. The candles burned brightly on the table to my left, and I gingerly walked forward. I was amazed to see the candles appear to move, and when they merged into one, I turned left with some trepidation. To my surprise all went well, and when the candles were two again, I turned north again.

"Amazing," I said after the other tapers were lit and the furniture put back to rights.

"Well, you must appreciate that this was a crude example of how a light-in-one works," Cork said, taking some more usquebaugh. "This student, this Knox fellow, has obviously made precise calculations, to place the lights in their proper positions."

"He was at it for weeks, spending nights out in a skiff while my son Secundus and I lit fires from rude poles placed ashore at different angles and heights. Once we had the proper mathematics, we started construction. In the last three weeks of operation we personally have traversed the channel at least fifty times. Three ships' masters have also taken their crafts through successfully.

"Copies of the charts were sent to all the major ports to the south and the harbourmasters have written back that they have made the information known to north-bound ships."

"And what of fog or heavy rain?" I asked.

"I am sorry to say that the lights are useless in foul weather, but we have tried to overcome that weakness by firing a star rocket every hour on the hour. At least it will be some warning, and will keep the taint of malicious rumour from my good name. Being accused of placing false lights to lure ships upon the rocks is a heinous charge."

"And punishable by death under Admiralty Law," Cork added with a note of grimness. "But it seems your troubles are over. Is John Knox still with you? I should like to meet him."

"To be sure. He is manning Tower One, while Secundus is in Tower Two. We have decided to hire keepers, but not for a while."

I smiled to myself at the Squire's penchant for naming things by number. A less precise man would have called the first tower the forward tower, and the second the aft, or rear, tower. But what could you expect from a man who had named his seven sons Primus, Secundus, Tertius, and so on? He once told me that he originally had planned to use the names of the Apostles, but was forewarned by his wife that he was overreaching himself. The female Delaneys were being named for the nine Muses. The Squire is clearly a man of stern determination.

"So, my lads," he said, raising his mug, "I give you the Point Judith Pharos, long may it shine." As he said it, Delaney walked to a large bow window and threw back the drapes. "There are my beauties," he said and raised his glass anew.

Out in the distance, through a starless night, were the dark landsides of the towers, eerie halos of light radiating above their silhouettes as their fiery faces shone out to sea. As we watched the halos glistening, Cork explained that the halo was called a corona, and the rears of the lanterns were much like a view from the dark side of the moon.

Then suddenly a toll of bells and the wail of handhorns sounded off in the distance.

"Why, it's like New Year's Eve," I said, jokingly. Cork touched my arm and cocked his head into the sounds. He turned and looked at the Squire, who was white with fear.

"Oh, God," Delaney said, lips trembling, "a shipwreck!"

The ensuing hours of that horror-filled night will never be erased from my memory. Out in the darkness lay a sinking ship, its timbers grinding chillingly like the broken spine of a wounded and thrashing beast. Small boats with survivors bobbled in the surf as citizens from the surrounding countryside rushed to aid them. It was near dawn when the last of the longboats dispatched from shore returned from a sweep of the wreck area.

As the longboat was hauled onto the beach, the last survivors tumbled out. One was a young sailor of no more than 20. His hand was bleeding, and one of the countrymen came forward to help him. As he lifted the lad to carry him, he cried out in anger, "It's Primus Delaney, it is. The old devil Squire is at it again!"

By noon the Squire and Primus had been placed under arrest and locked in the brig of a Royal Frigate in Narragansett harbour. The charges were barratry, collusion to shipwreck, and murder, since three hands were lost in the tragedy. The towers were closed by Royal Navy order, and the Delaney household was in chaos.

Before the two Delaneys were clapped in irons, however, Cork was able to piece together the gist of what had happened at sea.

The doomed ship was the *Queen of Tortuga*, out of New York, bound for Narragansett. Her master, who was injured but alive, was Captain Amos Whittleby. At the time of the wreck he had been below deck, having left Primus as the watch officer, and helmsman Fergus Kirk at the wheel.

According to Primus, he had been given charts of his father's new enterprise and was anxious to use the navigation aid. On sighting the two beacons, he sounded the ship's bell and ordered Kirk into the channel-crossing manoeuvre.

"The lights were joining beautifully," he told us earlier that morning, while being fed hot broth by his mother. All the survivors had been taken to the Delancy home for care, but it was obvious that most of the crew were suspicious and angry. "I kept the lights in sight until they were one, and then told the helmsman to bring her into the west. All went well, and when the lights started to part again, I thought we were through the channel. In fact, I could see the fore and aft lights of a smaller craft still further west. I was about to order us back north, when the crunch of the bottom came, and—well, after that it was hell."

"And now, in broad daylight," Cork said at the time, "we can see that the wreck lies hundreds of feet from the entrance of the channel. So you were on a dead heading for the shoal all the time."

"Yet I couldn't have mistaken the lights' merge, Captain Cork. Fergus Kirk can tell you the same thing."

But it seemed the helmsman couldn't.

"Aye, the boy may be telling the truth," the Scotsman told us later. "I kept my eyes peeled to the compass, and could nae say what the lights done. This I do ken, sirs. No wee laddie should have say on the course of a bark under sail."

Cork interrogated the rest of the crew, but at the time of the wreck all were at meal or asleep in the fo'c'sle. A second hand on the night watch admitted to being asleep on the forward hatch. The others on the watch were lost in the disaster.

Captain Whittleby refused to answer any questions, and replaced cooperation with threats and castigation.

"You have one of two choices, Captain Cork," he snarled as his battered head was being bandaged by a crewman. "Either the light scheme is faulty, or the boy was derelict in his duty. In either case, one of the Delaneys will swing for it, and I want to be there to see the execution."

"We are assured the lights were operating properly, and the system has been tested time and again, Captain Whittleby," Cork had said with some annoyance. "But while we are speaking of dereliction, may I ask why the youngest mate in your crew was given command of the ship in a difficult passage? Surely you should have been on deck, or at the least your first mate."

"The setting of watches is my own business, Captain Cork, and I resent the accusation of dereliction. Why wouldn't I trust young Delaney? He was in home waters and following his father's charts. And I'm sure, if you are a mariner, you well know the youngest eyes and ears in the crew are called on when needed in a rough crossing."

"Then you admit to a rough crossing."

"He admits to nothing, sir." The speaker was the local man who had helped young Primus from the boat. His name was Myles Swaith, and he was truly no friend of the Delaneys. "I have heard of your reputation, Captain Cork —how you are able to twist and contort things to fit your own ends. But not this time. Delaney has lorded it over this vicinity for years, but now he's for it, and there's no help for him."

"There really isn't, you know," I said to Cork when we left the room. "We ourselves are witness to the lighthouses working, and if Knox's calculations are correct, then it's error on Primus's part. But if the calculations are wrong, it's the Squire's neck."

"Yes," Cork said, stroking his barba in thought, "but when you have spent time at sea, Oaks, you learn not to trust the surface of the waves. It's what's below that counts. Let's talk to Knox and Secundus."

The lighthouse keepers were in a bedroom on the second floor. John Knox was in his mid-twenties, with flaxen blond hair and an aquiline nose. Secundus Delaney needed no description once you had seen the Squire or any of his offspring. The same red hair and round pixie face. It was as if they had all come from the same mould, which, when you thought about it, was precisely the case.

Knox sat in a chair with his head in his hands. Secundus, a lad of 18, lay despondently on the bed.

"I can't believe it, Captain," Knox said after we had introduced ourselves. "I am positive of my calculations. We tested them over and over again. If anyone should be blamed, it should be me."

"That's not true," Secundus said, getting up and patting his friend's shoulder. "My father and I have also used the system, and we know it works. And several ships' masters have done the same."

"All it proves is that your brother made an error," Knox said. "So what does that solve?"

"Mr. Knox," Cork broke in, "self-pity is a poor companion in dire straits. The Squire tells me that copies of the charts were sent to harbourmasters of all major ports to the south. Did you draw those charts?"

"Why, yes, I did. Oh, I see what you mean. I must have made an error on one of them, and somehow it got to New York and on to the *Queen of Tortuga*. Then I *am* to blame!"

"Possibly. But there is another aspect. The New York chart could have been changed. How were they sent?"

"By coaster, sir," Secundus explained, "out of 'Gansett. It was the quickest way."

"And Primus' copy of the chart went down with the *Queen of Tortuga*. How fortunate." Cork smiled.

"Fortunate?" Knox looked perplexed.

"Fortunate for Primus' neck. I believe there will be a trial, and I plan to defend him. I have that right, as a ship's master and owner. Now we have a point of doubt in our favour. If the Court will accept the argument that the chart could have been changed—ever so slightly, for a jot on a chart is hundreds of yards at sea—then we introduce the possibility of collusion from a third party."

Knox's face took on brightness for the first time. "Why, I never thought of that. But wait, Captain, the harbourmaster at New York—wouldn't he know?"

"I doubt that he would remember. Most seamen do not memorize charts they will never use."

Secundus smacked his hands together and let out a howl of glee. "Captain, sir, you're a marvel," he cried.

There was a commotion downstairs, and we all went down to find Primus and his father chained together and guarded by six towering Royal Marines. An English Captain named Cricker read formal charges and led the men away over the shrieks and wails of the Delaney women.

The rest of the day was spent within the legal machinery in preparation for a naval inquiry. Once in the town of Narragansett, we called on a local lawyer of some reputation. Giles Pomfret was an old eagle, trained in the Inns of Court, and regarded as a sound scholar. His offices were on the second floor of the Blue Whale, and after an explanation of the situation he sat back slowly touching the fingers of one hand to the other.

"I bow to you, Captain, in marine law, but this doubt-casting element about a chart being mysteriously changed —well, it is a thin line, sir. A very thin line, indeed, since the chart itself is fathoms down."

"That is only my first line, Mr. Pomfret, and I think you will agree that a good defense is the sum of many ramparts."

The old man nodded and then smiled. "To show you how ill equipped I am for the case, when you first said 'barratry,' my mind immediately went to the civil-law interpretation—the habitual maintenance of lawsuits or quarrels. Now in marine law, it means to sink a ship, does it not?"

"Technically, it is the use of fraud or gross or criminal negligence on the part of the master or mariners of a ship to the owner's prejudice."

"Yes. Yes, of course. And the Delaney boy being on the deck watch is the mariner in this case. But what of the charge of wrecking and murder?"

"The changed-chart theory, if proved, will obliterate all charges."

"Well, Captain"—Pomfret shook his head—"I wish you good fortune, but I'll also pray for the Delaneys at the same time. I will, however, prepare the necessary papers to allow you to represent them at the inquiry. If, however, this goes to a full Court, I suggest that you hire the finest marine lawyer money can buy."

We bid him goodbye on that sour note, and, when we were on the street, Cork walked in silence.

Finally he stopped for a moment and said, more to himself than to me, "Strange, a lawyer in a busy port, and he knows nothing of marine law."

"It could be his age. He seems in his dotage."

"That may be," he said, and then stopped a young boy. "Hey, my lad, who is the harbourmaster in these waters?"

"That be old Peg and Patch, sir," the boy replied with a shudder.

"Old Peg and Patch, hey? And I suppose you address him so when you bid him good day?"

The lad lowered his head and then shot it up again. "When I sees him I brings myself about, sir. Beware churned waters, my old man says," he told us through a toothless grin.

"A fearsome fellow, then?"

"Like the devil himself, sir. Some says he was a pirate and lived with wild natives on a far-off isle where he was a cannyball."

"And where would his headquarters be, lad?"

"At the foot of Tillford's dock, sir, but you won't find 'im there. Best look in Sadie's, by the Front Street." Then he said, wide-eyed, "If ye have the heart, for you 'pear to be of quality."

"Mere clothes, my lad," Cork said, tossing a coin to him.

One of the outstanding aspects of New England life is the righteous piety of the population. Yet, in its port towns, there is usually one low place where evil flourishes and slakes the appetites of men home from long voyages. Sadie's was buried deep in the cellar of an old warehouse. Through the thick and acrid smoke I could see a stairway that led to the upper part of the building, and dared not think of the evil doings that must occur up there. A crone with tousled hair paid court to our obvious means, and directed us to the harbourmaster at a table in a far corner.

From the boy's description I expected to see a demonic sot, racked with depravity. However, Captain Robert Tinker (for that was his true name) was a well kept man of 60. The appellation of Peg and Patch sprang from the spotless patch over his left eye and the ivory stump that served as his left leg from the knee down. To my further surprise he was a reasonably well-spoken Englishman of some education.

After we had taken seats, he must have noticed my own amazement, or sensed it.

"From the look on your face, Mr. Oaks, I take it you have been talking to the townspeople. I am no ogre, sirs. The eye and the limb were lost to gunfire in the service of King and Country. I guess I am resented because I was granted my post by Royal Appointment. Let me assure you, it is no sinecure."

An unbelievably buxom wench came to the table, and Captain Tinker ordered a bottle of madeira. *His* madeira.

"I take it you are here on the Delaney business, gentlemen. What service can I do for you?"

"I am told," Cork began, "that copies of the Point Judith charts were put aboard coasters and taken to southern ports."

"Aye. Four in all. Put them aboard myself, explaining in each case the Pharos to the ship's master."

"Do you recall the ships?"

"Ah, let me see, the *Tarrymae* was one."

"Excuse me, Captain," Cork interrupted, "to simplify it, which ship was New York bound?"

"The *Ice Cloud*, under Master Swaith."

"Miles Swaith?"

"Nay, his brother, Ishmael."

"Interesting. There were four wrecks in this area over the summer months, I gather."

"Aye. The Judith shoals were becoming a graveyard, until the Squire came along with this Pharos idea."

"Now I'm told that Delaney took salvage rights on the first bottom, but who took rights in the other wrecks?"

"The 'Gansett Corporation. After the rumours started when the *Bristol Girl* went down, Delaney wouldn't put an oar in the water. So Miles Swaith and a few local businessmen formed a group and took the jobs. Damned shame about young Delaney, though. Shouldn't put the deck under a youngster, I always say."

"Then you believe it to have been an accident?"

"What else, sir? I myself put the Pharos plan to the test and went through the channel like it was the Thames. Say now, don't go taking on this bilge that the Squire was a wrecker. He's as true as magnetic north."

"To be sure. You will be called as a witness if there is a trial, and I trust you will hold that position."

"You have my bond, sir."

When Cork offered to pay for the madeira, which was excellent, Tinker refused. "First one's free, Captain," he said. "It's good for business. You see, I own this place."

That evening, on our return to the Delaney ranch, we took a meagre supper in our rooms. The hearty familial spirit that had been drawn from the home had left only bleakness in its aftertide.

"It appears that the name Swaith abounds in this affair," I said, over the cold turkey and corn bread.

"Yes, the brother could have changed the charts, but we are on slanderous grounds. I want something with more meat to it."

"Your second rampart?"

"And a third, if we can find one."

With this, there was a tap at the window, which at first I thought was rain. Getting up, Cork opened the casement to admit Tunxis. Despite the fact that we were on the second floor, the Indian's sudden appearance was not in the least jarring to me. To come to the second floor like a normal person he would have to enter under a roof, so it was natural that he would scale the trellis to converse with Cork. The climb up must have winded him slightly, or set his mind a-bubble, for he spoke in English. Thrusting a sack through the window, he said, "Here, like you say, lower beach."

"Good fellow, Chawcua, and who was with you?"

"White man named Clint."

"Good. Wait below."

When Cork had closed the window again, he returned to the table with the sack and sat down.

"What's in that thing?" I asked, sniffing the air. "A skunk?"

"No. My second line of defense, Oaks."

I reached across, opened the sack, and quickly closed it. "Animal droppings. Dung is your second rampart?"

"Evidence is often as repulsive as the crime, Oaks. Now I'm off for the third."

"Not without me," I said, getting to my feet.

"You're a stout fellow, my lad, but not this time."

"And why not? Am I some slip of a girl, some piece of frippery? I may not have the woodsy wiles of that redskin, but I'm man enough to a given task."

There were few times in my long relationship with him that I experienced true camaraderie. He reached out, clapped my shoulder, looked at me with those cold blue eyes, and smiled. "I never doubted that, my friend. Come, we have some climbing of our own to do."

My moment of gallantry stuck in my throat as we approached the base of the forward tower on the Point. With the ground-level hatches of both structures sealed tight with Royal lead, Cork proposed to scale the side of the thirty-foot edifice fronting the sea.

"Not only is it dangerous, but pointless," I said, as Tunxis uncurled roping lines.

"Wrong on both counts, Oaks. The facing is of fine hammered sandstone with a wide bond, so, despite the mist, the footing is sure. As for examining the light room, it is crucial to the case. I will go first, Tunxis to follow. Once up, we will haul you up by rope."

"If you climb, I climb."

He looked at the Indian, and Tunxis nodded. A savage was giving his accord to my own valour. Perhaps, at last, I was accepted by him.

I will not embarrass myself by describing the toil and fear of the ascent. From one slippery stone to the next, never looking down into the blackness, I inched my way up into more blackness. Above me I heard the shatter of glass, as Cork broke one of the panes in the tower windows, and a sharp tug on the guy line around my waist alerted me that the end of the climb was near.

"Take care of the broken pane, Oaks," Cork whispered. "Reach above your head and you will find a rod running around the ceiling on the inside."

I swung into the window frame and got to my feet. Cork was examining the apparatus with a shielded candle. The now dark light was a wondrous machine. Twelve large candles were imbedded in a holding plate before a concave plate of polished brass. The candles, when lit, must have reflected a most powerful light out to sea.

"What are you doing, Captain?" I asked, as he tugged at the base of the holding plate.

"Solid as Gibraltar," he said. "Let's take the ladder below."

One by one we descended into a round room directly below the light chamber. It had been fitted out as living quarters for a permanent keeper, when he was eventually hired. A chair and a writing table were at one side of the room. Tunxis lit the lamp with his candle while Cork rummaged around. He found nothing in the table drawer, and obviously nothing of interest in the few books on the shelf.

"Looks like a wild goose," I said, sitting on the chair, still winded from the climb and the excitement.

"Perhaps," Cork muttered as he pulled back a curtain hanging on ring hoops to expose a bed.

"Are lighthouse keepers allowed to sleep?"

"We all must, eventually, Oaks. With the coal-fired beacons along the English coast, there is little chance of the light going out, so the keepers sleep. I'm sure that when Delaney hires a regular keeper, he will keep a night watch."

"Keepers, you mean," I corrected him. An opportunity I rarely have.

He looked at me from the shadows cast by the lamp and gave me that smirk-a-mouth again. "You! A man of ledgers and coin! My word, Oaks, that is astounding. One man can handle both towers. Stationed in this forward tower, he could see if the rear tower was lit at all times. What's below there, Tunxis?"

The Indian's head poked up the ladderway hatch from the deck below.

"Supplies, candles."

"Well," I said, "what next? I hope we are not going to climb the other tower."

"No need. Come, lads, there is nothing more here." Cork snuffed the lamp.

When we arrived back at the house, Tunxis went whereever he goes, and we entered to find a note from Lawyer Pomfret. Cork did not read it in front of Madame Delaney, but waited till we were in our rooms. He then tore open the sealed envelope and read quickly.

"They move with great haste in this matter." He tossed the paper to me and I read it with a sinking heart. Disregarding all the niceties and legal terms, its essence was that a Naval Court of Inquiry would convene two days hence to take advantage of the fact that Admiral Fenley-Blore, of his Majesty's fleet, was in the area, and had agreed to preside over the panel.

"My, my, a flag officer, no less. Is that good or bad, Captain?"

He shrugged. "All bad pennies have an obverse. If we lose, there is little chance for appeal in London. A Fleet Admiral's stamp will settle it forever."

"And if we win, that also ends it forever. But two days is so short a time to prepare."

"For us, yes. I feel other forces have been planning for weeks. But no use wailing over it. We must set some things to our advantage. Fetch me Secundus, will you, while I pen a note."

A note indeed. It was a missive of polite flattery and obeisance to Admiral Fenley-Blore. Cork expressed concern over the meagre accommodations available in Narragansett to a naval hero of the Admiral's stature. He went on to describe the luxury of the Delaney home and extended its hospitality to further add to the Admiral's comfort, and suggested that the Court be convened in the main hall of the Delaney mansion in order that the Admiral's august presence have the proper dignified surroundings. The most amusing part was his signing it, "Your obedient servant." Cork has bowed to no man, and I am sure he has never been obedient.

Secundus was dressed for the night ride, and took the letter. "Mind, lad, for the Admiral's hands, and no other's. By the bye, before you go. Was anyone aware that your brother's ship was making for these waters?"

"Surely. It was posted in the harbourmaster's office. Not the exact day, but on or about, you know."

"Estimated date of return, yes. Well, off you go."

The Admiral arrived the next afternoon with two aides. Fenley-Blore was an English sailor of the old line. In the days of Queen Bess he would surely have been one of the Sea Dogs. A shortish man, he tended toward portliness in his twilight years. But the weight of girth and age had not slowed his step or his agile mind. Cork, the sly fox, fawned over him like a lass to a fiddler.

It wasn't until the next morning that I saw through the reason for Cork's uncommon actions. We were at breakfast, and Fenley-Blore was saying, "Wild turkey, you say? Now that should be good sport, hunting from horseback. But I'm afraid we will have to get on with this inquiry business. I enjoy these sojourns ashore, but I must get back to sea."

"I understand, Admiral," Cork soothed him, "but why not have the best of all possible worlds? We can hunt to-day and hold the inquiry to-night. You have the power to convene at any hour, so why not at your leisure?"

"Well put. To-night it is. Feel a bit sheepish at trying a man in his own home, though."

"Command is not always easy, Admiral."

He had hooked him. The inquest was to be held that night.

Before I describe that evening of surprises, dejections, and finally, of an uncanny solution, I must explain that I have simplified the text to avoid all the technical terms that fog understanding for the layman. I myself kept copious notes, and it took Cork three days to explain them to me. The air in the main hall that night was thick with such phrases as "points to the larboard," "keel lines," "true and magnetic course," and "lines of divination," as well as an hour's worth of talks and arguments about sails and winds and cross-winds.

The main point is that a ship was wrecked due either to negligence or to a faulty system—or so the Court claimed.

Cork went immediately to work on the changed-chart theory. He carefully laid the groundwork by describing how the copies of the chart sent to New York *could* have been changed. He was about to strengthen his question of doubt when one of the Admiral's aides leaned over and whispered into his superior's ear.

"Excuse me, Captain Cork," Fenley-Blore said, "but this line that the chart used aboard the *Queen of Tortuga* by young Delaney being missing is not correct."

I looked up at Cork, who was standing at our table facing the Court. His face showed surprise, and a chart was handed down the line of nine officers on the panel to the Admiral.

"Captain Cork," the Admiral continued, picking up the chart, "this was found with the flotsam of the *Tortuga*. It bears the inscription: *Delaney, Point Judith Pharos*. Would you kindly verify that it is the same as the original chart?"

Cork called John Knox, who was sworn in. The student

looked at the chart carefully and said, "I'm afraid it's accurate, Captain," causing a murmur from the small group of townsmen who sat at the back of the long room. It appeared that Cork's first line of defense was breached, and I could see no rampart to fall back upon.

The Captain now went into skirmish manoeuvres. He called the Delaneys, and Primus and his father both took an oath to their stories. He also put on the stand a Captain Jeggs, one of the mariners who had tested the system, and he too swore to Heaven that it was a genuine chart.

Next came Fergus Kirk, who would swear to nothing except that he was Fergus Kirk. He stuck to his story that he had been watching the compass. As Kirk stepped down, a voice from the back of the room said, "If it pleases the Admiral and the panel, sir, may I be recognized?"

I turned to see Lawyer Pomfret walking slowly forward. The Admiral recognised Pomfret, who stood facing Cork.

"Gentlemen, I am Giles Pomfret, counsellor-at-law, representing the Virron Shipping concern of Maiden Lane, New York, owners of the *Queen of Tortuga*."

He shifted on his feet like a nervous bird, and faced the panel.

"We, of course, have an interest in this matter and its outcome, and it seems to me that the good Captain here has everyone in sight taking an oath. We can't believe both Delaneys and still have a logical explanation of the matter. Now I'm a local man and would like to see fairness tendered, but my clients demand justice."

"And, from justice, restitution?" Cork asked.

"Captain, you're a fine fellow and a superior host," the Admiral smiled, "but we will have to get more answers than we have so far."

Cork was about to resume, when Captain Jeggs motioned to him, and both men talked in low whispers for a few moments. "Admiral, I have no further need of Captain Jeggs. We have his testimony, and he has a tide to catch."

"Excused, and good weather, Captain," the Admiral said, tossing him a half salute.

"Now, gentlemen." Cork walked forward as a chair was brought up for Pomfret, who sat and crossed his spindly legs. "The crux of the matter is the Pharos system itself, and to fully understand it, the panel should see it in operation."

The Admiral pointed his finger at Cork. "Now see here, Captain, I have no intention of setting sail to watch lights."

"No need, Admiral. We can exhibit it right here, with your permission. It's very simple. All we will need is two candles and total darkness. I would use my friend Oaks to demonstrate, but that could be viewed as prejudice, so I will call on a man who has asked for Justice, Lawyer Pomfret."

The lawyer gladly accepted, and the room was set up much as we had it when I played the part of the ship. One major exception was that Cork had the panel table moved forward. That put us all facing the wall along which Pomfret would walk in darkness.

"Now, to truly imitate the conditions of the night in question," Cork said, before the tapers were extinguished, "I have fashioned a shield for the back of the candle holders. In that way, only Mr. Pomfret will be able to tell us what he sees. Now remember, Pomfret, when the lights are one, make your turn, not before or after, for those chairs could give you a nasty knock."

The lawyer left the room, and we waited, adjusting our eyes to the darkness. Cork lit the candles, for we could all see the halos above the shields. "Come ahead," he shouted, and a door opened and I could hear Pomfret slowly shuffling across the room ahead. Four, five seconds, and then he said, "I'm turning now," and then the crash of old bones and heavy mahogany chairs followed instantly.

It would have been a comic sight to see the old man lying on the floor rubbing his painful leg, had it not sunk the Squire once and for all. But then it occurred to me that Pomfret had deliberately turned too soon, in order to create a negative impression. I went forward in the low-lighted room and informed Cork in a low tone.

"Excuse me, gentlemen," Cork said to the Court, while he helped the snarling man to his feet. "It has been suggested to me that our legal friend here may have resorted to deceit to prejudice the case."

"That's a lie," Pomfret shouted, dusting himself off.

"You are correct, sir. I believe you did turn when the lights became one. Just as young Delaney did."

"Then you have proved the case against the Squire," the Admiral said.

"I have proved *a* case, sir. Let us see who fits the mould."

He walked over to the window and drew back the drapes to the oh's and ah's of everyone. The Admiral came to his feet and hurried to the window. "What are those lights doing on?" he roared. The two towers had glowing halos above their tops. "They were ordered sealed, and by the gods, I'll hang any man who has broken them open."

"There are ways around seals, just as there are ways around systems, Admiral. Say, isn't that a ship out there? See the fore-and-aft running lights riding the waves?"

"You're right, Cork." The Admiral spoke with sudden anxiety.

An aide who had come to the Admiral's side muttered, "He'll have her on the beach in a moment."

The Admiral was now purple with rage. "Cork, I hold you responsible for the safety of that ship. It was lured into the area by those blasted lights."

"I take the responsibility, sir. May I produce the master of that 'ship'?"

"How? By magic?"

"No, by voice." Cork opened the window and called, "Ahoy!"

It *seemed* like magic, for the ship turned its prow into the beach and headed straight for the window. Then, as it got closer, we could see the trick.

"It's a donkey!" the Admiral cried. "A beast with lanterns hung over its head and tail."

"And the movement of a donkey walking on the beach would give an observer at sea the illusion that he was looking at a distant ship riding the waves."

"That's an old wrecker's trick, a damnable one," Fenley-Blore swore. "But what has this demonstration to do with the Pharos being faulty?"

"If we will all take our seats again, I will explain," Cork replied.

When the room was back to order, Cork addressed us. He now knew he was in safe water, and he played like a dolphin.

"Actually, I am presenting the evidence for acquittal in reverse. You will recall that Primus felt he was on a safe course when the beacons were joined, because he saw the running lights of a ship ahead. That disturbed me, because the over-all plot was so well conceived, so wondrously scientific, that I couldn't believe such a shoddy element would be allowed to mar it. It was just too much sugar in the bun.

"The man out there with the animal is named Clint. On the morning after the wreck he and my Indian friend searched the beach area and found what my yeoman calls 'filthy evidence' that a beast of burden had traversed the ground. Now, Admiral, you are correct that this has nothing to do with the performance of the Pharos. I say it worked perfectly that night, and will continue to work perfectly."

"My shin seems to give that a sound argument," Pomfret put in.

"I am sorry about that, Mr. Pomfret. It was not done in malice, but perhaps with a touch—only a touch, mind you—of indignation at your performance in your office two days ago. I am sure you are skilled in marine law, and I do not like to be lied to. But leave it, sir. This conspiracy required a genius and a fool, and you are neither."

"Cork, get to the point," the Admiral admonished, irritably.

"I beg pardon. Would you be kind enough to walk the same course which was so painful to Mr. Pomfret? Oh, no, I will not have the lights out this time. Please, sir."

The Admiral got to his feet with a look of simmering anger and took a place at the far wall. Cork re-lit the candles and nodded for the old sailor to start. Fenley-Blore was a quarter of the way across when he stopped.

"What the devil are you doing, Cork? You're passing a screen over the forward candle."

"Yes, exactly as I did when Pomfret was our ship. Only in the lit room you can see the trick. Just as Primus Delaney could not see the trick out over the blackness of the sea. Seize him, Oaks."

John Knox was a slippery fellow, but I held him fast.

"You can't prove a thing, Cork," Knox said. "How

could I hold a screen in front of the candles up there? It's too big for one man to do."

"When I said this conspiracy needed a genius and a fool, I should have added a dupe, but I didn't want to forewarn you, Mr. Knox. You have told us that you went to Yale College. Did you graduate?"

"No, I went only two years."

"That's strange. Yale is a fine school, but more regarded for its humanities and theology than for its science."

"My father was a master builder, and taught me his trade."

"Builder, yes. The construction of the towers is sound. But what of seamanship, navigation?"

"I've read books."

"Good sailors learn their trade before the mast, as soldiers learn their craft in battle." This last drew smiles from the entire panel.

"I suggest you are a dupe, Mr. Knox. To devise this plan would require years at sea, years of experience with difficult passages. And, I might add, an accurate mathematical ability.

"As for holding a screen in front of the lamp, I agree that it would be impossible for one man to do it alone, and if you blew out the candles, there would be no corona, or halo, to be seen from the back of the tower to gull us all into thinking that the light was in proper working order.

"Also, if you were simply to hold up a screen in front of the light, no purpose would be served. A ship running on a parallel line would see it one second and not the next. The abruptness of the change would make a mere cabin boy suspicious. No, Knox, the screen would have to move slowly between the lights from left to right to give the illusion that the lights were joining, long before that would really happen."

"That would be some trick," Knox said contemptuously. "What would I use? I took nothing from the tower that night, and it has been sealed since."

"You had no need to take anything away. The tools are still there in all their innocence. One thing I noted about your tower when I broke in the other night is that it is efficient. Yet the only purpose of a rod that runs around the ceiling of the front wall seems to be to give intruders a handhold. Another inefficiency is a bed that gives the sleeper privacy, when a lone keeper needs no privacy. Thus we have your screen, or curtain, which could be attached to the rod in the light chamber and used to slowly eclipse the light source from the front, while still providing a halo at the back."

"That's fanciful conjecture, Cork."

"No, I think the two gentlemen entering the room will back it up. Did it work, Captain Jeggs?"

Jeggs and a naval officer came forward and told of sailing out off the Point while Tunxis worked the curtain in Tower One.

"You are the dupe, Knox, and you have the privilege of going to the hanging string alone if you choose. Shall I produce the fool and the genius, or would you care to throw yourself on the Admiral's mercy?"

Knox looked at Fenley-Blore and back at Cork. He was frightened now, like an animal in a trap.

"Swaith! Miles Swaith is the culprit!" he screamed. "When I came here to build only one tower, he offered me money to advise the Squire against it, because he had been wrecking the ships with that donkey trick and spreading rumours about the Delaneys. When the Squire insisted on going ahead, Miles Swaith brought me the Pharos scheme, plans, charts, and all. Believe me, Squire, I didn't know Primus was aboard that ship. When I saw the running lights through the long glass, I didn't know it was the *Queen of Tortuga*."

Miles Swaith was on his feet frothing at the mouth. "He can't bring me into this, he can't! I deny everything he says, and it's his word against mine."

"And your donkey against whose, Swaith? When I sent Tunxis to scour the neighbourhood with Mr. Clint, he learned that you are the only one in the immediate vicinity who keeps such a beast. Oxen are used hereabouts, which, as any wrecker knows, are too slow and too even-footed to give the illusion of a cruising ship. Admiral, I give you Miles Swaith, the fool in the plot. If he had followed his master's plan, and trusted the light system alone, without using the donkey trick, we would have never uncovered the plot."

"By the Duke's guns!" The Admiral thumped the table. "When I first laid eyes on you I said, 'There is a remarkable fellow.' Now I double it, sir. You are a genius."

"I thank you, sir, but there is only one genius abounding, and we must pin him before we have the lot."

"If you can do that, my boy, I'll give you a man-of-war for a toy. I don't know when I've enjoyed myself more. Well, go on, go on." The Admiral was as gleeful as a small lad on Christmas morning.

"I have given profound thought to his identity. Swaith is discounted, for he is merely a rude and greedy bumpkin. Our student is too limited in skill. So who have we? Let me see. We need a master mariner, to be sure, and a scientist of some prowess. Forgive me, Admiral, if this description seems to fit you."

For a moment the old boy looked concerned, and then he broke into laughter. "Very remarkable fellow," he said to the aide at his side.

"But, combined with these laudable attributes, we need also a man with a smidgen of evil, with an attraction to the low life. The criminal mind operates that way. A cut-purse or a highwayman will risk his life for a bag of gold, and then squander it on wine and whores. Another forgiveness, Admiral, but when I asked your naval lieutenant to accompany Captain Jeggs on to-night's cruise, I also requested that he have your Captain of Marines arrest a suspect—the only one who qualifies as a master mariner and a scientist with a touch of evil. May I produce him?"

The commotion at the back of the room turned all our heads. There, between two Marines, was Captain Robert Tinker, the harbourmaster, old Peg and Patch, as the street urchin had so aptly named him. . .

Well, nothing is more jubilant than an Irishman who has just escaped the noose, and since both Delaneys were free, it was merriment in double time at the ranch. Fiddlers were called, punch-bowls filled, and great sides of meat were put to the spits. The celebration lasted until past dawn, when the Admiral and his party took their leave.

"Technically, he owes you a ship of the line," I said as

we repaired to our rooms. "He made you that promise before witnesses."

"What would we do with it, Oaks? Start a navy? You know, this idea of closing off the Pharos light with a screen is intriguing when properly done. If a clock mechanism could be devised to shield the beacon for a specific amount of time—say, seconds or minutes—ships could recognise the seamark by the frequency of the light flashes."

"Excellent idea, and possibly profitable. Put it to paper to-morrow."

"It *is* to-morrow, and I'm for sleep."

So, I fear, it is to be with all his to-morrows. Sleep. Drink. Carouse. And, of course, solve. I shall persevere in spite of him.

THREE

The Georgia Resurrection

"To be sure, Captain Cork, I agree," Tolliver Smyth said, readjusting himself in the high-back cane chair after refilling our drinks. "Superstition is a weakness in the chain of reality, but even a weak link is better than none, especially here in the Georgia plantations."

Out in the darkness, through the heavy muslin screens that gave entry to a slight breeze and yet protected us from the fierce insects that churned out of the swamps, came the rhythms of drums. They had been beating since supper, and although a bit unnerving, the crude timpani was oddly hypnotic. Suddenly Smyth chuckled to himself.

"Was that meant to be a pun, Captain?" he asked. "Calling it *black* magic? Very clever when you come to think of it. The slaves call it *vodo*."

"Yes," Cork said. "I have run into it in the Indies, especially on Hispaniola. It is outlawed there, I believe."

"And frowned on here, sorry to say. What harm can a few drumbeats and a chant or two do, yet it scares the locals hereabout out of their skins. I say, if it keeps the slaves happy and productive, let them conjure away."

"You are most progressive, sir," Cork remarked, hiding his pejorative intent in mild observation. I, of course, could interpret his true feelings, for I know my employer better than any other man in the American colonies. Cork detests the concept of slavery; in fact, it was this abhorrence that had brought us to the Georgia colony in the summer of 1761.

When he first devised a machine for the harvesting of rice, I thought he had finally decided to put his mind to industry rather than the solution of what he calls "social puzzles." But the fervour with which he approached the task and the speed with which he implemented it soon told me his real mission. If he could successfully prove the economy of his intention, he would render slavery unnecessary in these terribly hot and dank deltas, where no white man could toil more than an hour or two at a time.

Tolliver Smyth's plantation was near the Brunswick settlement several miles up one of the many small rivers that finger this remote and sparsely populated area. The Tolliver lands were called a "spread" by its master, in contrast to the smaller farms scattered about the back country. Smyth himself was an amiable young man of 30 who had recently come out from England to try his hand at a frontier fortune. And he had the strong hands for it, despite all his gentlemanly ways.

During supper, before the drums from the slave quarters had started, our main topic of conversation had centered on the harvesting scheme itself, and there was much chiding at my expense because I was the only one of the trio who was beardless. Before we left Charleston, Cork had begun to allow his usually trim barba to spread into a full beard. I found the suggestion that I too grow a beard ludicrous, since the excessive heat of this semitropical place would roast a man to the bone.

Cork hadn't prepared me for the mosquitoes and gnats which had been eating me alive since we arrived. However, the bugs did not seem to bother Tunxis, the tamed Quinnipiac Indian who serves as the Captain's shadow. His method is to smear himself with a foul mixture of skunk oil and berry juice. It not only helps keep the insects away, but all humankind as well. As usual, he was out of doors somewheres—he refuses to enter under a roof.

We had arrived at Finderlay, as the plantation was called, earlier that day, and were now relaxing as best we could in the incessant heat. Overhead, from the verandah ceiling, swung a broad woven-reed plank that served as a fan, its locomotion provided by some unseen black hand. We were sipping dark rum, Smyth and I having refused to join Cork in his own ritual of eating raw clams liberally laced with vinegar.

"Well, I can see where a Christian community would be upset by occult arts being practiced in their midst," I put in.

Cork looked up from a clamshell. "The only thing that doesn't upset a Christian is another Christian, Oaks," he said, devouring the clam meat, "and then only if he totally agrees with him. It seems you are the only white man on the place, Smyth."

"I plan to marry one of these days, but I have to get Finderlay in shape for womankind, I'm afraid. What is it, Neela? You look like a startled fidget."

The tall black woman who had just come out onto the verandah was indeed astir. When we arrived earlier, I had noticed that her button-brown eyes were bright and minikin gay; they were now horse-wide with fear. She didn't speak, and merely cocked her head towards the front of the house.

"What the deuce has gotten into you, girl?" Smyth said impatiently. "Are there callers?"

She merely nodded.

"Then show them out here," Smyth told her. "Must be the devil himself," he said as we waited. "She's usually a calm woman."

Seconds later we had evidence of her consternation. I felt my own throat tighten as they loomed into view through the candle haze, presenting us with a bizarre duo of ominous dimensions.

Though the temperature had to be well over 90 degrees, and the humidity thickly oppressive, both men were dressed in winter greatcoats of immense bulk and mourning blackness. Despite their out-of-season bundlement, they showed no sign of discomfort; their alabaster faces glistened like hoarfrost on chipped stone. They could have been citizens of the netherworld, and instinctively I was repelled by them.

The taller of the two was heavyset, with a leonine head and a cavernous mouth that echoed his speech in deep drum tones. The other man was snipe-like in stature, with pathetically thin legs supporting an immense upper torso; when he spoke, he had a habit of turning his oblong head from side to side as if he were unable to see over his sharply pointed nose.

The latter announced himself as Zachary Gooms, and the black scarf trailing from the rim of his tricorner had already told us his profession of gravesman. The taller one announced that he was Simon Cratch, who made his living as a hangman. This was certainly strange postprandial companionship, and Smyth seemed annoyed at the intrusion by men of such low station.

"We bury our own here at Finderlay, Gooms, and slaves are too expensive to hang, Cratch, no matter what the crime."

"Well, sir," Cratch said uneasily, "we thought we could save you some trouble, since we understand you let your nigras practice heathen religion."

"What my people do on Finderlay is my affair," Smyth said sternly. "What *trouble* are you talking about?"

"Well, sir, Gooms is the local man, so I'll let him tell it," Cratch acceded to his companion.

Smyth raised a hand in tacit approval. "Go on, Gooms, I thought you looked familiar. You have a coffin shop in Brunswick."

"Correct, sir, coffins and burials and fine furniture, if you wish. But even as the official county gravesman, it's a poor living. Now the coffins are gaining favour with the townsfolk, although you people out in the back country still make your own. But the furniture's another matter, with people sending to England for it."

"At least you can make a living," Cratch lamented. "I purposely came to Georgia thinking there would be a great need for my services."

"Why is that?" Cork queried.

Cratch looked at Smyth, who said, "This is Captain Jeremy Cork and his yeoman, Wellman Oaks."

"Well, Captain Cork," Cratch went on, "it seemed to me that since many of the felons were being transported from our gaols at home to Georgia, and felons never changing their ways, as you know, there would be a brisk business for me.

"But it turned out not to be the case, and I near starved for lack of commissions. To add to my misfortune and a stroke of bad timing, I requested transfer back to England and was granted it. Of course now the Escape Commission is a-comin' over and there'll be lots of work for the new man at the derrick."

"Escape Commission? Sounds royal and self-contradictory," I said.

"Its mission has received quite a broadcast in these parts, gentlemen," Smyth explained. "Not only are the colonists perturbed by the legally-transported convicts, but terror is slowly building up over the escaped cutthroats who somehow make it to these shores and seek refuge among old criminal friends."

"Yes," Cork said, "several newspapers in the north have come out quite strongly for an end to transportation."

"Aye, and woe to my timing of transfer," Cratch consoled himself. "The Commission will bring with them a warder from each of the main prisons who know these escaped scoundrels on sight. They'll be full gibbets from here to Canada, they will. Now as luck would have it I missed my ship at Brunswick and happened by Mr. Gooms's shop. I wouldn't want the foul deed on my record."

"Foul deed? What are you talking about, man?" Smyth was irritated and abrupt. Cork seemed interested, however, and tried to calm our host.

"Perhaps these fellows have a tale to tell, Smyth. It will pass the evening. Why don't you two sit down?"

Smyth nodded agreement and they took seats.

"Well, gentlemen, the problem seems to be Arthur Briddleton here." As Gooms said it, he took a white plaster sculpture from under his greatcoat and laid it on the table. The object was a man's face in repose. The nose was aquiline, the skin smooth and unlined. It was the death mask of a man in his late twenties.

"You are quite expert in the art of death masks, Gooms. Is that one of your services to clients?" Cork asked.

"No, sir, it's more trouble than it's worth to me, but the Governor has ordered that one be made of every executed criminal."

I shot a quick glance in Cork's direction, but he ignored me. Just six months ago he had suggested this method of verifying the death of criminals to Major Philip Tell, a special King's agent at large. I could see that Tell had wasted no time in turning Cork's advice to his own advantage. However, I could not fault the Major, for I could see little profit in the business. Cork was speaking again. "And this, you say, is Arthur Briddleton's face?"

"Well, sir," Simon Cratch's voice boomed over us like cannon fire, "that's the heart of the matter, so to speak. I say that's *not* the face of the man called Briddleton who I hanged on Monday last, and Mr. Gooms insists that it is."

"Nay, Mr. Cratch, that's not correct. I claim that is the death mask of the body I picked up at the gibbet at Landsdown crossing at sundown on Monday last. I never knew Arthur Briddleton and could not swear what he looked like. I say the man hanging there bore the face you see in the mask."

"Gentlemen," Cork said, raising an open palm, "if you will let me ask a few questions to put the problem in its traces, I think we can be of help. Would you care for a drink?"

Gooms said no, but Cratch eyed the bottle near Cork's plate of clams. "Would that be vinegar I smell, sir?"

Cork nodded. "Yes, I believe a red wine gone sour, and quite tart."

"Then I'll happily take a cup. Helps with the heat."

My own mouth felt like cotton as I watched him drink down the acetose liquid and wondered if indeed it did keep one cool. Cork proceeded with a methodical interrogation, from which I have summarized the following.

On the previous Sunday (this being a Thursday evening), a stranger to the locality, who gave his name as Arthur Briddleton, was seized while stealing a horse in an inland village known as Landsdown. He was immediately brought to the local Justice of the Peace, who tried and convicted him. The punishment, as usual, was hanging.

There was some argument about executing a man on the Sabbath, and it was decided to hold it on the following day.

"And most fortunate for Briddleton at that," Cratch said. "I was on my way up from Waverly to take ship at Brunswick for England when I heard there was supposed to be a hanging at Landsdown. Believe me, I'm not one to miss a fee. Lucky lad, Briddleton."

"Lucky?" I echoed unconsciously.

"Certainly, Mr. Oaks," Cratch said with a wink. "A man condemned to death can suffer on the string, for if the noose is applied by some amateur, the hanging can be most unpleasant. But old Simon Cratch was handy, and he went swiftly and sweetly. But that mask isn't Arthur Briddleton."

"And just what did your Briddleton look like?" Cork asked.

"Well, the first thing I noticed when I happened to stop by Gooms's shop and saw the mask was that the scar along the left cheek was missing. Then the nose was different. This one is quite pointed, whereas the nose of the man on the gallows was flatlike."

"Of course this was a public execution," Cork said.

"Out in the open, but with no witnesses except the J.P., Bill Tooks. Folks want justice, gentlemen, but they don't like to see it dispatched. I put him on the string about two in the afternoon and went my way, for I had the ship to catch. As luck would have it, I missed her. Now, by the look you're aiming at me, Captain, I know you're asking yourself, was the man dead, and I can assure you he was. I've put fifty men on the derrick in my day, and not a manjack of them ever walked away." He sat back with a self-satisfied smug, "I'll take some more of that vinegar, if you please, sir. It's got a fine bite."

Cork refilled the cup and turned to Zachary Gooms. "Now will you tell your part in all this?"

"Glad to," the gravesman said, clearing his throat. "When I heard the nine tolls plus one for a dead man on the Landsdown bell, I knew I was needed for a felon burial. It's part of my contract to care for public graves, and when the bell is rung nine times and one, it's to tell me to come at sundown. The body is left on the gibbet till that time as an example, although most people avoid the Crossing when a body has swung.

"Well, sir, I took my cart out there to that deserted gibbet and brought the corpse back to Brunswick. As I was passing through the delta road by your bottom acreage, Mr. Smyth, I came upon a group of your nigras dancing and cavorting in a grove just off the road. It was like a witch's sabbath, it was, with drums and rattles and the like. Most hellish.

"I can't tell you how uneasy I was, and I gave the horse a crack to get out of the neighbourhood, for I wanted no truck with black devils. Then, damnation, my old Ned rears up and pushes the cart into a gulley. The noises attracted the nigras, and they came running to see. I'll say this for your boys, Mr. Smyth, they were most helpful. They got the cart back on the road and I was off like cannot-shot. I got back to Brunswick, made the mask, and buried the body outside town to the west, in the poor field, in an unmarked grave. The face you see in that mask is the face of the man I buried. I swear to it, sir!"

Tolliver Smyth, who had been sitting with his booted feet spread in front of him during the narration, now stood up menacingly. "Are you implying that my slaves had something to do with this?"

"Now, Mr. Smyth, sir," Gooms said hesitantly, "I just state the facts."

"Despite the heat," Cork put in, "let's keep cool heads. Did you look at the corpse when you took it down at the gibbet, Gooms?"

"It was hard to see in lanternlight, Captain. The first good look I got of him was when I reached my shop."

"Then the bodies could have been switched on the gibbet," Cork suggested.

"Switched!" Gooms said in confusion, "I never thought of that. I thought those black devils put a spell on the body. You know, used magic."

"Gooms," Cork said, "it is best to look to reality for an answer before bringing in the occult. Consider your own precarious position, sir. You bury a body that does not resemble the hanged man. That, my lad, is suspicious."

Gooms was visibly disturbed. "Why would I do anything like that? I made the mask, didn't I?"

"Of course, but you assumed that Cratch would be off to England and the J.P. at Landsdown would never see the mask, since it would be sent to the officials in Savannah."

"I beg you, sir," the gravesman pleaded, "I am an honest man."

"And you shall have a chance to prove it."

"Thank God for that," Gooms said fervently, "but how can I?"

"With the greatest ease—by resurrection." As Cork said the word, a sudden silence fell over the company. Gooms looked horrified, and Cratch—yes, even that grim hangman seemed uneasy. Tolliver Smyth was shocked. For myself, I was appalled.

"Dig up the body?" I said. "Why, that's sacrilegious!"

"Well, my fellows, you can't have it both ways," the Captain admonished us all. "We have a dispute over identity, so we must let the corpse speak for itself."

"Begging the Captain's pardon," Cratch said, "I'm as hard a man as any—but resurrection! I'd as soon forget the whole affair. In fact, the more I look at this mask, the only thing different is the scar and the nose."

"But I can't forget it; nor can you, Smyth," Cork said. "These fellows have made a serious accusation against your slaves, and it's bound to start disquieting rumours. No, the body *must* be resurrected at once. Let's see, buried just four days ago. Hmmm, should be still in fine condition for identification."

"Well, an official will have to pass on it," Gooms said humbly. "I'm all for it, but I'll not take it on my own head."

"To be sure. Let us keep it legal," Cork advised. "And who better to order Briddleton resurrected than the man who sentenced him to the grave? Now get you both to this J.P. and resolve the issue."

Both men got up to leave when Cork stopped them. "Oh, yes, you lads had better leave the death mask here, for safekeeping."

After our eerie visitors had left, Smyth suggested we turn in, for we had a long day ahead of us in the rice fields. I was all for it and, despite the heat, dropped off to sleep in minutes. It was still dark of night when I sat bolt upright in bed, a hand covering my mouth.

"By Jerusalem, Oaks, be quiet," Cork's voice whispered. "Come, get dressed, we have work to do."

Minutes later we were out of the main house, prowling about the outbuildings. We came upon a small shed, and Cork slipped inside, returned in a trice, and tapped my shoulder. "Come in, I've found it," he said.

Once inside he shut the door and relit a candle. It was nothing more than a workshed, quite like any that one would expect to find on a self-sustaining plantation which makes everything from shoes to shingles for itself. I watched the Captain as he uncovered a barrel of chalky white powder and scooped some into a bowl. To this he added water from a bucket in a corner, and proceeded to beat the mixture into a paste.

"It is fortunate that the Smyth main house has plaster walls, and that the materials are at hand," Cork said.

He dumped the paste onto a worktable, and then, to my surprise, took the Briddleton mask from inside his shirt. He lay the mask next to the heap of white paste and began to shape the stuff into a facsimile, smoothing the features of a face on it. I watched him work in silence, and after half an hour he stepped back and cupped his bearded chin with his hand, as if admiring a masterpiece.

"If your creation is supposed to match the original, I can assure you that you are no sculptor, Captain."

"It will do. Same general shape, similar nose, eyes. Yes, it will do fine. Now this will have to dry before we can move it." He picked up the original and tucked it back into his shirt. "Now we shall take a little stroll, old son," he said, going out into the moonlit, drum-beating night.

We were only ten yards from the workshed when he stopped and put both hands to his mouth, one cupped over the other, and delivered the most perfect imitation of a lake loon I have ever heard. I have tried it myself several times and failed, to Tunxis' amusement, for this is how the savage and Cork sometimes communicate. At the edge of a clearing I could hear the return call and knew that Tunxis was nearby. Cork walked off to meet him. When he returned to me, I said, "This is all so befuddling."

"That is because your mind is on other things. Come, our stroll is not over."

I followed him across the clearing into the underbrush, and ten minutes later found myself in a deep swamp, gingerly trodding along a hummock that snaked its way across the dark black water, hiding God knows what in its depths. Ahead of us the drums grew louder. I was amazed at the way Cork so assuredly picked his way along, till I realized that Tunxis must have marked the trail for him. We stopped for a moment while he got his bearings, and I asked him where we were headed.

"One of the sad thoughts in my life, Oaks, is that my adventures have kept you from romance. Tonight we shall rectify the oversight. Ah, there are lights ahead, and our destination."

The hummock suddenly broadened into a small island that rose slowly out of the swamps. Giant mangroves tentacled out of the water to make it a fortress, an evil bastion.

When we came into the clearing, the drums suddenly stopped. A group of black men and women were sitting by a fire, looking at us in wonderment. A huge muscular fellow rose slowly to his feet and came towards us.

"Why, it's the Cappin' who's visitin' the mastah," he said with a smile of relief. "You musta lost your way. Load a danger in the swamp at night, sirs. Come, I take you back so's you don't get ate by a 'gator."

"You are called Big Blue, I believe. I saw you this afternoon in the fields. You're a good worker."

The man smiled at the flattery. "Big Blue worth ten men, the mastah say. Make's Big Blue head man. Come, I take you back, sirs."

"No. First I must see the *mambo*."

Big Blue's amiable face froze in terror. "No *mambo* here at Finderlay, sir. No *vodo*. No priest woman, no sir."

"A *zohop* then, one who knows the plants and leaves. My friend here is in need of *vervain*." As he said it, he placed his hands over his heart and feigned a swoon, which brought hearty laughter from the campfire. Although it broke the tension, I didn't like having it done at my expense. I assumed *vervain* had something to do with the romance he had alluded to.

Amid all the laughter an ancient negress emerged from

the shack and sat herself on a tree stump. She was old and wizened; a bright red bandanna covered her head, while a gingham shawl hid her shrunken body. She let out a cackle and motioned us forward.

When we reached her, Cork bowed slightly and handed her two coins. "This is Mamabin," Big Blue said. "Very old, very much head for dreams."

The crone looked up at Cork and told him, "You are as high as a tree, which means your head always clear. How do you come by the tongue of the swamps?"

"I have put time in the Indies, old mother."

"Pirate?" she shouted.

"No, mother, a traveller. Please, a *vervain* for my friend."

She cocked an eye at me and looked me over from head to toe. "Hard to do, hard to do, but we try." She put her hand into a grass-woven satchel at her feet and took out a handful of leaves. She scrutinized her palm and then selected five leaves of equal size and handed them to me. They were nothing more than oleander leaves.

"Pin one each to the corner of your pillow and one in the center. Then you sleep and dream of lady you will marry." It was all nonsense, but I took them and thanked her.

"Tell me, old mother," Cork said, "what is the way to make a zombi walk?"

She immediately cringed, and he was quick to calm her.

"I know you don't make zombi, but I have great interest, and it may help your master."

"Masta Tolliver good man," she said. "No whips here at Finderlay. Make Blue head man. Good masta. Someone has spell on him?"

"Not yet, but in case it happens."

"They say make zombi drink salt water and he speak."

"You are very wise, old mother. I am told you can make zombi if you hang a dead man from his heels and take three drops from his nose."

She tossed her head back and cackled. "That would be a pizen, child."

"Or is it a pin stuck into a lime while still on the tree from sunup to sunup and then squeezing the juice?"

She cackled again. "More pizen."

"Or is it the black-leaf tea, old mother?"

At this remark she went silent. "Houngan. You houngan."

"I know more of magic than these people should hear, old mother. Come, let us go inside where we can talk."

He was in with her for almost half an hour, while I stood in the campfire-lit grove a bit uneasily. He finally came out, and we left the place hurriedly. Once back at the main plantation, we picked up the now dry, rude copy of the death mask, and crept up to our rooms.

"I take it she is a witch of some kind," I said to him before going into my own bedchamber.

"More an herbal magician, or a *docteur feuilles*, as the French colonists call them. These old tribal rites and beliefs brought over from Africa have been diluted and fragmented by time and locale, but the basics are still there. That's what I was after to-night."

"And did you get it?"

"Sweet dreams, old son," he said, shutting his door.

All this confusion had muddled my mind, and only sleep could clear it. I fell asleep for the second time that night with a bit of difficulty, for the oleander leaves on my pillow kept scratching my ear.

For the next two days we heard nothing from Cratch or Gooms and had little time to think of their problems. We were up with the sun and into the rice fields, where Cork made elaborate calculations and closely observed the method of harvesting. I spent most of my time swatting bugs. Each night Cork spent long hours at his drawings, leaving me to bide my time with Tolliver Smyth, who proved to be a well-read fellow.

Even Saturday night could not drag the Captain from his work, and Smyth and I repaired to drink once again on the verandah.

"One of my men, Big Blue, tells me that you paid a visit to the old woman in the swamps," he said, lighting a seegar. "Best be careful back in there. Hundred of quicksand places that could swallow a man forever."

I shuddered inwardly and thanked the Lord for Tunxis' trailblazing ability. I hadn't seen the savage since that night, and wondered where he was off to. But he does that now and again, so I paid it no heed.

"I'm afraid your visit has spoiled me, for I shall miss our talks and fellowship when you are gone," Smyth said.

"Not many neighbours?"

"These plantations are so vast that there is little sociality, and then in the small villages they don't take to strangers, at least not to me."

"They think you are too easy on the slaves?"

"Yes. Always talk of keeping them down for fear of an uprising. If the poor devils do a day's work, let them be. But then maybe it's me personally they don't like. After all, Bill Tooks is as new out here as I am, and the locals took to him like a duck to water. Elected him J.P. and all that."

"Never confuse competence with popularity." We looked up to see Cork coming out onto the verandah from the house. "It is one of the flaws of the human race. We seem to have visitors, gentlemen."

Out in the darkness was the sound of horse hooves, and one of the house slaves ran into the yard with a torch illuminating the arriving party. Three men were ahorse— Gooms, Cratch, and an unknown man. The fourth person on foot was known well to me.

"Take a care, sirs!" Cork shouted. "That's a war chief of the Quinnipiac you have bound by rope and lead on a halter."

"Runaway slave from the West Indies, if I have it right," growled the stranger. He was a fierce man with a black beard and wore rough back-country clothes. Smyth got to his feet and was seemingly about to corroborate Cork, when the Captain stopped him.

"Never shout a truth when you can exhibit it," he said to our host. "Very well, sir, you operate at your own peril."

Then, to Tunxis he said something in Indian jabber, and in a second the redskin's hands were not only free, but whipping the tether and the stranger from his horse.

"Help the gentleman up, Tunxis, and dust him off a bit. I suggest you let him do it, sir, for he could have your scalp in a trice if he cared to."

"It's all right, Bill, the Indian is with Captain Cork!" Smyth shouted.

There was much swearing from Justice of the Peace

Tooks as the three men climbed to the verandah. Cork went into the yard and talked with Tunxis, who handed him a piece of paper he had concealed in his moccasin.

Tooks was saying, "How was I to know he was a bloody prince or something?" when Cork returned.

"No harm done, Mr. Tooks. An Indian in unfamiliar country walking alone is, of course, suspicious, since the redman is used as a slave in the Indies. I can see that you were only doing your duty as a J.P."

This seemed to placate the man for a few moments, and then he became irritable again. "And I'm here to do my duty, I can assure you. These are strange doings indeed. Never saw the like of it. Gooms and Cratch arguing over who's hung and who's buried. I've been off in the wilderness for two days or I'd have been on this sooner. I'm not opening a man's grave, felon or not, until I find out which one's lying. I'm told you have the death mask, Cork, and I want it produced now."

"Of course, Justice Tooks, I'll fetch it and along the way I'll make you some of my own Apple Knock. Would you rather have more vinegar, Mr. Cratch?"

The hangman smiled. "I'm not against a bit of liquor, sir."

Cork asked me to assist him, and, as we left the verandah, Tooks was growling at Smyth, "If any of your damned darkies had anything to do with this, they'll all hang."

Once inside, Cork sent me to his room to get the mask. He was mixing the Knock when I returned below stairs. How he expected to pass off this childish copy as a death mask, I had no idea. I was preceding him out the door when he tripped me and sent me sprawling forward. The mask flew from my hands and smashed to pieces.

"Oaks, you jackanapes!" he shouted at me. "Now look what you've done. You'll be flogged for this!"

"Is that the mask?" Tooks cried.

"*Was* the mask, I'm afraid, Mr. Justice," Cork apologized. "You must forgive this menial of mine."

I was stunned at such treatment from the man I considered my friend. Seeing my anger, Cork admonished me, "Hold your tongue, man, that's an order!"

"Now that's done it." Tooks was red with anger. "Now I'll have to open the grave."

"I think not, sir," Cork said, handing the drinks around. "The explanation to this is quite simple. Tell me, Mr. Cratch, when did you arrive at Landsdown?"

"Why, Sunday in the forenoon, right after the trial."

"And how did you spend your time, sir? The hanging wasn't until Monday afternoon, which in itself is strange, since executions are normally at dawn."

"I'll tell you what he did, he got himself drunk as a lord." Tooks pointed a finger at Cratch. "Couldn't get the sot awake till almost one on Monday. I wouldn't have paid him a fee in advance if I knew he was a drunkard."

"So we have a bleary-eyed rumpot who says the man hanged is not the man buried. Your proclivity for vinegar is not uncommon among men who drink too much, Cratch. It is the fool's notion that acid thins the blood and makes one sober. In the Pennsylvania colony sauerkraut juice is the common remedy."

"You mean all this trouble was caused by a drunken hangman?" Tooks was now livid. "By thunderation I'll put *him* on the gibbet, I will!"

"Have a care, Mr. Justice, you may not be so lucky next time."

"Lucky? What do you mean, lucky?"

"Well, Mr. Tooks—" Cork took a piece of paper from his pocket "—two days ago I dispatched my Indian friend to Savannah by coaster with an accurate description of the death mask. Now in my report to the Governor, I failed to mention that you tried Arthur Briddleton on a Sunday, which is illegal, and thus so was his sentence. I did not mention that you might have committed judicial murder, for it was not my purpose to bring the Royal Governor down on your head. I have an interest in this death-mask system, sir, because I am its inventor. Well, lo and behold, you are a bit of a hero, for Tunxis brings me word that you have successfully tried, convicted, and hung none other than Black Jack Herleigh."

"The escaped highwayman? My word!" Tooks beamed. "He was one of the blackguards mentioned in the Escape Commission's proclamation. Think of it, gentlemen—me, Bill Tooks, captured and hung a notorious robber that all the King's men couldn't keep or find!"

He took a long draught to his success from his Knock and smiled anew. Suddenly, in the instant of a swallow, his face went white and he fell forward on the floor.

"Quick, you two! To the well for cool water!"

"It's no use, Captain Cork," the gravesman said, looking down at Tooks's face. "I knows a corpse when I sees one."

"I said water and fast!" Cork said with a roar that sent both men scurrying outside.

Smyth bent over the body, rolled back the eyelids, then put his head to Tooks's chest.

"Too much excitement, I would guess," Cork said.

Smyth got to his feet and rushed indoors, mumbling, "Damn fool." He returned seconds later and poured liquid from a small blue philtre into Tooks's mouth. The man's eyes began to flutter and his breath came heavy at first and then steadied.

"You're all right, Mr. Tooks," Cork said, kneeling down. "You've had a bit of a fright, that's all. You should take things easier in the future, for I think you may have some trouble with your heart."

Within the hour the Justice of the Peace was on his feet again and as feisty as ever. "You, Cratch, had better be on the next boat out of Brunswick, if you know what's good for you. And you, Zachary Gooms, help me to home. I'm sorry to have caused you trouble, Tolliver. Drop over soon to meet the folks at Landsdown. There's a young widow I'd like you to meet."

When the hoofbeats were out of earshot, we all sat down again to our drinks and relaxed.

"Well, I must say all's well that ends well," I chuckled. "But this affair must have had little zest for you, Captain, since it proved to be no puzzle at all."

He gave me that smirk-a-mouth. "More of a puzzle than you think, old son." He turned to Smyth. "Why don't you take off the false beard, Black Jack? Your own must be grown in fairly well by now."

"Black Jack? Black Jack Herleigh? Come now, Captain."

Then, before my eyes, the planter removed his thick beard and revealed a good seven-days' growth.

"When did you get on to me?" he asked.

"I was sure when you went for the antidote to the datura and gave it to Tooks. If you hadn't, I would have administered my own concoction."

I was astounded. "I don't understand this at all. Isn't Herleigh supposed to be in his grave?"

"Hold fast, Oaks. Let us start from the beginning. You will recall when Cratch and Gooms first brought us the problem, I offered the simplest of solutions. One body, probably Briddleton's, was replaced by another. But whose, and, more pointedly, why? The who, of course, would have required clairvoyance; the why, however, although a puzzling question, was not beyond *all* conjecture."

"Well, I've thought about that," I said, "and fell upon the idea that someone had been murdered and that his corpse had somehow gotten into Gooms's hands for a legal burial."

"Then you didn't think hard enough, Oaks. A murdered corpse could be hidden eternally in the quicksand of the swamps. No, the purpose of the replacement was one of *identity*. Either to hide Briddleton's or to expose the face on the mask. And the answer leans to the latter in light of the Escape Commission's imminent arrival. Briddleton was a complete stranger hereabouts with no friends to identify him. And even if he were an escaped felon, what could be gained by hiding his identity after death?"

"And that's why you sent the original mask to Savannah?" I asked.

Smyth-Herleigh looked agitated. "I thought you said you sent a description, and that those smashed bits of plaster are the remains of the mask."

"A mere diversion, Jack Herleigh, or should I say Tolliver Smyth, for you are for ever safe in your new identity. The Commission has now written you off as dead, and will not look for a man who has been officially buried. Hanged and buried. You can be assured that Tooks is so inflated by his capturing and hanging a notorious highwayman that nothing could convince him to the contrary. Black Jack Herleigh is 'dead.' "

"But that's what I don't understand," I said. "If Herleigh —that is, Smyth—posed as a corpse to have his freshly-shaved face cast in a mask, how could he fool a gravesman?"

"Because to all intents and purposes he *was* dead, Oaks. He was a zombi until his slaves could dig him out of the grave and put Briddleton's body in his place."

"A zombi? Why, zombis are mere superstition!"

"To the uninitiated, yes, but a person can be suspended in a death-like trance with any of several tropical drugs. In South America it is curare; in Hispaniola, datura is used."

"Or mancenillier," Smyth-Herleigh interjected.

"I see you know herbal medicine as well as Mamabin."

"Not really, but she made the sleep draught for me when I learned of the Escape Commission's coming. I was a wild lad in the old days, and took to the highway more for the adventure than for the profit. I never killed anyone, despite the reports of my savagery. My main sin seems to have been escaping from Newgate and cheating the hangman. Out here I planned a new life."

"And you have it, sir."

"Thanks to you, yes. When I learned that a man near my age and build was going to be hanged in Landsdown, I saw my chance to throw the Escape Commission off my trail, so I took the draught and had the slaves put my 'dead' body in place of Briddleton's during the slaves' diversion on the Delta road. But how could you know it was my face in the mask? I had to shave clean for the death mask. Is this false beard so bad?"

"No," Cork said, "it's quite good, in fact. Until Tunxis returned, I had no inkling of a man named Black Jack Herleigh. But I did suspect that the affair had something to do with a run-away criminal, and both yourself and Tooks were new to the neighbourhood. I decided on you, for Tooks, in his official capacity, could have made a mask of his own face and sent it along to Savannah without any hanging at all. You proved your mettle to-night when you gave Tooks the antidote for the death-sleep potion I put in his Knock."

"I thought Neela had done it to protect me."

"Your slaves think well of you, Smyth, and I suspect your attitude comes from having spent some time in chains yourself. If you perfect this new scheme of mine for rice production, you may well have no need for them. What the devil are you doing, Oaks?"

"I'm rubbing my shin where you tripped me."

"Sorry, old son, but I had to trip you. It was necessary to the charade."

I was truly touched until he gave me that smirk-a-mouth again.

"Of course, you can trot off to the swamps and have Mamabin fix you a poultice. And while you're there, have her give you new oleander leaves for your pillow. The old ones have scratched the back of your neck, and you are dreaming of the wrong things."

I decided to ignore him, but he is uncanny. How could he know that I had dreamed of my account books?

FOUR

The Bright Silver of Maryland

THE REASONS FOR OUR peregrinations about the colonies are usually too little tied to business dealings and too often spurred by Captain Jeremy Cork's involvement with what he calls "social puzzles." As his financial yeoman, my main dedication is to make him the wealthiest man in the Americas, while his bent, indeed his avocation, is to be perpetually concerned with the solution of crimes. These expeditions invariably bring us into contact with all manner of devious and unscrupulous persons.

Our arrival in Annapolis in the spring of 1750 was neither for crime nor commerce; we had come to eat terrapin. That may sound frivolous, but if you knew the nature of my employer, you would see it as just another jig-a-jot on his journey to perdition. But in the depths of me, I know that he will probably escape Lucifer's last grasp, and not by a penitent deathbed plea, mind you. Oh, no, Cork will talk his way out of Hades and charm his way into Heaven, and I intend to be right at his side to take advantage of the moment and slip into glory unnoticed.

This annual terrapin orgy has become ritualized for us over the years, and the most important part of the liturgy is our argument with Silas Randall, the owner of the Terrapin Inn on Dock Street. Randall is an even-tempered fellow of great girth and hearty hospitality. Yet his patience is tested whenever Cork shows up and puts sherry in his terrapin. To the people of the Maryland colony that is heresy.

"I hope, Mr. Oaks, that the Captain will not insist on the sherry this year," Randall said to me as I was unpacking in our rooms. Cork was below stairs showing a new barkeep how to make Apple Knock, a potation of his own invention, and not recommended for the faint-hearted.

"I would not mention it," I said, shaking my head. "It will only make him more obstinate. Remember, he once threatened to use madeira."

Randall closed his eyes and shuddered.

"Of course, he only said that," I added quickly to lessen the sting, "to bring you to heel about the sherry."

As we talked, Cork entered, stooping as usual to get his six-foot-six frame through the doorway. He was carrying a tray with a large pitcher and three tankards on it. Setting his burden on a table, he poured us each a drink of the Apple Knock, its heady aroma already filling the room.

"Good health, mine host," Cork toasted, lifting the tankard, "and who would Rutherford P. White be?"

The innkeeper quaffed his liquor and smacked his lips. "Excellent, Captain, truly excellent. I would not dare stray from your personal receipt. It would be a blasphemy."

I could see Randall's sly drift towards a touchy subject, but I feared it was only a hare out to trap a fox.

"My dear Randall," Cork said, taking a chair, "I am not a constructor of Procrustean beds."

Randall looked over at the bed in a corner of the room and then turned back to Cork with a confused expression on his normally jolly face.

"Not *that* bed, sir," Cork chuckled. "Although, when you consider my height, all beds are Procrustean. You have not read your Greek mythology, I see. Procrustes was a fabulous giant who stretched or shortened his captives to make them fit one of his iron beds. But I use the phrase figuratively to mean any arbitrary standard to which an exact conformity is forced. You make a Procrustean bed of your method for eating terrapin, with no regard for personal tastes. I do not make that claim for Apple Knock. Now, who is Rutherford P. White?"

Poor Randall, the hare, had been defeated, and he retreated from the argument. I suspect that he did so hoping not to goad Cork into breaking other house taboos, such as never putting cream gravy directly on fried chicken, but restricting it to the attendant johnnycake.

"Rutherford P. White?" Randall stroked his chin in thought. "Oh, yes—a young fellow, a lawyer. From Philadelphia, I believe. Just opened an office here."

I sent my eyes heavenward. With lawyers come lawbreakers, and lawbreaking is criminal, and anything criminal is Cork's delight.

"Word travels swiftly in your Annapolis, Randall. We have not been here an hour, and a boy handed me a note from this White saying he would stop by this afternoon."

"Well, I did mention around the public taproom that you would be visiting the neighbourhood, sir, and he might have heard me. Your name is not unknown hereabouts since you took a hand in the Bristol Herring affair."

Well, I was at least happy to know that we got some celebrity out of the case; we got little else except the chills and fever I suffered from spending two nights in an open rowboat while Cork was tracking down a cutthroat.

Cork spent the next two hours before White's arrival playing dice with himself. He has a theory that, if he throws them enough times and carefully records each outcome, he will find a pattern on which he can rely for making bets. *This*, to him, is industry at work. Paying attention to the spermacite candle factory he owns in Rhode Island, or spending some time at the copper mine up on the Hudson, not to mention the ship he owns and never sails in—all those things are mere incidentals.

It was close to three o'clock—or more accurately, two pitchers of Apple Knock and a thousand tosses of the dice later—when Rutherford P. White was shown into our rooms.

He was pleasant-looking enough, with fair hair and slate-blue eyes, but certainly he lacked the reserve and maturity so necessary in the legal trade. He tried to appear convincing by carrying the green bag which is a symbol of his calling.

"Captain Cork," he said enthusiastically, "I am delighted to meet you." He shook Cork's hand like a pump handle. "I believe you have the acquaintance of my uncle, Thomas Crosley, of Philadelphia. He has told me about you and your exploits over the years. Fascinating, simply fascinating." He went on in a rapid, almost breathless, pace, convincing me that his courtroom style was probably based more on bombast than expertise.

Cork offered him some Apple Knock, and asked what he could do for him. It turned out that he wanted not only the moon, but several stars as well.

"When I heard you would be in Annapolis, Captain, I saw it as an answer to an unspoken prayer. You may be able to help save a family fortune and a venerable reputation as well."

"Gold and honour have a way of cancelling each other out," Cork said, "but let's have the particulars."

The young man smiled. "Silver, sir, not gold, is at the bottom of the problem. Geddies Silver, to be exact. You have heard of it, of course."

"And who has not? The Geddies name has been in the forefront of silversmithing for years. The Geddies family discovered some method for producing a silver that is brighter than any other and less apt to tarnish," I put in.

"Correct, Mr. Oaks. It was discovered by old Farley Geddies back at the turn of the century, and has been kept a close family secret from father to son. Trevor Geddies, my client, is the last remaining Geddies, and now heads the firm. I am here on his behalf because he is in danger of losing the fortune that took almost fifty years to amass. Of more concern to him is the fact that, if the charges are true, his grandfather, so well remembered as an honourable man, will be branded a thief."

"Formal charges? I assume someone accuses the elder Geddies of stealing the process," Cork said.

"No, nothing formal yet, but Oliver Dunne threatens to go to law, and I fear his case is painfully clear. Let me start at the beginning. Five days ago, a young man named Oliver Dunne arrived from London, and claimed that his grandfather, David Dunne, had discovered the process for 'bright silver,' as it is called. I say he 'claimed,' gentlemen, but it is more accurate to say he *proved* it.

"He had in his possession a journal kept by his grandfather in his youth. The book had been lying, unnoticed and unread, in a trunk all these years. An entry for 4 August, 1707 gives a detailed explanation for making 'bright silver.' "

"Two questions, Mr. White," Cork said. "Is the method in Dunne's journal correct, and does not Geddies have a patent?"

"I'll answer the second one first, for that's the problem. Old Farley received a patent from the first Lord Baltimore on 10 December, 1708 in gratitude for some handsome silver plates that were presented to him. The patent does not divulge the actual process. It merely says: 'a method known only to the Geddies family.' It was granted for four lifetimes in the Geddies family. I have shown the method described in the Dunne journal to Trevor Geddies, and he admits, in confidence, that it is correct in every particular."

"But why did Dunne's grandfather let his process lie fallow all these years?" I asked.

"Because he died before he could use it. Now, here is the important point, as far as I am concerned. He died aboard ship while returning to England on 14 August, 1707. He left from Annapolis. The Geddies firm kept accurate records, and I went back over the years and found that David Dunne's name and signature are in their paybook from 5 July to 9 August, 1707."

"Aha," I chuckled. "He stole the secret and was going to England to exploit it."

"More likely the Continent, Oaks," Cork injected. "But your charge of theft also works in the reverse, does it not? It could be said that Dunne did indeed discover the method, and it was usurped by Farley Geddies."

"Precisely, Captain Cork," White said.

"Tell me, Mr. White, how is the method applied in the Geddies shop? Are the workmen involved?"

"No, sir, and never have been. Each succeeding Geddies

used it alone in a locked room. Of course, I can't describe
the process, but it has to do with adding certain chemicals
to the molten silver."

"The Dunne signature in the paybook was compared
with the holograph in the journal?" Cork wanted to know.

"Yes, of course. Forgery was our first suspicion. I had
two expert calligraphers study the pages of the journal,
masking only the portions of the pages that detailed the
process. They are positive the signature and the writing are
in the same hand. Further, three different papermakers are
convinced that the paper in the journal was made in the
colonies in the early 1700's."

Cork smiled at White and complimented him. "You are
very thorough, sir. Now, how precisely is the Geddies'
copy of the process recorded? Certainly old Farley would
not have trusted it to memory."

"It is carefully noted in a copybook which is kept in a
locked box. Of course, over the years, each Geddies has
learned it by heart, so the box is seldom out of safekeeping."

"And this copybook has no mention of date?"

"None at all."

"Strange. The old-time artisans were quite careful, and
I would say the original Geddies certainly was."

"How can you know that?" I asked.

"Because he kept detailed paybook records, and his
orderliness has been passed on to his heirs, since those old
documents, though of little value, are still extant."

"Absolutely correct, Captain," White assured him.
"Trevor tells me that, before their deaths, both his father
and grandfather were terrors about keeping meticulous
records."

"Yes, blood will tell. But how about the lineage of the
Dunne family?"

"If his journal is any guide, David Dunne was a restless
fellow. He left England shortly after his marriage in 1705
and was an itinerant silversmith in Boston, Philadelphia,
and then here in Annapolis. He didn't even seem to know
that he had fathered the child who became Oliver's father."

We all turned to a knock on the door. Cork called,
"Come in," and it opened to admit Host Randall and a

spare, dark-haired fellow who was dressed rather gaudily, like a strolling player.

"Ah, *there* you are, White," the man said, coming into the room. "I've been scampering all over this dusty town looking for you."

White introduced him as Oliver Dunne, but that was obvious from his London Cheapside accent. He nodded to me and then said to Cork, "Captain? You don't look like a toy soldier."

Cork ignored the thrust and said, "Randall, another pitcher, please. Pray sit down, Mr. Dunne. White has been telling us of your lucky find."

"Well, I hope it's lucky. Damnedest thing, the old rascal being a genius, isn't it? My old grandma'm would be twirling in her grave if she knew the family fortune has been gathering dust in an old trunk for forty years. She didn't speak very well of the old governor, she didn't."

"Are you a silversimth, Mr. Dunne?" Cork asked. I could tell he didn't care for the fellow, and was watching for a trap.

"Me?" He laughed aloud. "Ollie Dunne a silversmith? No, sir, rags is my calling. Ragmonger. That's how I come to find the journal. Poking around in my ma'm's things after the funeral. I was looking for old cloth that might bring a price. Well, upsy-daisy-Scarborough-Fair, there it is, in a pile of old clothes that must have come back with the old man's body long ago. My own old man never bothered with the stuff, the fool. Here them Geddies been making a fortune off the sweat of old Dave's brow all these years."

"How did you know that you were looking at the secret of Geddies Silver, Mr. Dunne, since you are not a silversmith?"

"Ah, you're a sly one, Captain," Dunne said, winking. "I didn't know. But the Geddies name was mentioned in the journal, and we've heard of Geddies Silver in London. Well, Ollie, I says to myself, you may have something here in your hands, me boy. So I goes to a solicitor and he checks the Royal Patents. Then he finds a record of the Lord Baltimore grant, but the thing is dated almost a year and a half after the entry in my grandfather's journal. Well, here I am, and from the look on Mr. White's face,

I think I have a good case. Geddies hasn't admitted that the methods are the same, but I'll wager they are. How do you and Mr. Oaks stand in this, Captain?"

"Mr. White and I have mutual friends. But I am curious. If you were proved true, what would you consider a fair settlement?"

Dunne broke into a broad smile, showing two missing teeth. "Now, that's the talk I like to hear! Well, I'm a fair fellow. I could take everything, I suppose. But why be a hog? Now what would I do with a silversmith's shop? No, for me, Captain, it's a healthy slice of all the coin that's been made in the last forty years, and a large nip of the yearly take from now on. Mr. White, I've been waiting now for five days, and I can't sit no longer. If I don't have an answer by to-night, I'll have to go to law in the morning."

Dunne got to his feet, bid us good day, and was abruptly gone. Randall passed him as he brought more Apple Knock to the table.

Cork mused into his empty mug and said, "This is most interesting. We have a forty-year-old crime to which all witnesses are dead, and yet they speak to us."

"Do you hear voices?" I asked.

"In a way. David Dunne gives us a picture of himself. He is a man with a reputable trade, yet he leaves England to come to the Americas. A man seeking advancement in silversmithing would find more fertile soil at home than in these climes, where most shops are rudimentary and have few customers of wealth. Remember, our forefathers were too busy breaking soil and abuilding to collect amenities. Yet here is a fellow who leaves a pregnant wife and goes off. From Oliver's description of his grandmother's feelings, I'm sure there was no love lost between them. Then, once here, David Dunne drifts about from city to city until he 'discovers' a process. Mr. White, you described him as restless, but I think it well might have been an inability to stay honest."

White nodded his head. "Of course, this is all conjecture, sir, and will do us very little good in court. I'm afraid we are done for."

"Dunne for, is more like it," I said, spelling out the name; but no one laughed.

"Possibly." Cork got up and stretched, which in itself is quite a sight. "But since we have had the advantage of meeting the Dunne offspring, perhaps we should now look at the Geddies issue."

The Geddies establishment was but a few blocks away, in Cornhill Street, and we walked there in the mildness of the afternoon.

It was a snug shop with two bow windows flanking the doorway. Travellers from the European continent are often shocked by the smallness of a colonial silversmith's shop and the lack of merchandise for sale about the place. I once had to explain to a visitor from the Lowlands that, since no silver is mined in the colonies and since the only sources are Spanish coins from the West Indies and the few English coins that filter through, converting the coins to decorative pieces is a practical method of protection.

A candlestick or a spoon is more recognizable than a common coin, if stolen. And, if coins are needed at some later date, the spoon or candlestick can be melted down and the coins struck. This, of course, by the authorized colonial Mint. Several silversmiths have swung for reversing the process and bypassing the Mint. Few Geddies creations made their way back into coins, however, for the workmanship and, of course, the brightness, made them worth more than common pieces of eight.

I assumed it was the original shop of old Farley Geddies, for a weather-worn sign hung across the top of the windows that used the curious lettering I have often noticed on old sentimental establishments. It read:

DeLICate
siLversMithing

Trevor Geddies met us in his short sleeves and invited us back to a small nook that served as his office. He was a strongly built young man of 20-odd years, and mildly handsome. Two miniature portraits hung over his desk, showing the common features of the Geddies' line. Trevor, however, looked tired and worried in comparison with his forebears.

"I see no hope for us, Rutherford," he said to the lawyer, after being told of Dunne's visit and his demands. "The process in the journal is the very same as the one put down by my grandfather."

"Your grandsire was quite careful about records, it seems," Cork said. "Yet he did not date the paper on which the method was written."

"I never thought about it, Captain Cork. Until this came up. I always assumed that the 1708 date on the patent covered everything."

"But that is beguiling to me, Mr. Geddies. Let us make an assumption here. David Dunne came to work for old Farley, or young Farley then, in July of 1707, and left the next month. Do your records indicate why?"

"No, sir."

"Did Farley keep a diary of his own?"

"No, not to my knowledge. And we've searched everywhere."

"Well, let us go on with the assumption, which is that David Dunne somehow got access to the process which existed in the summer of 1707, or possibly before. Were any pieces made from Geddies Silver, the 'bright silver,' sold prior to July, 1707?"

"The first recorded pieces were the plates given to Lord Baltimore."

"Which were presented in December of 1708. But there could have been others. How long would it take to make the plates, Mr. Geddies?"

"In those days? Hmmm. Well, it was a twelve-piece setting with matching goblets, and of course, the hand engraving. Possibly a year. More, if not worked on full time."

"Excellent. So we know the method probably existed in December of 1707."

"But, Captain," White put in, "that proves nothing, since Dunne's journal reads 4 August, 1707—five months earlier."

"Yes, but let us stay with our assumption that Dunne was a thief. Now, would you say that the method is a very complex one, involving ingredients that would have to be tested as to specific amounts in order to achieve the right mix?"

"Well, of course," Geddies said. "But I'm so familiar with it that it seems simple to me."

"So does the making of bread to any chit of a girl, sir. But the first loaf in creation—that was a different matter! Determining the right amounts of water, flour, and salt could have taken aeons. Now, your grandfather opened this shop in 1701—"

"How did you know that, sir? I didn't know it myself," White put in.

"It *was* 1701, Captain," Geddies told him. "In this very building."

"Of course." Cork was matter-of-fact. "And I am sure the first few years were lean?"

"Exceedingly so."

"But in the July of 1707 your grandfather hired another silversmith, so business must have been better, or its outlook rosier. A man enlarges his business with apprentices, and only hires a journeyman when the future is promising. Now I go back to my assumption. Farley, after months or possibly years, develops 'bright silver,' makes the Baltimore plates to ensure a patent, and hires a man equal to his skill to help with the project.

"But he does not know that his new journeyman is a scoundrel, and when Dunne suddenly departs for England, Farley is none the wiser that his secret method has been stolen. Do not ask me how, gentlemen. My assumption will not stretch that far. Now we have two documents in combat with each other: one clearly dated and the other not. May I see the Geddies method document, sir?"

Trevor shot a glance at Rutherford who, in turn, looked at Cork.

"Come, my dear fellow," the Captain said. "You have already admitted to Mr. White in confidence that the Dunne entry is correct, and he to me. If you stand where you are, the court will make you produce it, or you will lose by default."

With a solemn look on his face Trevor Geddies went to a back room and returned with a small metal box, banded in brass straps, and made fast with three separate locks.

He took one key from a chain around his neck and unlocked the first fastener. A second key was produced from
his pocket, and the second lock was undone. A third key
was ingeniously hidden in Trevor's ornate belt buckle, and
it went into service with the third lock. With the box lid
lifted, three pieces of faded copybook paper appeared.
Cork took them gently into his hands and read each sheet
carefully, scrutinizing each line of careful penmanship.

"As I thought, a simple task for you, but it must have
taken years to arrive at. Your grandsire had a touch of
the romantic about him, sir."

Trevor smiled for the first time, although weakly. "I call
that Farley's Folly," he said. "But I guess it was of no
help where Dunne was concerned."

Cork handed me the sheets and I smiled myself at the
old silversmith's bent for the heroic. It read:

> Verily
> I Issue Venomous wrath
> upon any Man Designing Calamity
> for our Claim for Virtuous Initiallity

The rest were instructions for preparing and adding
elements, and signed by Farley Geddies, Silversmith.

"If he had only put the date after his name, as is the
custom," I said, "and that date was prior to 4 August,
1707, we could tell Mr. Oliver Dunne to go fish in other
waters."

"And so we can, Oaks." Cork took a breath and shook
his head. "It's a shame that old Farley was so subtle, but
then he never meant this document to substantiate his
claim. He was merely having some fun."

"You mean he *has* put the date in there?" Trevor asked,
snatching the paper from me.

"Of course, and you are saved, sir. He wrote that down
on 5 July, 1706, a full year before Dunne was hired. Don't
look so astounded, gentlemen. I have no genius, but I do
have eyes. When I said the firm was founded in 1701,
Mr. White showed surprise because he had not mentioned
it to me. He didn't have to, because old Farley told every-

one who passed his door. The sign on the front of the shop reads:

DeLICate
siLversMithing

and it is a chronogram, gentlemen, often used in old documents to conceal the date. You merely add the purposely capitalized letters which then represent Roman numerals. In the sign we have D, which equals 500, L equals 50, I equals one, C equals 100, L equals 50, and M equals 1000. Added together, they equal 1701. What is often taken for old-style lettering is really a chronogram.

"Now in Farley's case, he refined the practice. Note he ends with the word 'initiallity,' when it might have been 'initiative' or 'invention.' But he says 'initiallity,' so we take him at his word and add up all the initials, in terms of their values as Roman numerals. On the first line we have the V in Verily. V is five—the day of the month.

"The month itself is found in the capital letters beginning 'I Issue Venomous'—I plus I plus V equal seven, or July. Apply the same system to the last two lines, and you have M for 1000, D for 500, C for 100, another C for 100, V for 5, and I for one—or, all together, 1706."

"By jing," I cried. "You are a genius, a veritable wizard!" I noted that lawyer White looked a bit happier, but then his brow furrowed in puzzlement.

"But is this enough for the court?" he asked.

"Perhaps. But let us put more raisins into the bun. You have a family Bible, I trust, Mr. Geddies?"

Trevor Geddies looked insulted that anyone could think otherwise. Then his eyes lit up. "Of course, when a new child was born, Farley would always write some bit of verse after the new entry."

"Once a man acquires a little habit, he finds it often takes him over, and he uses it everywhere," Cork said. "Shall we look in the Bible, sir?"

To be sure, Cork's theory proved true, for the entries in the Bible in chronograms matched the birthdates of the children born before Farley's death. The entry for Trevor Geddies' father, George, read:

George—
>   sound and lIVIng I
>   Vouch
>   thIs Comfort Comes,
>   MaDe as heaven's conVIvial

George Geddies *was* born on 8 May, 1707, as was also borne out by a Baptismal record. Now even the legal-minded Mr. White was jubilant.

The good feeling did not abate there, but persisted, indeed grew full-blown, as we all sat down to dinner at Randall's that evening. Our host gingerly put the plates of terrapin before Cork and closed his eyes as the Captain reached for the sherry

"Sherry in terrapin!" Trevor Geddies was appalled.

"Consider it a habit I have gotten into, sir. Like your grandfather's chronograms, it has taken me over."

That is surely not his only bad habit. There is this indulging in idleness, for one thing. I did, however, brave Randall's glare and used some of the sherry myself. If I must go to the gates of perdition with Cork, I, too, will not go in a Procrustean bed.

Later that night, when we were in our rooms, I suggested to Cork that we might convert some of his coin into Geddies silver.

"And what would we do with candlesticks, sir, or a salt-cellar? It would be that much baggage. Besides, I would take advantage of a trust, for the Geddies Silver now on tables in this land will be worth a high price thirty or forty years from now."

I looked a bit puzzled, and he went on.

"It is in old Farley's instructions for using the process that you did not see. Since the patent runs out with the death of the fourth son, old Farley left clear wishes that the pages be burned, and the process destroyed forever."

"My Lord, how selfish!" I cried.

"How so? He made capital on his own idea and enriched others, as well. And now I am to bed, or half a bed. Perhaps we should invent a bed that expands and contracts to fit the user. It could be done with rollers."

There you are. Another idea for money-making that will go nowhere. Where Geddies kept his idea alive for four lifetimes, I know that Cork would forget his by morning. I made note of it anyway. Could be, in his dotage, he will begin to see things my way.

FIVE

The Margrave of Virginia

OUR ARRIVAL in the Virginia colony in the autumn of 1751 was another submission to one of Captain Cork's many fancies. Of course, his first love is the solution of crime, but his second is unmistakably the theatre. When word reached us in New York that the famous Lewis Hallam and his family had arrived from England to perform *The Merchant of Venice* for the Royal Governor of Virginia, nothing could deter our coming to Williamsburg.

Although the trip south was uncomfortably passed aboard an ancient and ill-equipt coaster, the sparkle and gaiety of Williamsburg soon erased the foul memory of the journey.

Autumn is the gay season in this peninsula city where the old Tidewater gentry and the new Piedmont rich compete in extravagant outings. Balls, races, fairs, and other entertainment bloomed everywhere, and reportedly were not greatly inferior to London's in amusement and elegance.

We had taken rooms at the home of Telford Sheffield on the easterly end of Duke of Gloucester Street. It was a strategic move, for it put us only a few steps from the Raleigh Tavern, a focal point for revelry and good food. Eating, drinking, and carousing are some of Cork's other vices, and he likes to have them handy.

After thirteen days of gadding about, I began to excuse myself from Cork's torrent of social activities. I don't mean that I was bored; nay, I was exhausted. In the race for good times, I am but a quarter horse, good for a fast sprint, whereas my employer is a veritable thoroughbred, who must finish the whole course and then some.

One particular Thursday evening after dinner, I returned to our rooms alone. The Captain was off on another romp with a new lady friend—an association I hoped would not bring on another duel with another irate husband. As you can see, Cork's paean to life is a song of many verses.

I was immersed in an accounting of Cork's financial holdings when a knock on the door brought Mary, the Sheffields' serving girl, into the chamber. Mary is a perky piece of frippery, but I find the serving-girl fashion of wearing the skirts above the ankle a bit disturbing.

"There's a gentleman below, Mr. Oaks," she said with a movement that could hardly be called a curtsey. "Wants to see Captain Cork, he does."

"You could have saved yourself the stair climb, my girl. You know the Captain is out."

"I told him, sir, but he insists on waiting, and I know my mistress wouldn't want Sweet John Spunton left waiting on the porch."

"*Sweet John* Spunton?" I asked querulously.

"That's what he's called, Mr. Oaks. He's the Margrave's son, sir, Colonel Spunton."

The name sunk into my brain and re-emerged in a more familiar form. Colonel William Spunton was one of the largest landholders in the Southern colonies, a man of immense power, who was often called "Baron Bill" by his detractors.

"Well, in that case, you had better show him up, Mary," I said.

He entered the room a few minutes later, a tall, strikingly handsome fellow of twenty-odd. He had the patrician manner so common to the landed gentry. With some Southern gentlemen, it borders on the imperious, but my visitor carried his quality in an easy-going way.

"Mr. Oaks?" he asked, in the typical pronunciation of the Virginian. I extended my hand and he shook it. "I'm sorry to intrude on you, sir, but I must see Captain Cork. Where can I find him?"

I bid him a seat. "In any of a hundred places. I suggest that you wait here. He should be back around midnight. Perhaps I can help you? I serve as the Captain's financial yeoman, and transact most of his business affairs."

"I'm afraid I have need for Cork's more well-known talents," he said, his voice dropping lower.

He didn't have to tell me more. The sudden change in his eyes and the tightening of the muscles in his face bespoke a demeanour I had seen before. This man was in trouble—trouble so vexing that he needed the services of the most agile mind in the Americas. Yet this situation was uncomfortable for me. Without Cork's ready ears available, I was hesitant to broach the young man's problem. I hid instead in the boskage of small talk.

"Tell me, Mr. Spunton, the serving girl referred to your father as the 'Margrave.' I believe that is a German title. Is your family in the European peerage?"

"No," he smiled sardonically. "We are of the Virginia peerage, where power is land, and wealth is measured by the surveyor's chain. God knows we have enough of it—over 200,000 acres."

I *was* impressed. That was formidable acreage.

Spunton went on: "Margrave is an old colonial title. It dates back to the early days when the Cavaliers first came over. It meant that you owned more than 48,000 acres. My father inherited his first 12,000 acres from an uncle, and built it up to 62,000 by head right. The rest was purchased on and off over the years."

"That's interesting. You have a fine education, sir. Inns of Court in London?"

"No, I'm locally planted. William and Mary."

"As I understand it, head right allowed a man to receive fifty acres for every person he brought into the colony, but that was some time back. Your father must be quite elderly."

"Almost seventy-five. My mother was much younger."
At the mention of his mother, his newly relaxed face went
rigid in tension again.

"I take it your mother has passed on."

"Five days ago. That's why I'm here. I think . . . I know
. . . my father murdered her."

If someone had thrust a hot poker in my face, I could
not have been more seared with shock. In all my years
with Cork, I have heard a litany of horrible crimes, but
this, if true, was one of the worst. Yet those same years
had taught me to be wary, indeed suspicious, of loose
charges often delivered out of well-intentioned, but incor-
rect assumptions.

"That is a grim charge, Mr. Spunton. On what do you
base it?"

The outpouring that followed tested my mettle for dis-
criminating between fact and fancy. Five days ago, Mrs.
Spunton had fallen from a second-floor window at the
family estate, Spunton Hall. The Hall had been occupied
by the elderly Colonel, his wife, who was in her mid-
forties, the Spunton sons, John aged 22 and Brace aged
24, their younger sister Carrie, a girl of 18, and twenty
house slaves.

The death of the mistress would have been put down
to an unfortunate accident had it not been for the presence
of Rachel Broom. The Broom girl had come to Spunton
Hall six months before to serve as Mrs. Spunton's personal
lady-in-waiting. According to John, Rachel was a poorly
educated and uncouth woman of 20. She was lax in her
duties, insubordinate to her mistress, and ran roughshod
over the household.

"Is she a bondswoman?" I asked. "Sounds like a good
thrashing would put her to rights."

"No, Rachel is a freewoman. Her father was a sea captain of my father's acquaintance," John said as he wound
down his tale. "My mother complained, but the Colonel
turned a deaf ear. Anything Rachel did was tolerable to
him. I didn't understand it all until this morning. Then it
was clear that my mother was a victim of murder. My
father admits he was near my mother's bedroom when

she fell to her death. He said she was reaching out to feed a squirrel when she toppled.

"That is plausible, Mr. Oaks. She was a quiet woman who loved animals. We didn't see much of her these past few years. You see, she never got over the death of my youngest brother, Jed, back in '48. She'd spend most of her days sitting in her rooms feeding the small animals and birds that came up to the house."

"Poor woman," I said, "but what turned your thoughts to murder, sir, if her death was plausibly accidental?"

"This morning at breakfast Rachel Broom announced that she was betrothed to my father. Don't you see, he wanted my mother out of the way to marry this—this scullery maid?"

"Did your father confirm her statement?"

"Indeed. My brother Brace and I confronted him, and he indicated it was true. He became enraged when we pressed him. I had heard that Captain Cork was in Williamsburg, and I rode in to seek his help."

Well, by jing, if I was serving as Cork's proxy, I told myself, I might as well think like him.

"Tell me, Mr. Spunton," I said, leaning back in my chair and folding my hands in Cork's manner when interrogating a subject, "where was Rachel Broom at the time of your mother's accident?"

"*Murder*, sir, and you can mark it. I believe she was in her own room. It adjoins my mother's."

"You say you 'believe,' sir, but you don't know. Did your father actually see your mother fall?"

"He said he was passing her doorway when he heard her cry out. He rushed in, but it was too late—at least, that is his story, and I believed it until Rachel's announcement this morning. Now I can see that he was so filled with lust for that witch that he was willing to kill for her."

I have often been critical of the Captain's exercises in criminal investigation, but now, I must confess, I found it most exhilarating. In point of fact, it was quite simple, once you got the hang of it.

"Was your mother's bedroom door opened or closed when your father said he heard the scream?"

When John replied that the door was closed, I almost clapped my hands with glee; but, owing to Spunton's obvious grief, I resisted.

"It would seem to me, Mr. Spunton, that you have overlooked a more obvious culprit."

"Who, sir?"

"Rachel Broom herself. If she occupies an adjoining room, she could easily have pushed your mother out the window and scampered back to her own room in a matter of seconds. You must admit that is a much more palatable solution."

"And how do you explain my father offering Rachel marriage just five days after my mother's death? If Rachel is the culprit, he could have known about it. Perhaps it was collusion."

"Not necessarily, sir. You are a young man with many fertile years ahead of you. Your father is an old fellow, and would reach out for feminine comfort in his loss. You said yourself that your mother had been more or less a recluse over the past few years. Well, put yourself in your father's place."

I was grateful when Spunton conceded that I had a valid argument, and I couldn't wait to boast a bit to Cork. That was not forthcoming, however, for it was now past midnight, and the Captain had not yet appeared. Spunton said that he was fatigued from his ride in from the plantation, and decided to get some rest and speak with Cork in the morning. His family maintained a townhouse in Botetourt Street, just around the corner.

I, too, was sleepy, so I left a note asking Cork to waken me on his return. I drifted into slumber, content with my night's work.

It was dawn when I felt the Captain's hand shaking my shoulder. For a man who had been abounding all night, he didn't look the worse for wear. In fact, you would think that he had spent the night sedately in bed.

I am not one to dawdle on awakening. I was on my feet in seconds and relating the Spunton affair. I told him everything young John had told me, and then sat down at the table with a self-satisfied look on my face.

"All we have to do is fetch the authorities and clamp the wench in irons," I said, cupping my kneecaps.

"Oaks," Cork roared, "you're an ass, a bloody jacka-napes. Get dressed! We ride for Spunton Hall within the hour."

"I don't understand, Captain."

"I haven't time to explain. Now move."

"All right," I said, getting into my breeches, "I'll get mounts and pick up John Spunton and be back shortly."

"You can stop by the Spunton townhouse," he said, his face growing dark, "but only to confirm my suspicion that he is no longer there."

John had indeed left, and the Captain and I rode speed-ily north-west as if to escape the rays of the rising sun.

The thrust of beauty is often blunted when the mind knows that the splendour-in-the-eye is but a façade for some unknown evil. My first view of Spunton Hall, as we entered the plantation's main park, should have taken my breath away, and would have, had I not ridden for some silent hours next to the sullen Cork. The main house, a thousand yards ahead, was framed at the end of an oak-lined drive. It was like a scene on a stage—a stage rimmed with floral footlights aglow with the vitelline warmth of late autumn flowers.

The structure itself was clean-lined and impressive. The architect had let the building's many equally-proportioned-and-spaced windows serve as its chief external ornamenta-tion. It had a steep hipped roof above two full storeys, and the roof was pierced by twelve dormers. Two huge chim-neys rose from either end of the house, and, as we drew nearer, the late afternoon sun glinted off the pink brick-work, which was carefully set in courses of Flemish and English bond. It was an architectural masterpiece, and fitted the power of the Margrave.

We reined in at the foot of the porch steps. A thin black child in light blue livery and powdered wig raced up to tend the mounts.

"Is your master to house?" Cork asked him.

"The Many-grave is home, sah."

"And Miss Broom?"

The boy looked up in amazement as Cork dismounted and stood facing him. The Captain is six foot six, but he must have looked twenty feet tall to the child.

"No, sah. She done be dead."

"Hesh. Hesh up, boy," a deep voice said from the main doorway. Its owner was a ramrod-straight black man. He, too, was in livery, but his cotton-white hair was his own. He was a very dignified-looking man, and his manner, though quiet, was one of authority.

"May I be of service, sirs?" he asked.

Cork was about to speak when a young woman appeared in the doorway. "Who is it, Uncle Robbie?" she asked.

Her hair was the same yellow as the autumn flowers, and her comely features bespoke her kinship to Sweet John. Carrie Spunton was a true beauty.

We introduced ourselves and she asked us to enter the main hall. She told the butler to show us to the parlour, and went off to inform her father. We were left alone amid the fine English- and French-made furniture, brocade draperies, and walls covered with Chinese silk. The extravagance was lost on me, for I was disheartened over the news of Miss Broom's death.

I slumped onto a divan and looked up at Cork, who was studying a curious red vase. "I sealed that poor girl's doom, didn't I?" I said. "If I had not given John my theory, he wouldn't have sought revenge."

Cork put the vase down, rubbed his hands, and smiled. "Then you are a double jackanapes, my lad. This morning, when I gave you that appellation, I was pricking you for faulty deduction, not for sic-ing John Spunton on like the devil's mad dog. My haste in getting here was on the assumption that there might be another murder, but I couldn't be certain who the victim might be." He stopped when he heard footsteps in the hall. "As Uncle Robbie so colorfully put it, 'Hesh up.' You may see me play the dunce in a few seconds, but follow my trail."

The footsteps stopped at the doorsill, and Colonel William Spunton surveyed us. His face was well lined in the manner of the elderly, and so might be the body beneath the silk shirt and claret waistcoat; but his carriage was boldly erect. If Sweet John and Carrie were his children, they must have favoured their mother. But the young man who stood at his side took after his father as a lead image from a mould. Both Brace Spunton and his father shared the same fierce black eyes, and stern, almost cruel, mouth.

There was only one word for this duo, and it was arrogance. The master and the heir apparent were fiercely regal, like the dukes of old.

"Captain Cork." The senior Spunton's voice was surprisingly young and resonant. "Your reputation precedes you, sir. This is my elder son, Brace."

We shook hands all around, and the Colonel shouted an order to some unseen slave for peach juleps.

"You'll have to forgive my younger son John's running off half-cocked," he said as we sat down around a black lacquered table. "Sweet John's like his mama. Makes for a handsome boy, but a flighty man."

"Yes," Cork said, "I could tell that from Oaks's report. This Broom woman did herself in?"

"Ha! You see, Brace, I told you he was a man of good mind!" The Colonel's hand came down on his son's leg. "Of course, I couldn't believe that Rachel had pushed my wife to her death. I assumed she fell, poor woman. But when Rachel heard that Sweet John had been to see you, she must have panicked. Threw herself from the same window. Now that's poetic justice, eh, lads?"

A young slave entered and put down a silver tray with bottles and goblets on it.

"It is a sad business." Brace spoke for the first time. "If I thought she had killed mama, I swear I would have run Rachel through myself. But God has a way of squaring things."

"Your wife was ill, as I understand it, Colonel," Cork said, accepting a goblet.

The Colonel nodded, but spoke of the julep. "It's the mint that does it. Damnedest combination—peach brandy and mint. But it does have something curious about it."

"Delicious, Colonel," I said. "Almost as tasty as the Captain's Apple Knock."

Cork then had to explain his concoction, which is highly potent.

"Splendid!" the Colonel cried. "You shall make it for us at supper. By the Lord, it's good to have folks in the house again. Haven't had guests since my youngest boy Jed died five years ago. Dang beautiful child. Thrown from a horse. Brace here shot the animal on the spot. My wife came down with what the old mammies call 'the awfuls.' Moody. Kept to herself. I guess the poor thing is better off in heaven with Jed. Emily will be happy there."

"Where is John?" Cork asked. "I was hoping to meet him."

"Asleep," Brace told him. "Came in riding hell-for-leather around sunup. Told us what Mr. Oaks had said. Rachel must have eavesdropped, because she flung herself out of that window a half hour later."

"Well, enough of this morbidity," the Colonel said. "You gentlemen will want a scrub and some rest before dinner."

Cork quaffed the rest of his drink. "Can we possibly have adjoining rooms, Colonel? Oaks and I sometimes use the night hours for business plans, and we wouldn't want to disturb the household."

Old Spunton furrowed his brows for a moment and then smiled. "There's only my wife's room. The adjoining room was Rachel's. I don't think their things have been moved out, though."

"Perhaps we impose upon the house," Cork said. "We could ride back to—"

Colonel Spunton threw his head back and laughed. "Imposition! Lord, man, you have little knowledge of Southern hospitality. When I first came out here, plantation owners used to haunt the crossroads, looking for guests. There was one fellow, up near York River, used to take 'em at gunpoint. That's how much he wanted people around him. My wife's daddy once had guests just for overnight, and they stayed until their second child was born. Stay, sir, the house is yours."

I had finished my bath and was astonished that my linens had been washed and dried and my clothes brushed. I dressed and popped my head into Cork's room. He was hastily going through the late Mrs. Spunton's clothes closets.

"I know you played on the Colonel's pride to get us the rooms occupied by the mistress and Rachel Broom, but don't you think you will arouse suspicion if a servant comes in?"

"Just a cursory look for now, Oaks. We'll have to wait till tonight for a minute examination."

"I didn't think you were taken in by this suicide fancy, but whom do you suspect?"

"All of them."

"A conspiracy?"

"No, each one is highly motivated and had probable opportunity in Rachel's death. The wife's death is more perplexing."

"Couldn't part of my original assessment stand? Rachel killed her mistress to replace her and one of the Spuntons took revenge?"

He had abandoned the closets and was busy at a writing desk and the contents of its drawer. He spread several items out upon the desktop. They were a miniature portrait of an extremely handsome woman, a seal ring, a snuff box, and an ivory pipe.

"What do you think, Oaks?" he asked.

"You are testing me again, aren't you? Well, let me try my hand. The miniature looks like Carrie, but from the costume, I take it to be Mrs. Spunton. The ring is a family memento, and the pipe—you think you have me there, don't you? Well, I'm not that obtuse. I am supposed to say that the pipe is the Colonel's, but I know these Southern women smoke a bowl or two. I remember a lady of your acquaintance in North Carolina who blatantly smoked these seegars you're so fond of."

"Well, done, Oaks. Don't be dismayed by foul habits. These people make their living from tobacco. Proximity, or rather availability, spurs usage."

There was a soft rap on the door, and Cork quickly replaced the items in the drawer. Uncle Robbie entered and announced dinner.

In the course of our adventures, Cork and I have supped under all conditions—by campfire, in rude tree-line cabins, and in the finest houses of New York and Philadelphia; yet nothing could match the exotic splendour of dinner at Spunton Hall.

Our arrival had altered the regular dinner schedule, which was normally at three o'clock, but the food did not suffer from the delay.

We were seated facing the two Spunton sons. The Colonel and Carrie sat at opposite ends of the long table. Behind each chair was a footman in full uniform. They were silent and efficient under the direction of Uncle Robbie. The Margrave may have been the master, but these was no doubt that young Carrie was the mistress of the plantation. I supposed that during the years of her mother's seclusion, she had filled her place, and she now handled it with grace and subtle charm.

The table was laid with lace cloth, and there was damask underneath. While the Colonel carved a saddle of mutton, Carrie ladled black bean soup and pork bits from a tureen of East India china. Considering the recent tragedy in the house, the conversation was remarkably light and cheerful.

The mutton and soup were delicious, and when finished the plates were removed and others quickly put in their place.

"Now, sirs, I have a treat for you," the Colonel said, as Uncle Robbie refilled his goblet with champagne. "Owing to your visit, I have asked my little Carrie to have a preserve of fowle made in your honour."

I had no idea what he was talking about, and when the kitchen servant carried in a large turkey on a silver platter, I put the Colonel's enthusiasm down to pride in his daughter. However, when the turkey was cut in transverse sections and served, I marvelled at the plate of morsels before me.

"Pray, Miss Carrie," I said, savouring the meat, "this is most curious. I first taste turkey, and then I swear it's goose."

Carrie's eyes sparkled above the white of her teeth as she laughed. "Mr. Oaks, you have a tongue for taste, sir. What else do you find?"

I could see it was a game, and that she loved a tease.

"Duck," Sweet John said, "definitely duck."

"A star for you, Sweet John darling. How about my other brother?"

Brace was the most sombre of the party. "Just turkey," he said, and went on eating.

"Oh, pooh. You're a wretch, Brace boy. Daddy, your turn."

The old man winked at her. "You can't fool me, you minx, there's capon, too."

Carrie clapped her hands. "Now you, Captain Cork. Daddy says you have a head for solving things."

"Dove, to be sure, Miss Carrie, and, let's see." He took another forkful as the girl watched him intently with anxious glee. "Don't tell me now," he said, and she giggled. "Now, let me see, this feast is much like some of my cases. All the elements are here. The trick is to identify them. So you started with a dove and stuffed it into a guinea hen. Then into a duck, and the duck into a capon, and that into a goose, and then into a turkey."

Carrie clapped her hands again. "You missed one, sir, you missed one!"

"You see," Cork said to us all, "it *is* like my cases. I haven't found the missing ingredient."

"Partridge!" Carrie Spunton was overcome with triumph. "I've put you up a stump, Captain."

"To be sure, ma'am, but I have been up there before. However, eventually I manage to get down. It's just a matter of time until I find the missing ingredient."

We finished the preserve of fowle to much laughter. This course was followed by a plum pudding, tarts, and brandied peaches. Then the damask was removed, and we continued small talk over figs, raisins, almonds, and madeira.

Later, having excused ourselves, we retired to our rooms, me to digest and Cork to ponder.

"You are not satisfied, are you?" I asked the Captain.

"I told you to follow my dunce's trail, and you did so admirably. No, I don't believe that Rachel Broom committed suicide out of remorse for having murdered Mrs. Spunton. The case offers a strange mixture of motives."

"The children wanting Rachel dead is certainly strong. Carrie doesn't appear to be the type to give up her mistress-ship to Rachel, and both John and Brace had a great deal to lose if the Colonel had married her and she produced another son."

He nodded. "But how can you reconcile the mother's death? Certainly the children had nothing to gain from her death. Which leaves us with Rachel and the Colonel."

"Then we have come full circle," I said.

"Not quite. Colonel Spunton is no fool. He—" Cork

was interrupted by a knock at the door, and Colonel Spunton himself entered, looking less merry than he had been at dinner.

"Excuse me, gentlemen," he said. "I remembered that my wife's Bible was in here. Since she died, I have taken to reading myself to sleep. Ah, there it is." He picked up the Good Book and caressed the soft leather cover.

"Odd, isn't it?" he said in a tired voice. "My Emily was always after me to read the good word with her, and now that she is gone, it is my only consolation."

"She must have been a beautiful woman," Cork said, picking up the miniature. "You'll forgive me, I found this while looking for some writing paper."

The old man took the picture and looked at it lovingly. "No older than Carrie when she first came to the Hall as a bride. She was such a fragile creature—so like the little creatures she fed each day."

"Was your wife's illness melancholia, Colonel?"

"Yes, you might say that. Each of us has his little ways." He walked over to the window and looked out at the gathering dusk. "I'm going to have this damnable portal walled in to-morrow. I'm sorry that my wife's things are still in this room. I don't like shrines. I told Rachel to pack up Emily's things, but she never got around to it."

"Colonel." Cork joined him at the window. "Perhaps Oaks misunderstood your son last night, but he said something about you having been betrothed to Rachel."

"A complete misunderstanding, I assure you, Captain. John is a good lad, but impetuous. Rachel was not a bad sort, a bit unpolished, but basically a nice girl."

"And this misunderstanding?"

"Youth has a way of hearing only what they want to hear. Two days after Emily's accident, I was talking to Rachel and said something about the void in my life and that I was counting on her to fill it. I guess the girl took that as an offer of marriage."

"I see, but wouldn't filling that void with Rachel be a snub to Miss Carrie? She certainly is the apple of her father's eye."

"Applecore, meat, pips, and skin, sir. But don't be taken in by Carrie's guileless ways. She inherits 50,000 acres from her mother directly, and a fine house in Clarewick. She loves me dearly, but I fear she will be off to be her own mistress shortly. Southern women are not as dependent and helpless as they appear."

"Nor women anywhere," Cork said. "I have always been clinically interested in melancholia, Colonel. It's a strange disease that may take manifest forms. Was your wife under a doctor's care?"

"Not lately. Dr. Gordon rode out from Williamsburg several times a few years back, but he said that physically there was nothing wrong with her. And now I am quite tired, gentlemen, if you'll excuse me."

"Of course," Cork said, crossing to the door to open it. "Will Rachel's remains be sent on to her family?"

The Colonel stopped at the doorsill and turned to Cork. "Who told you she had a family?"

"All of us do, at some time, sir."

"She had only her father, who went down with his ship, the *Bonnie Marie*, last spring. That's why she came to live here. You'll forgive me, but I do not care to talk any more about the Broom girl. Good-night."

"Good-night, sir. Oh, by the way, Colonel, a personal request, since we will be leaving in the morning. What perfume did your wife use? This room has an intoxicating smell—so sweet, and yet it is too late in the year for magnolia or honeysuckle, so I assume it is her scent. If I could have the name, I'm sure it would please a lady friend of my acquaintance."

"Probably sachet. I have no knowledge of ladies' toilettes, Captain. Good-night."

Cork had me up at dawn, and we found the cookhouse already abustle under the direction of Uncle Robbie.

"Colonel said you would be leaving, gentlemen," the black man said, with no trace of sadness at our departure. "They'll be eggs, slab pork, and grits ready right soon."

Cork nodded and took a seat at one of the rude slave tables. His acquiescence to eat was a Godsend for me, because I do not like to travel on an empty stomach, and I had feared from Cork's agitated mood on awakening that we would be condemned to a long, hungry ride back to Williamsburg.

Uncle Robbie served the plates himself. "I trust you'll enjoy it in health, gentlemen."

"Tell me, Uncle Robbie," Cork said as he sliced some bread, "you appear to have some book learning."

"Master Jim always said he wanted good talk around Miss Emily, so he had the preacher learn me."

"Master Jim?"

"Mrs. Spunton's daddy, Captain. Master Jim Leigh, sir. A fine man." The slave's smoky eyes squinted hard. "Belong to the Leighs, sir. Come here with Miss Emily when she married the Colonel. Old Master Jim said, 'Robbie, you go over there and take care of my girl, and see that no harm come.' Now she's gone, and looks like Miss Carrie is going back to Leigh Hall, and me with her."

"It must have been sad for you, Mrs. Spunton falling to her death that way."

"What's done is done. The Lord has her now."

"And Rachel Broom as well, eh?"

"She's not with the Lord, Captain Cork. That's a surety."

Cork might have pursued the subject further, but he was cut off by the slave's sudden departure. We were just finishing our breakfast when the stable boy, who had greeted us yesterday, came in to tell us our horses were ready.

We cantered down the main drive until we had come a few hundred yards. Cork reined up for a moment and turned in his saddle for a final look at Spunton Hall.

"Is that the end of it?" I asked, a bit dejected. "Is the case a stone wall?"

"No. Much like Carrie's fowle preserve, I have all the elements identified, but they are not yet in their proper order."

"What next, then?"

"First, we have to prove an assumption, and then find one thousand men."

"One thousand men!" I found myself saying it to the flank of Cork's mount, as he broke into a gallop towards Williamsburg.

Dr. Gordon's house was on Scotland Street, just off Boundary Street. He was a fussy little man with quick nervous hands and a breathless way of speaking that gave you the impression that he was rushing from crisis to crisis.

"Mrs. Spunton—the Margrave's wife—oh, yes, yes. Very sick woman—most ill." He was fidgeting with papers on his desk.

"I believe you told the Colonel that there was nothing physically wrong with her."

"Physically? Organically—well, no, Captain. More in the mind and heart, you know. Broken-hearted over her son's death. Seen cases like it before. Nothing one can do."

"Would you say she had a demeanour of malaise?"

"Oh, yes, yes."

"But did she appear to be unhappy? Sadness and tears?"

"No. More like living in another world. I think she was dwelling quite happily within herself. She—ah—stopped time, as it were. And speaking of time, I have little to spare, gentlemen. I must be off."

And so were we. The Royal Palace was only two blocks away, so we walked.

"The good doctor didn't make much sense, but he seemed to have corroborated what we already knew about Emily Spunton."

"Dr. Gordon is a fool," Cork snarled. "Or at least limited in his observation. Well, at least the assumption is proved, and now for the thousand men."

These are the times in which I could strangle Cork without regret. He was closing in on a solution, and yet he kept it entirely to himself. There had been a time when I took his silence, as he stalked the denouement, to be necessary to his concentration. Now I know that was nonsense. He just enjoys dangling me on a string.

He had scrawled a hasty note before we left Dr. Gordon's office, and, on arriving at the Governor's palace, he had it carried within by a footman.

Ten minutes later, a scholarly gentleman with a balding head appeared and announced that he was the Clerk of Records, and had been instructed by the Governor's secretary to extend us every courtesy. For the next two hours, Cork not only accepted the courtesy, he abused it unmercifully.

The Clerk of Records, whose name was Fowler, was not a spry man, but this did not deter Cork. He had him climbing ladders in the cellar vaults, and toting massive ledgers to a small candlelit table. The poor man looked near exhaustion before Cork sat back and smiled.

"The greatest gift to mankind is the written word, Oaks, but putting it to record-keeping is without doubt its supreme moment." Old Fowler beamed. "Now, Mr. Fowler, would you be good enough to fetch me a quill and paper? Oaks, go on to the Raleigh Tavern and send back any young fellow who wishes to earn a purse for a long ride. I'll join you at the Tavern for an early supper."

All was ready when Cork arrived at the Raleigh. A joint of beef was almost off the spit, and terrapin stew was bubbling.

"Do you plan to keep this case secret?" I asked him as he drew out a chair and sat down.

"From most society, yes. But justice will be served if all turns out as I expect."

"Well, tell me one thing. Did I seal Rachel Broom's fate when I deduced she could have killed Mrs. Spunton, and informed Sweet John?"

"I told you before, no. Rachel sealed her own doom. The problem with this case was that it had too many murders and too many motives. Let's take the murders first. Mrs. Spunton wasn't murdered. Opium smokers have a way of losing their bearings."

"Opium smokers? But how—"

"The ivory pipe and the cloying smell in her room indicated it. Dr. Gordon's statements that she 'had stopped time' and was happy were merely euphoria. Perhaps we were too hard on the doctor. Opium-smoking is a rare sight outside of the Orient."

"But Colonel Spunton *could* have killed her for Rachel."

"Nonsense. A man of his wealth can have a dozen mistresses, and still keep a wife. A recluse at that, giving little trouble. No, no one had anything to gain by her death except Carrie, and it is inconceivable that she would have killed her mother for her estate."

"All right, but suppose one of the Spuntons believed

Rachel killed their mother. The wedding announcement would make it seem that there was collusion between Rachel and the Colonel."

"One-sided collusion, Oaks. I asked myself what possible hold Rachel could have had over old Spunton to get a betrothal out of him. That's where I had to use some arithmetic."

"The one thousand men, eh? That's still a mystery to me. Something in the records you went through this afternoon?"

"The records confirmed it. Now, what weapon could the daughter of a poor ship captain use against a powerful aristocrat?"

"That he killed his wife."

"Oaks, you are a vexation. We have concluded that Mrs. Spunton's death was an accident. Now, review in your mind your initial conversation with John Spunton. What is the source of power and wealth in these parts?"

"Land."

"But John told you that his father inherited only 12,000 acres and built it up to 62,000 by head right."

"Yes?"

"Arithmetic, man, use your great love of sums! If a man got fifty acres of free land for each person brought into the county by head right, where are the men? Divide 50,000 additional acres by 50, and you have to account for one thousand new immigrants. Where are they?"

"I haven't the slightest idea," I said.

"Rachel Broom knew. Her father must have told her his secret, and she used it to blackmail Spunton."

"I admit that one thousand people don't just disappear. Perhaps they went into the hills."

"Perhaps. But the records don't show that. They do show that the *Bonnie Marie* was Spunton's main carrier for immigrants, and that she made port four times a year over a ten-year period. That would mean twenty-five passengers per trip. Packed to the gunnels, the *Bonnie Marie* could not have carried over ten passengers. Moreover, her bills of lading reveal that each passage she was also stowed tight with hard goods."

"So the land grants were made out on people who didn't exist."

"They had to exist. The people had to stand before a magistrate in the flesh and blood."

"Then how?"

"The crew, Oaks, the crew. When the *Bonnie Marie* made port, her crew came ashore and were logged in as Spunton immigrants. Then they went back on board for the return trip to whatever port and there they found themselves discharged and a new crew put on. Captain Broom himself appears as a Spunton immigrant on one of the trips, which caps it."

"And when the *Bonnie Marie* went down, Rachel Broom forced the Colonel to take her in."

"And when Mrs. Spunton fell to her death, she saw her chance to be the new mistress of the Hall. A scandal in bogus land grants would destroy Spunton's honour. I believe he agreed at first, and then saw the folly of it. Blackmailers never stop at one bite; they go on until they have everything—in this instance, possibly the disinheritance of Brace and John."

The joint was served, and I sliced off a piece. "Well, I admit it makes sense, Captain, but as you are always so fond of pointing out to me, conjecture is not proof."

"We'll have that by morning," he said, helping himself to more stew.

I guess it was technically morning, although I consider 2:00 A.M. the middle of the night. I rose from my bed to the knock on our door, and saw Cork admitting the young lad I had hired as a rider that afternoon. He was worn and breathless from hard galloping, and Cork shoved him into a chair and poured him some wine.

"Thank you, Captain," he said, after a deep swallow. "I near rode the horse into the earth. I gave the Margrave your note and he read it. Then he looked at me with tired eyes and handed the note back to me. 'I'll trust you to return this to Captain Cork,' he said, and, by God, he walked into the next room and put a pistol ball through his head. He's dead, sir."

When the lad had left, Cork held the note over the candle flame and watched it consume itself.

"So you sent him your findings," I said.

"I sent him a conjecture, and he returned it with proof. He may have been a land swindler, Oaks, but the Margrave was also a gentleman."

SIX

The South Carolina Cicisbeos

IT WAS ONE of those warm, butter-turning days that pop
up now and again in early May to remind humankind that
the heat of summer is not far off. I normally would have
enjoyed this prelude to the balmy season of 1758 had we
not been visiting in Charles Town in the South Carolina
colony. Visiting is perhaps an improper word; we were
languishing. Or Cork was. I, as his financial yeoman, was
busy caring for his many business interests which are scattered about the colonies.

This gay and bountiful port holds a fascination for my
employer, Captain Jeremy Cork, and this sudden burst of
early summer filled me with dread. Not that Cork would
pass an aestival here once the temperature rose into the
80's and the dank humidity descended. No, the peril lay
in the possibility that he would be coaxed into joining the
local gentry in its annual exodus to New Port, Rhode Island, where the merriment would continue in cooler climes.
Once in that company, I would not be able to get him to
pay attention to business until October.

Charles Town's heady atmosphere stems from the quick

and easy fortunes that have been made in the rice and indigo trades. Nobody in the town seems to be poor, and quite honestly no one seems to give a damn if school keeps or not. Captain Cork is suited to the place like a hand to the glove. Balls, fairs, banquets and outings are the main preoccupation of the quality, and even the humbler classes display a wont for a good time. It was imperative that I get Cork out of this Sodom-by-the-Sea.

Of course, when we are in Charles Town it is mandatory that we stay at the Halcyon Club, where Cork is a charter member. It is a sumptuous mansion which serves as the hub, if not the inventor, of much of the town's social hijinks.

I was pondering the profit and loss situation of his talc mill in Pennsylvania when he emerged from his bedchamber, ducking as usual to get his six-foot-six frame through the doorway. It was close to eleven in the forenoon, yet he was fully dressed and was carrying those dratted sticks again.

"Up with the birds, I see," I chided him, "and off to your chores without breakfast."

"I ate before retiring," he snapped, "and there is more work in this than you realize."

"I know, I know," I said. "Doctor Rush says it will add ten years to your life, but I don't think he meant that you should spend your entire life playing at it."

His latest passion is a game called golf. It is a puerile pastime wherein grown men knock a feather-filled leather ball about an open common in the laughable effort to hit it into a series of holes in the ground.

"I wouldn't call a few hours in the fresh air and sunshine an entire life. Besides, it relaxes me."

"Relaxes you for what? The strain of gallivanting from party to party? Or perhaps it helps clear your mind for your pok-ar game."

Pok-ar is a vice which is practised between midnight and dawn. A requisite to the ritual is seegar smoke and brandy fumes.

"Oaks," he grunted, "you are an abomination."

"That may be so, sir, but so is the talc mill. It lost almost 50 pounds last quarter."

"Ha!" he guffawed at me, taking a practise swing with his golf stick. "I made that and more at the tables last night. Confound it, you're worse than a wife."

"A wife would have left you years ago. A woman wouldn't have you about."

He knocked his imaginary ball with the stick, and, by jing, stood there following its flight. "Perfect," he said with self-satisfaction. "Speaking of wives, we will both have one this week. The cicisbeos drawing is tonight."

"Must I get involved in that nonsense?"

"Of course. It would be an insult to the fair ladies of this town not to. Well, I'm off." He strode to the door and was gone.

"Take deep breaths," I called after him. "Stretch those muscles. There's a long night ahead, and you must be relaxed."

I heard his descent on the hallway stairs and shook my head in despair. I almost wished for a note from Major Tell, asking us to hurry to Philadelphia or Boston to investigate some social puzzle, as Cork calls them. Actually, the puzzles are the detection of criminals in all manner of mayhem and skulduggery. That I, Wellman Oaks, who normally abhors that activity, would hope for a case to occur indicates the depth of my concern. This cicisbeos nonsense would keep us in Charles Town another week, and invitations to New Port were dangerously close.

Actually, I had forgotten all about Cicisbeos Week, and now I was informed that I would have to participate. It is one of the customs at the Halcyon Club to place all the married ladies' names in a bowl, and have each member draw from it. For one entire week, you are the lady's cicisbeo, her recognized *cavalier servante* and her escort to various functions. The thought of catering to a lady in the presence of her husband seems a bit loaded to me, but the locals enjoy it no end. All, that is, except the unmarried ladies, who are excluded from the custom. Once selected, you become the lady's property, and you must pay court to her every whim, call her "cara mia" and wear her ribbon on your belt like a branded steer. I have nothing against doting on a lady, mind you, but with my luck, I felt sure to draw a cranky old crone who would have me scurrying about for bonbons and sweetmeats to fill her ugly face.

Happily my fears proved unfounded, for that evening I had the good fortune to draw the name of Mrs. Margaret Fishingale, a young damsel and as pretty a piece of frippery as you will ever see. Called Peggy by her friends, she was the wife of Hal Fishingale, the scion of the Fishingale Plantation. They had been married but a few months, and I could see that her spouse was not overjoyed at the thought of having a squire around her for a week. But Cara Mia Margaret (I kept it as formal as possible and refrained from calling her Peggy in deference to her husband's feelings) seemed to enjoy the situation.

Cork was not as fortunate. He was paired with Mrs. India Rygate, the wife of a powerful shipping tsar, Alonzo Rygate. Mrs. Rygate was the grande dame of Charles Town's society, and well into her sixties. Cork was unfazed, however, for he has a remarkable ability to make the best of any situation. As he says, "Enough is as good as a feast."

And so our servitude began in earnest the next day, when we were invited (or ordered, to be more accurate) to a luncheon at the Rygate townhouse.

Joining us at the affair was Peter Goselowe, the importer, who squired Mrs. Sue Hammond, an attractive woman in her thirties, whose husband Matt seemed quite content to be rid of her for a week. All the husbands were there to present their wives to us and then withdraw, leaving the gallants to their tasks. Margaret Fishingale introduced me to two other ladies, who had to be the pride of the South. Mrs. Jessie Barstow was a comely thing, blonde, half woman, half child, who bubbled with excitement. The other was Dicey Darby, no more than eighteen, with coal black hair and alabaster skin. She could be described only as stunning.

I found myself feeling sorry for Jessie Barstow, for her cicisbeo was almost twice her age and portly. Then, to my surprise, he was introduced as her husband, Trevor Barstow. Dicey's husband was John Darby, a young man with extensive frontier holdings and a reputation as an Indian fighter.

"It seems that we have been abandoned," Jessie said to Dicey.

"Dahlin', Cole and Clay have been late for everything since they were children."

Jessie tossed her pretty head back and laughed. "It's Clay that was the first to be late, remember." She turned to me and explained. "The Severy brothers are twins, Mr. Oaks. Cole is my gallant and Clay is Dicey's. Cole was born two minutes before Clay, and Clay says he had the right to be late from then on."

Just then there was some noise in the center hall, and two young men appeared in the doorway. They looked like a brace of matched thoroughbreds, black-haired, dark-eyed and fiercely handsome. The birth of twins is not uncommon, but their chance survival made them a rare sight. The two ladies rushed to greet them.

We were quite a merry group, and Cork made Apple Knock for everyone. We toasted our cara mias and then Mrs. Rygate announced that it was time for the presentation of the tokens of honor and all the gallants lined up in a row. Every wife went to her husband, and Mrs. Rygate gave the signal to begin. It was all very ceremonial.

Mrs. Rygate was presented to Cork by her husband, and she then tied a bright red scarf to Cork's belt and said, "Wear my colors with honor, sir." Cork took her arm and led her to the other side of the room. I was next in line, and Hal Fishingale presented Margaret to me. She gave me a white scarf, saying with a smile, "For the innocence of our relationship." Her husband looked glum as I took her arm and rejoined Cork.

The next husband and wife were Jessie and Trevor Barstow. As he presented her to Cole Severy, she, to my surprise, did not present him with a scarf, but unashamedly slipped a blue garter on his arm. "Now you take care of that, Cole," she admonished him mockingly. "That's from my wedding trousseau, my 'something blue'."

"Oh, no," Margaret Fishingale murmured from my side.

"Madam?"

"I knew she'd do something like this," she whispered to me. "Jessie chased Cole for years, and couldn't get him to the altar. She's just trying to embarrass him."

"Her husband looks like the embarrassed one," I said. Trevor Barstow was blushing.

"More like bullet-biting angry, Mr. Oaks. Trevor knows Jessie married him for his money, but he adores her in spite of her antics. Now watch, Dicey Darby won't be outdone."

And sure enough, she wasn't. When she was presented to Clay Severy, she turned her back to us and lifted her skirts, turning back again with a blue polka-dot garter in her hand. This was turning into an orgy, and I was uncomfortable.

Dicey slipped the garter on Clay's arm and said, "Now we can tell you handsome boys apart."

Sue Ann Hammond broke the tension in the room when she gave Peter Goselowe a bright green scarf and told him it was for spring.

Thus we were joined to our ladies and flung into a round of parties, picnics, dances and all manner of jollity. By the third day, I was a bit winded, but the ladies were going strong. Although there were forty-two couples in all, our original group at Mrs. Rygate's tended to stick together. No one was having more fun than Jessie Barstow.

We were all at dinner at the Halcyon Club on the fourth evening when Jessie brought up the tournament idea.

"I don't play golf," I told her when she suggested that the gallants play a game the next day for a purse of 250 pounds. Each of the five cavaliers was to put up 50 pounds, and the winner was to fete the whole group to a sumptuous dinner on the final evening of Cicisbeos Week.

"Then you will have to learn, Mr. Oaks," Jessie scolded me. "The knights of old held tournaments too, and golf is certainly safer than jousting."

I couldn't quite see the logic in that statement, but it was useless to argue with a beautiful headstrong woman. Besides, Cork, Clay, Cole and Peter Goselowe were all for it, and the match was set to begin at ten o'clock the following morning, with all the ladies in attendance.

The Severy brothers were staying at the Club, and Cork joined them for pok-ar after the ladies had been taken to their homes. I went to our rooms to brood. After all, 50 pounds is a great deal of money.

When Cork came in, I was sitting at the desk with my personal ledger.

"If you lose," he said, "take it out of the general funds. After all, I got you into this."

"No, sir, I cannot accept the offer. It's a question of honor."

He gave me that smirk-a-mouth of his. "Well, it's only a matter of batting a little ball around. You said so yourself."

"I didn't know you made wagers on it."

"Oaks, betting in golf is like sex in marriage. Without it, things get dull."

He is truly a heathen. "That's a rather hedonistic way to put it. In a sense, I have been married all week without romance, and it's quite enjoyable. Although I am surprised at the brazenness of Jessie and Dicey. Jessie is practically throwing herself at Cole Severy."

"He's quite a rogue with the ladies, but I hear he is smart enough to avoid complications with a married woman."

I finished my calculations in the ledger and saw that the loss of 50 pounds from my personal account would almost make a pauper of me. "Are all those fellows, Clay, Cole and Peter Goselowe, competent golfers?"

"Excellent, I would say."

"I was thinking. Tomorrow morning could we rise early and go out to the Common? Perhaps you could give me some instructions."

"If you like. Wake me early."

I did, but when we had breakfasted and went outside at 8 A.M., there was a light ground-fog under the morning sun. Cork assured me that it would burn itself off before we got to the Common, which was a ten-minute walk out of the town. But there still was some fog when we arrived and the grass was quite dewy. I was surprised at the size of the course. It was a large open field, some 200 yards in depth. At various places large poles protruded from the ground to mark the location of the holes.

Cork showed me how to hold the club and how to swing it. After a few practice shots I put down the ball and took a swing, sending the missile up into the air in a wide arc.

"Was that good?" I asked.

"As they say in this game, you're in the rough. The ball is in the woods to the left. Come on, let's find it." We entered under the trees and started our search. I was about ten feet from Cork when I saw it. "Captain!" I cried. "Come over here! This is terrible!"

He came on the run and looked down at the body that was stretched out on the ground.

"It's Clay Severy," I said, kneeling down by the corpse. There was a gaping stab-wound in his chest and his face was cold and white. On his arm was the polka-dot garter that Dicey had given him, and I wondered if it could possibly have been the motive for his death. I looked up at Cork, who was staring down at the man's face.

"Could he have run afoul of Dicey's husband?"

"There are many possibilities, but the first problem is which brother this is."

"Why, it's Clay. See the polka-dot garter?"

"Yes, but his face tells me it's Cole."

"Cole! But they are identical twins. How could you tell?"

"I have been in their company for four days, and to identify them in my mind I determined that Cole is the right-hand brother and Clay is the left-hand brother."

"Left-handed? I don't see . . ."

"Not *handed*, Oaks. Twins share a common face; they come from a common seed. But if you put them together, side by side, and merge their faces in your mind, one is the right side of the face and the other the left. Nothing in nature is exactly the same. I may be wrong, but we will see."

Cork remained with the body while I summoned the magistrate in town. His name was Horace Binsbee, an elderly gentleman of great girth who did not enjoy having his breakfast interrupted. He grudgingly called for his carriage and ate a meat pie on the way to the Common.

"Well, it's most fortunate you are in our town, Captain Cork," Binsbee said after viewing the death scene. "Some brigand must have waylaid him when he came to play golf."

"I doubt that, Judge Binsbee," Cork retorted. "His purse is still on him. And he couldn't have been playing in the fog. I believe he came here to meet someone. Let's take care of the corpse and then deal with the living."

We took the body back to town and left it with a coffin maker before going back to the Halcyon Club. On our way up to the Severy rooms, Cork warned us to keep quiet and to let him handle the situation.

He knocked at the door, and it opened in seconds. The twin was still in his nightshirt.

"Good morning, Captain." He yawned. "What has raised you so early?"

"Bad news, I'm afraid. Your brother is dead."

"Cole? Cole dead?" His eyes went wide with shock. "How? Where?"

So Cork had been right. We were looking at Clay Severy, and it was Cole who had been stabbed to death. Cork told him of the circumstances and the young man's jaw became rigid. "Damn that Jessie Barstow!" he growled. "I was afraid of this. Trevor Barstow is no man to trifle with."

"There is one complication. The killer thought it was you, Clay. Cole was wearing the polka-dot garter that Dicey Darby gave you."

There was a noise outside the open chamber door, and a woman rushed in with tears running down her face. She screamed in a French-accented voice, "Cole, oh Cole! Clay is dead! I've been such a fool, Cole. It was Clay I loved, and now it's too late."

The twin put his hands on her shoulders to calm her.

"Annette, calm yourself, I'm . . ."

"I was a fool," she ranted. "*Mon Dieu*, Cole, what am I going to do?"

"Annette, I *am* Clay, it's Cole who is dead."

She looked at him and went silent. The blood drained from her face and she swooned to the floor. Cork scooped her up in his arms and placed her on the couch. Clay brought brandy. As she came to, Clay explained.

"This is Mademoiselle de Arbois, gentlemen. She is my brother's ah . . . lady friend."

"She sounds French," I said.

"She is. She is a coiffeuse, poor thing, forced to dress

hair for a living. She was once at the French Court." He brushed her hair back from her face and soothed her once her eyes were open. "I'm sorry, Annette, Cole seems to have worn my jacket by mistake. It is I who should be dead."

"I think not, Clay." We all turned to Cork, who had gone unnoticed into the bedchamber and come back holding a jacket in his hands. There was a polka-dot garter around the sleeve. "Either your brother had a garter to match yours and wore it there to trick someone or . . ."

"Whom would he try to trick?"

"I don't know, but it cost him his life. Do you have any enemies?"

Clay shrugged and Annette de Arbois spoke for him.

"Clay has no enemies, but Cole did. It was that *sorciere*. She couldn't have him so she killed him."

"Annette, you must not speak that way. Jessie wouldn't harm Cole."

"Clay, you are so kind and so foolish. I know women better than you. It's all over town that she was throwing herself at his head this week. Remember, I do the ladies' hair. I get all the gossip. Even her best friend, Dicey, thinks she is acting shamelessly. She told me so last night when I did her hair for your dinner party. Everyone knows she always wanted Cole."

"Perhaps we should leave these two to their grief," Cork suggested to the judge and myself.

When we were outside the room and the door closed behind us, I said, "It looks more like Trevor Barstow is under suspicion and not his wife."

"Except that Cole was wearing Clay's garter. A woman in love would know the difference between the two, but not an angry husband. Trevor Barstow was present when the garters were given to the brothers. If Cole were wearing a polka-dot garter, Barstow would have mistaken him for Clay. Well, Judge, we have work to do. I would appreciate your following up on some details."

"Of course, delighted, but lunch will be on us soon."

"Eat here at the Club as my guest, by all means, and while you are at it you might question the staff about Cole's departure this morning."

We left the judge to his task and I dutifully followed Cork downstairs to the street.

"Do you actually think Clay may have killed his brother?"

"What's so strange? The first murder in creation was between brothers."

"But they seemed on the best of terms all week. What possible motive could he have?"

"Any number of them. They obviously share an estate, and from the tenderness displayed by Clay toward Mlle. de Arbois, I would say he thinks highly of her."

"So we have three suspects—Jessie Barstow, Trevor Barstow and now Clay himself. Most confusing."

"It's even more tangled," Cork said as we walked along. "Consider that the murderer might have thought he was killing Clay. Does that bring Dicey Darby's husband into the picture? She's been quite kittenish with Clay all week."

"My word," I exclaimed, "and why not toss in Dicey herself? She might have been in love with Clay. It's all beyond me."

"Ah yes," he sighed, "on the face of it, it should be a simple hornbook exercise, and yet its answer lies hidden in subtle colors and damnable complexities—little squiggles and twists that confound the mind like a bashful bride in a maelstrom of honeymoon quilts. But have faith, old son, a well wrought challenge is but a cold night to make a man keen for conquest."

"Where are we walking to?" I asked.

"We need some background information. We must know our players more fully, their passions and strengths. When you are looking into a town's musty closets, your best source is an old woman, Oaks."

"Madam Rygate."

"Most astute, Oaks, most astute." He was smirking when he said it.

Madam India Rygate was at her morning coffee when we were shown into her sitting room. The grande dame poured cups for us. Cork was right about her abilities at gossip. She had not yet set foot outside the house, but she had all the details of the tragedy.

"It's disgraceful," she said, handing me the cup. "Brigands coming in from the back country to rob and kill.

It is truly getting out of hand. My husband and some of the others are thinking of forming a group called the Regulators to bring law and order to the hinterland."

Internally, I was chuckling. It seemed to me that if the leaders of society had spent more time on good government instead of gay frolics, they wouldn't have had the brigand problem in the first place. Cork was digging his mental spade into the town's dirt pile.

"Tell me, Madam," he asked offhandedly, "you have known the Severy twins for a long time. Can you tell them apart?"

"I've known them since birth. Certainly I can distinguish between them. They are as different as night and day."

"How so?"

"In demeanor. Clay is the serious one, always was. Cole was quite a hellion as a child and a womanizer when he grew up. After their father died, Clay's steady hand kept their plantations going. Cole would have gambled them away. Jessie Barstow, she was Jessie Stone then, didn't know how lucky she was when Cole threw her over."

"For this French woman—Mlle. de Arbois?"

She looked aghast. "Heavens no, Captain Cork! That courtesan? Not Cole Severy. Oh, I heard the talk. But when Cole settles down . . . oh dear, I mean if he had *lived* to settle down, I can assure you it would have been a woman of quality. In fact, there is a lovely widow in Taylorville not too much older than he who would have made him a good wife. Quite wealthy."

"Yes, I am sure you are quite the matchmaker."

Her face beamed. "Well, I matched Jessie to Trevor Barstow and then, after Cole had his fling with Dicey, I was lucky to get John Darby interested in her. Of course, Dicey has her own money, where Jessie did not, so her dowry was considerable."

"Then Cole threw Jessie over for Dicey?"

"Oh, yes. Not thrown over, really. Cole was very fickle. You probably noticed how Jessie and Dicey compete for attention. Take this nonsense with the garters. It was quite naughty of them."

"I thought they were the best of friends," I said.

"My dear Mr. Oaks." She wiggled a finger at me. "You bachelors are easily fooled by womankind. Those two are playing a cat's game in public. In private, they detest each other. Why, they've never even visited each other's homes."

"Tell me about the husbands, Madam. Are they the type to be jealous?"

She pursed her lips in thought. "John Darby is a man of action, as are all men from the frontier. A rough, quick, no-nonsense fellow. Trevor Barstow, on the other hand, is a moody type, steady, not much of a talker. I have to admit that Jessie has put some snap into him, and he revels in it."

"A while back you referred to Mlle. de Arbois as a courtesan. Were you speaking pejoratively?"

Her expression was pained. "I live and let live, Captain, but she's a little too Continental for my tastes. Maybe it's all an act, and she's merely a *grisette* put to raise her station. I believe she had her hooks into Clay Severy until his brother came back from Savannah two months ago. It was just as well. Cole could handle a woman like that without getting entangled. Not that I have any animosity toward her, mind you. She comes here to do my hair. I am not a snob, gentlemen. Live and let live, as I said."

"A good philosophy," Cork said with feeling. "One other point. Did Cole have anything to do with Mr. Oaks's cara mia, Peggy Fishingale?"

"No. Peg is a bit of a gossip, you know, but she and Hal have been sweethearts since childhood."

"And Mrs. Hammond, Mr. Goselowe's escort?"

"No. They are woodsy people, and new to our circle. I don't think Cole ever met them. But Peter Goselowe was once one of Cole's best friends. His lawyer, in fact."

"They had a falling out?"

"Yes. Some business dealing or other. You know how silly men can be over a contract. Clay settled the matter somehow but Peter and Cole have been cool to each other of late."

We had finished our coffee and our hostess offered more. Cork refused, and I took his lead.

"This has been most enjoyable, Madam," Cork said, bowing.

"I was charmed to have you both and pleased to have you as my cicisbeo, Captain. Perhaps next year we won't have any difficulties. This killing has certainly ruined the entire season. You really don't believe that Cole was killed by a brigand, do you?"

"No, Madam, nor do you. Any guesses?"

"Live and let live," she said with a smile.

Back on the street again, we were headed back to the Halcyon Club.

"The old cat certainly knows every nook and cranny in this town," I remarked.

"We have enough dirt in our ears this morning to sow an acre of potatoes, Oaks."

"It looks like Peter Goselowe has joined the cast of suspects, doesn't it?"

"Yes, it's like seven-card stud in pok-ar. I have too many capital cards. Three kings—Goselowe, Darby, and Barstow. Two queens—Dicey and Jessie. And," he added, "a knave in the form of a mythical brigand."

"What about Clay Severy?"

"For the moment, he is my ace in the hole, but something disturbs me. Pok-ar is more a game based on a knowledge of human nature, you know. You can bluff an opponent out of a secure position."

"And you are looking for the bluff?"

"I am begging my mind to find it. It's rather warm, is it not?"

"Yes," I replied with trepidation, visions of New Port looming before me.

Judge Binsbee was sitting in the main dining room of the club when we entered.

"What ho, Captain," he greeted us. "Come try these squabs. They are delectable."

"I prefer oysters at midday, sir. What have you discovered?"

"Well, the Madeira is not top quality this year . . ."

"I think the Captain is referring to the case at hand, Judge," I reminded him. He had the remains of four squabs on his plate and two more on the platter.

"Oh, the case! Yes, the case. Well, I've had my deputies out and about. The people concerned are all cleared. The Barstows and the Darbys were home in their beds when this tragedy occurred. Peter Goselowe, being an attorney, is above reproach. It was a brigand, to be sure."

"How about Clay Severy?" Cork wanted to know, and

so did I. Here we were paying for this glutton's lunch and had nothing to show for it. I have been around this murder business long enough to know that husbands' and wives' alibis are worthless, and the good judge may have known the law, but not lawyers.

"Oh, yes. Severy. Well, I was just getting to that." He turned to the rear of the dining room and beckoned Roland, the chief steward. The small mustached man came up to the table and bowed.

Roland had once been a chef to the Earl of Cumberland back home in England, and was quite proud of his association with royalty.

"Yes, your Honor?" he asked.

"Ah, Roland, have the boy bring two more of these succulent birds and more gravy. Hot, mind you."

"Roland," Cork said, "a moment please. Did you see Clay leave the Club early this morning?"

"Not Mr. Clay, sir, but poor Mr. Cole went out around seven. I knew it was he because he had that blue garter on his arm. It's the first time I could ever tell those twins apart. It is quite a tragedy."

"Certainly is," the judge muttered through a mouth packed with squab meat.

For a moment, Roland lost his normal reserve. He spoke to Cork. "Captain, I am hesitant to say this, but in the interests of justice . . ."

"Justice be damned man," Binsbee growled, "the birds!"

"Pray let the man speak, Judge," Cork cut him short. "What is it, Roland?"

"Well, sir, there is talk all over town about the murder, and I feel I must speak. It may mean nothing, Captain, but on the night of the Cicisbeos drawing, I took a bribe."

"Bribe!" snarked the judge. "Probably to get you to serve hot food. What is this Club coming to?"

"Please, Judge," Cork pleaded. "Yes, Roland, what was it about?"

"The drawing, sir. Remember, I drew the lots. I was paid to pair Mr. Cole Severy with Mrs. Barstow."

"Indeed! By whom?"

"Mrs. Barstow, sir."

I shot a glance at Cork, who was furrowing his brows. "Is that all?" he asked.

"No, sir. You see, Mrs. Darby made the same request an hour later. She offered a few shillings more, but I was committed to Mrs. Barstow. Of course, I didn't tell Mrs. Darby that. I know I could lose my position here, but Mr. Cole was always quite generous with me."

"Excellent!" Cork cried. "By the Duke's guns, Roland, bring me a plate of oysters and some vinegar."

"Then everything is all right?" Roland asked anxiously.

"Quite all right, Roland, You have sorted my cards well. Now, for heaven's sake, get those squabs for his Honor. He'll need his strength."

Roland went off to his duties and the magistrate looked puzzled. "You mean I have more to do, Captain?"

"Yes sir, you do. You are about to trap a murderer."

"That may well be, Captain, but I am first going to trap at least three more squab."

While the judge filled his face, Cork laid out his plan. By five that afternoon, everyone involved was to be gathered at the home of John and Dicey Darby.

"Jessie Barstow might not like that," I cautioned. "Remember what Madam Rygate said about Jessie and Dicey not visiting each other's homes."

"Precisely the point, Oaks. We are into the final act."

I know what he meant. He calls it a catastasis, and he loves it. It gives him a chance to play the hero. If he had the answer, and, from the look on his face, he certainly did, all he had to do was inform the judge and effect an arrest. That would be the practical way. Cork is not practical. He is an actor. Actors are extravagant, both in emotion and coin.

At half past four that afternoon, Dicey Darby looked like she was about to have a fit, but she begrudgingly played hostess to the herd of people that had invaded her beautiful townhouse. Her husband John seemed discomfited by the invasion, but he, too, bore it all with an artificial smile.

In fact, artificiality was the main ingredient of the group. Madam Rygate and her husband Alonzo remained pompously aloof. Jessie and Trevor spoke genteel words through gritted teeth, and Peter Goselowe, the lawyer, was politely sullen.

Clay Severy sat on a sofa comforting the still-stricken

Annette de Arbois, while Cork and Judge Binsbee sat at the table which had been pushed to the center of the salon. The judge was calling the group to order when four more people entered the room. The Fishingales and the Hammonds made their entry with apologies for being late.

"Dicey dahlin'," Peggy Fishingale babbled, "this is a dreadful hour for a party."

" 'Tisn't a party, Mrs. Fishingale," the judge said, " 'tis an inquest. Now let's all get comfortable. I'll have a mite more of that Madeira, ma'am," he said to Dicey, and a servant refilled his glass for the third time. He sipped and went on.

"Now you all know there's been a murder done, and it's been quite an inconvenience to us all."

"Mostly to my brother," Clay Severy snapped.

"I guess you're right, Clay. Sorry. Well, to my thinking, poor Cole was done in by a murderous brigand, but Captain Cork here has a notion or two and it can't hurt to hear him out."

"If it were an outlaw—" Alonzo Rygate on his feet "—why wasn't a hue and cry raised, Binsbee? You officials are too blasted lax in your . . ."

Binsbee rapped the table with his Madeira glass. "Alonzo, this is a judicial proceeding, so sit down and shut up unless you're recognized by the bench. Go ahead, Captain, it's your deal."

Your "show" would have been more accurate, for Cork rose from his chair like a mainmast, and towered over the room.

"Ladies and gentlemen, at the outset I must announce that we are in the presence of a murderer, and I am prepared to unmask the culprit. But first, let us get rid of this brigand idea. Cole had his purse on him when we found him, which rules out a thief. Also, the notion that Cole went out to play a practise round of golf has no substance. He had to have left the Halcyon Club when the fog was thick. Hardly a good time to play. More importantly, he did not have golf sticks with him."

"He could have been pacing the course," Peter Goselowe offered.

"To what end, sir? He had played on it countless times. No, it is manifest that he went there to meet someone.

Now, another myth that must be dispelled is that no one can tell the Severy twins apart. I have only known them for a few days and I could distinguish them. Most of you have known them for years. Whoever killed Cole knew he was killing Cole."

"I challenge that," John Darby cut in. "I couldn't tell them apart, and I understand Roland, the club steward, couldn't either."

"Ah yes, Roland. We will get to him in a minute. Let us first examine why Cole was killed. Was it jealousy on the part of a husband, hatred by a former business associate, or that oldest of motives, murder for profit?"

"It seems to me," Goselowe said, using a legalistic tone, "that you have conveniently brushed aside the brigand theory with conjecture. Cole could simply have been taking a walk."

"Would a brigand from the back country switch the garters to confuse the issue?"

"Switch?"

"Yes, Mr. Goselowe. Roland says the twin that left the club wore a blue garter on his sleeve, and yet when the body was found it had a polka-dot garter instead. That was done by someone intimate with the Cicisbeos ritual and your personal lives.

"Excuse me, Captain," Judge Binsbee said, "but we found the polka-dot thingamajig on Clay's coat. How could they be switched?"

"Garters are worn on both legs. Where is the other polka-dot garter, Mrs. Darby?"

She looked surprised, if not shocked. "Why, on my dressing table."

"Good. Judge, will you go with Mrs. Darby while she looks for it?"

The couple left the room and in their absence, John Darby became belligerent.

"See here, Cork, are you insinuating that my wife had anything to do with this? We were in our bed till near ten o'clock."

"Bed partners are mutually exclusive as alibi givers, sir. Ah, here is your wife."

Dicey and the judge returned and Dicey's face showed great puzzlement.

"I don't understand. It was there the other day. I seldom wear them."

"How convenient to have lost it," Jessie purred.

"By the way, Mrs. Barstow." Cork turned to her. "Where is your other blue garter?"

"There was only one. It was made for my wedding."

"I thought as much," Cork smirked, "and yet your impetuous act to embarrass Cole by making him wear your wedding garter precipitated the killer's plan. Or did you do it to irk your rival?"

Trevor Barstow started to grumble and Cork stopped him with an upraised hand. "Spare your breath, sir. Cole's rejection of both your wife and Dicey are common knowledge. Now let's get to the heart of the matter. Dicey's second garter is missing. I believe it was stolen by the killer and exchanged with the blue one on the body to make us think that Clay had been killed."

"But that doesn't make sense," Clay said. "I was alive and could say so."

"Of course, but the killer wanted us to think two things. One—that the person who killed your brother thought he was killing you and two, once his true identity was discovered, to throw suspicion on Dicey Darby or her husband, for they had access to the second garter. The first step was to convince you of the killer's affection for you. It worked, I see, for Mlle. de Arbois seems to be in your charge."

We all looked at the French coiffeuse, who glared at Cork. "*Absurde*," she said.

"Come now, Mademoiselle, the weight of logic will crush you. Cole had resisted Jessie's attentions all week, so why would he hasten to an early-morning meeting with a woman he cared nothing for? Besides, Jessie had no opportunity to steal the other garter, for she has never been in this house before. As for Dicey, why would she use her second garter to throw suspicion on herself? But you, Mademoiselle, by your own admission were in this house dressing Dicey's hair last night." He turned to Dicey. "I assume your hair is dressed in your bedchamber?"

"Of course, at my dressing table."

"So you see, Mlle. de Arbois, your Gallic romantic nature has undone you. An Anglo-Saxon woman would have killed Cole and taken her chances that Clay would take her back. But you needed that dramatic moment in Clay's room when you feigned that he was Cole and professed your love for Clay. It was over-reaching, but what could you do? The real Cole had used you as he did all women. You learned too late that the quiet, steady Clay was the better catch and wanted to insure that he would believe your love. In one plunge of the blade, you took revenge on the roué, eliminated him from a joint estate, and got your original man back. A good morning's work, Mademoiselle."

Later that night we were packing our things at the Club for our departure in the morning for Philadelphia. Cork's exposure of all the town gossip had made him *persona non grata* to the quality, and I was jubilant. "We will probably never be invited here again," I said.

"Stop gloating, Oaks," he snarked.

But I did gloat—to myself, of course. This was the first case he had solved that did us any good.

SEVEN

The Massachusetts Peep-O'Night

As I WATCHED the shameful procession go down the road under our second storey, front room windows at Witloe's Nook, I couldn't help but think that the people of Boston are hard put to learn a lesson. Here it was, exactly two years to the day, this being 5 March 1772, that British troops had to fire at a surly mob to quell what could have been a mass riot. Massacre indeed! Now here they were, these Bostonians, having a memorium march for the five *martyrs*. Ironically, things had never been better in these American Colonies since that black day. Trade was flourishing. Corn and wheat shortages in Europe had brought British specie into the colonies for the first time. Despite this moment of calm, nay, profitable tranquility, these rascals who call themselves the Sons of Liberty had the audacity to create a street spectacle. It was an affront to the Crown and dangerous sport. What's the worse, one of the paraders marching by, head and shoulders above the rest, was none other than Captain Jeremy Cork, my employer and friend—the man I would make the richest man in the Americas.

131

I turned from the window shaking my head in consternation and went back to work on the ledgers. At least one of us was employing his time gainfully.

Since our arrival in Boston three weeks back, I was surprised to find that much of the usual anti-British oratory had abated, as radicalism usually does in the face of prosperity. Even at home, William Pitt himself had taken America to task. I prayed that this procession was merely a symbolic gesture carried off by the diehards as a futile and empty gesture. If only that damnable Sam Adams would shut his mouth—even if he now only spoke in whispers each night at the Green Dragon Tavern.

When Cork returned around midnight, I ignored him and went on reading my copy of the *Evening Post.*

"Did you enjoy the procession, Oaks?" he asked, slumping into a chair.

I peered over the top of the newspaper at him. He must have spied me at the window when he marched by, and he was out to trick me. But I have been with him too long, watched him interrogate too many suspects in his solution of his damnable social puzzles, to be trapped into mendacity.

"I saw it, not enjoyed it. As you would say, *that* was a leading question."

"How so? I was looking for a spectator's opinion. I thought it well organized and orderly."

"And futile. Look here at the news. My God, Captain, the colonies teem with good fortune."

"*Taxed* fortune."

"The Crown's privilege, sir. And if we are so oppressed by customs taxes, how do you explain Boston happily paying £8,921 in duties this past year? Why, even more indentured servants are running away these days. Serves their owners right though, half of those scamps are transported felons and not worth ten minutes trust. The newspaper is filled with reward advertisements. Now that's a sign that times are flourishing," I chuckled.

He didn't enjoy my jest at all, and showed it. "That is a good analogy, Oaks. Excellent! The American, all Americans, are in danger of becoming indentured slaves to the Crown. Mark my words. First customs duties, next Crown-paid judges, and then. . ."

"I say let the Crown pay the judges. It's a saving for us to get them off the colonies payrolls."

"Bad logic and more so . . ."

I was thankful for the rap at our door, for it saved me from another argumentative evening. Cork opened the door to admit a well groomed but plainly dressed man of thirty-odd. He was vaguely familiar to me, but I couldn't quite place him. One thing, however, sent my thanks for his arrival up the chimney-fire. He bore the unmistakable stamp of a lawyer, and they always mean trouble. I felt some relief when Cork addressed him as "Mr. Adams." Sam Adams is known to me, and it certainly wasn't him.

"This is Wellman Oaks," Cork said, introducing us. "Mr. John Adams."

Certainly he was familiar; he was John Adams, Sam's cousin, who had successfully defended the British soldiers in the "massacre" affair two years ago. Of course, Cork had considered the verdict of that trial faulty, since only two of the soldiers had been found guilty, and were allowed to plead right of clergy at Adams's request, thus escaping the gallows. Not that Cork is bloodthirsty, but he detests the legal concept that, because a man can read and write, he is excused of a capital crime. I say better to brand and transport the culprit than to clog the jails and gibbets. Obviously, John Adams agreed with my viewpoint.

"I am most pleased to meet an illustrious barrister, sir," I said, shaking his hand. Cork took his coat and stepped back to the door to call down for libations.

"If only I had the luxury of being merely a courtroom barrister, Mr. Oaks," Adams said to me, taking the seat I offered. He looked quite tired. "I'm afraid the American law practitioner is but a ladened donkey, being solicitor, barrister, research clerk and bill collector rolled into one. Ah, Cork, it wasn't necessary to serve drinks."

Cork came in from the door, a tray in hand. "Hospitality is my strongest card, sir. Apple Knock for Oaks and myself and a Whistlebelly Vengeance for you."

"Many thanks, Captain," Adams said, taking the mug up, "but I fear hospitality is not your strongest card. It's your ability as a detector that I'm here to solicit."

Heaven help us! I thought him a rational man, and here

he drops a crime at our doorsill. Well, there's no going by appearances.

"Don't tell me your cousin Sam has gotten himself into a scrape over the processional?" Cork asked with a smile.

"If it were only that simple. Mind, that's not a rap on Sam. He's a sound man, not a rabble rouser. No, the problem is most complicated—and dangerous."

"My sentiments exactly," I said. "The procession should not have taken place at all."

Adams looked at me strangely. "Mr. Oaks, I sense that you have me out of perspective. Many people do, since I took up the defense of the British soldiers. I am an American, sir, but I believe in the rule of law, not courtroom passion. As for politics, I would rather remain retired and cautious, minding my farm and my own business, but this has nothing to do with the procession today. It does have much to do with the future of Massachusetts."

Cork was sipping Knock and his eyes were sparkling, not from the liquor, but from glee. He had a new case. Damn his dancing eyes. "Well, let's to it, man," he said.

Adams took a deep breath and hooked his thumbs into his waistcoat. "We have what appears to be a foul murder on our hands. You are familiar with Major General Sir Francis Moran of His Majesty's Army?"

"Well, well," Cork mused, "a Major General and a Knight to boot. Oaks and I did him a service back in—what was it, Oaks?"

" '60's sir, during the French and Indian wars. The theft of the Ishmael plan, you might recall. He was a Colonel then."

"Yes, of course. Oaks is a great recordkeeper, Mr. Adams. Has Moran murdered or been done so?"

"He was poisoned. This very night, of all nights, at the home of Titus Fairmont. A senior Crown officer murdered in the home of a leading Tory, and with a member of the Royal Family visiting in the house. The charge against Dobby Hayes will be more than murder, it will be political assassination. You can see how that will bring it down on the heads of the Sons of Liberty."

Cork raised a palm to halt him. "Mr. Adams, you are a skilled lawyer now in the grip of emotion. It's understandable from the morsels that you have proffered that the situation is grave but pray, man, order your facts. A brief—a prolusion at least."

Adams wiped his brow. "Quite right, and I thank you for reining me in. Very well, the facts, gentlemen, the facts."

The lawyer spoke now with courtroom precision, each pertinent point followed in step by another, like well drilled troops.

Sir Francis had suddenly arrived in the colonies on what was purported to be an inspection tour, although his presence was viewed by local patriots as another slap in the colonial face, for Moran was a soldier of war, not an ambassador. This evening, he was to be feted at the home of Titus Fairmont, a wealthy Tory (Tory was Adams's term; I would have called him a Loyalist). At the same dinner was to be none other than the Marchioness de Waldengrave, a member of the Germanic artistocracy and cousin to King George's wife, Queen Charlotte. The royal lady was a current house guest of the Fairmonts. At the opening of the dinner, Sir Francis rose to give a toast to the King and, having drunk from his goblet, fell into a convulsion. A doctor was one of the guests, and he rushed to the Knight's aid, but it was too late.

"From the manner in which Moran died," Adams went on, "the doctor suspected poisoning, and tested the remains of the goblet on a cat, which also went into convulsions and died. However, there was no poison in the wine decanter or the other goblets, so it became obvious that the poison had been introduced into Moran's goblet by a third party, and Dobby Hayes came immediately under suspicion. Dobby is the Fairmont's footman and he had poured the wine. But what is worse, he is the brother of one of the men killed in the massacre two years ago."

"An act of retribution," I said.

"Yes, or so the authorities claim. In fact, they see Hayes as the instrument of a Sons of Liberty plot, since he is a fervent member of that society. Of course it's rubbish, but the British can use that excuse to crush the last bit of colonial peaceful resistance left. If they can brand us as skulking assassins—some sinister cabal—our friends in other colonies will disown any allegiance to the cause. Most of the members have fled the city for fear of arrest. My cousin Sam and John Hancock arrived at my farm in Braintree and suggested that I come and ask your help. Sam has a high regard for your ability as a fact-finder."

Cork stretched his legs out in front of him, seemingly taking up half the room. "It would be futile to try to prove that Hayes acted alone, Mr. Adams. The suspicion of a plot would always loom large, as they have for centuries."

"Sir, I would ask you to prove that Dobby Hayes did not do it *at all*. I stopped by the jail where he is held and was able to speak with him. He says he is innocent, and I believe him."

"Most culprits say that, sir, as you well know," Cork admonished our guest. "What amazes me is that, if he did do it, why not go for the bigger target?"

Both Adams and I shared puzzled looks.

"The Marchioness herself, gentlemen. If Hayes were a crazed madman seeking revenge on the British for having killed his brother, why not strike closer to the throne?"

"Kill a woman!" I was horrified.

"Madmen have poor manners, Oaks. I was merely making a point in Hayes's favor. Admittedly a weak one, however."

"Non-existent," Adams explained. "You see, the Marchioness took ill during the afternoon and was not at the dinner party."

Cork looked stern. "It is an intriguing challenge, but I, too, marched in the procession today and the authorities would hardly cooperate with me, Mr. Adams. I'll need facts. Who else was at the dinner? Who might have a grudge against Moran? I'll need to talk to people, probe them."

"I think you will be given welcome, Captain. I am told that a Major Phillip Tell is in charge of the investigation. He is known to you, is he not?"

Known to us! He is a pox on us. Major Tell has been our companion on many occasions. As King's agent-at-large, he has involved Cork and me in a number of cases which diverted us from coin-turning enterprises. Now he pops up again. And he pops up just when the Captain himself has given a plausible reason for not getting involved in this current affair. Damn, there's no escaping the man.

"Ah, Tell," Cork said with a grin. "That *is* different. He owes us some favors, eh, Oaks?"

"More like owing us £50,000 for all the times we've spent saving his neck."

He gave me that smirk-a-mouth of his and I knew we were off again on the hunt.

"Confound it, Cork," Major Tell rankled, "I know I owe you more than I can ever repay, but dammit all, man, this is not a backstairs murder. A distinguished officer— a man that was dubbed into the peerage by George III only a month ago, has been foully slain. I am not in concert with this plot theory, although I don't dismiss it, but this Hayes fellow is guilty as sin. No one else could have done it, or have reason to."

"We've heard that many times before, old friend, and it doesn't always wash."

Cork had been at him for half an hour. We were in a small office off the jail's guardroom, having come there directly after parting from John Adams. He was off, I suspected, to inform his cousin and Hancock that Cork was at work. Tell had been courteous at first and even allowed us to speak with Hayes. But when Cork asked that all the dinner guests be assembled at the scene of the crime, Tell balked like an ox. Cork kept pressing him; he hadn't had that problem with Dobby Hayes, who was all talk and little sense.

"I'm for separation from Britain, Captain," Hayes told us in his cell after Cork had browbeaten Tell into allowing the interview, "but I'm not a fiend. I had no grudge against Sir Francis. I knew and liked him when he was Mr. Fairmont's guest back some eighteen years ago. He was just a Colonel then—gave me a sovereign when he left for Quebec. I actually admired the man."

"Times have changed, as well as attitudes, Dobby," Cork said with a shrug.

"You mean my brother's death," the prisoner said in disgust. "I had no affection for Davey, gentlemen. He was a King Street loafer, to my mind. When I came to the colonies, I worked out my time to Mr. Fairmont and he kept me on as the master of the servant hall. Would I repay him by killing a guest who had once been kind to me?"

As he spoke, I tried to study his face and eyes, as I knew Cork was doing. He certainly didn't look like a killer. Clean shaven, with a healthy complection, his chubby physique showing the munificence of the servant's hall table, Dobby Hayes looked the admirable footman, not the revengeful poisoner. Cork was digging.

"You were familiar with the guests?"

"To a fair turn, Captain Cork. 'T'weren't that many, since Sir Francis showed up unexpected."

"He just arrived at the Fairmonts' unexpectedly?"

"You might say that. The master, Titus Fairmont, had word that Sir Francis was to be in Boston Town and sent word to the General Staff that his house was open to the Knight. The Fairmont house is one of the finest about, as you may well know—finer even than Mr. Hancock's. Sir Francis's ship was four days early and there he was, with bag and baggage, at our sill. You can imagine the chaos that caused with the help. Here we are with a Knight of the realm newly arrived and a Marchioness getting ready to leave for New York. The laundry alone caused all manner of havoc, and on top of that, the mistress feels she must have a welcoming dinner party for Sir Francis. Thank heaven it turned out to be a small affair, with a grandiose ball planned for next week."

He stopped for a moment in thought. "Well, at least that's off the staff's back."

"And a murder charge clings to yours, Dobby," Cork reminded him. "Who was at the dinner?"

Dobby flicked a finger out and held its tip with his other hand, as if he were counting silverplate or bed linen.

"One, Sir Francis Moran; two and three were the master and mistress; four, the daughter of the house, Miss Priscilla; five, Mr. Milo Windam." He reversed hands. "Six, Mr. Colin Livingston; seven, the widow Chalmers; eight, Dr. Twilling, and Miss Rose Dribblon, a friend of Miss Priscilla's, makes nine."

"It seems Madam Fairmont is not socially skilled. There was one extra man at the table."

Dobby smiled benevolently. "Madam is no grand lady,

sirs, but she tries her best. 'Sides, she planned on the Marchioness not getting ill and then it was too late in the evening to invite another lady."

"Yes, of course. Tell me, Dobby, did you lay the table yourself?"

"Aye, me and Sadie did. She's Mrs. Fairmont's personal maid and my wife, I'm proud to say."

"Are there no downstairs help?"

"Sally the cook, two scullies and a boy of all work. Couldn't trust them to do it right with a princess and a knight at the table. Used the best plate, we did, polished to a turn. If only I hadn't knocked the General's goblet as I reached to pour the wine, I wouldn't be here."

"How so?"

"That's when they say I put the poison in. You see, I had the decanter ready to fill his goblet when I tipped it a mite. It didn't fall over because I steadied it with my right hand. The General let it pass, but Madam gave me a look that seared my hide. When I steadied the goblet, they say I put the poison in."

"Did you?"

"No, Captain, 'pon my soul I didn't."

"Confound it, Cork," Tell was still raging against Cork's request for an assembly of witnesses. "Lord, man, Fairmont is a powerful personage—not to mention the Marchioness. I can't herd them together for your convenience and have you question them to death. The case is closed satisfactorily."

"Is it?"

"Of course it is. Who else would have reason to kill Sir Francis?"

"Of course you're sure it *was* Sir Francis who was the intended victim?"

"What the devil are you suggesting, Cork?"

"I mentioned to Oaks earlier that if Dobby Hayes wanted symbolic revenge, why not go after a bigger target —the Marchioness herself?"

The Major actually shuddered. "By the Duke's guns, Cork, that would have tumbled the beehive. But of course, the royal lady was not at the table."

"Which is precisely my point. Let us put Hayes aside

for the moment. If he wanted to kill the Marchioness, he had ample opportunity during her visit. Let us assume for the moment that someone wanted the Marchioness dead."

"But she wasn't at the table!"

"Exactly, Tell, exactly. If she had been at the table, she would have had the seat of honor at Mr. Fairmont's right. But she had a last-minute spell of some sort, so obviously Moran would move up to that spot."

"Well, that's what did happen according to Mrs. Fairmont, but. . ."

"And suppose," Cork continued, "the poison was put in the goblet before the guests sat down to be served."

"*Before* the dinner?"

"When else, assuming Hayes is innocent?"

"That's preposterous, Cork. Sheer lunacy."

"No, Major, it is a possibility. Now, if someone attempted to take the Marchioness's life and was foiled by her sudden illness, is it not possible that he will try again? And if he succeeds, how will that stand in London?"

I'm sure, in his years of soldiering, the Major has lived through some dark moments, but if the expression now etched on his face was any indication, this was his greatest moment of despair. Cork can be relentless when he has found an opening and he drove home on his point. It took almost another hour, but finally Tell conceded that the murder should be investigated more fully. He would not, however, allow Cork to pursue the case openly. He finally agreed to Cork's suggestion that he pose as an *amicus curiae* who was helping to strengthen the case against Dobby Hayes.

As we walked back to Witloe's Nook and some needed sleep, I wondered how he was going to pursue one target while seemingly after another. I found out the next morning at ten, when we were admitted to the Fairmont home in Tell's company.

"Well, what more evidence would you ask for?" Titus Fairmont grumbled from his chair behind his massive oak desk. We had been shown into a small, well appointed room on the ground floor which served as the master's office. Fairmont's wealth was derived from a number of enterprises, and the papers and documents piled here and there gave evidence of his industry. Perhaps, I hoped futilely, some of this man's love of commerce would rub off on Cork. Fairmont was a spare fellow close on fifty years or so.

"Seems to me, Major," he went on," that you got Hayes dead to rights. He slipped the poison in when he toppled the cup on orders from these damned troublemakers."

"Not quite dead to rights, sir," Cork injected. "Many a criminal case has fallen when the preparation was not thorough. The Major wants to be crack-sure that we have Hayes pinned."

"No one can fault you for that," Fairmont sighed. "I just hope you're not going to turn the house topsy-turvy. With Hayes in jail, things are confused enough."

"We shall be careful, sir," Cork assured him. "Sir Francis was sitting to your right, as I understand. Did you observe Hayes's hands when he toppled the cup?"

"Can't say that I did. Too startled and embarrassed, I suppose. But I didn't have to *see* him. Man, he did it. My own footman!"

"Did you know he was a member of the Sons of Liberty, sir?"

"No, I did not! I knew his brother had been killed in that affair two years ago, but I always assumed Dobby to be a loyal subject."

"You were a friend of the General?"

"Not exactly. Well, yes, I guess you could say that. Knew him back during the French and Indian. He stayed with us a while before he went to Quebec. Then, of course, he went on to greater honors in Ireland and India."

"In addition to your family, you had other guests at table. A Miss Dribblon?"

"Rose Dribblon, a chum of my daughter. All agog over meeting royalty and a peer. Sort of scatterbrained like most of the young girls today. She wouldn't have noticed anything. And it was most fortunate that the Marchioness wasn't present to witness that awful thing. I can see her shocking the Queen with stories of how barbaric we are over here."

"How is Lady Caroline today?" Tell inquired.

"Tolerably well, considering all the chaos. I've con-

vinced her to rest a few days before going to New York.
If only she had left before Sir Francis arrived. Ah well,
it's done."

"There was a gentleman named Colin Livingston here
last night, too," Cork said, bringing the conversation back
to pertinent points.

"Yes, he's new in these parts. Mighty successful for a
young buck. Made a fortune in India and decided to come
over here. We could use more like him, I can tell you."

"India, hey?" Cork was stroking his barba. "Must have
known Moran out there."

"No, he says not. Seems he was in the north most of
the time. He'd heard of Moran, of course. Who hadn't?"

"Yes, I also had his acquaintance. What of Milo Windham?"

"See here, Cork, I know you're supposed to be a genius
at these things, but why all this interest in my guests?"

"Perhaps one of them saw Hayes put the poison in the
goblet."

"Well, if they did, they would have said so last night."
Fairmont's voice was showing irritation.

"They may not realize what they saw and I'll have to
jog their memories."

Fairmont gave a sly wink. "Yes, I see your method.
Not much to tell of Windham. Came here ten years ago
and has done well in naval timber and such. Sound fellow.
But the person to talk to is Cecily Chalmers. That woman
notices everything. Her late husband was a friend of my
father's. She's a hawk on details."

"I'll be sure to see her, sir," Cork assured him. "Now
could we interview the lady of the house and your daughter?"

"Well if you want to waste your time, Captain, go right
ahead. They're up in the sewing room doing more gossip-
ing than sewing, I'll warrant. That flippitygibbet Rose
Dribblon was back here at dawn, it seems, and they've
been chirping about this affair like magpies ever since."

A serving girl called Nellie was summoned and she
nervously led us up to the back of the house. Cork, en
route, asked her where Dobby's wife Sadie was, and was
told that she was below stairs.

"Poor woman's in a terrible state with the Hayes bein' dragged off. Put all the work on me and I'm dreadin' serving breakfast to the royal lady, having never been 'bout no great lady before. Here ye are, sirs."

The Fairmont sewing room was occupied by three well frocked ladies. Tell introduced us. Mrs. Fairmont was a plain woman with a touch of grey in her hair. Her daughter, Priscilla, favored neither parent, for she was a remarkably handsome young girl with well honed features and hair so blond and soft you were tempted to touch it. Her friend, Rose Dribblon, was a perky, pug-nosed imp with a coy smile. She truly was a bit of a magpie who tittered when she talked.

"I was at the other end of the table, of course," Mrs. Fairmont replied to Cork's question. "So my view was blocked by the centerpiece. Dobby was usually so correct in table service that I was shocked when he almost knocked over the goblet."

"He was nervous all day," Rose chirped. "Remember, Prissy, I mentioned it during the afternoon?"

"He was overworked, you mean!"

"Priscilla!" her mother chided her, "what will these gentlemen think of us? The servants aren't slaves. They were all nervous with such important people in the house."

"Oh, it's all so much bosh and bother over nothing," Priscilla stated firmly. "Royalty is a trick of fate. People born to the right parents."

"Priscilla!" Mrs. Fairmont was irked now. "I will not have that talk in your father's house. You must forgive my daughter, gentlemen. She expresses these wild views to bring attention to herself. An educated girl can be a burden."

She solicited our agreement and I, for one, gave it mentally. Cork, however, merely smirked.

"Just how did Dobby express his nervousness, Miss Dribblon?"

"In many ways, sir. I told him he had set the table wrong, and he told me I was wrong. Respectfully, of course, but. . ."

"You were wrong," Priscilla told her friend. "Even Her Royal Highness said so." Her reference to the Marchioness was definitely sarcastic. Rose's only rejoinder was to pout her mouth and say, "Oh pooh, Prissy."

Cork asked a few more questions which, to my mind, weren't pertinent, and we excused ourselves and retired to the hall.

"This all seems rather fruitless, doesn't it, Cork?" Tell asked impatiently. "We got nothing out of that encounter and I doubt we will with the others."

"You have lazy eyes, Major. You are committed to an assassination plot and can see nothing else, which is a pity. For myself, I have a thread of something, but it is not clear as yet."

"Well, the least you could do. . ." I was cut off by a resounding crash and a woman's voice screaming from upstairs.

"Look alive," Cork bellowed and made a bound for the back serving stairs. Tell and I followed with shocked obedience. My mind was ringing with Cork's prediction of the Marchioness being in danger. On the second floor landing we found Nellie, the serving girl, shaking uncontrollably. A breakfast tray lay on the floor outside an oak door, its former contents strewn about on the carpet.

"What happened, girl?" Tell demanded. He got nothing but more gasping sobs. Cork crossed the hall to the door and knocked on it.

"She threw a mirror at me, she did," Nellie pushed out the words. "Didn't know she was in her bath, sir."

In response to Cork's rapping, the door opened. In its frame stood an enraged woman in a satin morning wrapper. She was tall, dark-haired and fiercely beautiful.

"My lady," Cork said with a bow, "we feared for your safety, but it seems you were merely interrupted in your toilette. The girl meant no harm."

"She should be flogged. Don't your servants knock before entering a room?" The Marchioness's voice was sharp and officious.

The mention of flogging brought fresh wails from Nellie.

"Where is the other servant, Sadie? At least she has some training, but *that* clod is impossible."

"My lady, I extend the apologies of the house, though it is not mine." Cork was being charming which he is devil-ishly good at where ladies are concerned. I had moved next to his side, wondering if I should genuflect, then dismissed the thought. The Marchioness's boudoir was obviously the master bedroom, given over to her for her stay. Near the fireplace was a high-backed French bathtub from which the lady had obviously just emerged in a rage.

"Who are you?" she demanded of my employer.

"Captain Jeremy Cork, at your service, m'am. We colonials take some time getting used to. May I suggest we send for another breakfast tray and set your room to rights?"

"You may be a colonial, sir, but you know your manners," she said, softening her look of disdain.

Nellie was set to scooping up the dropped tray while Tell and I, at Cork's suggestion, carried the portable bathtub out of the chamber. When we returned, Cork was sitting opposite her. She reclined on a chaise longue. Cork was oozing with concern for her comfort.

"Most distressing," the royal lady said. "My two ladies in waiting taken ill in Philadelphia and I am left to the ministrations of scullery maids. Then this dreadful death downstairs."

"Did you happen to know Sir Francis at court, m'am?"

She looked startled. "Well, hardly an acquaintance. These peers created by the sword are, to my mind, to be only tolerated. Of course, my dear cousin . . ." she cast her eyes at a miniature on the bedside table. It was a well-executed portrait of Queen Charlotte. ". . . poor Charlotte must by her office suffer all courtiers, but I do not."

There was a knock on the door and a new tray and a new servant appeared. It was Sadie, Dobby's wife, to the rescue, which she handled expertly. We excused ourselves and left.

In a whisper, I said, "I hate to say it, but the Marchioness is a bit of a snob. I wonder if she really was ill last night at all."

"Probably thought the whole affair beneath her," Major Tell put in. "I'm relieved that you didn't mention your theory that the poison might have been meant for her."

"You do plan to protect her, however?"

"Do you think that necessary now, Cork?"

"Yes, a guard would guarantee her safety and protect *your* position should an attempt be made."

Tell agreed and left us to arrange for guards, and we descended the stairs and were let out of the house.

"Won't the sudden appearance of guards alarm her?" I asked as we strolled along.

"Oaks, that lofty lady will be pleased as punch. She'll love the spotlight and think it her due that she finally has an honor guard. But we have other trails to follow."

"To be sure, Colin Livingston. He may have run afoul of Sir Francis out in India, although Milo Windham seems to have had no relationship with the dead man."

"We shall see, old son, in due time, but for now, we seek the more important witness."

"Who, pray?"

"The hawk-eyed Widow Chalmers."

We made straight for the house pointed out to us by a servant back at the Fairmonts'. It sat in a side alley with its own small dooryard; more a large cottage than a town house.

The widow was quite old, but by no means feeble. She wore an old-fashioned dress with a matching cap on her cotton-white hair. Her eyes *were* quick and alert, much like a hawk's.

"Wondered when someone was going to get around to asking me some questions. Just 'cause a body's getting on don't think I don't see things, young man." She waggled a finger in Cork's direction.

"We share a bent for observation, madam," Cork said as we took chairs. "Too many people walk through life with their eyes half shut."

"Folks today, you mean. They wouldn't have lasted five minutes on the old frontier. Had to be alert in those days, watch every tree and bush for redskins."

"Had you met Sir Francis before last night, m'am?"

"Yes, when he was here back during the French and Indian."

"What was your opinion of him in those days?"

"Opinion!"

"Observation, then. Let me explain. I also knew Moran when he was a Colonel. Let me tell you what I saw. A dashing officer, a devilishly handsome blond Irishman with an eye for the ladies."

I expected the old lady to turn crimson at such a ribald

description. Of course, it was true, but why bring that up in front of this ancient widow? There was no embarrassment forthcoming, however. To my surprise, she gave a low cackle.

"He was all you say, I suppose, but that's a soldier's nature. You don't look a shrinking violet yourself, Captain Cork."

Cork smirked again and went on. "I was struck by something odd when at the Fairmont home this morning. I couldn't help thinking how heredity is strong and unerring."

"I agree that bloodlines will out," the widow said warily, "but I can't see where it figures in Moran's death."

"Really, Madam? I'm surprised you missed it, but no matter. Can you tell us exactly what happened at table last night?"

The old lady went through pretty much the same story of the fumbled goblet and Moran's drink of death. When we rose to leave, she looked straight into Cork's eyes. "I miss very little, sir, unless I care to. Some things should be overlooked, sir, and I trust you are a worthy gentleman."

"As worthy as conscience allows, m'am. Thank you and good day."

"That was quite a cryptic exchange. I trust I have missed something?"

"You usually do, Oaks. The old hawk has confirmed a suspicion of mine, first by her silence and then by her final appeal. Put some facts together, man. Moran was last here eighteen years ago when he lived in the Fairmont home."

"Yes, and you think something happened then. Why all this jabber about bloodlines?" The thought came back to me. When we had entered the sewing room, I had noticed that Priscilla Fairmont's handsomeness set her apart from both her father and her mother.

"By jing, Captain," I cried with amazement, "that child is the spitting image of a younger Francis Moran!"

"And she is eighteen years old, my lad."

"Is it possible? Mrs. Fairmont is certainly a proper Boston woman."

"Propriety be damned. Moran was a persuasive man and effective in war *and* love."

I shook my head in amazement. I know the human condition is fragile, but in Boston?

"Which one do you think, Cork? I'm for the wife. The wronged woman, and all that?"

"Or the revengeful daughter?"

"Oh no, she couldn't know her true parentage."

"Her eyes could have told her. But that goes for Fairmont himself," Cork explained.

"Yes, that makes more sense. He says he didn't know of Hayes's association with the Sons of Liberty, but he could have lied. Old Dobby would be suspect even if he hadn't tipped the goblet. By jing, you've done it again, Captain."

"Done what?"

"Solved the mystery, of course."

"Nonsense. I have put forward a conjecture that merely gives us a wider dimension to work with. There are some other facets that bother me. Let us see what some trolling in Colin Livingston's waters will bring."

When Titus Fairmont had described Colin Livingston as a young buck, he understated the case. He was almost a lad fresh to his maturity. But his youthful appearance was only skin covering. Inside the young fellow was a shrewd old man's insight and the bustle of his offices on Broad Street showed his business ability.

He, too, was fair-haired and blue-eyed, but his years in India had turned his skin nut brown, giving him a rugged appearance. He seemed to be engaged in the import-export trade and his clerks and warehouse men scurried about in an atmosphere of success which I admired deeply.

"Damndest thing I ever witnessed, I can tell you, gentlemen. Saw a fellow struck by a cobra out east who lasted longer than Sir Francis did. Certainly jarred the ladies, I can tell you. Don't mix in politics, haven't got the time, but this Hayes fellow seems to be the culprit. I can understand your wanting to build a stronger case, but I can help you little. Damn shame for the Fairmonts."

"You are a guest there often?"

"No," he smiled, "but I hope to be, as time goes on."

"Yes, Miss Fairmont *is* most attractive," Cork said. "What brings you to our shores, sir? I understand you found good fortune in India."

"The climate was not to my liking, sir. Bloody hot all the time, you know. The flaming sun would fry a man."

"Well, we appreciate your confirmation that Hayes had the only access to the lethal goblet, and we thank you."

We were on the street once more and I asked Cork if our final witness, Milo Windham, was next on the list.

"No, Oaks, but *list* is the appropriate word. We are off for the State House."

I followed like a loyal dog and when we reached the building on Market Street, he made his way to the Board of Trade offices. Ten minutes later, with the help of a clerk prodded by a shilling, he had confirmed that there had never been a Colin Livingston registered with the East India Company in the last five years.

"Our young soldier could not enter trade out there without a registration."

"Soldier? You think he was a soldier out there?"

"He has a soldier's speech, punctuated with 'sirs' and army curse words. Perhaps Tell could trace him on the Army lists. In any event, we know he has a past."

"You know, Captain, he also could have knowledge of exotic poisons. The east abounds in them, I fear."

"Not likely an exotic poison, Oaks. Anyone can put his hands on rat killer. Well, let's go back to Witloe's Nook for a lunch."

"And what of Milo Windham?"

"Two birds with one stone, my lad. The gentleman has rooms there and I left a note this morning inviting him to join us. I asked him to extend our invitation to Dr. Twilling as well."

When Cork designs a lunch, it turns into a feast of no mean proportion. Of course, the table he had prepared was simple fare, by his terms. Consider a Leaping Joint, a specialty at Witloe's Nook, wherein a haunch of venison is slow simmered in Toggleberry sauce. This masterpiece is preceded by mounds of shucked oysters, corn chowder, baked taters with gobs of butter and the inevitable beans with slab pork. This is simple?

"My, my, this is a fine spread for a midday repast," Dr. Twilling said, peeping over his eye specs. One wouldn't expect a dour old man's attitude to hide a trencherman's ability. Milo Windham merely toyed with his food and I suspected he thought a luncheon that lavish was a total waste of money. I liked Windham at first sight. He was a no-nonsense man of commerce who sat down, checked his timepiece and informed Cork that he could spare only thirty minutes. He got to the point immediately.

"I know your reputation, Captain Cork, or should I say your escapades, where you rescue the seemingly guilty from the gallows and replace them with the true culprits. I further think that you intend to do so in this Moran affair. I wish you good fortune, sir, and stand ready to answer any question to the best and fullest of my ability. First, let me say I did not notice Dobby Hayes's mischance with the goblet. Second, I knew no one at the dinner except Fairmont himself, and I suspect I was there to be impressed for commercial reasons, not social. It was the first and, I might add, the last time I shall dine under his roof. Damned insulting to invite a man to witness a murder."

"Come now," Dr. Twilling said, "old Titus couldn't have known what a servant would be up to. He is the embarrassed party, if anyone. Here's a lady of the blood royal who has offered to aid his interests at court. I don't think the murder of a knight, almost in her presence, will predispose her to Titus Fairmont's commercial cause now."

"Yes, and I have lost £2,000 in the process."

"Two thousand pounds?" Cork asked.

"Yes. That is royalty for you. Seems the Marchioness is short of cash and Titus thought it would be a fine idea if we joined forces in a 'loan.' He called it a royal offering of friendship. Now she is so angry she'll probably do us more harm than good back in London."

"Gifts to the royal family are not uncommon," the good doctor said, savoring the joint.

"Pishes and poshes, Doctor. Well, Captain, I have but ten minutes left."

"I have what I want from you, sir."

"But you haven't asked me anything."

"Right you are, Mr. Windham. Very well, one question. Were you ever a registered agent for the East India Company?"

"How strange. The answer is yes. In the period 1758 through 1760, I was a London agent for that company, but I can't for the life of me see why that is pertinent."

"Believe me, sir, it is quite pertinent and I thank you for your candor. There is a lovely trifle for dessert if you can wait."

Windham declined and left for some money-making conference or other—an activity we should be pursuing, but we finished our meal instead.

"Tell me, Doctor," Cork asked over the trifle, which I admit was expensively delicious, "have you determined the nature of the poison?"

"I am no expert, but it 'pears to be a quick acting substance used on vermin. I learned only an hour ago that this Major Tell has discovered a tin of the stuff in the sub-kitchen of the Fairmont house. Seems Dobby had it ready to hand."

"Many kitchens have vermin, Doctor. I take it you attend to the Fairmont household's medical needs?"

"Have for twenty years."

"Would you say that Mrs. Fairmont is a vengeful woman?"

The doctor looked perplexed. "Vengeful? Mercy no. I wouldn't say so. Mild woman, that. You don't think she had anything to do with this?"

"Forgive the implication. I was just curious about her emotional stand."

"Well, I can tell you she is the most proper of womankind, a truly gentle nature, sir."

"Yes, I think you are right. More trifle, gentlemen?"

Later that day, just after dark, Cork started to act strangely. All afternoon he had sat silently drinking Knock. At one point, he left our rooms and returned an hour later with a queer smile on his face.

"You've hit on something," I said after the supper dishes had been cleared.

"It's a preposterous long shot, my friend, and quite dangerous if I am wrong."

"Then I shall share the peril equally, sir, as always."

"No, not this time, Oaks. I will need you in reserve."

He got up and went to his sea chest and, to my amazement, took out his long glass.

"Going star-gazing?" I chided.

"Yes, in a way. A good navigator fixes his position before an action. I shall be back within the hour."

But he wasn't. Nor was he by ten o'clock. My worry was increasing when about midnight, a frantic rapping came at the door. It was the Fairmont's servant, Sadie Hayes, Dobby's wife. She was wide-eyed with agitation, and breathless.

"Your master has been taken by the sojers," she gasped. "Ye best come quick."

"Where, how?"

"Tarry not a moment. Come."

Twenty minutes later, we were at the Fairmont door and to my surprise, Major Tell opened it.

"Major, what's going on here? Where's Cork?"

"It's despicable, Oaks. To think that Cork is a common peep-o'night!"

"Cork peeping in ladies' windows! That's insane Major, and you know it."

"Oh, I wish it were. He was caught by a member of the guard mount I put about the house. Having a fine old time for himself observing ladies in their boudoirs."

The shame of it fell over me like an odiferous fog. The man I admired above all others had a baser side I had never known.

"Certainly it can be hushed up, Major?"

"How, man? He has demanded an immediate trial and, by God, he's going to get one. Judge Cooper is here at my request. That damned fool employer of yours has called character witnesses who don't even know him. I tell you, Oaks, the man's gone mad. Fairmont is livid that his women have been seen dressing for bed. And he'll prosecute to the limit."

I was appalled, of course, but also puzzled. Cork is no stranger to women preparing for bedtime, so why in heaven did he put himself in jeopardy? He is a loose living man, but no letcher. Or was he?

I became suspicious when I followed Tell into the main drawing room where Judge Cooper was to hold his informal court. There were all the guests of the tragic dinner—the Fairmont family, Rose Dribblon, the widow Chalmers, Colin Livingston, Dr. Twilling, Milo Windham and lastly, the Marchioness herself.

Rose Dribblon was saying to the judge, "I was horrified, your Honor, when I gazed into the garden and saw this *man* with a spy glass observing the house in moonlight. You are a filthy fellow, Captain Cork."

"Unethical, perhaps, young lady," Cork retorted and then turned to the judge. "Sir, shall we do the Bay Colony a service this night and solve a murder?"

Judge Cooper, a squat little man, looked galled. "Don't cloud the issue, Cork."

"Nay, sir, I'm the fresh breeze to dispel the fog. See here, we have put this royal lady to a great inconvenience. Before she leaves us tomorrow for New York, I think we should show her that we colonials are not the crude bumpkins we seem. Perhaps it will allay any hard feelings she would carry back to the Court of St. James."

"You mean you can prove conclusively that Hayes did it?" Titus Fairmont asked with glee. He obviously hoped to impress the Marchioness.

"I can prove the murderer out, sir." Cork said.

"Your Honor," Milo Windham joined his partner in protecting his investment, "perhaps we should hear him and take up the other charge later. Cork does have a knack in these affairs."

"This is most irregular," the judge mused aloud, "but if it would show our royal visitor that our courts are swift and fair. . ." He, too, was out to impress the Marchioness. "What have you to say for yourself, Cork?"

"Many mindsfull, sir; the winnowings of a hundred thoughts, dozens of conjectures and surmises and, at last, hopefully, a solution among the silt."

He was in high style, as he always is with an audience in attendance. So he had done it again. Contrived to bring things to a head by this peep-o'night ruse.

"Now let's to it," Cork went on. "In all fairness, we must put Dobby Hayes aside and explore other sectors. All here were in this house at the time of the murder and their names must be cleared beyond all doubt."

I thought Titus Fairmont would swallow his tongue as
he spluttered and fumed. "This is unpardonable, Cork. I
will not have my guests treated in this way."

"One of your guests was treated most shabbily and it
cost him his life. Now, sir, if you will be quiet and let me
proceed."

"Yes, Mr. Fairmont, let the man go on so we can be
done with it," the judge said wearily.

"Thank you, sir." Cork bowed. "First, I asked myself
what was the motive for the murder. Since Sir Francis
had not been in the colonies for eighteen years, it would
have to be for an old grudge. That would discount Messrs.
Windham and Livingston, for they are recent arrivals. On
the other hand, that would point to those people who
knew him years ago; the Fairmonts, Widow Chalmers
and, of course, Dr. Twilling."

I glanced from face to face. Fairmont glared, his wife
sat impassively. Widow Chalmers stared dead ahead as if
in a worrisome trance. Only Dr. Twilling spoke.

"And what possible grudge could I have, sir?" he asked
indignantly.

Cork shrugged his shoulders. "It is only that you, as a
medical man, are familiar with poisons and have access to
them."

"I told you, it seems to have been rat poison which was
found here in the house. What nonsense!"

"I agree, doctor," Cork replied. "I felt an eighteen-year-
old grudge murder *was* nonsense. As nonsensical as Dobby
Hayes committing murder to revenge a brother he didn't
care two pins about."

The judge interrupted with a grump. "Seems to me,
Cork, you've exonerated everyone."

"Yes, on the motive of revenge, although Colin Livingston was in that category for a while."

Livingston had a superior smile on his face. "Thank
you for exonerating me, Cork. I appreciate it."

"Delighted, sir. You see, at first, I believed that you
were an agent for the East India Company, but the records
at the Board of Trade do not list you. However, records
are marvelous things—one thing the British are expert in
is the listing of details. You were absent from the East

India list, but I'm afraid Major Tell has found your name on the Army lists. Subaltern Colin Livingston of the 234th Light Horse—cashiered over a year ago."

Livingston started up out of his chair. "You scoundrel," he snarled. He then stopped and looked hopelessly at Priscilla Fairmont.

"No sir, *I* did not steal money from my brother officers —I suggest you are the scoundrel and, I might add, one without further prospects in this house."

The young man sank back into his chair, seething in silence.

"I say," the judge perked up, "there's a motive for you. This young scamp killed Moran to avoid being detected as a cad."

"Well done, your Honor," Cork congratulated him. "That crossed my mind. But all he had to do was refuse the invitation to dinner. Yet he came and met Sir Francis quite boldly. No, it won't wash. Generals pay little or no attention to the sins of junior officers."

"Well then, confound it, Cork, where does that leave us?" The judge was irritated at the fallacy of his theory and the verbal rigamarole Cork was spinning. I admit I was getting a bit sick of it myself.

"It leaves us with Milo Windham. No, pray, sir, don't bestir yourself. The same East India list that exposed Livingston verified your story that you never left England until you came here. Which brings us to my little experiment this evening with my long glass."

"You dirty man," Rose Dribblon chastised him.

"I told you before, young lady, the word is *unethical*, and my act was necessary, for if I had been wrong, it would have cost me my head."

He started pacing nervously around the room as he spoke, and I feared he had run out of excuses for his actions.

"You see, your Honor, you had it quite right about the murderer wanting to escape detection by Sir Francis, and she almost did."

To our horror, Cork reached over and savagely tore the bodice of the Marchioness's dress, baring her shoulder and breast.

The woman screamed. The judge said, "Good Lord," but the royal lady sat there, not embarrassed, but shaking with rage.

It was then that I noticed the target of Cork's horrendous act. There, on the high section of her breast, was a bright red scar—a brand forming the letter F. "F" for felon.

"Madam, I know not your true name. It could be any one of twenty printed in the runaway indentured columns. But we'll find out, my girl."

And find out we did, just a fortnight later. Tell brought the news to our dinner table at Witloe's Nook.

"It was a Sarah Wilson," he said, taking a seat. "Ran away from her owner in Baltimore over six months ago."

"And she had served at court?" Cork asked.

"Bless my soul, you're a conjuror, Cork, pure magician."

"No, her speech was too perfect; she had been around quality all her life."

"To be sure. She had been a servant at court and absconded with her mistress's jewels. A lady in waiting, I believe. Then that she-devil posed as the Queen's cousin in leading houses from Charleston to New Port, borrowing money, promising royal offices. But you still haven't told us how you caught on to her."

"By elimination *and* one telling fact that everyone forgot."

Tell and I looked at each other in puzzlement.

"Sir Francis arrived four days early, did he not? She was trapped in the house. The sister of the Queen could not avoid a meeting with a knight of the realm, so she feigned illness."

"But the poison?"

"The young ladies told us she oversaw the laying of the table. She could coat her own goblet with poison knowing she wouldn't be there and that the one person who could expose her game would be moved to the spot."

"But you say elimination of suspects uncovered her," I said. "Surely no one would suspect a royal personage of murder."

Cork took a mouthful of roast goose and scoffed. "Put it together, Oaks. She travels without servants, becomes

enraged when a servant enters her bath. Her only cre-
dential seemed to be a miniature of the Queen. I suspect
we Americans *are* bumpkins."

"And you actually used your long glass to spy on her
when she was preparing for bed?" Tell leered.

"You can thank Oaks for putting me onto the fact that
she might have been a runaway servant. He, himself, said
they were mostly branded felons allowed to plead right
of clergy. In England, most women are branded on the
breast or shoulder. All I had to do was test the theory with
a little peep-o'night. Fortunately, it worked out."

"And if it hadn't?"

"We would have trailed her elsewhere, Oaks, a task
I'm sure you would have enjoyed."

AUTHOR'S NOTE: Although this is a fictional story, the exploits of Sarah Wilson, who was probably America's first
con woman, are quite true. She posed as the Marchioness
de Waldegrave quite successfully in the major cities of the
colonies during the late 1700s, although historical records
disagree whether she posed as the "sister" or "cousin" to
the Queen. In either case, she got away with it because
there is no evidence that she was ever caught.

EIGHT

The Witch of New Hampshire

"IT WOULD SEEM TO ME," I said to Captain Cork with general irritation, "that Parliament has overstepped itself. I say, let the Almighty take care of the calendar and let those august gentlemen sitting in London keep their noses out of our sunrises and sunsets."

The Captain sat across from me at the table in our rooms at the Sign of the Two Doves. On my side of the board were the ever-present account books, on his was a plate of steamed lobster. As usual, I was working and he was idling, with shellfish. We had come to the New Hampshire town of Berryport to scout for future refittings of *The Hawkers*, the ship Cork owns but never sails in. That is, *I* came for refitting arrangements; Cork was deeply involved in determining if lobster went better with drawn butter or a mixture of brine and vinegar. I had just finished reading a report in the Boston *Gazette* about Parliament's inane enactment to adjust our calendar to correct the inaccuracies the Julian calendar had made of timekeeping. Gregorian, indeed!

"You realize," I went on, "that we have all had our lives

shortened by eleven days. That's God's purlieu, not a legislature's."

He looked up from cracking a huge red claw with his pistol butt and smiled. "Don't saddle the Deity with the authorship of keeping time, Oaks. That's man's invention, and he's stuck with it. Having the calendar jump from September 2 to September 14, 1752 has its compensations. There isn't a manjack among us who wouldn't like to expunge a few days from his life here and there. I suspect your rancour stems from the fact that this is September 5, and your dratted ledgers now contain the jottings of three days that no longer exist. Your problem is easily solved however. Merely strike off the old dates and pen in the new ones."

Of course he was japing me. He knows that my "dratted ledgers" are the neatest and most scrupulously kept accounts in these colonies. Perhaps in the world at large. I, Wellman Oaks, financial yeoman, accept my fate as a crosser of t's and a dotter of i's. He is, on the other hand, Captain Jeremy Cork, six foot six inches of insouciance who mocks my efforts to make him the richest man in the Americas. All that truly stimulates him are these "social puzzles" which are always entangling us.

Had I know that, at the very moment, the town of Berryport was abrew with a bizarre mystery, I might have wished that Parliament had eliminated the year 1752 altogether.

My first clew that something foul was abroad in the vicinage was the appearance, later that afternoon, of Major Phillip Tell at our doorsill.

Major Tell is a King's colonial agent-at-large, but for me he is a vexing *avant courier* of crime and mayhem. Time and again he has dragged the Captain into investigations that divert our energies and produce not one half-joe to our coffers. This humid afternoon he outdid himself in presenting the macabre. Needless to say, his tale was a more interesting morsel to Cork than a lobster claw, and His Nibs gave up the shellfish to listen.

"Thank you, Oaks," Tell said when I poured him a mug of Cork's Apple Knock. He took a draught and let his lips shiver at its bite. Most people's eyes tear, but Tell is a seasoned field soldier. He turned to Cork. "As you know, Captain, I am not given to hysterical assumptions, but there seems no other answer to this Berryport problem."

"First, Major, what is the problem?"

"Witchcraft, and worse, I fear."

"That *is* hysteria, and sounds more like a conclusion. Can we have the legs on which it stands?"

Tell pulled his chair closer to us and lowered his voice. "Missing children—females. Six in all over the last half year. All between fourteen and sixteen. The last two, the Derby twins, disappeared two days ago without a trace."

"Kidnapping," I said.

"No ransom was asked, Oaks," Tell said, "making kidnapping unlikely. The countryside has been scoured and all outgoing vessels thoroughly searched after each disappearance, and of course, the Covenant is deeply distressed."

"The Covenant?" Cork asked. "Why not the populace?"

"The Covenant *is* the populace of Berryport, Captain, or most of it. The town was founded just twenty years ago by the Covenant of the Cleansed, and it is still the dominant factor in its daily life. All the girls were daughters of congregation members."

"And how does the witchcraft enter in?"

"Because, Captain"—Tell took another swallow of Knock—"it seems I have found a witch. You'll have to admit that's nothing new in this New England of yours."

"If you are referring to the Salem charade of over a hundred years ago, I can assure you its seeds were imported. But let's not quibble with history. Who is this witch and how is she spiriting these women away? Note I do not say 'children,' as you did, Major. It is a misleading word, considering their ages, and it's best to start a case with a proper eye."

"Women, granted," Tell said, "but virgins and children in the eyes of their parents and the congregation."

Cork grunted, put on that smirk-a-mouth of his, and Tell went on: "I was called in when the fourth *woman* disappeared in mid-August, and was as perplexed as anyone. I was determined that it would never happen again, and garrisoned two squads of troops in the town. Checkpoints were set up at the three roads leading out of town, all

goods going aboard vessels were searched, and random
patrols circulated in woods beyond the farmlands. And
yet, just two days ago, the Derby twins vanished." Tell
snapped his fingers for emphasis. "Of course, the answer
was there in front of us all the time. By the Duke's guns,
the children of this town even call her a witch—The Witch
of Weymore Alley."

"And the taunting chants of children become fiat identification? Come, Major, they call you and your fellow
redcoats 'lobsterbacks,' but I don't think you're in any
danger of the steaming pot."

Tell ignored the "lobsterback" quip and continued:
"The children's description merely piqued my interest in
the Weymore woman.

"The widow Weymore lives at the end of a cul-de-sac
known as Weymore Alley, and a more horrid hag I have
never seen. She was respectable in her time, I am told—
the wife of a ship's first mate who was lost at sea, leaving
her with an infant son. She raised the boy poorly, it seems,
for he grew to be a lout of a lad, fond of gaming and
carousing. Five years ago, when the son was eighteen or
so, he went out for his usual night of revels. His mother,
who doted on the lad, sat in her window with a candle, as
she did every night until he returned.

"On this particular night her son never did return, and
she's kept the candlelight vigil each and every night from
dusk till dawn ever since."

"What happened to the son?" I asked.

"No one is sure. It is thought that he fell to fighting
with some sailors and was killed and his body disposed
of."

"My, my," Cork chuckled. "This town abounds in disappearances. But, Major, how can you deduce that the
widow is a witch on the basis of some odd behaviour?"

Tell's face was beaming as he withdrew a fold of paper
from his tunic. "By direct testimony, my old friend. When
I first learned of the widow Weymore's existence, I quickly
procured a copy of Cotton Mather's study in witchcraft,
Memorable Providences, and, by jing, if some of the facts
of this case don't match those he encountered in Salem!"

He unfolded the paper and read aloud; "Item one. On
April 9, Sally Trent, the first girl to disappear, was ob-

served near Weymore Alley at dusk. It is assumed she was going to take the Witch Walk."

Both Cork and I looked puzzled.

"It's a local custom among the young girls hereabouts," Tell explained. "A single girl who walks down the alley alone and stares directly into the witch's eyes will be married within the next moon's last quarter. A harmless enough game, but on the morning of the tenth Sally was missing. Of course, a hue and cry was raised, but no one thought about the widow at first.

"Item two. Giles Cooper, a local farmer, recalls having spit while passing the alley on May 10. That night all his milk cows died of disease, and on the twelfth his youngest daughter was gone. Don't you see how the pattern forms? This list contains twelve different occasions when animals died or crops went bad after someone had passed through the alley and looked at the witch. There you have it, clear as crystal."

"There *you* have it," Cork said, "as clear as coincidence and superstition can muddle it. You're aware that Cotton Mather not only investigated witchcraft, he also created its American manifestations. I think you have swallowed a bad carp, Major. What's your next step? Perhaps you will toss the widow Weymore into the sea, and if she drowns, it will prove she is innocent. That's the approved method of judgment, is not not?"

Tell laughed aloud and shook a finger in Cork's direction. "You're japing me, Captain. I may not be able to pin her as a witch on the basis of this"—he tapped the paper—"but to-night I will have undeniable proof. I am convinced the Derby twins are still somewhere in this town. In fact, they are at the house at the end of Weymore Alley, and I intend to take it by storm and free those virgins. I thought perhaps you would like to be in on the hunt."

"Does the widow live alone?" Cork wanted to know. I could see from the squint of his eyes that he was honing his senses.

"Yes."

"And she is elderly, you say?"

"Ancient, Captain."

"And at what hour do you mount this attack?"

"Precisely at the stroke of eight. A full squad will be deployed."

"Only a squad! Well, best have each man wear a piece of hemlock on his person, just to play safe."

"Hemlock?" Tell thought for a moment and then it struck him. "Of course, hemlock as a bane against her powers. Excellent thinking. But does hemlock grow hereabouts?"

"I have no idea, since I have never been in Berryport before."

The Major was quite taken with the suggestion, and rushed away to implement it, promising to return for us before eight o'clock.

"Isn't wolfbane the thing to ward off evil?" I asked as Cork got up from the table to wash his hands in a side bucket.

"Or garlic, or roses, or a dead haddock, for all the good it would do. Tell is a competent soldier, but an ass at ratiocination. In his desperation he reaches for the occult to solve his problem. Do you actually believe that an ancient old crone could overpower healthy young women?"

"She could have lured them into her house. Young women are impressionable."

"And then what? No, Oaks, there are too many avenues of exploration open. Perhaps they left of their own accord—fled with lovers. This Covenant of the Cleansed doesn't sound like a group given to hot-blooded fancy, and might well be escaped from. But we'll have to nose about, my old son, and harvest some facts. Let's take a look at this infamous alley before darkness falls."

Directions were easily come by, and within ten minutes' walk of the Sign of the Two Doves we found ourselves in the waterfront area. Although the cul-de-sac bore no marking, it was undeniably the place. It was a narrow, cobbled walkway leading back some twenty yards to a small ramshackle house badly in need of repair. The house's frontage had one tiny window on the lower floor, and one door. The upper floor was blind. Flanking the alley on either side were shops in the nautical trades—to the left a ship's chandlery and to the right a food provisioner.

Cork was surveying the scene when a man emerged

from the chandlery and began to lock the door behind him.

"Excuse me, sir, are you shut for the day?" Cork asked him.

"That's what my sign says," the man said gruffly, pointing to a small sign that read: EBENEZER CUTLER. *Sunup to sunset, daily except Sabbath*. "If you have business, it will have to wait, for I have two ships just in that I must tend to."

"By all means, Mr. Cutler. My own vessel will not arrive for a week or so. I'm told you have fine spars available in Berryport."

"Finest money can buy." Seeing that we were potential customers, he had softened his stern tone, and almost smiled. He was as tall and spare as the ships' spars he was lauding.

Cork introduced us and got him into general conversation which he deftly steered towards the twins' recent disappearance. His ability to extract information through the manipulation of idle chatter marks him as a verbal helmsman of the first water.

"Six lassies, you say?" he chattered, "and all seen near this alley, Mr. Cutler? My, my, what are times coming to?"

"We of the Covenant have taken steps, I can assure you. A high-ranking King's officer is now in charge and he promises results within days."

"Excellent. When the King's hand is in, things are set to rights. Tell me, why is this called an 'alley'? It is not a thoroughfare."

"It was built by old Fergus Weymore before anything else was erected around here. Now I must be off, gentlemen. I look forward to doing business with you."

My timepiece said six o'clock, and I asked the Captain if we should return to the inn for supper.

"No, Oaks, we have other meat to chew on this day. Let us try the food provisioner's shop."

We strode across the alley and I chanced another glance—it was not yet dusk—and the window, that small, mysterious cyclops' eye of the house, was vacant. The doorstop bell of Mr. Giles Plunkett's shop tinkled as we entered, and a dark-haired woman with tawny skin and fierce black eyes came out from a back room where I could see all kinds of meat hanging on hooks and great head-cheese pots brewing.

"Good evening, Senorita," Cork said in the charming tone he uses when a woman strikes his fancy.

She smiled and corrected him. "Senora, sir. I am Mrs. Plunkett. What can I do for you?"

"I thought we might get a little sustenance, a *minestra*."

Throaty laughter. "We sell only in bulk, sir, although from your size, you look as if you could eat a galley bare. There is an inn up the town."

"And that I know, Mrs. Plunkett. My mission here is to sample. I am Captain Jeremy Cork, and my ship, *The Hawkers*, will make port here for a refitting within the month. I want to assure myself that fresh goods are available."

"Good or bad, it will have to come from this shop, Captain. It's the only one about. Strange, a ship's master walks ahead of his vessel?"

As she spoke, I was revising my original opinion of her. She was indeed a woman of uncommon acuity.

"The vessel is to me a child to be fed, not a mistress to be fawned over, Senora. We shall be placing a rather large order, and I—"

"What is all this, Dolores?" a voice asked from the back room. It was followed by its owner into the front of the shop.

He was short and powerful, with ox-like shoulders and massive forearms, and he was obviously perturbed with the woman's dalliance in idle chatter. When she had explained the situation and introduced him as her husband, Giles Plunkett, his mood became less suspicious, but certainly not more congenial.

"We'll be pleased to provision you, Captain Cork," he said, "but we've got two barks in the harbour now waiting on us. There's much corning to be done. Dolores!"

"Go back to your work and leave the front counter to me," she snapped, and to my surprise he responded with a docile shrug and returned to the back room.

"He gets pawky with strangers," she said. "I'll fetch

you a sample of my wares, Captain, but it will be a slim
portion, mind, for we have just enough for the two ships
in port." She went into the back room and returned shortly
with a plate containing a small piece of head cheese and
two thin slices of meat. The meat was far from delectable,
being slightly stringy and strong. Cork swallowed his
portion and asked, "Deer meat, Senora?"

"That's all that's available. Deer and bear, since the
cattle and chickens died off over the spring and summer."

"Oh, yes," Cork said. "I heard it was the result of
some sort of spell."

The woman's face became serious and hard-lined. "So
now they have started on the old lady, have they?" She
gritted her teeth in anger. "This Covenant crowd should
be horsewhipped. They put on their pious ways and show
no charity to a toothless old crone. Their children torment
her, and now the adults are at it. My Giles told them the
animals died of the pox, not of spells." She shrugged.
"They are fools, all of them. The old lady is harmless.
They just want to be rid of her, for fear she'll become a
public charge. The chandler across the way is always
after her to sell her house to him. But where would she
go? I take her scraps of food now and then and some
bread and milk. She needs little."

Her anger seemed to cool and she returned to business,
asking us particulars of *The Hawkers'* needs. Cork, however, was anxious to leave, and told her we would deal
with the precise details later. As we were leaving, Cork
bid her good day in Spanish, and to my surprise she threw
back her head and laughed. "I am Portuguese, not Spanish, sir," she proclaimed proudly.

"A thousand pardons." Cork bowed. "Lisbon is a beautiful city."

She laughed again. "Perhaps. I have never been there.
I am from Ponte Delgarda"—she shook a finger at Cork
—"so I know you sailors well."

"She's quite a spirited woman," I said when we were
once more on the street.

"Most of the woman of the Azores are," he chuckled.
"And I imagine she is the backbone of the shop's manage-
ment. Best keep an eye peeled when we deal with her

again." He started to stroll off towards the dock area, and I called after him. "The inn is the other way, Captain, and we just have time for a bite before eight o'clock."

"We've had our bite, Oaks, but now something bites at me. Come, let us find the port captain's headquarters."

"The port captain?" I asked, falling into step with him.

"Several times to-day, people have referred to 'two ships' in the harbour, but there is a third ship moored in the lee of that cove in the outer harbour. Let's find out about it."

Captain Lewis Fuller, the port captain, looked more the ship's cook than an ex-skipper. He was quite obese, and made little effort to waste movement. We sat opposite him sharing a mug of rum as he answered Cork's questions.

"That ship in yonder cove be the *Queen of Prussia*, lads. This is her home port, or maybe her graveyard. Ain't out of the harbour more than once the year for fishing. I understand she was a deep-water vessel in trade, but that was before I took over back in '35. Belongs to the Covenant."

"She looks a fifty-tonner," Cork said. "Shame to waste her in casual fishing."

The Portmaster grinned broadly. "Don't try to make no sense out of that lot of psalm singers, Captain Cork. I never could."

"Of what persuasion are they? I had never heard of the Covenant before coming here."

The old sailor tamped his clay bowl, relit, and puffed. " 'Pears to me they made it up all by themselves. They're God-fearing all right, too God-fearing for my likes. Take the rum works, for instance. When I came aboard this billet, I was looking forward to having a local source of supply. But then the Covenant shut the works down just a year or so after I came. How's that for bad navigating? Now I have to rely on a few coasters to keep my cup full."

"Tell me, Captain Fuller," Cork wanted to know, "do many ships make this their port of call?"

"We refit about six or seven a year. The woods here-abouts yield fine naval timber."

Cork then asked if either of the two ships now calling on the port had ever been here before. Fuller scratched his head, then rose and took down a logbook. Flipping through the pages, he stopped and looked up. "Wanted to put a fire under my memory bone," he said. "One of them has—the *Lady of Castile*, over four months ago. Trades in salt fish and madeira on the return passage. Pretty good madeira at that."

I checked my timepiece and reminded Cork that it was approaching eight o'clock and he rose to leave. "Thank you, Captain Fuller," he said. "One last question. When was the *Queen of Prussia* last on a fishing trip?"

"Last month. Had a bit of a meat shortage, and the town needed the fish. God, I hate cod!"

With some degree of understanding, Cork said he preferred shellfish himself.

We were again into the night air, and I suggested that we go directly to Weymore Alley, since it was almost time for the siege.

"A siege of shadows, Oaks. Our time is better spent on substance. We'll leave the witch hunt to Major Tell. Now we must find a dory and take a little exercise at the oars."

"Oars? Dory? Captain, I don't understand. Are we going out to the *Lady of Castile*?"

"Not the *Castile*, Oaks, the *Queen of Prussia*."

I followed him as usual, loyal but bewildered. He was on to a scent, but I had not a smell of it.

Half an hour later we had stolen aboard the deserted ship. Cork prowled about her decks and then led the way into the darkness below, our small lantern serving as a weak source of light as we made our way down the passage. We felt along the bulkhead until we were at the door of the most aft cabin, slipped inside, and Cork surveyed what was obviously the master's quarters.

"Are we looking for anything in particular?"

"Of course, Oaks. Ah, we are in luck! The master of this vessel follows tradition, and leaves his logbook aboard." He had lifted the object from a drawer, and, in the lantern's light, I saw his face break into a broad grin. He turned the pages as I held the light higher so we could read. He had turned to the earlier entires and read them quickly.

"Looks like an ordinary logbook to me," I said. Page after page recording common shipboard happenings and ports of call. Cargoes of fish en route to Europe, goods on return.

"Do you think so, my boy? Come, the light is not good, but what looks odd about this log?"

"Well, the pages are of vellum, which is a little expensive for a ship's log, but—"

"And that, added to the other facts, makes me suspicious."

"What other facts?"

"Well, for one, the first mate of this vessel was Fergus Weymore, the widow's husband, and her master was Mr. Ebenezer Cutler, our grumpy chandler, as it shows here. Strange, Weymore was lost at sea on the last Atlantic voyage, in 1732."

"I may be dense, but how is that strange? This was his home port."

"You know, Oaks, this started out to be a simple case, one easily solved, but now we have a double mystery, and the second is more intriguing than the first. Come, we have work to do."

"You're taking the log?"

"To be sure. If I have it right, it is you who have given me the answer."

How anyone could supply an answer when he didn't even know the question was beyond me. When we were back ashore, Cork made straight for the Two Doves, and proceeded to embark on a frenzy of activity. First, he commandeered a corner of the kitchen and had a large open kettle put to boil. Then he dispatched two kitchen boys on separate errands. One was to go to Giles Plunkett's shop and procure all the hooves and horns of the carcasses available, and the bile sac of any one animal. The second lad was sent to the local apothecary to bring back a large portion of brimstone.

When all the items had been assembled, Cork put the horns and hooves into the boiling kettle and added a fistful of sulphur.

"Now we shall let that cook while we repair to the public rooms for a libation," he said.

As we drank some Knock and shared some cheese and cornbread, I asked what all this hubabub in the kitchen was about. "Are you brewing up some witchcraft of your own, Captain?"

"On the contrary, we are about to embark on an endeavour as old as the Pharoahs, Oaks. We noted aboard the *Queen of Prussia* that the pages of the log were of expensive vellum, and not plain paper, as one would expect. When I told you earlier to-day about all of us wishing we could expunge some days out of our lives, I didn't realise it was an omen. You see, I believe the vellum pages were used by design to hide something."

"Secret writing!" I exclaimed.

"In a sense. The pages of the log may be a palimpsest. You look confused, Oaks. A palimpsest is a document, on parchment or vellum, from which the original writing has been scraped and new writing inscribed over it. The Egyptians used it as a method to reclaim a writing surface when the original document was considered outdated. The monks of the Middle Ages did the same thing. The original writing was removed by soaking the vellum in milk, then sprinkling the wet surface with flour. Once dry, the writing was rubbed off with pumice or chalk. When the cleansing process was completed, it gave them a blank page for re-use. Yet the old priests of Isis knew that the original message was not lost forever. Out there in the kitchen we are preparing the Mist of Ammon by boiling the hooves and horns of animals."

"Of course! I thought the odor was ammoniacal, but why the brimstone?"

"Be up to date, old son. Call it sulphur."

"And the bile sac and alcohol?"

"That is our second step. By treating the pages with this mixture, we will hopefully bring out the original entry."

"It sounds most ingenious, but you haven't soaked the pages in milk."

"Because I suspect we haven't all night to spare, since the Major is now storming the Weymore house. Besides, cleaning each page would take weeks. But we have several things to our advantage. If someone had cleansed the pages and wrote in a new entry, it would be impossible for them to cover the original completely, word for word, line for line. There would be gaps because the writer would be working with blank sheets of paper again."

"But which pages do you plan to treat? There are so many, stretching over several years of voyages."

He ruffled through the log pages and stopped at a place far back in the book. "This entry intrigues me for several reasons." He pushed the book over to me, and I read:

17 May, 1732—Lng. 20. Lat. 45. Nor'westerly heading, fair winds. Mr. Weymore went to the Lord today, taken by fever. Buried at sea and may God rest his soul. Main topsail fully repaired. Supplies are ample. Mr. Kittery, second mate, appointed to first mate's berth.

"I see the connection. Do you think Weymore was murdered, Captain? And even so, what has that to do with the missing girls?"

"Perhaps nothing. But it is the last Atlantic voyage of the *Queen of Prussia*, and the dead man's widow is Tell's prime suspect. Ah, here is our Major now. Best tuck that log under your jacket, my boy."

The Major strode across the public room with a pleased grin on his face. As he took a chair, we could see that he was breathless with excitement.

"Where the devil were you?" he exclaimed. "You weren't here when I came by earlier, and you missed the entire show."

"A fruitful endeavour then, Major? And I thought you were off on a sleeveless errand."

"Not this fellow, Cork." Tell thumped his tunic with a finger.

"Then the girls are safe and the problem solved, hey?"

The Major's grin lost all its support, and he pursed his mouth. "No, not exactly. The girls could be found nowhere in the house. My men tore it apart and found not a trace of them. But I think I have the answer, and I fear, gentlemen, that it is a gruesome business indeed." He turned and hailed a sergeant who had been standing by the taproom door. As he marched forward, I could see he carried a cloth sack in his hands. He deposited the sack on the table and returned to his station.

"She's a witch, all right," Tell said, emptying the sack's

contents onto the table, "for those are the tools of her devilish trade."

There before us was an odd, almost obscene, collection of items. A carved wooden statue of a grotesque monster in a man's form, something that looked like a child's rattle (save this odious thing was fashioned from bones that resembled human fingers), two human skulls, and a deadly sort of knife made from what appeared to be bone and carved with symbols beyond my ken. Cork picked up each piece and inspected it carefully.

"They certainly look ominous," I said.

"That she-devil used them in her evil rites, to be sure, Oaks. And you, Cork? What have you to say?"

"Simple enough. Where are the missing girls?"

"I venture we are going to find those poor innocents buried in her backyard. I have ten shovels at it now, and should have an answer by morning. I wish I had more troops, though. The townspeople have gotten wind of it, and they are in an angry mood."

"A suggestion then," Cork said. "I would enlist the aid of the two Captains moored in the harbour. Their crews could help you to maintain order."

"Excellent idea, Cork. At least, you've been of some help to me in this affair. I suspected from the first that I hadn't piqued your curiosity as in the past. What's the matter, Captain? Has Oaks finally turned you into a bookkeeper?"

As Tell refilled the sack and got up to leave, Cork smiled. "You might say it is just that, Major. This *is* your night for clever deductions."

Turned him into a bookkeeper, indeed. I could more readily fly to the moon. Cork sat there in silence, thinking, when Merton, the innkeeper, came up to us in a lather.

"Mind, Captain, I am honoured to have you under my roof, but this foul concoction you have brewing in my kitchen is enough to peel the insides of a body's nose."

"Not for long, mine host, it is almost ready. Tell me, I have heard about six girls who have disappeared from the area. Did you know them?"

"Indeed I did, sir—by name and sight, at least. I'm a newcomer, and not of the Covenant or any church."

"All pretty, I imagine."

"As pictures, sir."

"And fair-haired?"

The innkeeper nodded.

"You are the second person I've met today who is relatively new hereabouts. Are there others?"

"Well, I'd say quite a few. The Covenant folk settled the town and didn't invite new settlers for a number of years. I'd say most of the tradespeople are new—that is, in the last ten years or so."

Ten minutes later we were back in the kitchen, and Merton was right—the place reeked with noxious fumes. At his request I gave Cork the logbook, and he carefully held the page with the 17 May entry over the bubbling kettle.

"We may be on a false trail, sir," I said as my eyes began to tear. "The items Tell found certainly point to some kind of skulduggery, don't you think?"

"They point to witchcraft, to be sure, but—ah, that should do it. I don't want the ink to run. Now some of the bile mixture. Hand me that cloth there on the table."

He applied the reddish-purple substance carefully on the areas of the page that were blank and then gently dabbed it dry.

"We have something, my boy. Not much, but something."

I looked at the page and at first there seemed to be only blotches; but peering closer, I could see the fragmented remnants of part of the original entry. Some words stood out thusly:

> start of midd passage
> uprising   eymore dead
>   escape to sea
> suicides abound
>
>   set s

"A mutiny!" I cried. "There was a mutiny aboard the *Queen of Prussia*. But why try to hide it? The crew escaped to sea, it seems."

Cork was about to speak when a voice called our names from the doorway to the public rooms. It was the sergeant who had accompanied Major Tell earlier. He breathlessly described a desperate situation and delivered a message from the Major.

While the soldiers were digging in the widow Weymore's backyard, a group of townspeople had breached the house and taken the old woman off to the Church of the Covenant. The squad and the crews from the two ships had gone off in hot pursuit, but the Covenant's leaders refused to give their captive up, stating they intended to try her as a witch. Major Tell was hesitant to use force to save the widow, and requested that Cork come and make some suggestions.

It was a brisk walk to the church seven blocks away, and when we arrived, Tell looked grave. "A damnable dilemma, Cork."

"And of your own making, I'm afraid, Major. I think diplomacy will have to serve where force has failed."

"What should we do?" Tell asked somberly. "I am at your command."

That, I knew, was not an easy statement for a proud soldier to make, but, true to the breed, he was not about to purchase pride at the price of regret.

Cork took charge, always a spiriting sight. He stood there, casting a long shadow in the cloudless moonlight, stroking his barba. In the snap of a few seconds he moved.

"Major, I'll need eight stout soldiers under my direct orders. Keep these sailors and their Captains on hand, just in case." He then took the assigned soldiers aside and, having instructed them, sent them off at double-step.

"Now," he said, returning to us, "two more messengers will serve our needs. Have them fetch Captain Fuller, the Portmaster, Mr. and Mrs. Plunkett, and inkeeper Merton, telling them they can be of some assistance to me."

"What about Ebenezer Cutler?" I asked.

"I'm sure that stout member of the Covenant of the Cleansed is among the witch-triers within."

"He is that," Tell confirmed, "and his brother Amos, as well. He's the Pastor."

"Indeed," Cork mused. "A learned man, I assume?"

"Yes, quite."

"Well, let us knock on their gates and stir up the dust and cobwebs of this mystery."

When I finally make him a wealthy man, I am going to suggest to Cork that he enter the ambassadorial service, for his display of tact and courtesy is unparalleled. And when you consider that beneath it all is a fox-quick mind, you have the makings of a shrewd negotiator.

Amos Cutler was an older version of his brother, and as frostlike in countenance. Cork palavered with him for several minutes at the church door before persuading the man that we should be allowed to enter. His most telling point was that any trial must be open to the public, and that the defendant had a right to counsel, Cork being the counsel by virtue of his being a Justice of the Peace in our home colony of Connecticut. He has told that lie several times in the past, but never before in a church.

The congregation, which numbered some sixty-odd, sat in pews, woman to the left, men to the right. At the front of the church was a simple pulpit and, before it, a long table with chairs placed behind. Off to the right sat the withered old hag, who stared into nothingness, unmindful of her surroundings.

We followed the Reverend Cutler to the table and were offered seats. The Pastor explained to his flock that he concurred with Cork that any trial should be open. "Let the record show that we have nothing to hide."

There was much murmuring which quieted down and then started again when Mr. and Mrs. Plunkett, Captain Fuller, and innkeeper Merton were ushered in and seated at the rear. The witch trial was in session, and Cork was smirking again.

The Pastor arose and read a list of charges that ran the gamut of all we had heard before. Various people were called to give testimony about having seen the girls near the alley, about crops failing, about cattle dying, and all manner of catastrophes—and all of it attributed to the pitiable old woman sitting in the corner.

Cork did not challenge them, but merely took swigs from a flask that Merton had brought forward just before the proceedings began. The Captain told the Pastor it was medicine for his rheumatism. That was the second lie he had told in a house of worship, and I found myself checking the rafters for a sign of imminent collapse.

The last witness called was Ebenezer Cutler, who swore he had seen the Derby twins near the alley the night they disappeared. When he finished, he rose from the witness chair, and Cork finally spoke.

"A question, sir, if you will," he said, and the chandler reseated himself. "You were the master of the vessel *Queen of Prussia*, owned under charter by the Covenant?"

"Yes, but what has this to do—"

"Pray, sir, a mere point of curiosity. I have learned that on several occasions you have offered to buy the widow Weymore's house and property."

"I am a man of commerce, sir, and often deal in property."

"As we all do. My point is that you have something to gain if this poor wretch is convicted, for I am sure you would have first bid, owing to your stature in the community."

"That is preposterous, and I repeat—what has this to do with the missing children?"

"Ah, there's that word again—'children.' A girl of fifteen, sir, is nubile, a woman of marrying age. To give them infant status beclouds the issue. And I might add, comely women at that."

A woman in the back sobbed into her hands—obviously one of the distraught parents who considered that Cork was being exceptionally cruel.

"Are you suggesting that I had anything to do with their disappearances?" Cutler snarled.

"Indirectly, yes."

A gasp went up from one and all, and Cutler turned purple with rage. "The Major's men have turned over every stick and stone and peeked and poked into everything that has left my shop. *There's* your culprit"—he pointed to the widow—"the she-devil! Ask the Major what he found in her house!"

"Yes, I have seen them. In fact, they sealed the case for me. Let me test your memory, sir. What happened in your life on the seventeenth of May, 1732?"

Cutler's purple rage gave way to bloodless white. "I don't know what you are talking about."

"Come now, Mr. Cutler. Such a harrowing experience

would never be wiped from the mind. On that day the *Queen of Prussia* was in the thirty-sixth longitude at the twenty-fifth latitude, not the 20° and 45° heading your logbook shows. Don't be startled, sir, I have proof. The true reading would put you just south of the Azores. Now why, I ask myself, would someone want to falsify that location? But the answer is clear, is it not, Captain Cutler? The Azores would be the first port of call *after the African coast.*"

If Cutler had been unnerved before, he was in complete crumble now. His hands trembled and his breathing came heavy.

"I think I have the thread of it from the scant words I was able to raise from your doctored log. You were a slaver, Captain Cutler, a dealer in captive black flesh, and to me, no better than a jackal."

Tears were coming down Cutler's face as he spoke. "I have atoned these long years in prayer and piety. We were starting the middle passage with forty blackamoors below. Somehow they panicked and got free and were all over the ship like locusts. My first mate was struck down, and a dozen of the slaves jumped overboard. Then, may God help me, when we had the remaining ones under control, they started to commit suicide by horrible means."

There were moans from the congregation and cries to have him stop. Cork looked at the assemblage with scorn.

"What else would a frightened, terrified animal do?" he roared. "Ripped from their homes and villages and marched hundreds of miles to the sea to be stocked in pens until the ships arrived. And then locked aboard like cattle for the middle passage, that infamous run of ocean between Africa and the Sugar Islands of the West Indies where their backs were broken in the canefields. All of you look shocked and horrified, but I'll have none of it! Slaves are sold for molasses, and molasses is made into rum, which in turn, is used to buy more slaves. Where did you think the molasses came from for the rum works in your town? And where do you think the rum went? You closed your eyes, all of you, and enjoyed the prosperity that the trade produced. I am sickened by the lot of you!"

Usually he is play-acting in these circumstances, but not this time. His emotions were at full sail.

"Then, after this horror on May 17, this fiend tries to blot out the past. The log is altered and the ship berthed for good. I don't call that atonement, sir!"

Major Tell cleared his throat almost out of embarrassment and said, "There are people who share your views on slavery, Captain, but there is nothing illegal in it. We still have the missing-girls problem and the question of the paraphernalia found at the witch's house—"

"Major, you make noises like a blatherskate. The items found in the house are souvenirs from Weymore's trips to Africa. They were religious articles to their rightful owners. Perhaps that's why Cutler wanted to buy the Weymore house. He wasn't sure that his dead first mate hadn't left some damaging evidence or papers behind him."

"But our children," a woman moaned from one of the forward pews. "What has become of our babies?"

"I am coming to that, madam. When I saw this case clearly, I said to my associate that there were two crimes, one punishable by law and the other by irony. Oaks, will you have the sergeant bring in what I sent him for?"

I went to the door and opened it. To my surprise the squad of men had a large barrel with them that they carried into the church and put down at the head of the center aisle.

"Senora Plunkett," Cork called out to the rear of the church, "this container bears the mark of your shop. Have a care, woman, there are soldiers behind you." He called for a prying bar and another uniformed man brought one forward and opened the lid.

"Ah, head cheese," Cork said, looking in and taking a cut with his knife. He tasted it. "Not bad, but a bit too sweet for my palate. It seemed strange to me, Senora, that although a pox had destroyed the local meat supply, and only recently you had started to use game animals, how then you were able to provision ships. But now I think I know where your new supply came from."

There was a shriek from one woman, followed by another, and still another. In seconds the horror of the statement rippled through the entire congregation, which now was awash in tears and wailings. I felt a catch in my own throat, for I had eaten food at the Plunkett shop.

"Oh, Lord in heaven," the Reverend intoned. "Oh, God! Not the flesh of our children!"

"Stop it, all of you!" Cork's voice thundered, and silence ensued. He then reached into the barrel with both hands and lifted up what appeared to be a two-foot-deep basin. It was a false top, and the barrel area beneath was empty.

"Smugglers soon learn the ways of contraband agents, Major, and this is an old trick, but a well-kept one. A soldier might jab a sack with a rifle butt or probe a container of dry beans with his sword. But no spotlessly uniformed redcoat would dirty himself or his gear digging around in head cheese. Are the twins all right, Sergeant?"

"A bit groggy, sir, when we took them out of the false-topped barrels aboard the *Lady of Castile*. They had been drugged, as you guessed."

"You have the Captain in custody?"

"Yes, sir, outside."

"You mean the Derby twins are safe?" The Reverend folded his hands. "Thank Jehovah!"

"And where are the others?" a man shouted.

"I said a crime punishable by irony, sir. By now I am sure those fair-haired ladies are the pride and joy of some sultan's seraglio. The slave trade works two ways, although the girls' fate will be far better, I am sure, than that of the black souls you delivered to the swamps of the Indies. Senora Plunkett does not look in a confessional mood, but I'm certain she has connections in her native Azores to make the transfer to the slave markets of the Levant. Perhaps you recognised the *Queen of Prussia* when you arrived here to set up shop, and saw no evil in doing exactly what this town had done, but in reverse. Keep your silence, madam, I'm sure the Captain of the *Lady of Castile* will want to escape the hanging string. Come, Oaks, I want to leave this unclean place."

Around eleven that night Tell joined us in our rooms for a late supper. He was quite cowed by his blundering, and was solicitous to Cork.

"When did you get on to it, Captain?"

"The missing girls? That could have been solved easily enough. What intrigued me was the closed-down rum works, the ship that didn't go to sea, and a town that had isolated itself for a number of years and yet was as prosperous as any busy port. That's why I assured myself that no ship would leave here until I had time to work out the problem. To make sure one didn't slip away, I had you bring the crews ashore. The sergeant got no trouble from the skeleton crews left behind. The palimpsest gave us our answer. By the by, I said Cutler's crime was punishable only by irony, but it is illegal to alter a ship's log, and I hope you will bring it to the Admiralty's attention."

"I will indeed. But why did he keep accurate records in the first place?"

"He would have to protect himself from inspection in foreign ports or if stopped on the high seas by a British navy ship. It is legal, as you said, to carry slaves, but it had better square with the log."

"And the other girls are lost forever?" I asked.

"Damnation, now you are doing it, Oaks," he snapped. "In the Middle East they would be almost old ladies, but still desirable, I'm sure. Tell could check the Portmaster's records to trace all ships that called here in the last six months, but it will be a futile task. The price for white slaves is truly handsome, and would tempt a merchantman's master, but he would cover his tracks, to be sure. Have another lobster, Major."

"I haven't any appetite after your suggestion of cannibalism, Captain."

"I just wanted to rub their noses in horror—a small gesture to some poor souls now in the Indies. Oh, yes, Oaks, it occurs to me that you might try to expunge your erroneous dates from your account book. Just strike them out, lad. It may not be neat, but it's more in keeping with nature."

"It goes against my grain, sir."

"Well then, take solace in the philosopher who tells us rightly that the lightest act leaves at least a trace of stain behind it—a lesson this town learned, I'm happy to say, at my hands. Try the brine and vinegar, Major, it has a fine smack."

I sat there and shook my head. Here he tells us that one of his "suspicions" was a 50-tonner that sat idle at anchor. How about a six-foot-sixer who does the same thing? The brine and vinegar dip, by the way, is dreadful, and I'm sure it would stain your innards.

NINE

The Christmas Masque

As MUCH AS I PREFER the steady ways of New England, I have to agree with Captain Jeremy Cork that the Puritans certainly know how to avoid a good time. They just ignore it. That's why every 23rd of December we come to the New York colony from our home base in Connecticut to celebrate the midwinter holidays.

I am often critical of my employer's inattention to his many business enterprises and his preoccupation with the solution of crime—but I give him credit for the way he keeps Christmas. That is, as long as I can stop him from keeping it clear into February.

In our travels about these colonies, I have witnessed many merry parties, from the lush gentility of the Carolinas to the roughshod ribaldry of the New Hampshire tree line; but nothing can match the excitement of the Port of New York. The place teems with prosperous men who ply their fortunes in furs, potash, naval timber, and other prime goods. And the populace is drawn from everywhere: Sephardim from Brazil, Huguenots from France, visitors from London, expatriates from Naples,

Irishmen running to or from something. I once counted 18 different languages being spoken here.

And so it was in the Christmas week of 1754 that we took our usual rooms at Marshall's in John Street, a few steps from the Histrionic Academy, and let the yuletide roll over us. Cork's celebrity opens many doors to us, and there was the expected flood of invitations for one frivolity after another.

I was seated at a small work table in our rooms on December 23, attempting to arrange our social obligations into a reasonable program. My primary task was to sort out those invitations which begged our presence on Christmas Eve itself, for that would be our highpoint. Little did I realize that a knock on our door would not only decide the issue, but plunge us into one of the most bizarre of those damnable social puzzles Cork so thoroughly enjoys.

The messenger was a small lad, no more than seven or eight, and he was bundled against the elements from head to toe. Before I could open the envelope to see if an immediate reply was required, the child was gone.

I was opening the message when Cork walked in from the inner bedchamber. Marshall's is one of the few places on earth with doorways high enough to accommodate his six-foot-six frame.

"I take the liberty," I said. "It's addressed to us both."

"On fine French linen paper, I see."

"Well, well," I said, reading the fine handscript. "This is quite an honour."

"From the quality of the paper and the fact that you are 'honoured' just to read the message, I assume the reader is rich, money being the primer for your respect, Oaks."

That is not absolutely true. I find nothing wrong with poverty; however, it is a condition I do not wish to experience. In fact, as Cork's financial yeoman, it is my sworn duty to keep it from our door sill. The invitation was from none other than Dame Ilsa van Schooner, asking us to take part in her famous Christmas Eve Masque at her great house on the Broad Way. Considering that we had already been invited to such questionable activities as a cockfight, a party at a doss house, a drinking duel at Cosgrove's, and an evening of sport at the Gentlemen's

Club, I was indeed honoured to hear from a leader of New York quality.

Cork was glancing at the invitation when I discovered a smaller piece of paper still in the envelope.

"This is odd," I said, reading it:

> van Schooner Haus
> 22 December

Dear Sirs:
 I implore you to accept the enclosed, for I need you very much to investigate a situation of some calamity for us. I shall make myself known at the Masque.

It was unsigned. I passed it to the Captain, who studied it for a moment and then picked up the invitation again.

"I'm afraid your being honoured is misplaced, my old son," he said. "The invitation was written by a skilled hand, possibly an Ephrata penman, hired for such work. But our names have been fitted in by a less skilled writer. The author of the note has by some means invited us without the hostess's knowledge. Our *sub rosa* bidder must be in some dire difficulty, for she does not dare risk discovery by signing her name."

"Her?"

"No doubt about it. The hand is feminine and written in haste. I thought it odd that a mere boy should deliver this. It is usually the task of a footman, who would wait for a reply. This is truly intriguing—an impending calamity stalking the wealthy home in which she lives."

"How can you be sure of that, sir?"

"I can only surmise. She had access to the invitations and she says 'calamity for us,' which implies her family. Hello." He looked up suddenly as the door opened and a serving girl entered with a tray, followed by a man in royal red. "Sweet Jerusalem!" Cork got to his feet. "Major Tell in the flesh! Sally, my girl, you had better have Marshall send up extra Apple Knock and oysters. Tell, it is prophetic that you should appear just as a new puzzle emerges."

Prophetic indeed. Major Phillip Tell is a King's agent-at-large, and he invariably embroils us in some case of skulduggery whenever he is in our purlieu. But I bode him no ill this time, for he had nothing to do with the affair. In fact, his vast knowledge of the colonial scene might prove helpful.

"Well, lads," Tell said, taking off his *rogueloure* and tossing his heavy cloak onto a chair. "I knew Christmas would bring you to New York. You look fit, Captain, and I see Oaks is still at his account books."

When Cork told him of our invitation and the curious accompanying note, the officer gave a low whistle. "The van Schooners, no less! Well, we shall share the festivities, for I am also a guest at the affair. The note is a little disturbing, however. Dame Ilsa is the mistress of a large fortune and extensive land holdings, which could be the spark for foul play."

"You think she sent the note?" I asked.

"Nonsense," Cork interjected. "She would not have had to purloin her own invitation. What can you tell us of the household, Major?"

I don't know if Tell's fund of knowledge is part of his duties or his general nosiness, but he certainly keeps his ear to the ground. No gossip-monger could hold a candle to him.

"The family fortune was founded by her grandfather, Nils van der Malin—patroon of holdings up the Hudson, pearl potash, naval stores, that sort of old money. Under Charles the Second's Duke of York grant, Nils was rewarded for his support with a baronetcy. The title fell in the distaff side to Dame Ilsa's mother, old Gretchen van der Malin. She was a terror of a woman, who wore men's riding clothes and ran her estates with an iron fist and a riding crop. She had a young man of the Orange peerage brought over as consort, and they produced Ilsa. The current Dame is more genteel than her mother was, but just as stern and autocratic. She, in turn, married a van Schooner —Gustave, I believe, a soldier of some distinction in the Lowland campaigns. He died of drink after fathering two daughters, Gretchen and her younger sister, Wilda.

"The line is certainly Amazonite and breeds true," Cork said with a chuckle. "Not a climate I would relish, although strong women have their fascination."

"Breeds true is correct, Captain. The husbands were

little more than sire stallions; good blood but ruined by idleness."

This last, about being "ruined by idleness," was ignored by Cork, but I marked it, as well he knew.

"Young Gretchen," Tell went on, "is also true to her namesake. A beauty, but cold as a steel blade, and as well honed. They say she is a dead shot and an adept horse-woman."

"You have obviously been to the van Schooner haus, as our correspondent calls it."

"Oh, yes, on several occasions. It is truly a place to behold."

"No doubt, Major." Cork poured a glass of Apple Knock. "Who else lives there besides the servants?"

"The younger daughter Wilda, of course, and the Dame's spinster sister, Hetta van der Malin, and an ancient older brother of the dead husband—the brother is named Kaarl. I have only seen him once, but I am told he was quite the wastrel in his day, and suffers from the afflictions of such a life."

"Mmm," Cork murmured, offering the glass to Tell. "I change my original Amazonite observation to that of Queen Bee. Well, someone in that house feels in need of help, but we shall have to wait until to-morrow night to find out why."

"Or who," I said.

"That," Cork said, "is the heart of the mystery."

The snow started falling soon after dinner that night and kept falling into the dawn. By noon of the 24th, the wind had drifted nature's white blanket into knee-high banks. When it finally stopped in the late afternoon, New York was well covered under a blotchy sky. The inclemency, however, did not deter attendance at the van Schooner Ball.

I had seen the van Schooner home from the road many times, and always marveled at its striking architecture, which is in the Palladio style. The main section is a three-storey structure, and it is flanked by one-storey wings at both sides.

The lights and music emanating from the north wing

clearly marked it a ballroom of immense size. The front
entrance to the main house had a large raised enclosure
which people in these parts call a stoop. The interior was
as rich and well appointed as any manse I have ever seen.
The main hall was a gallery of statuary of the Greek and
Roman cast, collected, I assumed, when the family took
the mandatory Grand Tour.

Our outer clothes were taken at the main door, and we
were escorted through a sculptured archway across a large
salon towards the ballroom proper. We had purposely
come late to avoid the reception line and any possible
discovery by Dame van Schooner. We need not have bothered. There were more than 200 people there, making
individual acquaintance impossible. Not that some of the
guests were without celebrity. The Royal Governor was
in attendance, and I saw General Seaton and Solomon
deSilva, the fur king, talking with Reeves, the shipping
giant.

It was difficult to determine the identity of the majority
of the people, for most wore masks, although not all, in-
cluding Cork and myself. Tell fluttered off on his social
duties, and Cork fell to conversation with a man named
Downs, who had recently returned from Spanish America
and shared common friends there with the Captain.

I helped myself to some hot punch and leaned back to
take in the spectacle. It would be hard to say whether the
men or the women were the more lushly bedizened. The
males were adorned in the latest fashion with those large,
and, to my mind, cumbersome rolled coat cuffs. The materials of their plumage were a dazzling mixture of gold
and silver stuffs, bold brocades, and gaudy flowered vel-
vets. The women, not to be outdone by their peacocks,
were visions in fan-hooped gowns of silks and satins and
fine damask. Each woman's *tête-de-moutin* back curls
swung gaily as her partner spun her around the dance
floor to madcap tunes such as "Roger de Coverly," played
with spirit by a seven-piece ensemble. To the right of the
ballroom entrance was a long table with three different
punch bowls dispensing cheer.

The table was laden with all manner of great hams,
glistening roast goose, assorted tidbit meats and sweets of
unimaginable variety. Frothy syllabub was cupped up for

the ladies by liveried footmen, while the gentlemen had their choice of Madeira, rum, champagne, or Holland gin, the last served in small crystal thimbles which were embedded and cooled in a silver bowl mounded with snow.

"This is most lavish," I said to Cork when he disengaged himself from conversation with Downs. "It's a good example of what diligent attention to industry can produce."

"Whose industry, Oaks? Wealth has nothing more to do with industry than privilege has with merit. Our hostess over there does not appear to have ever perspired in her life."

He was true to the mark in his observation, for Dame van Schooner, who stood chatting with the Governor near the buffet, was indeed as cold as fine-cut crystal. Her well formed face was sternly beautiful, almost arrogantly defying anyone to marvel at its handsomeness and still maintain normal breathing.

"She *is* a fine figure of a woman, Captain, and, I might add, a widow."

He gave me a bored look and said, "A man would die of frostbite in her bedchamber. Ah, Major Tell, congratulations! You are a master at the jig!"

"It's a fantastical do, but good for the liver, I'm told. Has the mysterious sender of your invitation made herself known to you?"

"Not as yet. Is that young lady now talking with the Dame one of her daughters?"

"Both of them are daughters. The one lifting her mask is Gretchen, and, I might add, the catch of the year. I am told she has been elected Queen of the Bal, and will be crowned this evening."

The girl was the image of her mother. Her sister, however, must have followed the paternal line.

"The younger one is Wilda," Tell went on, "a dark pigeon in her own right, but Gretchen is the catch."

"Catch, you say." I winked at Cork. "Perhaps *her* bedchamber would be warmer?"

"You'll find no purchase there, gentlemen," Tell told us. "Along with being crowned Queen, her betrothal to Brock van Loon will probably be announced this evening."

"Hand-picked by her mother, no doubt?" Cork asked.

"Everything is hand-picked by the Dame. Van Loon is

a stout fellow, although a bit of a tailor's dummy. Family
is well landed across the river in Brueckelen. Say, they're
playing 'The Green Cockade,' Captain. Let me introduce
you to Miss Borden, one of our finest steppers."

I watched them walk over to a comely piece of frippery
and then Cork and the young lady stepped onto the dance
floor. "The Green Cockade" is one of Cork's favourite
tunes, and he dances it with gusto.

I drifted over to the serving table and took another cup
of punch, watching all the time for some sign from our
mysterious "hostess," whoever she was. I mused that the
calamity mentioned in the note might well have been pure
hyperbole, for I could not see how any misfortune could
befall this wealthy, joyous home.

With Cork off on the dance floor, Tell returned to my
side and offered to find a dance partner for me. I declined,
not being the most nimble of men, but did accept his bid
to introduce me to a lovely young woman named Lydia
Daws-Smith. The surname declared her to be the offspring
of a very prominent family in the fur trade, and her breed-
ing showed through a delightfully pretty face and pert figure. We were discussing the weather when I noticed four
footmen carrying what appeared to be a closed sedan chair
into the hall and through a door at the rear.

"My word, is a Sultan among the assemblage?" I asked
my companion.

"The sedan chair?" She giggled from behind her fan.
"No, Mr. Oaks, no Sultan. It's our Queen's throne. Gretchen
will be transported into the hall at the stroke of midnight,
and the Governor will proclaim her our New Year's Sovereign." She stopped for a moment, the smile gone. "Then
she will step forward to our acclaim and, of course, mandatory idolatry."

"I take it you do not like Gretchen very much, Miss
Daws-Smith."

"On the contrary, sir. She is one of my best friends. Now
you will have to excuse me, for I see Gretchen is getting
ready for the crowning, and I must help her."

I watched the young girl as she followed Gretchen to
the rear of the hall where they entered a portal and closed
the door behind them. Seconds later, Lydia Daws-Smith

came back into the main hall and spoke with the Dame, who then went through the rear door.

Cork had finished his dance and rejoined me. "This exercise may be good for the liver," he said, "but it plays hell with my thirst. Shall we get some refills?"

We walked back to the buffet table to slake his thirst, if that were ever possible. From the corner of my eye I caught sight of the Dame re-entering the hall from the rear door. She crossed over to the Governor and was about to speak to him when the orchestra struck up another tune. She seemed angry at the intrusion into what was obviously to have been the beginning of the coronation. But the Dame was ladylike and self-contained until the dancing was over. She then took a deep breath and nervously adjusted the neckline of her dress, which was shamefully bare from the bodice to the neck.

"Looks like the coronation is about to begin," Major Tell said, coming up to us. "I'll need a cup for the toast."

We were joking at the far end of the table when a tremendous crash sounded. We turned to see a distraught Wilda van Schooner looking down at the punch bowl she had just dropped. The punch had splashed down her beautiful velvet dress, leaving her drenched and mortified.

"Oh-oh," Tell said under his breath. "Now we'll hear some fireworks from Dame van Schooner."

True to his prediction, the Dame sailed across the floor and gave biting instructions to the footmen to bring mops and pails. A woman, who Tell told me in a whisper was Hetta van der Malin, the Dame's sister, came out of the crowd of tittering guests to cover her niece's embarrassment.

"She was only trying to help, Ilsa," the aunt said as she dabbed the girl's dress with a handkerchief.

The Dame glared at them. "You'd better help her change, Hetta, if she is going to attend the coronation."

The aunt and niece quickly left the ballroom and the Dame whirled her skirts and returned to the Governor's side. I overheard her say her apologies to him and then she added, "My children don't seem to know what servants are for. Well, shall we begin?"

At a wave of her hand, the orchestra struck up the

"Grenadier's March," and six young stalwarts lined up in two ranks before the Governor. At his command, the lads did a left turn and marched off towards the rear portal in the distinctive long step of the regiment whose music they had borrowed for the occasion.

They disappeared into the room where Gretchen waited for transport, and within seconds they returned, bearing the ornate screened sedan chair. "Aah's" filled the room over the beauty and pageantry of the piece. I shot a glance at Dame van Schooner and noted that she was beaming proudly at the impeccably executed production.

When the sedan chair had been placed before the Governor, he stepped forward, took the curtain drawstrings, and said, "Ladies and gentlemen, I give you our New Year's Queen."

The curtains were pulled open and there she sat in majesty. More "aah's" from the ladies until there was a screech and then another and, suddenly, pandemonium. Gretchen van Schooner sat on her portable throne, still beautiful, but horribly dead with a French bayonet through her chest.

"My Lord!" Major Tell gasped and started forward toward the sedan chair. Cork touched his arm.

"You can do no good there. The rear room, man, that's where the answer lies. Come, Oaks." He moved quickly through the crowd and I followed like a setter's tail on point. When we reached the door, Cork turned to Tell.

"Major, use your authority to guard this door. Let no one enter." He motioned me inside and closed the door behind us.

It was a small room, furnished in a masculine manner. Game trophies and the heads of local beasts protruded from the walls and were surrounded by a symmetrical display of weaponry such as daggers, blunderbusses, and swords.

"Our killer had not far to look for his instrument of death," Cork said, pointing to an empty spot on the wall about three feet from the fireplace and six feet up from the floor. "Move with care, Oaks, lest we disturb some piece of evidence."

I quickly looked around the rest of the chamber. There

was a door in the south wall and a small window some ten feet to the left of it.

"The window!" I cried. "The killer must have come in—"

"I'm afraid not, Oaks," Cork said, after examining it. "The snow on the sill and panes is undisturbed. Besides, the floor in here is dry. Come, let's open the other door."

He drew it open to reveal a short narrow passage that was dimly lit with one sconced candle and had another door at its end. I started toward it and found my way blocked by Cork's outthrust arm.

"Have a care, Oaks," he said. "Don't confound a trail with your own spore. Fetch a candelabrum from the table for more light."

I did so, and to my amazement he got down on his hands and knees and inched forward along the passageway. I, too, assumed this stance and we crept along like a brace of hounds.

The polished planked floor proved dry and bare of dust until we were in front of the outer door. There, just inside the portal, was a pool of liquid.

"My Lord, it is blood!" I said.

"Mostly water from melted snow."

"But, Captain, there is a red stain to it."

"Yes," he said. "Bloody snow and yet the bayonet in that woman's breast was driven with such force that no blood escaped from her body."

Cork got to his feet and lifted the door latch, opening the passageway to pale white moonlight which reflected off the granules of snow. He carefully looked at the doorstoop and then out into the yard.

"Damnation," he muttered, "it looks as if an army tramped through here."

Before us, the snow was a mass of furrows and upheavals with no one set of footprints discernible.

"Probably the servants coming and going from the wood yard down by the gate," I said, as we stepped out into the cold. At the opposite end of the house, in the left wing, was another door, obviously leading to the kitchen, for a clatter of plates and pots could be heard within the snug and frosty windowpanes. I turned to Cork and found myself alone. He was at the end of the yard opening a slatted gate in the rear garden wall.

"What ho, Captain," I called ahead, as I went to meet him.

"The place abounds in footprints," he snarled in frustration.

"Then the killer has escaped us," I muttered. "Now we have the whole population of this teeming port to consider."

He turned slowly, the moonlight glistening off his barba, his eyes taking on a sardonic glint. "For the moment, Oaks, for the moment. Besides, footprints are like empty boots. In the long run we would have had to fill them."

I started to answer when a voice called from our backs, at the passage doorway. It was Major Tell.

"Hello, is that you there, Cork? Have you caught the dastard?"

"Some gall," I said to the Captain. "As if we could pull the murderer out of our sleeves like a magician."

"Not yet, Major," Cork shouted and then turned to me. "Your powers of simile are improving, Oaks."

"Well," I said, with a bit of a splutter. "Do you think magic is involved?"

"No, you ass. Sleight of hand! The quick flick that the eye does not see nor the mind inscribe. We'll have to use our instincts on this one."

He strode off towards the house and I followed. I have seen him rely on instinct over hard evidence only two times in our years together, and in both cases, although he was successful, the things he uncovered were too gruesome to imagine.

The shock that had descended on the van Schooner manse at midnight still lingered three hours later when the fires in the great fireplaces were reduced to embers, the shocked guests had been questioned, and all but the key witnesses had been sent homeward. Cork, after consultation with the Royal Governor, had been given a free hand in the investigation, with Major Tell stirred in to keep the manner of things official.

Much to my surprise, the Captain didn't embark on a flurry of questions of all concerned, but rather drew up a large baronial chair to the ballroom hearth and brooded into its sinking glow.

"Two squads of cavalry are in the neighbourhood," Major Tell said. "If any stranger were in the vicinity, he must have been seen."

"You can discount a stranger, Major," Cork said, still gazing into the embers.

"How so?"

"Merely a surmise, but with stout legs to it. If a stranger came to kill, he would have brought a weapon with him. No, the murderer knew the contents of the den's walls. He also seems to have known the coronation schedule."

"The window," I interjected. "He could have spied the bayonet, and when the coast was clear, entered and struck."

"Except for the singular fact that the snow on the ground in front of the window is undisturbed."

"Well, obviously someone entered by the back passage," Tell said. "We have the pool of water and the blood."

"Then where are the wet footprints into the den, Major?"

"Boots!" I shouted louder than I meant to. "He took off his boots and then donned them again on leaving."

"Good thinking, Oaks," Tell complimented me. "And in the process, his bloody hands left a trace in the puddle."

"And what, pray, was the motive?" Cork asked. "Nothing of value was taken that we can determine. No, we will look within this house for an answer."

Tell was appalled. "Captain Cork, I must remind you that this is the home of a powerful woman, and she was hostess to-night to the cream of New York society. Have a care how you cast aspersions."

"The killer had best have a care, Major. For a moment, let us consider some *facts*. Mistress Gretchen went into the den to prepare for her coronation with the aid of—ah—"

"Lydia Daws-Smith," I supplied.

"So we have one person who saw her before she died. Then these six society bucks who were to transport her entered, and among their company was Brock van Loon, her affianced. Seven people involved between the time we all saw her enter the den and the time she was carried out dead."

"Eight," I said, and then could have bit my tongue.

"Who else?" Cork demanded.

"The Dame herself. I saw her enter after Miss Daws-Smith came out."

"That is highly irresponsible, Oaks," Tell admonished.

"And interesting," Cork said. "Thank you, Oaks, you have put some yeast into it with your observation."

"You're not suggesting that the Dame killed her own daughter!"

"Major," Cork said, "she-animals have been known to eat their young when they are endangered. But enough of this conjecture. Let us get down to rocks and hard places. We will have to take it step by step. First, let us have a go at the footmen who carried the chair into the den before Gretchen entered."

They were summoned, and the senior man, a portly fellow named Trask, spoke for the lot.

"No, sir," he answered Cork's question. "I am sure no one was lurking in the room when we entered. There is no place to hide."

"And the passage to the back door?"

"Empty, sir. You see, the door leading to the passage was open and I went over to close it against any draughts coming into the den. There was no one in the den, sir, I can swear to it."

"Is the outside door normally kept locked?"

"Oh, yes, sir. Leastways, it's supposed to be. It was locked earlier this afternoon when I made my rounds, preparing for the festivities."

"Tell me, Trask," Cork asked, "do you consider yourself a good servant, loyal to your mistress's household?"

The man's chubby face looked almost silly with its beaming pride. "Twenty-two years in this house, sir, from kitchen boy to head footman, and every day of it in the Dame's service."

"Very commendable, Trask, but you are most extravagant with tapers."

"Sir?" Trask looked surprised.

"If the backyard door was locked, why did you leave a candle burning in the passageway? Since no one could come in from the outside, no light would be needed as a guide. Certainly any one entering from the den would carry his own."

"But, Captain," the footman protested, "I left no light in the passageway. When I was closing the inner door, I held a candelabrum in my hand, and could see clear to the other end. There was no candle lit."

"My apologies, Trask. Thank you, that will be all."

When the footmen had left, I said, "Yet we found a lit candle out there right after the murder. The killer must have left it in his haste."

Cork merely shrugged. Then he said, "So we go a little further. Major, I would like to see Miss Daws-Smith next."

Despite the circumstances, I was looking forward to seeing the comely Miss Daws-Smith once more. However, she was not alone when she entered, and her escort made it clear by his protective manner that her beauty was his property alone. She sat down in a straight-backed chair opposite Cork, nervously fingering the fan in her lap. Brock van Loon took a stance behind her.

"I prefer to speak to this young lady alone," Cork said.

"I am aware of your reputation, Captain Cork," van Loon said defensively, "and I do not intend to have Lydia drawn into this."

"Young man, she *is* in it, and from your obvious concern for her, I'd say you are, too."

"It is more than concern, sir. I love Lydia and she loves me."

"Brock," the girl said, turning to him.

"I don't care, Lydia. I don't care what my father says and I don't care what the Dame thinks."

"That's a rather anti-climactic statement, young man. Since your betrothed is dead, you are free of that commitment."

"You see, Brock? Now he suspects that we had something to do with Gretchen's death. I swear, Captain, we had no hand in it."

"Possibly not as cohorts. Was Gretchen in love with this fellow?"

"No. I doubt Gretchen could love any man. She was like her mother, and was doing her bidding as far as a marriage went. The van Schooner women devour males.

Brock knows what would have become of him. He saw what happened to Gretchen's father."

"Her father?"

"Gustave van Schooner," Brock said, "died a worthless drunkard locked away on one of the family estates up the Hudson. He had been a valiant soldier, I am told, and yet, once married to the Dame, he was reduced to a captured stallion."

"Quite poetic," Cork said. "Now, my dear, can you tell me what happened when you and Gretchen entered the den this evening?"

The girl stopped toying with the fan and sent her left hand to her shoulder where Brock had placed his. "There's nothing to tell, really. We went into the den together and I asked her if she wanted a cup of syllabub. She said no."

"What was her demeanour? Was she excited?"

"About being the Queen? Mercy, no. She saw that as her due. Gretchen was not one to show emotion." She stopped suddenly in thought and then said, "But now that I think back, she was fidgety. She walked over to the fireplace and tapped on the mantel with her fingers. Then she turned and said, 'Tell the Dame I'm ready,' which was strange, because she never called her mother that."

"Was she being sarcastic?"

"No, Captain, more a poutiness. I went and gave Dame van Schooner the message. That was the last I saw of Gretchen." Her eyes started to moisten. "The shock is just wearing off, I suppose. She was spoiled and autocratic, but Gretchen was a good friend."

"Hardly, Miss Daws-Smith. She had appropriated your lover."

"No. She knew nothing of how I felt towards Brock. We were all children together, you see—Gretchen, Wilda, Brock, and I. When you grow up that way, you don't always know childish affection from romantic love. I admit that when plans were being made for the betrothal, love for Brock burned in me, but I hid it, Captain, I hid it well. Then, earlier this evening, Brock told me how he felt, and I was both elated and miserable. I decided that both Brock and I would go to the Dame to-morrow. Gretchen knew nothing of our love."

"And you, sir," Cork said to Brock, "you made no mention of your change of heart to Gretchen?"

The fellow bowed his head. "Not in so many words. This has been coming on me for weeks, this feeling I have for Lydia. Just now as you were talking to her, I wondered —God, how terrible!—if Gretchen could have committed suicide out of despair."

"Oh, Brock!" Lydia was aghast at his words.

"Come," Cork commanded sharply, "this affair is burdensome enough without the added baggage of melodrama. Use your obvious good sense, Miss Daws-Smith. Is it likely that this spoiled and haughty woman would take her own life? Over a man?"

Lydia raised her head and looked straight at Cork. "No. No, of course not. It's ridiculous."

"Now, Mr. van Loon, when you entered the den with the others in the escort party to bring in the sedan chair, were the curtains pulled shut?"

"Yes, they were."

"And no one spoke to its occupant?"

"No, we didn't."

"Strange, isn't it? Such a festive occasion, and yet no one spoke?"

"We were in a hurry to get her out to where the Governor was waiting. Wait, someone did say, 'Hang on, Gretchen' when we lifted the chair. I don't remember who said it, though."

"You heard no sound from inside the chair? No groan or murmur?"

"No, sir, not a sound."

"Well thank you for your candour. Oh, yes, Miss Daws-Smith, when you left Gretchen, was she still standing by the fire?"

"Yes, Captain."

"Was her mask on or off?"

She frowned. "Why, she had it on. What a queer question!"

"It's a queer case, young lady."

The great clock in the center hall had just tolled three when Cork finished talking with the other five young men who had carried the murdered girl in the sedan chair.

They all corroborated Brock's version. All were ignorant
of any expression of love between Brock and Lydia, and
they were unanimous in their relief that Brock, and not
one of them, had been Gretchen's intended. As one young
man named Langley put it, "At least Brock has an inheritance of his own, and would not have been dependent on
his wife and mother-in-law."

"Dependent?" Cork queried. "Would he not assume her
estate under law?"

"No, sir, not in this house," Langley explained. "I am
told it's a kind of morganatic arrangement and a tradition
with the old van der Malin line. I have little income, so
Gretchen would have been no bargain for me. Not that I
am up to the Dame's standards."

When Langley had left, Trask the footman entered to
tell us that rooms had been prepared for us at the Major's
request. Cork thanked him and said, "I know the hour is
late, but is your mistress available?"

He told us he would see, and showed us to a small
sitting-room off the main upstairs hall. It was a tight and
cozy chamber with a newly-stirred hearth and the accoutre-
ments of womankind—a small velvet couch with tiny pil-
lows, a secretaire in the corner, buckbaskets of knitting
and mending.

Unusual, however, was the portrait of the Dame herself
that hung on a wall over the secretaire. It was certainly
not the work of a local limner, for the controlled hand of
a master painter showed through. Each line was carefully
laid down, each colour blended one with the other, to produce a perfect likeness of the Dame. She was dressed in a
gown almost as beautiful as the one she had worn this
evening. At her throat was a remarkable diamond necklace which, despite the two dimensions of the portrait, was
lifelike in its cool, blue-white lustre.

Cork was drawn to the portrait and even lifted a candle
to study it more closely. I joined him and was about to
tell him to be careful of the flame when a voice from behind startled me.

"There are additional candles if you need more light."

We both turned to find Wilda van Schooner standing in
the doorway. She looked twice her 17 years with the ob-

vious woe she carried inside her. Her puffed eyes betrayed the tears of grief that had recently welled there.

"Forgive my curiosity, Miss van Schooner," Cork said, turning back to the portrait. "Inquisitiveness and a passion for details are my afflictions. This work was done in Europe, of course?"

"No, sir, here in New York, although Jan der Trogue is from the continent. He is—was—to have painted all of us eventually." She broke off into thought and then rejoined us. "My mother is with my sister, gentlemen, and is not available. She insists on seeing to Gretchen herself."

"That is most admirable." Cork bid her to seat herself, and she did so. She did not have her sister's or her mother's colouring, nor their chiseled beauty, but there was something strangely attractive about this tall dark-haired girl.

"I understand, Captain, that you are here to help us discover the fiend who did this thing, but you will have to bear with my mother's grief."

"To be sure. And what can you tell me, Miss Wilda?"

"I wish I could offer some clew, but my sister and I were not close—we did not exchange confidences."

"Was she in love with Brock van Loon?"

"Love!" she cried, and then did a strange thing. She giggled almost uncontrollably for a few seconds. "That's no word to use in this house, Captain."

"Wilda, my dear," a female voice said from the open door. "I think you are too upset to make much sense to-night. Perhaps in the morning, gentlemen?"

The speaker was the girls' aunt, Hetta van der Malin, and we rose as she entered.

"Forgive our intrusion into your sitting room, Ma'am," Cork said with a bow. "Perhaps you are right. Miss Wilda looks exhausted."

"I agree, Captain Cork," the aunt said, and she put her arm around the girl and ushered her out the door.

"Pray," Cork interrupted, "could *you* spare us some time in your niece's stead?"

Her smile went faint, but it was a smile all the same. "How did you know this was *my* room, Captain? Oh, of course, Trask must have—"

"On the contrary, my eyes told me. Your older sister

does not fit the image of a woman surrounded by knitting and mending and pert pillowcases."

"No, she doesn't. The den is Ilsa's sitting room. Our mother raised her that way. She is quite a capable person, you know."

"So it would seem. Miss Hetta, may I ask why you invited us here this evening?"

I was as caught off guard as she was.

"Whatever put that notion into your head? My sister dispatched the invitations herself."

"Precisely! That's why you had to purloin one and fill in our names yourself. Come, dear woman, the sample of your hand on the letters on your secretaire matches the hand that penned the unsigned note I received."

"You have looked through my things!"

"I snoop when forced to. Pretence will fail you, Ma'am, for the young lad who delivered this invitation will undoubtedly be found and will identify you. Come now, you wrote to invite me here and now you deny it. I will have an answer."

"Captain Cork," I cautioned him, for the woman was quivering.

"Yes, I sent it." Her voice was tiny and hollow. "But it had nothing to do with this horrible murder. It was trivial compared to it, and it is senseless to bring it up now. Please believe me, Captain. It was foolish of me."

"You said 'calamity' in your note, and now we have a murder done. Is that not the extreme of calamity?"

"Yes, of course it is. I used too strong a word in my note. I would gladly have told you about it after the coronation. But now it would just muddle things. I can't."

"Then, my dear woman, I must dig it out. Must I play the ferret while you play the mute?" His voice was getting sterner. I know how good an actor he is, but was he acting?

"Do you know what a colligation is, Madam?"

She shook her head.

"It is the orderly bringing together of isolated facts. Yet you blunt my efforts; half facts can lead to half truths. Do you want a half truth?" He paused and then spat it out. "Your sister may have killed her older daughter!"

"That is unbearable!" she cried.

"A surmise based on a half truth. She was the last person to see Gretchen alive, if the Daws-Smith girl is to be believed. And why not believe her? If Lydia had killed Gretchen, would she then send the mother into the room to her corpse? Take the honour guard who were to carry the sedan chair: if Gretchen were alive when her mother left her, could one of those young men have killed her in the presence of five witnesses?"

"Anyone could have come in from the outside." Miss Hetta's voice was frantic.

"Nonsense. The evidence is against it."

"Why would Ilsa want to kill her own flesh and blood? It is unthinkable!"

"And yet people will think it, rest assured. The whole ugly affair can be whitewashed and pinned to some mysterious assailant who stalked in the night season, but people will think it just the same, Madam."

She remained silent now, and I could feel Cork's mind turning from one tactic to another, searching for leverage. He got to his feet and walked over to the portrait.

"So in the face of silence, I must turn the ferret loose in my mind. Take, for example, the question of this necklace."

"The van der Malin Chain," she said, looking up at the portrait. "What about it?"

"If the painter was accurate, it seems of great worth, both in pounds sterling and family prestige. Its very name proclaims it an heirloom."

"It is. It has been in our family for generations."

"Do you wear it at times?"

"No, of course not. It is my sister's property."

"Your estates are not commingled?"

"Our family holds with primogeniture."

"I do not. Exclusive rights to a first born make a fetish of nature's caprice. But that is philosophy, and beyond a ferret. Where is the necklace, Madam?"

"Why, in my sister's strong box, I assume. This is most confusing, Captain Cork."

I could have added my vote to that. I have seen Cork search for answers with hopscratch questions, but this display seemed futile.

"It is I who am confused, Madam. I am muddled by many things in this case. Why, for instance, didn't your sister wear this necklace to the year's most important social function? She thought enough of it to have it painted in a portrait for posterity."

"Our minds sometimes work that way, Captain. Perhaps it didn't suit her costume."

Cork turned from the picture as if he had had enough of it. "I am told there is an Uncle Kaarl in this household, yet he was not in attendance at the Bal to-night. Did he not suit the occasion?"

"You are most rude, sir. Kaarl is an ill man, confined to his bed for several years." She got to her feet. "I am very tired, gentlemen."

"I, too, grow weary, Madam. One last question. Your late niece was irritable this evening, I am told. Did something particular happen recently to cause that demeanour?"

"No. What would she have to sulk about? She was the centre of attraction. I really must retire now. Good night."

When the rustle of her skirts had faded down the silent hallway, I said, "Well, Captain, we've certainly had a turn around the mulberry bush."

He gave me that smirk-a-mouth of his. "Some day, Oaks, you will learn to read between the lines where women are concerned. I am sure you thought me a bully for mistreating her, but it was necessary, and it worked."

"Worked?"

"To a fair degree. I started on her with several assumptions. Some have more weight now, others are discounted. Don't look so perplexed. I am sure that Hetta's note to us did not concern Gretchen directly. She did not fear for the girl's life in this calamity she now chooses to keep secret."

"How is that?"

"Use your common sense, man. If she had suspected an attempt on her niece's life, would she stand mute? No, she would screech her accusations to the sky. Her seeking outside aid from us must have been for another problem. Yes, Trask?"

I hadn't seen the footman in the shadows, nor had I any idea how long he had been there.

"Beg pardon, Captain Cork, but Major Tell has retired to his room and would like to see you when you have a moment."

"Thank you, Trask. Is your mistress available to us now?"

"Her maid tells me she is abed, sir."

"A shame. Maybe you can help me, Trask. My friend and I were wondering why the Dame's picture hangs in this small room. I say it was executed in such a large size to hang in a larger room. Mr. Oaks, however, says it was meant for Miss Hetta's room as an expression of love between the two sisters."

"Well, there is an affection between them, sirs, but the fact is that the portrait hung in the Grand Salon until the Dame ordered it destroyed."

"When was this, Trask?"

"Two days ago. 'Trask,' she said to me, 'take that abomination out and burn it.' Strange, she did like it originally, then, just like that, she hated it. Of course, Miss Hetta wouldn't let me burn it, so we spirited it in here, where the Dame never comes."

"Ha, you see I was right, Oaks. Thanks for settling the argument, Trask. Where is Major Tell's room?"

"Right next to yours, if you'll follow me, gentlemen."

Tell's chamber was at the back of the house where we found him sitting in the unlighted room, looking out at the moonlit yard.

"Nothing yet, Major?" Cork asked, walking to the window to join him.

"Not a sign or a shadow. I have men hiding at the front and down there near the garden gate and over to the left by the stable. Do you really expect him to make a move?"

"Conjecture costs us nothing, although I have more information now."

Although the room was bathed in moonlight, as usual I was in the dark. "Would either of you gentlemen mind telling me what this is all about? *Who* is coming?"

"Going would be more like it," the Major said.

"Going—ah, I see! The killer hid himself in the house somewhere and you expect him to make a break for it when everyone is bedded down. But where could he have hidden? Your men searched the den and passageway for secret panels, did they not?"

"Ask your employer," Tell said. "I am only following his orders—hold on, Cork, look down by the passage door."

I looked over Cork's shoulder to catch a glimpse of a cloaked figure in a cockade, moving among the shadows towards the stable.

"Our mounts are ready, Major?" Tell nodded. "Excellent. Let us be off."

As I followed them downstairs, I remarked on my own puzzlement. "Why are we going to *follow* this scoundrel? Why not stop him and unmask him?"

"Because I know who our mysterious figure is, Oaks. It is the destination that is the heart of the matter," Cork said as we hurried into the ballroom and back to the den door.

Once inside, I saw that Tell had placed our greatcoats in readiness and we bustled into them. Cork walked over to the weapon wall and looked at two empty hooks.

"A brace of pistols are gone. Our shadow is armed, as expected," he said.

"I'll take this one," I said, reaching for a ball-shot handgun.

"No need, Oaks," Cork said. "We are not the targets. Come, fellows, we want to be mounted and ready."

The night was cold as we waited behind a small knoll 20 yards down from the stable yard. Suddenly the doors of the stable burst open and a black stallion charged into the moonlight, bearing its rider to the south. "Now keep a small distance, but do not lose sight for a second," Cork commanded, and spurred his horse forward.

We followed through the drifts for ten minutes and saw our quarry turn into a small alley. When we reached the spot, we found the lathered mount tied to a stairway which went up the side of the building to a door on the second-storey landing. With Cork in the lead, we went up the icy stairs and assembled ourselves in front of the door. "Now!" Cork whispered, and we butted our shoulders against the wood panelling and fell into the room.

Our cloaked figure had a terrified man at gunpoint. The victim was a man in his forties, coiled into a corner. I was about to rush the person with the pistols when the tri-cornered hat turned to reveal the chiselled face and cold blue eyes of Dame Ilsa van Schooner.

"Drop the pistols, Madam, you are only compounding your problem," Cork said firmly.

"He murdered my child!"

"I swear, Dame Ilsa!" The man groveled before her. His voice was foreign in inflection. "Please, you must hear me out. Yes, I am scum, but I am not a murderer."

Cork walked forward and put his hands over the pistol barrels. For a split second, the Dame looked up at him and her stern face went soft. "He's going to pay," she said.

"Yes, but not for your daughter's death."

"But only he could have—" She caught herself up in a flash of thought. Her lips quivered and she released the pistol butts into Cork's control. He took her by the arm and guided her to a chair.

The tension was broken, and I took my first look about. It was a large and comfortable bachelor's room. Then I saw the work area at the far end—with an easel, palettes, and paint pots.

"The painter! He's Jan der Trogue, the one who painted the portrait."

"You know about the painting?" the Dame said with surprise.

I started to tell her about seeing it in her sister's sitting-room, but never got it out. Der Trogue had grabbed the pistol that Cork had stupidly left on the table and pointed it at us as he edged towards the open door. "Stay where you are," he warned. "I owe you my life, sir." He bowed to Cork. "But it is not fitting to die at a woman's hands."

"Nor a hangman's," Cork said. "For you will surely go to the gallows for your other crime."

"Not this man, my fine fellow. Now stay where you are and no one will get hurt." He whirled out onto the landing and started to race down the stairs. Cork walked to the door. To my surprise, he had the other pistol in his hand. He stepped out onto the snowy landing.

"Defend yourself!" Cork cried. Then, after a tense mo-

ment, Cork took careful aim and fired. I grimaced as I
heard der Trogue's body tumbling down the rest of the
stairs.

Cork came back into the room with the smoking pistol
in his hand. "Be sure your report says 'fleeing arrest,'
Major," he said, shutting the door.

"Escape from what? You said he didn't kill the girl!
This is most confusing and, to say the least, irregular!"

"Precisely put, Major. Confusing from the start and
irregular for a finish. But first to the irregularity. What
we say, see, and do here to-night stays with us alone." He
turned to the Dame. "We will have to search the room.
Will you help, since you have been here before?"

"Yes." She got up and started to open drawers and
cupboards. She turned to us and held out a black felt bag
which Cork opened.

"Gentlemen, I give you the van der Malin Chain, and
quite exquisite it is."

"So he did steal it," I said.

"In a manner of speaking, Oaks, yes. But, Madam,
should we not also find what you were so willing to pay
a king's ransom for?"

"Perhaps it is on the easel. I only saw the miniature."

Cork took the drape from the easel and revealed a portrait of a nude woman reposing on a couch.

"It's Gretchen!" I gasped. "Was that der Trogue's game?
Blackmail?"

"Yes, Mr. Oaks, it was," the Dame said. "I knew it was
not an artist's trick of painting one head on another's body.
That strawberry mark on the thigh was Gretchen's. How
did you know of its existence, Captain? I told no one, not
even my sister."

"Your actions helped tell me. You ordered your own
portrait burned two days ago, the same day your sister
sent me a note and an invitation to the Masque."

"A note?"

"Portending calamity," I added.

"Oh, the fool. She must have learned about my failure
to raise enough cash to meet that fiend's demands."

"Your sudden disdain for a fine portrait betrayed your
disgust with the artist, not with the art. Then Wilda told
us that you had planned to have your daughters painted

by the same man and, considering the time elapsed since your portrait was finished, I assumed that Gretchen's had been started."

"It was, and he seduced her. She confessed it to me after I saw the miniature he brought to me."

"Why did you not demand its delivery when you gave him the necklace to-night?"

"I never said I gave it to him to-night."

"But you did. You went into the den, not to see your daughter, but to meet der Trogue at the outside passage door. You lit a taper there, and he examined his booty at the entryway, and then left, probably promising to turn over that scandalous painting when he had verified that the necklace was not an imitation."

"Captain, you sound as if you were there."

"The clews were. In the puddle just inside the door, there was a red substance. Oaks believed it was blood. It was a natural assumption, but when the question of your anger with a painter came to light, I considered what my eyes now confirm. Painters are sloppy fellows; look at this floor. Besides, blood is rarely magenta. It was paint, red paint from his boot soles. Then, Madam, your part of the bargain completed, you returned to the den. Your daughter was still by the fire."

"Yes."

"And you returned to the ballroom."

"Yes, leaving my soiled child to be murdered! He came back and killed her!"

"No, Dame van Schooner, he did not, although that is the way it will be recorded officially. The report will show that you entered the den and presented the van der Malin Chain to your daughter to wear on her night of triumph. My observation of the paint in the puddle will stand as the deduction that led us to der Trogue. We will say he gained entry into the house, killed your daughter, and took the necklace. And was later killed resisting capture."

"But he *did* kill her!" the Dame insisted. "He had to be the one! She was alive when I left her. No one else entered the room until the honour guard went for her."

Cork took both her hands.

"Dame van Schooner, I have twisted truth beyond reason for your sake to-night, but now you must face the hard truth. Der Trogue was a scoundrel, but he had no reason to kill Gretchen. What would he gain? And how could he get back in without leaving snow tracks? Gretchen's executioner was in the den all the time—when Lydia was there, when you were. I think in your heart you know the answer—if you have the courage to face it."

To watch her face was to see ice melt. Her eyes, her cold, diamond-blue eyes watered. "I can. But must it be said—here?"

"Yes."

"Wilda. Oh, my God, Wilda."

"Yes, Wilda. You have a great burden to bear, my dear lady."

Her tears came freely now. "The curse of the van Schooners," she cried. "Her father was insane, and his brother Kaarl lives in his lunatic's attic. My mother thought she was infusing quality by our union."

"Thus your stern exterior and addiction to purifying the blood-line with good stock."

"Yes, I have been the man in our family far too long. I have had to be hard. I thank you for your consideration, Captain. Wilda will have to be put away, of course. Poor child, I saw the van Schooner blood curse in her years ago, but I never thought it would come to this." The last was a sob. Then she took a deep breath. "I think I am needed at home." She rose. "Thank you again, Captain. Will you destroy that?" She pointed to the portrait.

"Rest assured."

As he opened the door for her, she turned back with the breaking dawn framing her. "I wish it was I who had invited you to the Bal. I saw you dancing and wondered who you were. You are quite tall."

"Not too tall to bow, Madam," Cork said, and all six-foot-six of him bent down and kissed her cheek. She left us with an escort from the detachment of soldiers that had followed our trail.

The room was quiet for a moment before Major Tell exploded. "Confound it, Cork, what the deuce is this? I am to falsify records to show der Trogue was a thief and a murderer and yet you say it was Wilda who killed her sister. What's your proof, man?"

Cork walked over to the painting and smashed it on a chair back. "You deserve particulars, both of you. I said that Wilda was in the den all the time. Your natural query is how did she get there unseen? Well, we all saw her. She was carried in—in the curtained sedan chair. In her twisted mind, she hated her sister, who would inherit everything by her mother's design. One does not put a great fortune into a madwoman's hands."

"Very well," Tell said, "I can see her entry. How the deuce did she get out?"

"Incipient madness sometimes makes the mind clever, Major. She stayed in the sedan chair until her mother had left, then presented herself to Gretchen."

"And killed her," I interjected. "But she was back in the ballroom before the honour guard went in to get her sister."

"There is the nub of it, Oaks. She left the den by the back passage, crossed the yard, and re-entered the house by the kitchen in the far wing. Who would take any notice of a daughter of the house in a room filled with bustling cooks and servants coming and going with vittles for the buffet?"

"But she would have gotten her skirts wet in the snow," I started to object. "Of course! The spilled punch bowl! It drenched her!"

Cork smiled broadly. "Yes, my lad. She entered the kitchen, scooped up the punch bowl, carried it into the ballroom, and then deliberately dropped it."

'Well," Tell grumped, "she may be sprung in the mind, but she understands the theory of tactical diversion."

"Self-preservation is the last instinct to go, Major."

"Yes, I believe you are right, Cork, but how are we to explain all this and still shield the Dame's secret?"

Cork looked dead at me. "You, Oaks, have given us the answer."

"I? Oh, when I said the killer took off his boots to avoid tracks in the den? You rejected that out of hand when I mentioned it."

"I rejected it as a probability, not a possibility. Anything is possible, but not everything is probable. Is it probable that a killer bent on not leaving tracks would take off his boots *inside* the entry where they would leave a puddle? No, I couldn't accept it, but I'm sure the general public will."

The major looked disturbed. "I can appreciate your desire to protect the Dame," he said, "but to *suppress* evidence—"

"Calm yourself, Major, we are just balancing the books of human nature. I have saved the Crown the time and expense of trying and executing an extortionist. God knows how many victims he has fleeced by his artistic trickery over the years. And we have prevented the Dame from the commission of a homicide that any jury, I think, would have found justifiable. Let it stand as it is, Major, it is a neater package. The Dame has had enough tragedy in her life."

The last of his words were soft and low-toned, and I watched as he stared into the flames. By jing, could it possibly be that this gallivanting, sunburnt American had fallen in love? But I quickly dismissed the thought. We are fated to our roles, we two—he, the unbroken stallion frolicking from pasture to pasture, and I, the frantic ostler following with an empty halter, hoping some day to put the beast to work. I persist.

TEN

The Doleful Duelist of Delaware

"THAT BOY is as good as dead," I said to Cork in exaspera-
tion. He sat there calmly cleaning and polishing the pistols.
They were a matched brace with silver banded mahogany
grips made by Kiltey's in Boston Town and presented to
him by our friend Squire Delaney in gratitude for having
saved his son from a charge of barratry back in 1736.
Now, twenty years later, one of these full stocked, smooth
bore engines was to be the instrument of death in what
could only be termed legal murder.

Crick. Snick. Snack. The three ominous sounds filled
our rooms as Cork cocked the hammer with the crook of
his experienced thumb, caressed the hair trigger and sent
the uncharged piece into sterile action. Crick, snick, snack,
he tested the other pistol and I shuddered as a goose
walked over my grave.

To think we had come to the lower region of Pennsylvania called Delaware to the town of Dover to do pleasant
business in the china dish pottery trade, only to become
players in a ridiculous test of honour and courage. What's
the worse of it was Captain Cork was only a second in the

affair, while I had full responsibility as the proctor of the killing ground.

The combatants, who would meet at dawn, were young Billy Douglas, a skilled artisan in the art of pottery and crockery at the Argyle Manufactory in Dover, and Dander MacCloud, scion of the MacCloud glassware fortune and the fiercest of the redheaded MacCloud clan of West New Jersey. No two men on the face of the earth were more mismatched for combat.

Billy Douglas was barely twenty, slight of build and girlishly handsome. He had the quiet temperament of a man who works with fragile things. Dander MacCloud, on the other hand, was a rugged chunk of Highland rock, with enough flint in him to spark at the slightest touch. To make matters worse, MacCloud was an experienced duelist, while young Billy had never stood in the paces in his life.

Crick! Snick! Snack! I shuddered again as Cork went on with the testing. We were waiting in our rooms at the Sign of the Green Rooster for the arrival of Bo Briggs, Dander's second. Our meeting was to set the terms and conditions of the contest, and while Cork cleaned and oiled his pistols, I was racking my brain for a way to neutralize the imminent conflict.

I am no stranger to duels and their protocol. On four occasions, my employer has gone to dawn's judgement and walked away unscathed. In those encounters, two men have fallen mortally, another never to use his left arm again, and the last was left with a scar on his cheek to remind him that Captain Jeremy Cork, when pushed to the extremity of patience, acquitted himself with dispatch.

Crick! Snick. . . "Must you keep playing with those things?" I snapped at him.

Snack! "I only hope I can convince Bo Briggs that the contest be with pistols, Oaks," he said. "Dander MacCloud has choice of weapons since he is the challenged party. He'll undoubtedly want to use claymores, since he's been trained since birth in their use."

Another goose was walking, and the hair rose on my nape. The claymore, the double-edged great sword of the ancient Highlanders, could cleave a man in two. I doubted that Billy Douglas could even pick one up.

"Tsk, tsk," I shook my head, "all this nonsense just to prove courage." I looked at Cork, who was chuckling. "I find nothing risible in that, sir."

"No, my old son, nothing laughable at all. I was thinking about Plato's view of courage as being 'the virtue of fleeing from inevitable danger.' "

"Inevitable death's more correct, Captain."

"That's redundant, Oaks, but I see your pain in all this and I share it. But the die is cast, and we must make the best of it."

He was putting the pistols in their velvet-lined case, and I fell back to thought. How strange, the trick of fate and the frailty of man's senses. Just that afternoon, we were sitting in the public room of the Green Rooster, talking business with Angus Travis and Billy Douglas, and now, seven hours later, we were preparing to stand witness to the resolution of a stupid insult.

The trick of fate was that Dander MacCloud was in Delaware in the first place, his lands and manufactory being in West New Jersey. As we later learned, he was in Dover to meet with Bo Briggs, his agent-in-commerce for the entire Piedmont. The frailty of man's senses was that an idle remark made by young Billy about his own fiancee would bring him to the brink of death.

The lady at the center of this madness was Heather Travis, the comely daughter of Angus Travis, owner of the Argyle Manufactory, who employed Billy as his master foreman. Perhaps "employed" is not correct. Billy had come to Travis as an orphan-apprentice and had learned his trade from the old man. There was no doubt of Travis's affection for the lad, since he was about to give him his daughter's hand and with it, future control of his lands and business. Angus was an expert potter and glazer who, by hard industry, had made the name "Travisware" a by-word in all the colonies and England as well.

We had spent the morning on a tour of his prodigious facility and I was thoroughly impressed with its sophistication. We rejoined to the Green Rooster for a mid-day meal and negotiations for shipping Travisware aboard *The Hawkers*, the ship Cork owns and never sails in.

Cork, as usual, instructed the tapman in the making of Apple Knock, a potation of his own invention. Since it was early autumn, he gave him the summer formulation, which omits the slabs of butter and fist of sugar as well as the hot poker. The winter formula goes into effect December 22 on the first day of the solstice. The tapman, a lanky fellow named Davy, was loyal to the receipt, and we drank a toast.

"So you see, Mr. Oaks," Angus Travis was saying, "the Travisware is just a beginning. I want to get into the flint and glass business now that I have this laddy-buck to carry on."

Billy Douglas shot a wary glance at his father-in-law-to-be and shook his head. "That's just in the talking stage, and to my mind, that's where it ought to stay."

"Ho ho." Old Angus cocked a white eyebrow over a crinkly blue eye. "That's a raw spot with Billy, gentlemen. But that's why my lassie and this fellow will make a good pair. She's full of fire and ideas, my Heather is. Always looking to the future, while Billy is more steady like. She'll bring him around, just like she did her Da. Have some eggs, gentlemen. They're free." Angus was a frugal gnome. He pointed to a basket of hard boiled eggs that sat on each table. I took one and cracked the shell. Cork ordered oysters, three dozen, as usual.

"There's too much competition in glassware to my thinking." Billy stopped and looked over his shoulder. "Speak of the devil. The MacCloud himself and his resident toady, Bo Briggs."

I looked at the two men who were taking chairs to our left in the near-empty taproom. "The MacCloud himself" could apply only to the huge man who removed his pommed bonnet to show the world a mass of hair as red as a well-stoked hearth. I had heard of the MacCloud fortune, and here was its future heir sitting not two feet from us. If his companion was truly a toady, he didn't look the part. He was well clad, on the tall side, and darkly handsome.

"Pay them no mind, Billy," Angus cautioned and then resumed his conversation with us. "So when we get the flintglass production underway, gentlemen, we can *really* use your help, for I understand you deal in potash lead, Captain."

Cork was lacing his oysters with vinegar, and he nodded. That's how interested he is in business—a nodding acquaintanceship. The details always fall to me as his financial yeoman. We'd be in a pauper's jail if I didn't oversee his money enterprises and curb his maliferous appetites. Oysters are one of his *minor* vices, as is nodding when business and profit are in the air. And what does this six-foot-six devotee of the flesh say to the man who has just offered him an opening to trade?

"I hear the quail run good around here."

He said it between oysters. An opening proferred and he changes the subject, or rather, avoids it. I could strangle him at times. Quail, indeed!

"Oh, yes. Took a fancy to raising prize quail a few years back, but just for the sport of it, mind. We aren't much on shooting. I finally turned them loose in the woods on my upper forty, so you're welcome to try your hand, if the poachers haven't taken them all. Say, you two have got to come out tomorrow night to my place for the doings. This laddy-buck here and my Heather have come to an agreement, and I'm getting up a party to announce the engagement. Heaven knows why they want to get married. They've been fighting like cats and dogs since this boy came on as an apprentice." He cocked his head at Billy and winked. "Are ye two not on speaking terms again, I wonder? Is that why Heather sent us here to eat?"

Billy had a mock frown on his face and a twinkle in his eye. "Sir, your daughter has the sense of a mudhen, the soul of a witch and the patience of a bitch hound on scent."

Angus Travis's face broke into a broad smile. "Ye see what I mean, gentlemen? They fight all. . ."

"You'll retract that, sir, or answer to me!" The voice boomed like a cannon's report. We looked up in confusion to find Dander MacCloud standing behind Billy's chair. Billy turned his head and looked up at the intruder. "Retract what?"

"That Heather Travis is a bitch hound, a witch, and a mudhen. She is a lady, sir."

"Ah, go on with ye, MacCloud," Angus said with a wave of his hand, the smile still on his face. "The lad was just joshing."

"I don't take to hearing a lady's name bandied about a taproom," MacCloud boomed anew.

Now Angus's smile was replaced with a scowl. "I'll remind ye, Dander MacCloud, that the *lady* is my daughter, and warn ye that we'll brook none of your wild New Jersey ways here in Dover."

"And you call yourself a Scotsman, Angus Travis. It's shame you should have. I'll not have my future bride's name given coarse usage."

"Future bride!" Billy was on his feet. "She'll be no bride of yours, you pompous ass, she's rejected you twice already."

"Have a care with your words, lad." This was from Bo Briggs, who had come to stand by his employer's side.

"Don't call me 'lad,' Briggs." Billy's mouth curled in anger. "And I'll warn him not to defend *my* future wife's name if he knows what's good for him."

"Come now, Billy Douglas," Briggs put up his palms and pushed back the words just uttered. "You mustn't threaten the Laird."

"Laird! That's a laugh," Billy smirked. "He may be your 'laird' Briggs, but to me he's a pompous ass who had better keep his nose out of my affairs."

MacCloud's neck tubes bulged in rage. "You little scud, I'm a Laird by lineal descent and to mock it is to insult the MacClouds to a man."

Cork rose up like a tree and tried to calm the situation. "Gentlemen, I think this is out of hand. Let's keep cool heads. Perhaps you would care to sit and taste a concoction of my own invention."

"No thank you, sir," MacCloud said, giving us a half glance. Cork's sudden interruption seemed to calm his anger a mite.

"A good cup would give us clearer and cooler heads, gentlemen," Cork insisted and extended a mug of Knock to MacCloud. The scotsman accepted it and took a long pull.

"Now that, sir, must have bear blood in it," he said with obvious relish.

Bo Briggs took a sip and agreed. "Well, I'm glad to drink to tranquility," he said. "I wouldn't want to see blood shed over loose words."

"Bloodshed? Who said anything about bloodshed?" Angus Travis bellowed.

"Now, now," Briggs said. "The Laird has let it pass, Angus. I'm sure Billy spoke in haste."

Billy grimaced. "I said what I meant. Laird or no laird, he's sticking his nose into my business and he'd better pull it out."

"Or what?" Dander roared anew, his anger refueled. I stood praying that Billy would watch his mouth. He didn't.

"Or answer to me. . ."

"Billy. . ."

"Be quiet, Angus," the lad said to the older man with half-hearted authority. "This red-combed cock of the walk invades our meal, insults my affianced. . ."

"Are you demanding an apology?" Bo Briggs asked incredulously.

"Two. One from him and one from you, Briggs. I'm not to be called 'lad' by anyone."

The next move was as if a thunderbolt had suddenly struck the room leaving all of us mute as we listened to Dander MacCloud's rumbling roar.

"You can go to hell in a buckbasket. Go twice if you like. You'll have your satisfaction, sir." As he turned, he said, "Briggs, you stand as my second," and strode from the public room.

"Good Lord, Billy, what have ye doone, laddic," Angus moaned in remorse. "Are ye daft, man?"

Billy Douglas looked at his employer with surprise and his face started to drain of its color. The reality of the situation bore down on his shoulders like a lead yoke. What had been to his young mind a shouting match of careless words now cannonaded into the realization that he had just made a wager with fate. A wager to be paid in blood.

"I warned you to watch your mouth, Billy," Bo Briggs said quietly. "But it's done. Who will stand for you?"

The lad slumped into his chair. "Why I. . ." He looked almost pleadingly at Cork. ". . .would you mind, sir?"

"Honoured, sir."

"Very well, Captain," Briggs said, starting to leave. "I will call at your rooms this evening to work out the details. We will need a field proctor."

Cork thought for a moment. "Since Oaks and I are strangers in these parts, I would suggest Wellman Oaks for proctor to keep the contest neutral."

"Good idea," Briggs said, and left.

I didn't think it was a good idea at all.

And so the *duorum bellum* was joined, and we found ourselves seven hours later cleaning pistols and waiting for Briggs's arrival at our rooms.

"You know, I'm not sure Billy is quite twenty years old," I said after Cork returned to the table from placing the pistol box on the sideboard. "If he's only nineteen, he would be exempt."

"Only under the rules of a judicial duel, Oaks, which this is not."

"I had another idea. How about a surrogate? Yourself, for that matter?"

"To be sure Billy is frightened, but he is not a coward. Besides, his pride would keep him from letting me take his place. You are very generous with my life, I might add."

"At least you would stand a chance."

"Billy's chances are not that grim, Oaks. Believe it or not, very few people die in duels, especially gun duels."

"It's hard to believe when you yourself have put two men in their graves."

"I did not consider der Trogue's killing a duel. It was a pleasure to expunge an extortionist's existence. The other was a mishap; the fool moved his head. I was aiming for his ear."

He was a little rankled that I had brought up the Broad Way Blemish affair, not so much on der Trogue's account, but because it reminds him of a certain Dame Ilse van Schooner, of whom he never speaks, but I suspect he often thinks.

"You know, it might be a good idea for you to give Billy some lessons before dawn, Captain. Of course, as proctor, I can take no part in it, but you could instruct him in handling the pistols and aiming them."

There was a knock at our door and I opened it to admit Bo Briggs. He bowed slightly to Cork and said, "May we carry out our duties with honor, sir?"

Cork followed ritual and returned the bow. "May we so, sir. Have you prepared the document?"

"Yes sir, I have." Briggs withdrew a parchment and handed it to me as proctor. I read the challenge aloud:

Be it known that one Dander MacCloud, Laird of the Clan MacCloud, has suffered grievous insult from one William Douglas in my hearing and the former accepts his demand for satisfaction on a field of honor at a time and place selected by myself and the opponent's second, one Captain Jeremy Cork.

(Signed) Bo Briggs

I finished and looked at Cork. "Do you accept this in the name of the combatant?"

"I do."

"Well, gentlemen, as proctor, I must first ask if there is no settling this matter in any other way."

"I'm afraid not, Mr. Oaks. The laird is adamant."

"Very well." I winced when I said "What is the weapon of your choice, sir?" I shot a glance of apprehension at Cork.

"Pistols with swan shot at twelves paces," Briggs replied, and I felt immediately relieved. Swan shot was larger and more lethal than ballshot, but it was better than claymores.

"Agreed, Captain Cork?"

"Agreed, Mr. Oaks. Now, Mr. Briggs, time and place. Dawn?"

"Yes, it's better to get it over with early in the day. I might suggest a stretch of ground at the north end of town. If there is morning fog tomorrow, it will be clear to the north. Would you care to inspect it, Captain?"

"No. You know the area better than I. May I make one suggestion. Could this contest be fought from horseback?"

"Pray tell why?" Briggs queried.

"I believe it balances the competition, and it is our duty to make the match as even as possible. But swan shot at that range can be quite deadly, and my contestant is little used to pistols."

"Nor is my champion, sir. The Douglas lad is fortunate that there are no claymores readily available hereabouts. The Laird excels in them."

"Yes, I've heard tell," Cork said, "but if the Laird is no expert, would it not be to his benefit as well to shoot from horseback. They would both have to steady their mounts and aim at the same time. We would have a bloodless contest."

Briggs stroked his jaw. "Yes, I can see the sense of it. I'll chance the Laird's anger and agree to it."

"It's done then," Cork said. "We'll leave the mounts' selection to the proctor. Now I have a fine set of pistols for your inspection."

And so the ceremony went on for another half hour or so with everyone being very formal and Cork calling me 'Mr. Oaks' all over the place. When Briggs finally gave us his last bow and 'sir' and left, it was close to ten o'clock.

"It seems a bit late to give Billy any lessons," I said.

"It won't be necessary now that Briggs has agreed to the horses. I doubt that there will be a killing."

But long before dawn we had a complication that would alter Cork's prediction. The duel would not take place after all or, according to the local magistrate, it had already taken place by then.

We were summoned from our beds at three that morning by a pounding at our door. It was Heather Travis in a state of high anxiety, if not near panic. When we had met her the day before, she had seemed an even-tempered girl, but the poor child could not be blamed for her present consternation; her father and her future husband were under arrest for murder. Their alleged victim was Dander MacCloud.

"You must do something, Captain Cork," she sobbed. "The magistrate came to the house an hour ago and accused Billy and my da and had men search the house." She stopped to catch her breath, for her next words were difficult for her to utter. "They found a pistol—a pistol that had been fired recently—it belongs to my da!"

Cork tried to calm her but to little avail. With some difficulty, we learned that both men had been taken to the magistrate's house for questioning. We left Heather in the care of the innkeeper's wife and departed.

Twenty minutes later, we were in the parlor of Thomas Pettibone, an aged magistrate for Dover. With him was

Daniel Cooper, captain of the Night Watch who had found Dander's body in a meadow at the south end of town.

"It's a bad business, Captain," Cooper said from an easy chair. We sat on a settee; the magistrate sat in a straight-backed chair near the fire.

"One of the local fellows had a skinful of rum and lost his way home. He stumbled over the body in the dark. The whole town knew about the duel between MacCloud and young Billy, so I sent one of my men for Doctor Dermot and hotfooted it here for the magistrate."

The magistrate cleared his throat and took up the narrative. "Not everyone in town knew about the duel. I didn't. But when Dan informed me, I could see that either Billy or old Angus, either separately or in collusion, might have had a hand in it and went to the Travis house immediately. Young Billy lives there too. Members of the Night Watch searched the house and in a desk in the parlor we found that." He pointed to the table with the stem of his clay pipe. On it was a pistol.

Cork rose, walked over and picked the weapon up. "Recently fired," he said, smelling the bore. "Can either man account for it?"

"Aye, Captain," Daniel Cooper said. "Billy says he was off in the woods around twilight using it for target practise. More's the likely he was using it on Dander MacCloud. In a way, you can't blame the lad; he'd have been dead by dawn if he hadn't done MacCloud in. He says he cleaned it after practising, but he should have been more thorough."

Cork handed it to me and I examined it. I am not the expert at firearms that Cork is, but it was easy to see that Billy Douglas knew even less. The attempted cleaning was inept; there were even fresh scorchmarks on the muzzle.

We returned to our seats. "If the evidence is so damaging against Billy, why are you holding Angus Travis?"

"Well, Captain, I've known Billy Douglas since he was a tad, and he's not the type to sneak up on a man in the dark and shoot him. But old Angus has a temper, and he might have had MacCloud meet him out there at a glen that's south of town by some trick and done him in. Then there's the possibility they planned it together. Finding the pistol at the house pins it to one of them."

"Has Angus no alibi?" I queried.

"If he can call down the Almighty, he has. He says he spent most of the evening at the kirk, but no one saw him there. Says he was praying for the Lord's intervention."

"More's the likely Angus intervened himself," Cooper said with a sneer.

"We'll just have to sort it out," Pettibone said. He turned to Cork. "Your prowess in these affairs is known to me, Captain, and I'd appreciate your lending a hand. I'd rather not hang two men if one will do."

Cork looked at me and then said, "My hand is already in, sir."

Well, normally I detest his getting involved in these affairs, but this was different. One of these men was a future customer.

"Where is the body?" Cork wanted to know. He was told that it was still at the death scene, awaiting the arrival of the town doctor.

"Excellent!" Cork cried. "We can start fresh. Will you show us the way, Mr. Cooper?"

The night watchman agreed, but I could see that he was not enamoured of Cork's intrusion into his case. He fetched a lantern and reluctantly led us out of the town to the south.

It was past five o'clock when we reached the glen, and the first light was breaking across the sky. Two men with muskets stood over a form on the ground; a third man was on his knees, examining the body. He got to his feet as we approached and was introduced by Cooper as Dr. Dermot.

Cooper explained our involvement in the case at the magistrate's request.

"Delighted, Captain," the elderly medical man said. "Just got here myself. Been over in Hilton all night helping a farmer with a calving. First a cow, now a corpse. What a week. What a week. Looks like he was shot in the back of the head. Here, you fellows, turn him over."

The guards pitched the body onto its back. Dander MacCloud's face was frozen in a curious expression; his right eye was gone, leaving a bloody, ragged crater in its place.

"Straight through the skull," the doctor said as he went through the man's shirt to feel for the empty possibility of a heartbeat. "Dead as a mackerel he is, fellows, and not even a local man. What a week, and winter's not even here yet. Everything is popping up—epizoo, ticks and heaves. Ringbone, pink-eye, it's enough to try Hippocrates himself."

"Can the time of death be established, doctor?" Cork asked.

"To the minute, it seems. Careful, don't cut your finger on the broken glass." He held up a smashed timepiece which showed the time as 9:10.

"Must have smashed it on that small rock there when he fell forward," Cooper offered.

"Well, I can't stand about all day," Dr. Dermot said impatiently. "Come on, you boys, let's get the corpse back to my shop. Does he have any kin hereabouts, Cooper?"

"Bo Briggs has sent word to his father in New Jersey."

We watched as the guards made a litter with a blanket slung between their muskets and placed the body on it with some effort, due to Dander's size and rigidity.

"Coming, Captain Cork?" Cooper asked and was surprised to find Cork on his knees where the body had been. He was picking up something.

"What is it, sir?" I asked, looking into his outspread hands.

"Eggshells," Cork said.

"You'll find lots of them in the woods, Captain. Squirrels getting into birds' nests, the devils. I must get back, gentlemen."

"Yes, of course." Cork got to his feet. "We'll tarry a while here, Mr. Cooper."

Cooper had a sly grin on his face. "Expect the birds to tell you who did it? No parrots in these parts, I'm afraid." He walked off with the doctor, chuckling to himself. I looked into Cork's eyes and could see that gleam that comes into them when he puts his mind to work. He walked slowly over the area, stopping now and then to turn and stare at me.

"What about the eggshells?" I called to him.

"They may well be from a nest. Or they may help us

hatch something. Well, let's get back to town and some breakfast."

The serving girl at the Green Rooster laid the table with hot johnnycakes, slab bacon, beans and Indian rye. When Cork breaks his fast, he prefers beer, while I favor coffee made from the beans I carry about with us. Davy, the tapman, brought a tankard of beer to the table.

"Morning, Captain," he said, putting the tankard down. "I hear there was some doings last night."

"Yes, a bit of homicide. Tell, me, Davy, a tapman is usually a very clever, knowledgeable fellow in local affairs."

The man was a lanky fellow with a bony face that looked like a skeleton when he smiled.

"Aws, sir, I keep my ear to the ground, I do. But I'm no idle gossip, mind."

"To be sure. But can you tell me how the entire town knew about the duel? This room was empty except for the two parties and yourself when the challenge was given."

The bony face took on a scarlet tinge. "Waren't me, sir. I don't go carrying tales about squabbles among gentlemen."

"Heaven forbid. I thought, as a good citizen, you might have reported it to a town official."

"Yer reading my mind, sir, and that's a fact. I mentioned it to Daniel Cooper, seeing he's the head of the Night Watch and all. I wondered if it was legal to have a duel. He told me he didn't know of no law again it."

"Good man. Say, where are those delicious hard boiled eggs you had out yesterday?"

"Only puts 'em out at midday meal, Cappin. Don't do much trade at that time of day. So it don't hurt to be generous."

"Did you notice when Briggs and MacCloud had left if they had eaten any eggs?"

"Can't say for sure about MacCloud, Cappin, but Bo Briggs don't like eggs. He says we ought to have free fruit instead. Some nerve, I say. You sure are interested in them henfruit, Cappin. . ." He ambled off to his chores and Cork started on the johnnycakes.

"He put it rather well," I said. "You sure are interested."

"It rankles at me, and now there is only one way to prove a conjecture."

"How?"

He didn't answer because Dr. Dermot had come over to our table. "Well, we meet again," he said. He sat down when Cork gestured to a chair. "What a week. Now I'm off to Tottentown without a wink of sleep. Malignant fever all over the place and the frost isn't even on the ground. Hey, Davy, have the girl dish up some vittles here. I'm in a hurry. Hear there's going to be an inquest tomorrow."

The girl put food in front of him and he dug into it.

"Can't be too soon for me," he said through a mouthful of beans. "Don't like cadavers hanging round my shop."

"Yes, I can see where it would unnerve your assistant," Cork said.

"Assistance! The only assistance I get is a horse, and thank God she knows the way to most places, or else I never would get any sleep."

"Yes, a surgeon needs a steady hand." Cork was after something.

"Don't hold with intruding a knife in the Lord's corporeal creations, Captain. Phlebotomy is the only way to cure them, draw off a little blood and hope for the best." As he talked, he kept shoveling food in his mouth so fast that I doubted he even tasted it.

"It seems Daniel Cooper has the situation well in hand."

"Well, he was quick enough to nab Billy Douglas and Angus Travis. Be a shame if both men swing it; it would leave Heather an orphan."

"I'm sure there are enough gallants about to protect her."

The doctor chewed some bacon and winked. "Well, if Billy goes to the derrick, and with MacCloud gone, the field is sorely narrowed."

Cork chuckled. "How about yourself? You're obviously a bachelor, since you take your meals here."

"A widower. Wife carried away five years back with the fever. I'm not that old that I can't appreciate a young woman, but where would I find the time man? Hey, Davy, have the girl make up a sack of grub. I'll be gone more than two days this time. No, marriage is out for me, gentlemen. Well, I'm off." At the rate he was going he could soon trade his pet phrase in for "what a month."

I scooped up the last of my beans and said, "I've never

known you to dwell in idle chatter, but you're certainly the conversationalist this morning."

"Collecting facts, my lad."

"Like what? That the doctor prefers widowerhood and is having 'what a week'?"

"Your drollery gets in the way of your awareness. We have learned many bits and pieces, but the most essential is that the doctor works alone and will be away for two days. Now we can view the body without interruption. Best get some sleep, Oaks, we'll be busy once darkness falls. Make sure you have a ruler handy."

He always does this to me. He plans some nocturnal caper and sends me off to bed in daylight without a hint of what's going on in his mind. Thus, I lay on a pillow unable to sleep because of frustrated curiosity. We finished the meal and went off to see Heather Travis. She had been given a room at the inn, since she refused to return home.

The poor girl was sitting in an easy chair sipping tea. Her face showed that she had had a sleepless night.

"Tell me, Miss Heather," Cork said after we had declined tea and taken seats instead, "when did Dander MacCloud propose marriage to you?"

"Why, two summers ago. I would have none of him, yet he returned this spring and asked again. That's why my da decided to announce the banns with Billy. Poor da, they can't think he would kill a man, could they Captain Cork? He's a religious man—I believe him when he says he was at kirk last night. And Billy is innocent as well. You must help them, Captain."

"I'm trying to, Miss. Sorely trying. You're an attractive and, if I might add, fairly well-off young woman. Were there no other suitors in your train?"

The girl blushed despite her despondency. "Why, Captain, you make me sound quite brazen."

"A flower need not explain its attraction for bees, ma'am. Say, Daniel Cooper or this fellow Davy downstairs?"

"A tapman? Sir, that is insulting. And as for Daniel Cooper, he has his eyes above buttons since he became head of the Night Watch."

"What of Bo Briggs?"

"He is what Billy calls him, Dander's toady. We have nothing to do with his kind."

"Well, I thank you for your help." Cork got to his feet, crossed the room and then stopped and took something from his pocket. "The serving girl told me that you didn't want breakfast, so I took the liberty of bringing you some hard boiled eggs. Do you like them?"

The young woman took them in her hands. "Not very much, but thank you, Captain."

Outside her room, Cork said he was going downstairs for a minute, so I went to my chambers to stare at the ceiling and attempt to put together the details of this affair.

First I considered the suspects. Did Billy lurk in that wood and shoot his pistol. Somehow he didn't seem the type. And then Angus truly loved the lad. It came over me like a thunderclap. Of course! It was a surrogate duel. Angus had stood in for Billy and took his man. But why didn't he just admit it? And who would believe him? Then there was this Cooper fellow. He knew about the duel in advance and saw a chance to pin a murder on Billy. He was a young, robust man who might turn a grieving lady's head, even though she didn't seem to care for him at the moment.

But why, then, was Cork so all fired up over eggshells. Why did he need a ruler? Questions, questions, and no answers. I was tired, since we had been up and about since three o'clock that morning, and closed my eyes and felt sleep overtaking me. I yawned and agreed—what a week!

It was close on midnight as we watched a member of the Night Watch stroll by on his tour of the main street. From our vantage point in the alley, we could see Dr. Dermot's darkened shop across the way. The building was distinguished by the brightly painted blue and white striped pole topped with a red flag. We watched as the guard turned the corner into the next street. I felt a poke from Cork's elbow. "Now! Make for the back of the building!"

We raced across the road, slipped through a picket gate and followed the building's wall toward the rear of the structure. Cork, for all his lazy faults, could certainly support himself as a portico burglar. He had the rear door opened in seconds, and we were safely inside.

He pulled back the shield of his lucifer lantern and

shone its ray around the room. We were in the back chamber, which was windowless, and there on a table lay a shrouded form. Cork pulled the drape from the body.

"You have the ruler?" he asked.

"Yes," I whispered.

"Then measure his length. Be accurate, mind."

I went to work laying the rule along the body, foot by foot. When I finished, I said, "Six feet, two and three-quarter inches."

"Double check, please."

I did so, and it came out the same. I looked up from where I had stopped measuring at the corpse's feet and was aghast. Cork had turned the head as best he could and was inserting what looked like a knitting needle into the exit wound at the back of the skull. He withdrew it and looked pleased in the half shadows. "Borrowed from the serving girl at the inn," he said, "but best we keep its employment secret or she'll never knit again."

"I may never eat again," I said as my supper turned over in my gut.

"Nonsense. Come, help me with his shirt."

"You're going to undress him?"

"Just the upper torso. Quickly now, Oaks."

Now I'm as hard as the next man, but undressing a corpse—a stiff one at that—is no easy task. We struggled with it for ten minutes and finally Dander MacCloud's hairy chest and stomach were exposed.

"Now bring that lantern closer, Oaks. If I'm right in my conjecture, we'll know on the first try."

"Know what? Oh my God, oh heaven forgive you."

He must have had the razor in his pocket, and as I watched in horror, he drew its sharp edge into the flesh. My throat was fighting back my own stomach and I shut my eyes to blot out the awful sight. I heard Cork saying, "By jing, I was right, my old son."

I couldn't answer. I couldn't make my throat work. My body was damp all over. I was going to swoon. I did swoon.

The next thing I knew, Cork was slapping my cheeks. "Snap to, Oaks, it's finished." I shakily got to my feet, not knowing how long I had been unconscious, but I could see it was long enough to give Cork time to mop up the mess. The shirt was back on Dander's body.

I tested my voice. "Won't the incision bleed?"

"No, I sail stitched it."

I felt faint again at the casual report of this last atrocity. "Come, I'll give you a hand back to the inn and we will get some Knock and oysters into you."

"Captain Cork," I groaned, "would you kindly shut up, sir?"

After stopping in three different alleys, I arrived at the Green Rooster still shaky but feeling better. Cork had Knock sent up to our rooms.

"Here, drink this down," he bade me.

"We have some usquebauth in our kit, do we not?"

"Yes, but Irish whiskey is a bit rough."

"It's exactly what I need. I am going to sit here and drink until I can't remember anything; not this night, not even my name."

And I did. I drank all we had—perhaps a quart—and felt the peace of alcoholic forgetfulness.

Despite the fact that I had slept most of the day, I was exhausted and limp. I vaguely remember trying to stagger to my bedchamber and Cork's offer to help me which I refused on the drunken premise that he might want to practice his butchery on me.

The angle of the sunlight on my bed told me that the day I greeted with a parched throat and pounding head was well into the forenoon. I said "enter" to a tapping at my chamber door and it was Sally, the serving wench from below stairs. She had a tray with a pot of hot coffee and sugar buns on it.

"Good morning, Mr. Oaks," she curtsied. "Captain Cork said to wake you around noon, and it is almost to it. He says you are to meet him at Magistrate Pettibone's house at one o'clock for the re-quest."

"Oh, the inquest, yes." I took the merciful coffee and drank it down in three gulps. She refilled the cup and asked, "What is a request, Mr. Oaks? Is it like a party?"

Here my head was coming apart at the seams and I am being questioned by this ignorant woman. No wonder I'm a bachelor. I shooed her out, got bathed, shod and dressed.

There was no hope for me, the coffee wouldn't work. I
repaired to the taproom below. To my surprise, Sally, and
not Davy, was behind the bar.

"Where is the tapman?" I asked her.

"He's gone to the request too. Seems everybody but
me's got an invitation. The young lady, Heather Travis,
she's gone too."

"Give me a glass of rum," I pleaded.

Her voice, although normally not loud, seemed like a
cracked bell inside my head.

"I just gave you coffee."

Why do women tell you things you already know?

"Oh, hair of the hound, is it, sir? Well, step right up. I
heard you singing away last night up in your rooms. Must
be jolly to be a traveling man. Parties all night, requests
all day."

As she prattled on, I grasped the glass of rum from
her, tossed it into my throat and fled her tolling voice. I
walked into the sunlight and breathed deeply, letting the
rum course through me to steady my nerves. My head
stopped aching after a while and I kept walking and
breathing. I was startled when the church clock struck
one. I had become so engrossed in my physical rehabilita-
tion that time had slipped by me. I made straight for the
magistrate's house and was admitted by one of the night
watchmen who had been at the murder scene.

The inquest was already underway in a large room off
the main hall on the first floor. Everyone concerned was
present, as well as a stranger and, oddly enough, an old
acquaintance, Major Philip Tell, the King's agent-at-large.
The stranger was a tall bulky man and his red hair bespoke
him as Dervis MacCloud, Dander's father. Cork and Pettibone sat at a table in the center of the room before rows
of chairs which seated Billy Douglas, old Angus, and
Heather. Across the aisle, next to the elder MacCloud,
sat Bo Briggs, Daniel Cooper and Davy, the tapman.

Tell was seated near the door, and I slipped into a
chair near him. The redcoat turned and whispered a
hello to me. "I see Cork is in the middle of things again.
Was on my way down to Charles Town when I heard of
this problem and wouldn't miss one of Cork's shows for
the world."

"Yes," I grunted. "And God knows what he's up to this time."

Our attention was drawn to the front of the room where Daniel Cooper had been called and sworn and was giving testimony about the death scene.

"Shot in the back of the skull," he told the magistrate. "When the body fell forward, MacCloud's timepiece was smashed on a rock, fixing the time of death at 9:10." He went on with a recapitulation of searching the Travis house and finding the pistol.

Davy was then called and recited the facts of how the duel came about in the taproom. He was followed by Bo Briggs, who corroborated the facts of the duel.

Suddenly a loud voice boomed in the room. It was Dervis MacCloud.

"Damn me, judge, we know all this. Let's get to them." He cocked a finger at Angus and Billy.

"We'll go by the rules, if you don't mind, sir," the magistrate growled. "Step up here, Billy Douglas, and speak your piece."

The young fellow's face was red as he went forward and took a seat at the side of the table.

"All right, lad," the magistrate said, "where were you last night around nine o'clock?"

"It's hard to tell, sir. You see, I knew I was no marksman, and decided around twilight to do some practising. I took the old pistol Angus kept in the workshop to try my hand at target shooting. That was around six o'clock, and I guess I kept at it until the daylight went. Then—well, I guess I was scared. I sat up there for a long time thinking about death."

"Planning one's the more likely," Dervis MacCloud muttered audibly.

"Here, here," the magistrate admonished him. Then, to Billy, "What time did you get back to the house?"

"Round about half past nine, but I'm not sure. I stopped at the manufactory and cleaned the pistol and then went up to the house."

"You took the pistol to the house?" Cork asked.

"Yes, Captain. I thought I would have to use it at dawn for the duel."

I noticed Daniel Cooper shaking his head and Cork

must have, too, because he asked, "Do you have a comment, Mr. Cooper?"

"No," the night watchman said with a sneer. "Except that we only have his word for it."

"Not so!"

We all turned to a new voice and personage. He was a bearded man in buckskins, a truly woodsy type.

Pettibone shot a searing glance at the newcomer. "Do you have business here, Gully McCabe?"

"Thinks I do, yer honor. You see, I was up on Forty Acres Ridge last night and saw this young feller pot-shotting at a tree."

"And what were you doing there?" Cork queried.

"Poaching, most likely," the magistrate snapped. "This lazy fellow has been before this court time and again, Captain. Seems he likes prize turkeys and such."

"Yer honor," the woodsman said with bowed head, "yer right, I'm admitting it because my conscience wouldn't let me see this young tad swing for a crime he couldn't have committed."

"Take the word of a poacher," Dervis MacCloud growled.

"Seems reasonable to me," Cork put in. "His admission will get him a day in the stocks, or worse."

"I'll have to take my medicine," McCabe said with too much piety. "I was up there around six o'clock looking to bag a few of Angus's birds, when Billy comes moping along. He shot at a tree till it got dark and I thought he'd leave, so I lurked about, but danged if he didn't build up a fire and set there half the night, at least till nine o'clock or so, by the moonrise."

"You're sure of this, Gully?" the magistrate demanded sternly.

" 'Pon my honour, sir."

"Well, that seems to unhook Billy," the judge went on. "He couldn't have gotten from those woods to the death scene in fifteen minutes." He stopped and looked dead-eyed at Angus Travis. "It looks a might darker for you, Angus. Now why don't you come forward and confess. It will be good for your soul and will save us time as well."

"My father is innocent," Heather shouted and put her

arms around the old man who looked like he had taken on twenty extra years.

"The circumstances rule out everyone else," the magistrate said. "At the time of the murder, Daniel Cooper happened to be at the Green Rooster, and confirms the comings and goings of all else here."

"Then you must put me back in your deck and shuffle again, sir," Cork said. "Did the sedulous Mr. Cooper establish the whereabouts of all gathered here for six twenty-two last evening?"

"Six twenty-two?" The magistrate was perplexed as were the rest of us.

"Yes, your honor, my nautical charts show that the sun set at precisely that hour at this latitude on this date."

"Is this man sprung in his mind?" Dervis MacCloud roared. "Charts and sunsets be damned."

"Sir," Cork said to him "if you want to punish the murderer of your son, bear with me. We have a common cause." He rose from the table and dominated the room. Here it comes, I thought, his topgallants were unreefed and billowing. Cork was under sail and loving every moment of it

"First off, can everyone account for himself from say, 6:20 to 6:30?"

Indeed a quick check around the room showed that no one could give a corroborated account. Davy said he was working alone in the inn's barn; Cooper was at home resting up for his tour on the night watch. Angus was heading for the kirk. Even Bo Briggs was at a loss, for his witness was dead. All the men resented Cork's suspicion, but he really got a rise out of everyone when he asked, "And what of you, Miss Heather?"

"See here, Captain," Angus said sharply, "leave my child out of this."

"Miss Heather?"

"I was at home with three servants to prove it and went to bed early with a headache over this horrible duel."

"Thank you, young lady. As for Oaks and myself, we have mutually exclusive alibis, so we are in the stew as well. Now let us clear up some misleading points. First, there is the time of death. I am sorry to say that your local sawbones is more adept at calving than he is at examining cadavers. I arrived at the glen around 5:00 A.M. That would make the time lapse between 9:10 P.M. and 5:00 A.M. a little under eight hours. Yet, when the guards moved the corpse, it was stiff as a board. Medical men at such schools as Edinburgh have determined that rigor mortis takes over the body in about ten hours, although they caution that it is an unreliable indicator of the time of death. But it was the start of my mental process. After all, the watch could have been set ahead and smashed to confuse the time of the shooting.

"The second misconception was that Dander was shot from behind the head, with the bullet exiting through the right eye. A careful examination of the skull shows that the bullet entered through the eye.

"But let us put the time element aside for a moment. We have other fires to attend. Our killer was crafty, but untidy with details. For instance, since the body was found face down, it was assumed that the shot was fired from behind by some skulking coward. Nonsense. A ball striking the back bone of the skull would lose most of its velocity upon impact, and bury itself in the brain, as any experienced field soldier could tell. Wouldn't you say so, Major Tell?"

"Of course," the redcoat said with authority. "Even the heaviest charged pistol couldn't put a ball straight through a skull. I'm sure any army surgeon would agree."

"And I'm sure any qualified doctor, seasoned in battle, would concur that the reverse is highly probable. A ball striking the eye would meet little or no resistance, and still have enough speed to pierce the back of the skull. And if shot from the front, the impact of the shot would have pitched the body onto its back. This I can attest to on my own experience.

"So we have two points in hand. The time of death could have been earlier and the victim was shot from the front. I favor the sunset theory for I can't construct a plausible reason why Dander, a relative stranger to the area, would go walking in a strange wood in the darkness of nine o'clock at night to eat eggs."

"Now let me remind you, Captain," the magistrate shook a finger at Cork, "that I'll not have this proceeding marred by jocosity."

"I am deadly serious, sir. Dander MacCloud ate hard boiled eggs almost within three or four minutes of his death."

He went on to explain our midnight invasion of Dr. Dermot's shop and his having performed an autopsy on the corpse. Even the judge looked pale.

"Purely in the interest of justice," Cork apologized to Dervis MacCloud. "It was a small incision."

"And just where did you learn this despicable art?" the magistrate demanded.

"Any woodsman who has dressed out his game can attest that it is sensible to deduce what the animal ate last. So we have a man standing in a remote glen at sundown eating eggs. I can understand his hunger, for he had no mid-day meal and refreshed himself with the eggs he had taken from the inn's table."

"Aye," Dervis said with a sigh. "That would be Dander's way, all right."

"Your son was an experienced duelist, sir," Cork continued, "but was he a dead shot?"

"No. No, he favored the claymore."

"So we come to the final construction of the actual crime. I believe Dander MacCloud went out there at sunset to practise for the duel. He calmly ate eggs."

"And shot himself accidentally, I suppose," Cooper's tone was laden with derision.

"No. Earlier last night, Oaks suggested that I put Billy through the dueling paces and teach him aiming with a steady hand. Was that how it happened with you and Dander, Bo Briggs? Dander confidently held an unloaded pistol, while yours was loaded. He stood there as a duped target while you fired."

"Hogslop," Bo sneered. He turned to Dervis MacCloud. "Why would I want to murder my benefactor?"

"You might check his account books," Cork suggested to Dervis.

"That's the first thing I did when I got word of Dander's death. There are no monies missing."

"You see, Cork, you *are* spinning fairy tales," Briggs said haughtily.

"You might remind him, your honor, that motive need not be proved."

"That is true, but it is still conjecture."

"Very well, we will have to summon up Euclid." We all looked surprised. "Yes, ladies and gentlemen, the geometry of matter is irrefutable. Both Angus and Billy are short men and Cooper is of average height. A shot aimed at a tall man's head by any of these men would have had an upward trajectory through the skull. Dander's height was close to my own, yet his wound goes straight through his skull. How tall are you, Mr. Briggs?"

It was obvious that he was over six-two and fit Cork's premise, but then so did Cork himself. I felt the Captain had at long last come up against a case in which he knew the culprit, but could not prove it. I doubted that a jury of country bumpkins would be able to follow the geometric logic of Cork's proof. I looked at him with a feeling of compassion. He hates to be blocked and will use trickery if he has to pin his man, but he was out of tricks. Or was he?

He scribbled something on a piece of paper, walked over to Briggs and handed it to him. The man read it and looked up at Cork with the look of a trapped animal.

"Take your choice, sir," Cork said to him.

All the spirit drained out of Briggs and he slumped forward. "You win, you devil," he said.

Bo Briggs's confession was taken down and his sentencing set for two days hence. It never took place. He hanged himself that night.

Magistrate Pettibone was livid on two counts. One, that Briggs had cheated the hangman, and two, that Cork refused to tell him what was on the paper that had brought about Briggs's confession.

"You realize that I can bring you to trial for mutilating a body," he threatened Cork on the day of our departure from Dover. "You also withheld evidence."

"Come, come, judge, it is your curiosity that is piqued and not your sense of jurisprudence. I gave you your murderer—your justice. Let it rest, sir."

We were eating a cold lunch in a coach heading north to Philadelphia two hours later when I reached my breaking point.

"Well!" I said.

"Well what?"

"You mean you're not going to tell *me?*"

"If you had been alert, you would have the answer."

"I don't."

"Think back, my old son. What piece of the puzzle was left out of place?"

I shrugged.

"The newly fired pistol found at the Travis house. Billy said he cleaned it, but he is not incompetent. There was burned powder on the muzzle. Would Billy Douglas, an artisan, be that careless? I think his cleaning would have been quite adequate. The gun was fired a second time after he cleaned it."

"By whom, for heaven's sake?" I stopped. Of course. By the only person able to. "Heather Travis?"

"I assumed so. Remember our luncheon conversation with Angus and Billy. Angus was going into the flint glass business at his daughter's prodding and over Billy's objections. Since Briggs had extensive contacts in that business, it suggested a connection between him and Heather. I asked Briggs in the note if he wanted the girl implicated, suggesting that I could prove she had sneaked the pistol out and refired it to fix blame on Billy. Remember, she showed no emotion while Billy was the prime suspect, but when the poacher supplied the lad with an alibi and her father became the target of suspicion, she became quite vocal.

"There were other points that bothered me from the first. Briggs did play the toady when Dander confronted Billy at the inn. In fact, he helped worsen the situation by injecting the fact that Dander was a laird. Yet the toady rather cavalierly accepted my proposal that the duel be fought from horseback without consulting his principal. How could he? Dander was already dead. I saw the horseback agreement as a lucky coup at the time, but a flaw once the murder was discovered. A clever plot indeed. Briggs eliminates his employer whom he probably hated, takes over his flint glass accounts, eliminates Billy as a suitor, and eventually gets Heather and her father's estates."

"My word," I said, sinking back into the pitching coach seat. "She is going ahead with her marriage to Billy?"

"And a dutiful wife she'll be since she suspects I know of her part in the affair."

"But she is an accomplice to murder!"

"And she must live with it on her soul. I was merely thinking of old Angus in my deception."

He had that smirk-a-mouth look on his face.

"Did you contrive that poacher's testimony to put pressure on Heather by giving Billy an alibi and making her father the prime suspect?"

"That would be subornation, my old son."

He went on smirking and munching on a breast of smoked quail. I let it pass. I had had enough of duels, mental *or* physical.

ELEVEN

The North Carolina Corruption

THE HORRENDOUS SLAM of the door shuddered an echo throughout the sitting room, mayhaps the entire Inn of the Bashful Swan. Cork shot a lazy glance at the closed portal which had just told him resoundingly that he was curt and rude. He shrugged at it and the woman who had just stormed out of it.

"You must forgive her, sir," Mr. Amos Afflack, the lawyer, said apologetically and with magisterial calm. "She is young and impetuous."

Cork drained the Apple Knock from his cup and gave forth with what I would call an insufferable sigh. "Of course," he said, "but don't put it down to some caprice of youth. It's really the pressure that boils up when a child finally realises it is not immortal. It's really a good sign that something of worth will come of them."

I put my own cup down with an emphatic thud. "It's all very well of you, Captain Cork, to wax philosophic, but you have just insulted a troubled young lady by calling her a fool. Where are your manners, sir?"

"My manners are akin to shopping for a hat, Oaks. I can only don what fits. Miss MacGregor's talk of visions and monsters is not of my size, so I deem her foolish—not a fool. There is a difference, you know. While you are asking forgiveness for Miss MacGregor's hasty exit, Afflack, I will have to ask you to overlook my friend's pique with me. You see, we are not supposed to be here in North Carolina at all. No sir, this gentleman, Mr. Wellman Oaks, is my financial yeoman. His horizon is a balanced ledger and our sojourn here in Beauford vexes him. Now tell me, Afflack, is there such a thing out there off the coast called the Red Soaring Fish?"

"Ah, you are a fisherman," Afflack said. "Yes, Captain, it's a wondrous denizen requiring two stout men to boat. You'll enjoy the battle."

"Hell, man, I came here to eat them, not fight them," he grumped.

Afflack looked appalled. I was not. I well knew this six-foot-six fakir who would rather devour seafood than make money. I have him well on his way to being the richest man in the colonies, and he shuns industry as the Red-whatever would repel a lure. This was June 1, marking the initial day of the second quarter of 1758, and we had much to do. First, there was the problem of delivery at the chocklit factory he owns in Connecticut. Then consider the fact that the Horse Protection Agency had not turned a profit in two years. That was only a start on our complications. While on our way up from the Sugar Islands, a fellow passenger had told him about a strange fish that had suddenly come into waters off Beauford, and his mind stopped dead like a rundown clock. Nothing else would do but that we be put ashore and here we were, waiting for Red something-or-other to be broiled and buttered and stuffed into his lazy maw.

"You say you haven't ever tasted the fish," Cork was saying, "but I can only assume that it is active and runs deep, so we can expect good, dark and oily musculature. Now vinegar could well temper that."

I glowered anew at him. "This is preposterous and absolutely inane. Here this young woman is in the grip of a terror and you babble on about vinegar. Captain, I must protest; you have to help her."

Now there was that smirk-a-mouth of his. He didn't have to fish for red soaring things. He had me, Wellman Oaks, on his line. He hauled me in, damn him.

"Well, well, you are actually asking me to become embrangled in a social puzzle, Oaks? What of all your entrepreneurial schemes? What of profits and ledgers and goading me to gold?"

"The girl needs help, Captain," I pleaded.

"Well, if you insist, Oaks," he smirked again. I was boated. I could have bashed him with a buckbasket for his maneuvering me into finally sanctioning his idle dalliance in the solution of mysteries. Damn his eyes, he's clever.

"I'm just trying to be humane," I said defensively. "Someone is trying to cheat Miss MacGregor out of a vast estate."

"All right," Cork said, "then let's to it. Mr. Afflack, your client was a bit agitated, so be good enough to put this matter in perspective for us. Would you like some more Knock?"

"Mercy, no," the lawyer put up his palm. He was a curious specimen; compact as a young, stunted bull. He had sure hands hanging from strong arms and stronger shoulders. He was in the latter part of his third decade, yet his teeth seemed good and his eyes quick. What made him curious was his uncertainty. I had put it down to bashfulness. In Cork's neighborhood, most people fall into that demeanor.

Since Afflack had refused the drink, Cork felt obligated to honor the flacon so it would not become lonely, and poured. The lawyer started to give us the perspective.

"Mind you, gentlemen, I have only what I have been told, and hearsay, sirs, is dangerous. First as a prolusion."

"Spare us the Inns of Court procedure, Mr. Afflack," Cork said. "Just cough it up, man. All I have now is that your client spent a night in a castle on an island off this coast, and was beset by monsters. I detest tales told *in medias res*; they are cruises without bearings."

"She's a woman is all," I said.

Cork cast a stern eye at me. "Mulierbrity is a poor defense, Oaks, and one that Miss MacGregor would reject. Despite her fiery temper and obvious confusion, she is a strong individual."

"Precisely!" Afflack said. "Otherwise, I would have dismissed her case as the rantings of a lunatic. . ."

He stopped short because the door opened and Amy MacGregor stood squarely in its frame. Her angered expression on exit was now changed to one of calm with a hint of embarrassment blushing her buttermilk complection. Her Celtic red hair fell loosely about her sharply sculptured face and draped over her remarkably broad shoulders. Her sea-green eyes leveled at Cork. We were witnessing a rare event; a Scotswoman was about to apologize.

"I'm sorry my temper got the best of me, gentlemen," she said, stepping forward. "I know it sounds like madness, Captain Cork, and I don't blame you for not believing me."

"Miss MacGregor," Cork rose like a tree to his full height and brought a chair to the table, "when I said that belief in monsters was foolish, you didn't let me finish. Things can *appear* to be monstrous. Now please, ma'am, sit down and tell us the problem from the beginning."

She sat and she did. It was an eerie tale fit for All Hallow's Eve and not a warm summer afternoon. Yet as she told us in a soft voice flecked with a Highland burr, I felt a slight horripilation up my back.

Amy MacGregor had arrived in Beauford only twenty-four hours before, having come down by coaster from Philadelphia. She had recently arrived in the American colonies in search of her uncle, Fergus Doone.

"My mother's brother went to sea from our home in Talisker on the Isle of Skye before I was born. The family assumed he was lost at sea, for not a word was heard from him in fifteen years or more. Then, out of the blue, a sailor arrived at our doorstep seven years ago with a packet of gold coins. The man told my mother that they were from her brother, Fergus, who was now a captain in the American whaling trade. The money was gladly welcomed, gentlemen, for my father had passed on, leaving my mother and me to dip and scrape for a living at the washing tubs. The sailor, Rob Dougal by name, told us that he had served in my uncle's ship and was entrusted with his errand on his way home to Edinburgh.

Of course my mother was anxious to write to her brother, but Dougal said that was impossible, since the *Scimitar* roved the seven seas."

"Surely Captain Doone had a home port?" I queried.

"My mother's exact words, Mr. Oaks, but it seems that my uncle sold his catch at any port handy."

Cork grunted and sipped more Knock.

"Well, there we were with a sack of good fortune, but my mother was chagrined that her beloved benefactor was out of her reach for thank you's and affection. I was only twelve at the time, and in poor health. Had I not been so, I think she would have come to the colonies to search for him.

"Last winter, the fevers carried my mother off, and I was left to myself alone in the world. The Isle of Skye held nothing for me and I decided to use what money I had left to come out here for a new life and possible word of my uncle."

As she spoke, I found myself wondering if all the young bucks on the Isle of Skye were blind. Certainly this lassie was worth a wooing to keep her to home.

"I landed in Philadelphia and found work as a serving girl at the Inn of the Hanging Dog to conserve my funds. I guess I became an oddity around the Inn, for I was always inquiring after my uncle from travelers. Then, two weeks ago, what I thought was good fortune came my way. A seafaring man on his way to New York told me that he had heard of Captain Doone, and told me that he lived in a great castle on an island off the coast of North Carolina. I was overjoyed, gentlemen, and took passage on the next coaster for this place."

"The island is known as Twisted Lip," Afflack explained. "It gets its name from two rugged ridges that flank its small harbor. It lies about a mile to the southeast and I am told that the castle was actually a monastery built by monks from St. Augustine in the Floridas. It was abandoned years ago. Of course, that's also hearsay; I'm new in this area myself." Afflack seemed to be new to the law as well, for he surely loved its terminology.

Miss MacGregor's face grew dark as she went on.

"I was anxious to get to the island and hired a boy with

a small sailboat and set off for my uncle's home. The lad put me ashore in the late afternoon and went back to the mainland, for a heavy fog was settling in. It was near dark when I reached the great stone house and pounded for admission. Finally, a man answered the door and he was both shocked and puzzled to see me standing there.

"I told him my name and mission and asked to see my uncle. You can imagine how I felt when he told me that my uncle was dead, lost at sea five years ago. Basker, that was the fellow's name, a tall, dark-eyed man, told me that I would have to return to the mainland immediately. He was quite upset when he learned that I had dismissed my transport. He wasn't even going to let me in until I insisted.

" 'I'll take you back myself,' he snarled, but when he saw the heavy fog banks rolling up to his door, he knew a return passage was impossible.

"Everything I said seemed to upset him. Being tired and hungry, I offered to make myself some dinner, and he became alarmed beyond reason. He told me to follow him and, instead of taking me deeper into the house, he led me outside and along the west wall. My heart was pounding with fear, for the man could have been a scoundrel. We walked a short way in the fog until we reached an outside staircase. Ascending it, he led me to a wooden door in the castle wall, and then into a small chamber—no bigger than a cell.

"As frightened as I was, I demanded an explanation of why I was being treated in such a rude way. After all, I was the niece of the owner, I told him.

" 'Former owner,' he corrected me. 'You see, ma'am, your uncle left this place to me for loyal service as his first mate on the *Scimitar*. Now I can't take you back mainside till morning, so you are welcome to spend the night, but you must stay in this room. I will have food sent to you.' "

She stopped for a moment and closed her eyes. "The food was simple fare brought to me by a small creature of Oriental cast. He spoke not a word, placed the tray on a small table, and left. I was about to pour some cider when I heard the door being locked from the outside. I was a virtual prisoner in a strange house. The room was solid stone from floor to ceiling with no way of escape, and indeed, even if I got out, where would I go? But tears are not in my make-up, gentlemen, and I calmed myself and ate the meal. I was so tired from the long trip that the simple cot in the corner looked inviting. Perhaps I should have feared for my life, but fatigue had me in its grip and I drifted off in slumber."

"My, my," I complimented her, "you are a brave young woman, Miss MacGregor. Most men would have cringed in a corner."

"Any bravery I may have had was drained from me before the night was over, Mr. Oaks. I do not know how long I had slept, but it must have been hours, when something woke me. It was a noise, or maybe something inside me that sensed danger. I opened my eyes and there before me was a living gargoyle in the candlelight. You say monsters don't exist, Captain Cork, but this ogre did. The nose and lips were bloated and twisted out of shape and the cheeks were shriveled. It was horrible."

Afflack was on his feet pouring her a drink, which she took.

"Thank you. No matter how many times I tell it—relive it—it never gets easier. Of course I screamed, and the foul thing disappeared in a puff and I was left in the darkness until I heard the door being unlocked. Basker entered with a lantern and calmed me, suggesting I had experienced a bad dream, which of course was nonsense. I saw what I saw. At dawn, Basker ferried me back here. He was full of apologies for having been a poor host and gave me a sack of coins. To my surprise, it was a small fortune.

"He said my uncle would have wanted me to have it. It was all so strange that I sought out legal assistance, and after relating my story to Mr. Afflack, he said we were in good luck because he had heard that the famous Captain Cork was in Beauford and brought me here."

"I suspect some wrongdoing, Captain," the lawyer said. "As I said, when we first met, this Basker fellow could be doing the woman out of an estate."

"Yes, of course," I agreed. "And this monster's appearance could have been a trick to scare her off."

Cork sighed again. "First, the man scares her and then

he gives her money! How much did he give you, Miss MacGregor?"

"If it's a question of paying a fee for your services," she said, untieing a small pouch from her belt and tossing several coins on the table, "I have plenty. Over £400. The rest is in a strong-box at Mr. Afflack's office."

Cork picked up one of the coins and fondled it. "I don't charge fees, ma'am. I was interested in how far Basker would go to be rid of you." He stopped for a moment and then examined the coin more closely. "Is this dubloon one of the coins Basker gave you?"

"It is."

"Strange, this coin is many years old, and yet it looks newly minted."

I picked up one and, sure enough, it was a Spanish dubloon bearing an imprint A.D. 1690 (in Roman figures). "It looks like it has been polished," I commented.

"They are *all* like that," the young woman said.

"Polished or not," Afflack put in, "they bespeak an intent to bribe her. I feel that this Basker may have more than an island and a castle under his control. I intend to demand to see Captain Doone's last will and testament. None was ever filed for probate at the courthouse. I checked. Furthermore, I suspect that Captain Doone's death might not have been by natural causes."

Cork seemed not to be listening. "Tell me," he asked of Miss MacGregor, "do you remember if the coins sent to your mother were bright like these?"

She smiled at a long buried memory. "Definitely not. I remember because my mama scolded me for biting one. She said they were filthy, and they were. Why do you ask?"

"It is the curse of the fact-finder. Do you have any knowledge of Basker, Mr. Afflack? Ah, personal *or* hearsay."

"Very little. All I could gather is that Judd Basker suddenly appeared here one day and took possession of the island. He had the deed transferring it from Captain Doone to himself. It could have been forged, however. There is an Oriental fellow whom Miss MacGregor mentioned, who lives out there with him.

"When Doone lived on the island between trips to sea, the only contact he had with any of the locals was with Diddlefield, the owner of this inn."

"Then, by all means, let's have at him. Oaks, will you fetch mine host. Thank you, Miss MacGregor. I suggest you put those coins away. Oh, Oaks, don't waste the trip. Have some more Knock sent up."

Five minutes later, I had Myles Diddlefield and the Knock in Cork's presence and he gave them both his scrutiny with equal zeal.

Most innkeepers of our acquaintance seem to follow a common demeanor; they are usually round and hearty as plum puddings and cheery as their own firesides. Myles Diddlefield, however, looked more like a curate in a pot-poor parish; aloof and dour, tall and thin, and the worst walking advertisement for hospitality in God's creation. Despite the physical drawbacks of its owner, the Bashful Swan offered well-laid tables, fluffy clean beds, hot water at one's beck and call and a general air of efficiency. Cork once said of Diddlefield that he would make an exemplary ship's master, for what he lacks in solicitude, he makes up in sedulity. An admirable trait for a man in charge.

"I trust everything is to your satisfaction, Captain," the innkeeper said with suspicion on being asked into our rooms.

"Quite passable, mine host, although I had hoped to find the Great Red Fish on my supper board before this."

"Your offer of £20 has been broadcast to the fishermen hereabout, and should set them stirring for the prize."

I was ired, and my glance at Cork told him so. If he was going to pay out £20 in good coin for a fish, it had better be as big as a whale and have gold teeth. Of course he ignored my scathing glance and dug into the innkeeper.

"Why is this red sea creature so illusive, Diddlefield? Perhaps the trollers don't fish in proper waters. Now how about the lee of Twisted Lip? I've heard rumors it might be a feeding bed."

Diddlefield smiled as best he could. "Not a chance, Captain. No one hereabouts boats in there anymore. Mr. Basker won't have it and he has a cannon to enforce it."

"Why that's—that's illegal," Afflack sputtered.

Cork calmed him. "Cannons have a quick repeal to law, sir." He turned his head back to our host. "Tell me about Mr. Basker. I hear you provision his island, or should I say Captain Doone's island."

"It's Basker's island now sure enough since the *Scimitar* went down."

"Where did the vessel sink?"

"I couldn't tell you, Captain. Captain Doone didn't spend much time on the island. They were always away at sea for two and three months at a time, and then home again for several weeks. Doone bought the island and the castle from the monks who lived out there. They gave up trying to convert people and went back to St. Augustine. Mr. Basker told me that the *Scimitar* went down in the Caribbean with all hands except himself and the Chinese fellow, One Step Ho."

"Did you provision the ship when she was home?"

"Of course, and a fine account it was, sir. The hands on the *Scimitar* ate like Royal Governors. Of course, with the ship gone and just two men living out there now, it's a piddling business. They come in twice a month for staples and a bit of meat."

"Nothing else?"

"Oh yes, some tools now and then, Captain, and of course the lye." He chuckled as much as his sour face would allow. "They take as much of that as they do flour and sugar. They must be plagued with rats out there, I can tell you."

"You're paid in gold coin, no doubt?" Cork asked.

"To be sure. Shiny ones at that."

"You look like a shrewd man, Diddlefield. Have you ever had those coins assayed?"

He was obviously flattered and forced another smile. "Each and every one as I get them. Those old dubloons are genuine, sir. It seems Mr. Basker likes to polish his money, which is all right with me. Captain Doone never did, but each man has his own ways."

"And I have mine. I think I will try my hand at catching that fish. Can you arrange for a boat for us?"

The innkeeper said he could and went to see to it.

"I have a suspicion," Amos Afflack said, "that this

Basker might have led a mutiny against his master, killed him and took over his estate. When Miss MacGregor popped up, he quickly gave her a large sum of money, thinking to be rid of her."

"Perhaps, but the fact that he gave her money at all puzzles me," Cork said, frowning his brows. "She told him *and* us that she is Captain Doone's niece. Can you prove it, Miss MacGregor?"

The girl raised her eyebrows at what she felt was an impertinence. "Well, I *know* who I am, Captain!"

"We all do, I hope, but take me, for example. Because I *say* I am Captain Cork does not stand any test of proof. Oaks here can vouch for me, as can numerous friends. But you are new in these colonies, no friends, no vouchers, so to speak."

"I'm sure her birth is recorded," our lawyer interjected. "Did you bring letters or any momento to prove you are Doone's niece?"

The girl was truly angry. "Why no, I didn't. I didn't come to claim an estate, you know. I came to see my mother's brother. Anyone on the Isle of Skye can attest to my identity."

"That is a geographical difficulty, my dear woman," Cork retorted. "But calm yourself. I am not questioning your word, but I doubt I would simply give you a bag of gold just because you say who you are."

"Well, I think we are overlooking one point," I said. "Doone could have told Basker about his niece."

"How so? She wasn't even born when he left Skye. True, Basker could have known of Doone's sister and assumed she had a child, but it just doesn't add up. Suppose you could make a case at law, Afflack. How would you proceed?"

"We would first have to substantiate her birth and lineage with records on Skye. That, of course, would take time. That done, we would demand to see the will and testament of Captain Doone."

"And if there is none?"

"All the better, Captain. If Doone died intestate, we would claim a *per stirpes* share of the estate."

"I'm sorry," Miss MacGregor said, "but I'm confused."

"Lawyers have a way of doing that," Cork smirked. "A *per stirpes* share is a division of an estate to heirs in respect to their order of descent from the ancestor. It does not have to be an equal share."

"Correct, but in this case her mother was the only heir and Miss MacGregor is next in line. As I see it, she stands to take it *in toto*."

"Unless our sinister Mr. Basker states that he was given a deathbed testament by Doone. He conveniently has the Oriental as a witness to back him up. It might be wiser to take your £400 and be satisfied, Miss MacGregor, for there are aspects of this case that tell me there are some secrets on that island that you might not care to know."

"What secrets? Have you an inkling, Captain?"

"No, Oaks, just a mere whiff. Some inconsistencies and disorders. Well, Miss MacGregor? It is your decision."

"If that man had something to do with my uncle's death, I owe it to my mother's memory to avenge him. In fact, gentlemen, with you at my side, I am going back to the island and confront Basker."

"Confront him with what, madam?" Cork wanted to know. "Have a care lest you put zeal before common sense. I would suggest that Mr. Afflack proceed with his paperwork, and he will need particulars from you. In the meantime, Oaks and I will put our heads together and present you with a plan tomorrow."

When I had shut the door after them, I turned to Cork. "You must be losing your touch, sir. This is the first time you've had to *think* about a plan of action. Usually we are off on the scent with the first . . . are you going to bed? It's only six o'clock."

He was turning down the covers of his bed and then, to my surprise, stripped it of its sheets.

"The plan is in place and operating, Oaks, but it will work better if Miss MacGregor is employed elsewhere. She's a strong willed woman and not disposed to follow orders. . ."

As he talked, I watched him with great curiosity. He took one of the sheets and cut a hole at its center and then put his head through it, letting the material drape around him like a tent. He tied the waist with a belt and then took a pillowcase and with the knife blade, cut diagonally across it. He then fitted the larger piece into the neck opening of his new garment and pulled it up over his head.

"By jing, you look like a monk, sir."

He bowed humbly. "Friar Jeremy at your service. Come, Oaks, take your sheets and join the order. We have a date with a monastery."

It was past nine o'clock that same night when we pushed off in the boat that Diddlefield had procured for us. Cork chose that hour to catch the outgoing tide which would minimize our rowing to Twisted Lip. The night was moonless and fog was rolling in from the sea, which could make navigation difficult, had Cork not had two stable boys build a large bonfire on the beach. Using the fire as a guide, he was sure he could hit the island by dead reckoning.

His plan was simple, yet ingenious. We would present ourselves as traveling monks who thought the castle was still a monastery. It was enough to get us in the door without arousing suspicion, and then, as Cork put it, "we will make our chances as best we can." It was the part about "making our chances" that made me a bit anxious. We had rowed for almost an hour, and the beach fire was a vague dot through the wisps of fog.

"It can't be much further, Oaks," he said from behind. "I can feel the current changing now. Now hold up, boat your oars." He whispered the last part and I obeyed in confusion. Ahead in the water, I could hear and see nothing, and yet Cork scrambled to the prow and peered out into the blackness, his ear cocked into the wind.

Then, suddenly, I heard it above the plangence of the waves. It sounded like a moan or a droning noise and as it grew louder, it was a chant: "Hee stroke, hee stroke, hee stroke." It came across the water on a chilled wind like a ghostly whine. Now I could hear oars cutting into water and the sea-sweep against a hull. Then, through a break in the fog, I saw it, and felt a grab in my chest. There before us was a large longboat being sent through the water by twelve oarsmen. A helmsman sat at the tiller under a lantern which hung from a short pole. "Hee stroke, hee stroke." The chant grew louder as the boat slipped past without noticing us. I watched the scene with surprise and, I admit, a touch of terror. All the men wore monk's robes with cowls hooding their heads and shadowing their faces.

"What do you make of it?" I asked Cork as the chant faded in my ears.

"It confounds one premise, and yet props up another. Come, lad, to the oars."

He was right about being close to the island, for we drew into a small cove with twenty more strokes. Above the beach standing clear of the fog and mist loomed Doone's Castle, although from its vague outline the word "castle" was loosely applied. It was a two-storey structure running some fifty yards in length. At one end was a bell tower that rose twenty or so feet above the main house. Lights shone in the left wing near the tower.

We beached our boat and dragged it onto the sand.

"Are you clairvoyant?" I asked him as we rested. "Did you expect to find monks out here when you dreamed up these get-ups?"

"It was the last thing I expected, Oaks. We are not dealing with just two men, we have fifteen on our hands, and that calls for new tactics. Come, let us see if we can find the stairway that leads to the outside room where Miss MacGregor spent her night."

We scaled the hill to the house and after some prowling in the dark, we came upon the wooden staircase and ascended it. The door was unlocked and we entered. Cork struck the flint on his Lucifer light and cast its beam about the room. Miss MacGregor's description of the place was accurate. It was stone from floor to ceiling, containing only a simple cot, a chair and a rude table. There was a strong chemical odor in the air and Cork was sniffing like a hound.

"Look here," he said, casting light on a section of the floor next to the back wall. "This area has been washed recently, but only these three squares of stone. They are almost bleached."

"They smell awful."

"There *is* a strong lye odor. And see, Oaks, the washed squares lead out from the wall."

"Did Miss MacGregor's monster disappear through the wall?" I chuckled.

"Of course," he muttered. "Damnation, here we are, dressed as monks, standing in what was once a monastery, and it never occurred to me. It should have come to mind when the young woman told us her tale. A room cut off from the main house sounded strange at the time, but now that I see it in a monastic context. . . Yes, Oaks, we are standing in a *salle des pas perdus*." As he spoke, he began tapping at the square wall bricks.

"What in creation is a *salle des pas perdus*?" I asked.

"Literally, the hall of the lost footsteps," he answered, and went on with his wall tapping. "Before a religious novice took his final vows, he could elect to leave the order, but not before a night of contemplation. A separate room, separate from the monastery, but still connected to it, was set up for the vigil. Symbolically, the contemplating novice still had the right to remain or leave—ah, here is an iron ring affixed to this top block."

He tugged at it and a section of the wall opened into a dark passage. "This explains the monster's sudden disappearance. Come quietly and be ready, Oaks," he said, and I followed him into the opening.

Cork was moving ahead quickly as if he knew where he was going, and I whispered, "I can still smell that odor."

"We also have a trail. See the floor? A two foot path has been washed along here."

And so it was. We followed it across the hall and turned with it down a corridor. At its end, I could see a speck of light and like moths, we were drawn to it. When we reached its source, it proved to be a small barred window high up in the wall. Cork's immense height allowed him to peer through easily.

"As I thought," he murmured.

"What is it, Captain?"

He turned to me with a grave expression. "Perhaps it's best you don't look," he said.

"I have come this far," I said. "Give me a hand, please."

"As you please," he said, and made a stirrup with his hand.

If through some injustice, I should find myself sentenced to hell at the final judgement, I could enter that underworld without a flinch. The sight before my eyes had hardened my senses to stone.

I was looking into a large chamber with a cooking hearth ablaze at one end. At its center was a long dining board and around it sat the thirteen boatmen, their cowls tossed back to expose their features. It was a congregation of monsters, ogres. Their faces were bloated and twisted into horrible masks of evil disfigurement. My flesh crept as Cork lowered me to the floor. My gut was so tight I could hardly speak.

"Heaven help us," I finally managed to say. Cork did not get a chance to reply, for a voice behind us said, "Put your hands over your heads and turn slowly."

We did so and found ourselves facing a dark-haired man and a short Oriental, both holding a brace of pistols.

"Mr. Basker, I presume," Cork said quite coolly. "You are indeed a brave man. I think we should talk; it will be in the best interests of your secret."

Five minutes later, after we had been led back through the darkened house, we were ushered into a homey chamber that appeared to be the sitting room of a small apartment. For all the ferocity of his eyes, Basker was limp. He sat in an easy chair while the Oriental, One Step Ho, brought wine. Cork had introduced ourselves on the way back from the horror chamber, and his reputation was known to our host.

"It was the girl, wasn't it?" he said with an air of defeat. "I knew she wasn't satisfied."

"Nor am I, completely," Cork said.

"Well, you know the worst," Basker's voice took on the color of despair. "What can I tell you?"

One Step Ho had put down goblets for us, and I seized mine, hoping the liquor would calm my nerves.

"How long have Captain Doone and his crew been like this?"

"Those ogres are Doone and the crew of the *Scimitar*?" I said. "Impossible."

"Good Lord, Oaks, has it not dawned on you yet that you are in a lazaretto?"

"Lepers!" I cried, dropping the goblet. "This is a leprosaurium." I clutched my throat in panic.

"Keep your head, man," Cork admonished. "Basker here has taken great care to isolate this end of the house. As I said, he is a brave man."

Basker sat forward and put his head in his hands, and then looked up.

"Five years. Five long years. I wasn't on the last cruise of the *Scimitar*. I was laid up with monkey fever and Doone left One Step Ho behind to nurse me. The Captain took the ship around the Cape and into the Pacific. They put in at a small island which they thought was a paradise and stayed on for over three months. When they found that there was leprosy among the natives, they fled the place and put to sea, but it was too late. One by one, they came down with the dread disease and were unable to make any port, for people would shun them.

"They sailed back here, scuttled the *Scimitar* and walled themselves at the far end of the house. We communicate through the window."

Cork smiled, no, smirked, in triumph. "And when Miss MacGregor suddenly arrived, you shut her away in the *salle des pas perdus* and informed your Captain. Then he came in at night to see her and she woke and screamed and he made a hasty retreat through the hidden passage. He must have noticed a family resemblance in the girl and ordered you to give her the money. The crew was careful to holystone and lye the floor areas on which he walked, leaving me a fine trail marking."

"You are most observant. You intimated that you intend to keep our secret."

"Nothing would be gained by exposing you. I suggest that, when you soak the gold coins brought back on the *Scimitar* in lye water to insure they do not carry the disease, you dirty them up again. People take note of such things."

"I never thought of that," Basker said. "I am careful about buying enough food for two people to allay Diddlefield's suspicions. Those poor devils live on the fish that they catch each night. Can the girl be trusted?"

"Yes, I'll handle her. Well, Oaks, I think we have our answers."

Basker got to his feet. "I'll have One Step Ho show you to the door."

Cork put his palm up. "I confess to a flair for the dramatic. We will spend the few hours till dawn in the *salle*, and take our leave from there."

We were shown back through the secret door and watched it rumble to a close.

"What a nightmare," I said, shaking my head. "We are safe from contamination, are we not?"

"Yes, my old worry-wart, you touched nothing they had handled."

"You know, I'm not a religious man, but it might be fitting if we said a prayer for these poor souls. To think of their agony over the years to come. Why, it's a living hell."

"Don't waste your time, Oaks. There is a perfect irony at work here."

"How can you be so callous, sir?"

"I don't waste my sympathy on cutthroats and pirates, my old son."

"Pirates?"

"Yes. That's what initially roused my curiosity. Diddlefield told us that the *Scimitar* was at sea for two or three months and then came back to port. Didn't that tell you something?"

"Of course I was caught up in other details; the cleansed coins and the lye purchases. Whaling ships are at sea for a year or more, until they've filled their rendering barrels with oil."

"And very few are paid off in Spanish dubloons, but it's common booty in the Caribbean. And what better place for a pirate's lair than an island?"

"I see the perfect irony, Captain. These men who have killed and pillaged for plunder now are chained to their lair and doomed to their fate."

"Ah, Oaks, there is hope for you as a poet yet. But the washing of the gold would have been better symbology. They can wash the blood off it and use it to buy lye to wash their clothes and chambers."

"Why the monk's robes, I wonder? Are they seeking expiation?"

Cork shrugged. "Probably more comfortable on their diseased bodies. Well, it's almost dawn, so we'll leave our footsteps lost behind us."

He opened the outer door and the cool morning sea air blew in, if only for a moment to freshen that dismal place. It is a good thing to breathe on a dawn's air. Smacking and alive. I followed him thinking to myself that I could be a poet. The dawn, like Cork, was definitely smacking and alive.

TWELVE

The Curse of the Connecticut Clock

THE FACT THAT Captain Jeremy Cork, my employer, avoids profitable endeavors in favor of dabbling in the solution of social puzzles is my cross to bear, and I accept it and persevere in spite of him. However, the pawky methods he uses to resist my making him the richest man in the American colonies are downright frustrating, although admittedly ingenious.

No better example of his cleverness at resisting industry, while thoroughly enjoying a crime, exists than in the Autumn of 1762, when we returned to the Oar and Eagle on the Connecticut coast. Cork considers this his home port, although we pass no more time there than anywhere else. The only reason for giving this snug inn *dominium* status is that it contains the only bed in the Americas that will accommodate his six-foot-six frame. That massive sleeping couch is part of the private rooms, fitted as a ship's cabin, that he rents on an annual basis. His apartment is on the ground floor, off the public rooms. Mine is above stairs, although I work at an accounts dais in his chambers during the daylight hours and take my meals there.

It was in the forenoon of a crisp October day when I decided to broach the subject of manufacturing his Apple Knock and shipping it about the colonies. It is a potent potable which has gained great favor with his friends, and it occurred to me that a good profit could be turned from the venture.

"I believe we would gain more if we barrel it by the percheon or pipe rather than by hogshead," I said, bringing a rather brilliant analysis to a close. "That would mean lower cost per gallon shipped and. . ."

"You would involve me in barter and score?" he roared. "*Sell* liquor? By Jerusalem, Wellman Oaks, you are without soul. TEDDERHORN!"

Bertram Tedderhorn is the innkeeper of the Oar and Eagle who believes Cork is the next best thing to the Divinity. Considering the rent and the lavish meals the Captain pays for, he may be right. He burst into the chamber within seconds of Cork's shout.

"Yes, Captain?" He was breathless because his corpulence is not given to quick movements.

"After this moment, we are now to use the winter formulation for the Knock." Cork took up a quill. Tedderhorn looked confused.

"But sir, it is only October 30. The solstice is weeks away."

"True, Tedderhorn," Cork said as he wrote on a piece of paper, "but we are victims of habit, and be wary that habit becomes ritual, and ritual breeds dogma, and that is not healthy for the mind *or* body. The receipt is as before with the addition of one new ingredient which I have written here and will be known only to you and me."

As he handed the innkeeper the paper, Tedderhorn gave me a sheepish look. As well he should, for I am Cork's confidential yeoman, and usually nothing is privy from me. Yet I held my tongue and bore no ill will for the innkeeper. He was merely a pawn in my employer's playful game.

It was what you can expect from Captain Jeremy Cork. All he had to say was "no" to the venture, but that wouldn't have been dramatic enough. A simple negative response would have robbed him of a chance to jape me.

Tedderhorn was leaving the room when he suddenly turned. " 'Pon my word, I forgot, Captain. There's a man to see you. I was coming in to tell you when you called."

"Show him in, by all means." Cork went back to his book with a self-satisfied look on his face.

I am not a man to waste energy in hurt feelings. "I assure you I have no intention of skulduggering around to learn the new receipt," I told him. "It was only a suggestion."

"Your suggestions, Oaks, have a way of becoming burdensome realities. People who sell liquor are in the same class as people who sell love, and they share a common name. One may traffic with whores without becoming one. Hello, sir, come in, I think we have met before."

This last statement was to the man who had entered the room. My heart sank, for now, on the heels of my idea having been scuttled, was a person obviously distraught and in need of help. Before he even spoke, I knew it, for I have come to recognize the characteristics of a new puzzle looming into view.

"Yes, Captain, we met several years ago at the Widow Chandler's in Fairfield. My name is Gerret Hull."

"Of course. What can I do for you, Mr. Hull?" Cork indicated a chair and Hull sat. He was a shortish man, clean shaven and dressed in a plain suit and obviously fresh linen for his visit.

"I have had a great tragedy in my life recently, and until today, I was convinced it was God's will, and humbly accepted it. Now . . ." he drew something from his coat which turned out to be a copybook. ". . . well, now I'm not sure that my fourteen-year-old son's death was accidentally caused by a schoolboy prank."

Cork requested details, and I sat there and listened to the father tell his sad story with but mild interest.

Gerret Hull went on. "I am not a wealthy man, gentlemen. Just a small farm and a fair sized cooperage. But if life had limited my horizons, I was bound that it would not be so for my oldest boy, Chad. It was hard on my purse, but I enrolled him at the Fenway School above New Haven in the hope that he would go on to Yale and then to a profession. He was not happy at Fenway during his first year, for he was a poor boy among the sons of wealthy families, which is not always an easy road. But Chad stuck to his books and returned to Fenway this September with high hopes. Then, last week, the awful news came. Chad had been killed while performing the foolish prank of scaling a belltower in the middle of the night. It is not uncommon for a boy to try to place a chamberpot or underdrawer on the spire for all to see in the morning."

"He fell?" I asked.

The father closed his eyes as if in the grip of some horrible mental picture. "No, Mr. Oaks, he was stabbed to death by a jacamart."

For an instant I shared Hull's horrible picture. A jacamart is a life-sized statue, usually a knight in armor, that moves across the face of a tower clock to strike the hour bell with a sword or lance.

"The school officials told me that Chad must have reached the clock face platform at precisely one o'clock, and was impaled on the jacamart's sword as he stood there preparing to scale higher."

"How ghastly," I said, "and unfortunate that the poor boy was there just at the stroke of one."

"Precisely as I felt, Mr. Oaks. I saw it as fate. Although Chad was not a wild boy, I assumed he wanted to be one of the fellows, and fell victim to the accursed clock."

"But now you have reason to question the accidental aspects of the affair? What is the source of your suspicion?" Cork wanted to know.

"Suspicion is a strong word, Captain, for I wouldn't want to cast any shadows over Fenway's reputation. It's more a feeling that I do not have the whole story." He opened the copybook and withdrew a piece of notepaper. "I received this letter from Chad earlier this week. On the face of it, it is a dutiful son informing his father that he is trying his best." He handed the letter to Cork, who read it through and passed it to me. It was in a neat hand without the scholarly flourishes so common to academicians.

Fenway School
Derby, Connecticut
21 October 1762

Father:
All is much the same here, but I persevere. But take
heart, for I have come onto something which may
take the burden of my education from your shoulders.
Be of good spirit, sir, and wish me well. My best to
all.

Your son,
Chad

P.S. I shall try my best to put my mind to the task.

"You see, gentlemen, Chad had previously mentioned
that there was the possibility of receiving emoluments for
good scholarship, and I assumed he was in competition for
one. A student grant would obviously ease my financial
load."

"That is certainly a reasonable interpretation," I said,
giving him back the letter.

"I agree, Mr. Oaks, but yesterday, I finally overcame
my grief enough to go through the clothes and things I
brought back home with Chad's remains. In this copybook, I came across some queer notations which puzzle
me. I have heard of your reasoning powers, Captain Cork,
and wondered if you could make something of it."

Cork took the book, and I leaned over his shoulder as
he leafed through it. It appeared to be a typical lesson
book, with each page containing daily lessons.

"The Fenway curricula seems to be well rounded," Cork
remarked as he perused page after page of Latin transla-
tion, Ancient History, Mathematics, and Physics.

"To be sure, Captain, the school is the finest of its kind.
The notations to which I refer are in the back of the copybook, where the boys are allowed to make their own scrib-
blings and work out problems."

Cork turned to the back pages and finally found one
bearing a very peculiar inscription. It read:

Blandersfield Program

Sept 19

EF/FG/GA/AB/BC/CD/DE/EF ?

Oct 10

$$78-34=44=GB?$$
$$78-32=46=GA?$$

Oct 20

VI=EF!

The Captain furrowed his brows and studied the symbols for some minutes. "It's quite cryptic, of course," he said at last, "but schoolboys are often given to secret writings as a pastime, Mr. Hull. What makes this suspicious in connection with your son's death?"

"The 'Blandersfield Program' overline, Captain. Blandersfield is what the boys at Fenway call the jacamart, 'Sir Jack Blandersfield'."

Rarely have I ever seen Cork shift from mild interest to intense occupation so rapidly. "Most interesting indeed. Tell me, on what date did Chad meet his death?"

"So you've noticed it then. October 21, the evening after the last notation, or really the morning of the 22nd, since he died at one o'clock in the morning. All I can make of it is that Chad had an interest in the jacamart beyond a prank."

"Yes, that seems patent," Cork agreed. "If he were merely trying to put a chamberpot atop a spire, why all the hocus-pocus with codes?"

"Perhaps he was trying to compute the proper time for the jacamart's movements," I put in.

Cork looked up at me with that smirk-a-mouth of his. "Hardly, Oaks. That could be done by a child of no education. These notations are a thought progression. The first, on September 19, obviously did not give him an answer since he ends it with an interrogation mark. Then, on the 10th of October, he has refined his thinking, but still we have an interrogation mark. But on the 20th of October, Chad discovered something in the VI=EF equation, for he ends it with an exclamative. And then he dies in the process of putting his theory to a test."

"But what does the last entry mean, Captain?" Hull asked.

"Several notions present themselves, but to speak now would be to conjecture, based on a paucity of facts. It looks as if we shall be going to school again, Oaks."

"Then you believe there is foul play involved, Captain?" Hull was obviously agitated.

"No, sir, I venture no such idea, for the minds of young boys are labyrinths, full of twists and turns which can be confounding to the adult who ventures in there. This I *will* say, Mr. Hull. Initially, it struck me as odd that Chad was on the clock face platform at the exact stroke of one. Now this Blandersfield enigma adds more to the mystery. Mind you, my inquiries may produce aspects of your son that you might not care to know. Will you chance it?"

Hull bowed his head as if in prayer; his voice was low as he piously intoned, "I swear by his soul that Chad was a good boy."

"To be sure. Tell me, sir, was the boy a musician of any kind?"

The father smiled, recalling an old thought. "No, sir, no ear for it at all. My wife has taught the children to sing, but poor Chad had a voice like a strangled bird."

"I see. Then it is done. Go about your business, sir, and try to balm your grief. I should have something for you in a few days."

When the farmer-cooper had left, I went back to my place at the accounts dais. Tedderhorn came in bearing a tray with two tankards on it and set them down, one before each of us. I sipped the Knock and said, "Do you think it could be murder?"

Cork shrugged and took a deep draught. "What I said about the minds of boys still holds. They can be a pack of scoundrels at times. Chad could have been put up to it by his school chums, but his letter to his father indicates that he expected to be in funds very soon."

"The emolument, of course."

"I think not. His lesson book shows an average mind, and certainly not one of high scholarship. No, if he was to soon be in funds to alleviate his father's burden, it had to come from another source."

"Blackmail, possibly?"

"Very perceptive, Oaks. It's a possibility. Boys have eyes and ears, and they sometimes use them effectively."

"But whom would he blackmail?"

"A schoolmaster? A classmate? The students are all wealthy."

"But the Blandersfield notations. They confuse it."

"No, Oaks, they put more raisins in the bun. These alphabetical notations are some sort of progression. Note the September 19 notation. The first two are EF, the second set repeats the last of the first and adds a new letter, becoming FG. In the third, the "G" has become the initial letter, and "A" is added. Actually, he is only dealing with the letters E,F,G,A,B,C, and D in a repeating pattern."

"Perhaps the letters, properly arranged, spell out a word."

"I think not, at least not a meaningful word. And that does not seem to have been Chad's thinking either, for, on October 10, he tries a completely different trick, using two sets of subtractions. But where did he get the numerals? No matter, for the moment. It is obvious that he took the two remainders, 44 and 46, and went back to his September 19 progression to count the fourth and eighth letters to arrive at 44=GB and 46=GA."

"And you feel that Chad wasn't a bright student, Captain? This certainly seems to indicate an inquiring mind of some subtlety at work."

"An embrangled mind, Oaks. One that has mired itself in a complex approach to a solution. It is not limited to schoolboys. Too many times, seemingly intelligent people cannot find an answer when it lies in front of them. Obviously, Chad woke up to his error on October 20, for a new element, 'VI,' has jumped into his mind. The first two notations on September 19 and October 10 are mere exercises in garbled logic. I am sure the October 20 thought was a stroke of luck. He even matches it with an exclamative to prove the point, like someone stepping back and saying, 'My, my, there it is!' No, the boy was no genius, and indeed, may have been a fool. How is the Knock?"

I smacked my lips. "It tastes the same to me."

"That's the subtlety of it. Well, we shall be off for Fenway at dawn with a short stop off in New Haven."

"For lunch?"

"No, my old son, I think it is time we had your watch cleaned."

The trade of Jared Elliot was proclaimed by a wooden sign displaying a clockface fixed forever at twenty minutes after eight o'clock. The shop itself was a small bow-windowed establishment tucked into a commercial alley just off High Street. Its owner was a gnome-like, white-thatched man with thick spectacles and a scratchy voice. The interior of the place was filled with timepieces of all description, lantern clocks of brass and long case instruments of beautiful floral marquetry. One unique item was an elephant clock with the dial and bell in the howdah and the beast's eyes moving with every tick of each minute. Cork's attention was on the watchmaker as he opened the case of my pocketwatch and peered into the works through an optical glass.

"I see you travel a bit, Mr. Oaks, for many a watchmaker has put his hand to this piece."

I was fascinated by the elephant's eye movements and merely agreed with a nod. Cork, on the other hand, showed great interest in Jared Elliot's work, and enjoined him in conversation. As he put questions to the old man, I could see the reason for our visit.

"You seem to be a master at watches, sir, and house clocks. Do you have any knowledge of tower clocks?"

"Great Clocks is the proper name," Elliot grumped. "I don't build them. Too old."

"I hear there is one of great interest out at the Fenway School. Well worth seeing."

"That old monstrosity! Ha, it's something out of the fourteenth century, son."

"That old? It must have been brought over from the old country."

"It's only a score and some. Twenty-five's the more like it. Built by an old faker named deJoonge."

"Didn't know his business, I take it?"

"That's a mild way to put it, son. That clock has a

foliot for a time controller, mind you, as if the man never heard of the pendulum. It's only been around since old Christian Huygen invented it in 1656."

"I'm sorry, but I've just gotten interested in clocks. What is a foliot?"

"The old makers used to employ them centuries ago. It's a swing bar that has an unpredictable period of swing or vibration. It's the pendulum that makes present day clocks accurate. Old deJoonge had some gall, passing himself off as an 'orologier,' he did. That monster has stone weights," he started to chuckle and shake his head to emphasize his incredulousness. "Never saw the like of it."

Cork continued to coax information from him. "I'm told the clock has an ingenious jacamart."

"Ingenious! Now that's a bold face concoction. It's not a true jacamart at all because it doesn't really strike the chimes. They are in the spire above the clock. All the jacamart does is come out of a guardhouse on the hour and cross the face of the clock where its sword fits into a slot in the far buttress. It's a fake, like deJoonge himself."

"Did this deJoonge move on after the Great Clock was built?"

"No, son, he stayed right out there at Fenway. Still there, six feet under. He died just after the clock was finished." Elliot closed the inner dome of my pocketwatch and snapped the outer silver back with a snap. "Just a bit of dust was all. Hardly worth the charge."

"Perhaps we can remunerate you in another way. Would you rent me those books back there on your shelf?"

The old watchmaker turned his head and looked at the two volumes. "You must surely be interested in clocks and watches, sir. *The Horologium* by Huygens is in Latin, and makes rough reading. The other, *A Compendium of Watchmaking*, is easier going."

"Two pence for each, per day," Cork suggested.

"To be sure. But don't waste your time on that Fenway clock. You'll learn nothing from it."

"Probably not." Cork gave him some coins. "I am told there was some sort of misfortune out there recently."

"Could have been. I keep to myself and my clocks. They are more reliable than people. What was the misfortune? Did the clock cave in?"

"No," I said. "Some poor lad was accidentally killed by the jacamart."

His wizened old face grew dark and his eyes behind the spectacles popped wide. "Killed by the jacamart! My Lord, that's just the way old deJoonge died. Yes sir, the day after the clock was completed. He was making an adjustment on the face when the jacamart broke loose and ran him through." He gazed off in space for a moment and then turned to us. "Maybe the stories are true that the clock is cursed. My, my. But they do have a heart of their own, you know, and their own logic. My, my."

Captain Cork has many skills, and one of them is the uncanny ability to read while riding a horse. I tried it the once and got a headache for my efforts. All the way to Fenway, he had his nose buried in the books he had rented from the old clockmaker.

It was drawing near to four in the afternoon when we turned off the King's Highway at a rude sign that indicated the school lay to the northwest. All afternoon, during our silent ride, I had been thinking about this mystery the Captain had created. It could be nutmeg, or possibly cinnamon, but I was damned if I could taste it. Now if he had changed the formulation for the summer Knock, the new ingredient would have been more easily discernible, since the summer version does not have a slab of butter and a fist of sugar to mask any subtle additives.

"You amaze me, Oaks," I heard his voice say as we turned off to the northwest. "Here we are, heading into what might be a most tantalizing confrontation, and you waste your time toying with the new Knock receipt."

I looked at him with some amazement. "You have learned to read minds from these new books of yours?"

"No, but you have been moving your lips and tongue in a manner to suggest you were trying to remember the taste of something. When you are trying to discover a hidden substance or meaning, it is better to rely on facts, and not vague memory. Ho, there is our nemesis hoving into view in that vale."

We had come over a small rise, and there below in a gentle dip in the earth was a large quadrangle of field-stone masonry; its only entrance being an iron gate flanked

by a belltower that rose out of the main structure some
forty feet into free air. The clock, I assumed, faced the
inner courtyard, for the towerside in our view was solid
stone; an ominous grey finger becoming hazy in the descending autumnal dusk. We were about to start into the
vale when we heard the grim tolling of four o'clock from
the tower top.

"Do you confirm it?" Cork asked me and I checked my
newly cleaned timepiece.

"No, I show five minutes after the hour."

Cork smiled and put spurs to his horse. "Come, old son,"
he said as he galloped away, "I want to see this jacamart
at work."

We clattered through the gate at Fenway seconds later
in time to see the clock sentinel still poised at the far side
of the clockface. Jack Blandersfield was garbed as a fourteenth century knight with a coat of mail covering the
upper torso and jambs and sollerets at the cuffs and feet. A
two-edged sword held upright in the right gauntlet withdrew from a slot in the far buttress as the deadly knight
moved slowly backward to its guardhouse. We were both
looking up at this instrument of death when an elderly
gatekeeper raced up to us, shouting, "Here, here, you men.
What's this racing in here like a thunderstorm? You'll
have Headmaster to answer to, my fine swift fellows."

He had been dealing with schoolboys for so long that
he obviously treated everyone as a child. Cork slid from
his saddle and his immense height seemed to prove he was
no adolescent. The man was undismayed, however. "Fine
thing, fine doings. You'll catch a switching for this, mind
you, and I hope Mr. Crisp lays it on, for he's the best at
it."

"Mr. Crisp is the headmaster then?" Cork asked.

"None of your devilment. All knows who the headmaster be. Now come away with me, you scuds, the Reverend will do for you."

The Reverend Obadiah Travistock, the headmaster of
Fenway School, looked like a willow tree in winter. His
limbs and trunk were thin and grey, but you detected a
certain resilience in his very marrow, which is uncommon
among men of the cloth in New England. Stern, to be

sure, dedicated, no doubt, but long years of teaching boys to be men had mellowed him to a point of amused acceptance. His chambers were an admixture of religious simplicity and scholarly messiness. There were piles of paper everywhere.

"You will have to excuse Amos, gentlemen. He has been at his gate duties so long he has lost track of time. When I took over here from my late father, over fifteen years ago, it took him a long time to accept me. Well, you have an interest in old Great Clocks, you say."

"Yes," Cork said it with aplomb and without the hesitation of a man about to lie to a man of God. "I was considering doing a treatise on clocks in the colonies. Mr. Oaks is aiding in the preparation."

"Admirable undertaking, Captain, but I must be honest and ask you to be judicious when writing about the Fenway clock."

Cork feigned a puzzled look and the headmaster smiled. "You see, the clock has a rather sordid history, and a more recent notoriety that could foul the school's reputation if broadcast about like seed. In fact, I had a mind to tear the cursed thing down, but the undermasters have dissuaded me. Perhaps they are right. Accidents will happen."

"Accidents?" Cork asked. "With the clock? Pray, Reverend Travistock, anything you tell me will be held in confidence."

The headmaster then related all that we already knew, with the addition of another student who had fallen from the tower twelve years ago when engaged in a midnight attempt to affix a pair of ladies' undergarments to the weathervane atop the spire.

"What was this latest boy . . . er, Hull, I think you said . . . what was the object he attempted to use in his prank?"

The headmaster looked a bit embarrassed. "A chamberpot, I'm sorry to say. It was found on the clockface platform where he dropped it when the jacamart struck."

"Tell me," Cork leaned forward in his chair. "Is there no way to get to the upper tower other than by scaling it?"

"Of course. There is a ladderway on the inside that leads up to the clockworks and a door opening onto the clockface, but the tower is locked at night, so the only way up is to scale the outside."

"And what of deJoonge? Did you know him?"

"I was just a child when he built the tower and the clock. A Dutchman who wandered by one day and offered to do the work for my father at cost and room and board. Then, just when it was done, he was killed. I'm still not sure the tower shouldn't be torn down." He looked up at a woman who had just entered the room carrying a tea service. "Ah, Manites, how good of you. Gentlemen, my sister, Manites Travistock."

Miss Travistock was a familial copy of her older brother, but her eyes were blacker and her bearing more erect. She nodded when we bowed and we all resumed our seats. I watched her as she poured and handed the cups to us. There was a flintiness in her speech that indicated a taciturn nature, and the darting movements of her black eyes could be taken for suspicion.

"I hope, Obadiah dear, that you have not been boring our guests with that talk about the clock," she said. "You must forgive my brother, good sirs, but there are times when he prattles on like one of his own students."

"Not at all, Miss Travistock," Cork sipped the tea without making a face. "How many boys do you have here at Fenway?"

"Forty-four, Captain," she said. "In four forms. All from the finest families, I might add."

"Now, Manites," the headmaster wagged a finger at her, "there is no such thing as quality in heaven, so let's not have it here on earth."

"I am merely stating that it is our duty to provide for those who know their station. These upstarts who have their souls above buttons have no place here. Next we'll have farriers' sons among us."

The headmaster was about to chastise her when the room was filled with the ringing of a loud gong. Miss Travistock reached for the watch attached to the chatelaine belt around her waist. She checked the time and muttered, "Seven minutes late now. Such a watch."

Confused, I took my own timepiece from my pocket.

It was quarter past five, and yet the tower clock had rung only once.

"I see you are a bit dismayed by our queer clock, Mr. Oaks," the headmaster chuckled. "Old deJoonge was a frugal Dutchman, and used a Roman strike in the tower clock instead of the conventional system."

"Roman strike?" I asked.

Cork nodded his head. "Of course, most ingenious, and very rare, Reverend. A Roman strike, Oaks, uses two bells, one low toned and another of a higher pitch. The low bell stands for five, and when struck twice, it means it is ten o'clock."

"Quite correct, Captain," Travistock beamed. "Thus, Mr. Oaks, the hours one through four are struck on the high bell, one for each hour. Five o'clock is sounded just as you heard, once on the low bell."

"Ah," I said, "and eleven o'clock would be two low and one high bells."

"Let me see," Cork did a quick mental calculation. "Yes, frugal indeed. Instead of the regular seventy-eight strikes required to sound out individual hours, this Roman system needs only thirty-four blows to run through the hours."

The Reverend chuckled. "Oh, that's not correct, I'm afraid. You see, the clock doesn't strike at six o'clock at all, so there are only thirty-two blows in the Fenway run of hours, since six o'clock would be one low and one high bell."

"Was it always so?" Cork asked.

"Yes. It was one of those things left unfinished by deJoonge's death. And we are all quite used to it."

Cork turned to Miss Travistock. "But you said your watch was wrong, m'am."

"Always is, sir." She corrected the watch hands with the stem. "I will never understand how deJoonge could have made a tower clock that is always right, and a watch that is always wrong."

"Do tell. May I see it, please?"

She freed the timepiece from the chain and handed it to him. It was an elaborate thing in a beautifully tooled case that hung from a metal fob to which the winding key was attached.

"It is a lovely thing," the Captain handed it back, "but it is not strange that it is inferior, for clockmakers rarely make good watch mechanisitions. Do you have a music master on faculty, Reverend?"

"Music! Heavens no. It is difficult enough getting Latin and Greek and history and mathematics into their heads. However, my sister has taught the boys their scales for choir practice. Why do you ask? Are you interested in music, too, Captain?"

"Only of late. I take it that forty-four boys require a large staff."

"Oh, that it were possible." The headmaster looked rueful. "There is just myself, Mr. Crisp for mathematics, Mr. Goselow for languages, and young Biggard for everything else. Quite proud of Biggard we are. One of our own boys who went up to Yale from here and came back to his alma mater to teach. Always hoped he would be drawn to the ministry. Well, I see that darkness is upon us, and the boys will be at supper in a few minutes. We will take supper when they are finished. Of course, you won't be able to examine the tower clock now in the dark, so I offer you our humble hospitality for the evening. In the meantime, I have my evening meditations to attend to, and my sister must oversee the dining hall. Perhaps you would care to spend some time in our common room. The faculty uses it for lesson preparations and social talk. Come, I'll introduce you around."

The common room was a roomy hall with exposed beams. At its center was a long mahogany table where the staff obviously took their meals. In each of the four corners was an alcove with a writing table and chairs, which we learned was the working area for the undermasters and Miss Travistock. The walls of each alcove were lined with books, as was most of the main room. A fire blazed in the north wall fireplace, but its cheeriness did little to warm the greeting of the room's two inhabitants. Tom Biggard, we were told, was on proctor duty at the boys' mess in the far wing. Mr. Moses Crisp and Mr. Alonzo Goselow were hard at work on the boys' copybooks.

"Dolts, pure and simple," Mr. Crisp said, handing a pile of the copybooks to his colleague. "I hope they did better with declensions than they have with my fluctions today, Goselow." Crisp was a heavy florid man of forty odd years who had been at Fenway for the past six. Alonzo Goselow was decidedly Crisp's junior in age, but not in pedanticism.

"I haven't the heart to read them tonight," he said, "but I have a duty to the ancients. You are here to see the clock, Captain?"

"And just in time. I understand the Reverend is thinking of tearing it down since the unfortunate episode recently."

"The headmaster has become a bit over-excited," Goselow said with a prissy grin. He was no more than thirty, and thin and pale as a flounder's belly. "It's ludicrous, isn't it? Tear down a perfectly good clock because some jackanapes decides to play a prank and gets himself killed. Hull was a common boy—a mere farmer, and what he was doing here, I'll never. . ."

"For an education, Mr. Goselow, which is not an exclusive preserve."

The speaker was a young blond fellow who had just entered the room.

"Ah," Goselow said, turning toward the new arrival, "enter the schoolboys' hero, our own Mr. Biggard. Have your darlings been fed and bedded?"

Tom Biggard ignored Goselow and strode across the room toward us.

"You must be Captain Cork and Mr. Oaks," he said, shaking our hands. "You'll have to forgive my colleagues, gentlemen. The dust of antiquity clouds their humanity."

"Schoolboys have no humanity," Crisp said, yawning. "When do we eat?"

There was a knock at the door and it opened without anyone having answered. Amos, the gatekeeper, shuffled in carrying a large keyring. "All's secured, Tommy," he said. "Tower, dorm, and main gate." He hung the ring on a hook to the left of the door. "Nighty to you, Tommy and all," he mumbled over his shoulder as he left.

"Why you allow that ignorant old fool to call you by

your Christian name, I'll never know," Crisp said. "It's disgraceful."

"Amos knew me when I was here as a lad, Mr. Crisp. I take no offense."

"Do I understand that the main gate is locked?" Cork got to his feet. "You see, Oaks and I must be leaving."

"I understood you were to spend the night here. Reverend Travistock just told me so."

"He offered, Mr. Biggard, but I must apologize that we cannot accept. We have business to the north and will stop to see the clock on our way back. Tomorrow, or the next day at the latest. You will give our regards to the headmaster and his sister. No, don't bother, gentlemen, I see your supper has arrived. Just give me the key and I will give it to Amos to return to you when we have passed through."

"But it's after dark," Mr. Crisp warned us.

"Things are more interesting by moonlight at times. Here, Oaks, we'll take some of these hot biscuits to tide us over on the ride."

I thought it quite rude of him when he took several rolls from the basket that a serving girl had placed on the table. He then took the keyring, and we were off like a gust of wind. Amos was locking the gate behind us when Cork steadied his mount and said, "Tell me, good fellow, is there a farrier in the neighbourhood? Our horses are still summer shod, and there seems to be a heavy frost up."

"A mile north, ya night birds, ya. Don't go for unlocking and locking and unlocking all night, so you're out to stay and that's the end of it. Horseshoes at night. Bah. Look for the sign of the Inn of the Hanging Dog and you're there."

The moon was at the full when we reached the Inn of the Hanging Dog. It was a rude one-storied structure quite unlike the accommodations we were used to. The host was a morose fellow named Jobbot who was not happy to have tired and hungry guests at his doorsill. A few coins from Cork's purse rekindled any hospitality the scoundrel ever had. He told us that he had but one sleeping room, for the place was more a country tavern than a hostelry, and he sent his wife to prepare it.

The Captain and I took a table in the deserted public rooms where we were promised cold pork and beans. Sly dog that he is, Cork ordered straight rum lest he have to divulge his precious Knock's secret ingredient in front of me.

"Is there a blacksmith in these parts, innkeeper?" Cork asked when the plates were put down before us.

"Aye, Lemuel Stroud has a forge nearby."

When he had left us to our meal, I asked, "A smith? I thought you wanted a farrier to shoe the mounts, and while I'm at it, have we convinced ourselves that Chad Hull's death was an accident?"

"Our needing a blacksmith should answer your question." He reached into his pocket and brought forth one of the biscuits he had taken from the table. He had torn it in two, and a curious imprint was sunk into the soft bread.

"The key, you made an impression of the key when we were on our way to the gate. But why? And if Chad was played foul, shouldn't we have stayed to see it through?"

"Best to allay any suspicions. I believe the boy was done in, but I do not yet know why. The rest is aii in place, but the reason eludes me, damn it."

"The whole affair eludes me. How are you so sure he was killed . . . ouch . . ." he had poked me soundly in the ribs, and I dropped my mug of rum. "What the devil. . . ?"

"Precisely the point, my old son. If you had a chamber-pot in your hand, you would certainly have dropped it when a jacamart's sword pierced your back, and it would have been smashed to a million pieces. Chad would have dropped the pot off the platform and yet it was found lay-ing next to his body."

"Possibly, but it could have happened."

"Also consider that the tower was locked, so he had to scale the outside of the edifice carrying the item. It's an impossible task, I feel."

"But if not out to make a prank, then why climb the tower in the first place?"

"Good Lord, man, use your memory. The boy sends a letter home implying that money will soon be his. His copybook contains a cryptic progression of thought that now makes sense."

He suddenly looked up at the innkeeper who was just leaving the tap with a tray of mugs. "So there we have it. I should have guessed."

"Guessed what, the meaning of the notations?"

"No, the reason why an innkeeper would be drawing four mugs of cider for the third time in an hour."

"It is an inn, is it not?"

"An empty inn, Oaks, and a one-storey inn at that. And yet, while we sit here talking, you can hear shuffling up in the eaves."

"Squirrels, no doubt."

"Well, a nest, at least. Come, Oaks, quickly."

I followed him out of the public room and stopped behind him in the shadows of the passageway. Suddenly the passage ceiling seemed to lower itself, and by the gods, it was a hidden ladderway that lowered on ropes. The innkeeper was descending, and we let him pass in the half light, and then Cork raced to stop the stairway from ascending to the ceiling again. We slowly made our way up the stairs; voices could be heard somewhere above. A chill went up my back as we listened to the voices chanting in unison:

> "Find my measure
> Find my treasure
> Know no pleasure
> Death, death, death"

"Now!" Cork cried, and we rushed up the last two steps and into one of the most bizarre rooms I have ever seen in my life.

The candlelight from atop a circular table cast eerie shadows about the walls and danced upon a life-sized painting. I gave a gasp, for the image was that of Blandersfield, the jacamart. The four figures around the table jumped up in startlement at our bounding in on them.

"Please be seated, gentlemen," Cork commanded. "I believe I have the pleasure of addressing the leading members of the Fenway School Fourth Form, do I not?"

What then ensued was a jumble of tumbled chairs, frightened faces, and much calming by the Captain. When he had convinced the lads that he meant them no harm, the students took their seats and introduced themselves and explained the ritual. As Cork surmised, they were all fourth form members: Lemfent Pieterse, Pardee Davis, Edmund Edwards, and Jonathan Lott. Pieterse was the eldest at sixteen, Lott the youngest at fourteen.

"We are doing no harm, Captain Cork," Pieterse said. "Blandersfield's Ba . . ." he stopped and looked at his cohorts.

"You are among men, Master Pieterse," Cork chuckled.

"Blandersfield's Bastards has been a school club for years. All our fathers belonged to it. It's just a spot of fun, sir."

"And what of the incantation?"

"Well, Captain," Pardee Davis spoke up, "it's just an old tale that's as old as the school."

The boy went on to tell the same story that had been handed down from member to member over the years. Hector deJoonge, so the legend went, was a Dutch pirate who used the Fenway School to hide from his fellow cutthroats from whom he had stolen a sack of jewels. Having been trained as a clockmaker in his youth, he posed as a benevolent man wanting to make a contribution to the school, and built the Great Clock. He had hidden his treasure somewhere in or near the tower and set Jack Blandersfield to guard it.

"All these years, no one has ever found it, but the club goes on just for fun," Pardee Davis concluded.

"Was Chad Hull a member?" Cork asked.

"Hull!" Jonathan Lott said. "That clod?"

"He was all right, Johno," Pieterse corrected him. "Just a bit awkward."

"But he could have known about the legend?"

"Oh, to be sure, Captain," Pieterse answered for all. "Most of the young 'uns have heard about it, but no one seriously believes about the treasure."

"I have a feeling that Chad Hull did, and it cost him his life, lads. How would you like to help me snare a killer?"

Their eyes went wide in wonder and the answer was a resounding yes.

"Good, now which is the best sneak here? No modesty, please, my lads."

"Johno, to be sure," Pieterse said with admiration, and all eyes turned to young Lott.

"The envy of your peers is a compliment indeed, Johno. Do you think you can slip into the common room tomorrow night and take the keyring?"

The boy's smile showed that the task was not a maiden voyage for him.

Cork returned the grin. "Excellent, now, tell me, are your copybooks turned in at the end of each day?"

"At three on the dot," Johno assured him.

"You have pen and paper there on the table. May I please? Tomorrow, Johno, you will copy what I write here exactly into the back of your book and turn it in as usual. Then, at night, just after the clock strikes ten o'clock, you will borrow the key from the common room and let yourself into the clock tower and climb to the clock face platform."

"Whatever for, Captain?"

"To meet Mr. Oaks, who will be there waiting for you. Now this notation is done, and take care to copy it exactly."

I looked on as the boys read it:

BLANDERSFIELD PROGRAM 10/31

```
                              DO
                        TI
                  LA
             SO
          FA
       ME
    RE
 DO
 V      I!
```

"Makes little sense to me," I said after the boys had left and we were in our room. "And how am I to get to the top of the tower . . . oh yes, I see, the key impression in the bread and your need for a blacksmith. And where might you be, may I ask?"

"Tripping my snare."

"One thing hasn't gotten past me. You asked at the school if the boys studied music, and tonight you wrote out the do-re-me's for Johno (what an appalling hypocorism) to copy. So we now know that Chad was after this mythical treasure and someone stopped him."

"Who said it was mythical?"

"But Captain, the boys implied that it was only an old tale perpetuated by a secret club."

"People are seldom murdered over myths, Oaks. Over the years, these true stories take on the trappings of myth, but some are true all the same." He took out his rented books and began to read again.

"And you think the treasure is hidden in the clock?"

"I *know* where the treasure is. I don't need a snare for that. Now why don't you get some sleep? You'll need it."

"Yes, of course. One thing, though. If the students are locked in every night, how the deuce did these four get out?"

He gave me that smirk-a-mouth again. "Wellman Oaks, I am now convinced that you came into this world a fully grown man with a ledger book under each arm. Man has dictated many a rule and many a circumscription, but these do not apply to boys, for boyhood is the epitome of cleverness. At least not on this night, man. The date, man, think. It is All Hallow's Eve."

I closed my eyes thinking there had been one extra boy at the meeting of the Blandersfield Bastards this night.

I woke the next morning to the chagrin that I had overslept, and to my surprise, Cork was gone. A note and a large iron key were at my bedside table:

Oaks:
Herewith your means of entry to gate and tower. Stay here till nine tonight and thence to Fenway. Enter the tower after the stroke of ten and await Johno on the clockface platform. I am about other business, but shall be there when needed. Mind, lock the tower and gate behind you.

Godspeed,
Cork

It was ten-ten by my timepiece as I stood huddled against the clockface. The wind had turned from west to nor'west, and the fingers of coming winter played upon me. The moon was slipping behind high clouds, leaving me with alternate light and sudden dark. To be sure, I was truly shaken. Here I had climbed a perilously long ladder inside the tower and fumbled in the darkness to find the opening to the outer platform. That was wearing enough, but now I stood on a platform of very small width looking down at the quad, which seemed miles away. On the right side of the clock platform was the ominous jacamart's guardhouse, its shadow standing in deadly stillness in the intermittent moonlight.

A fissure of panic started to crease my brain. If for some reason young Lott could not get the key, and perchance I miscalculated the time, I could well meet the same fate as Chad Hull. Suddenly, my ears harked. I could hear a muggled noise down below, and, minutes later, the creak of the ladder within the tower. My heart was a'bump and the creak came closer and closer.

"Mr. Oaks," a voice whispered. "It's Johno, Mr. Oaks."

"Out here, lad," I said. "Take care the edge now."

"Where is the Captain?" the boy asked when he reached me. "I thought he would be here too." His voice sounded more than disappointed. More excited or nervous. My Lord, the thought struck me, could this stripling be the murderer? Had Cork used me as the lure for his snare, and if so, where was he? "Don't stand too close, my boy," I told him gingerly, "this is a small platform indeed."

"I know, sir, I've been up here before."

"When?"

"Last . . . what's that? Someone's coming up the ladder-way!"

Thank God, I told myself, Cork hadn't failed me. The two of us could handle this young murderer.

"Johno," a voice whispered, "you out there, lad?"

"Yes, who is it?"

"Where in the dome, Johno, my boy? Where is it? We could split the treasure, laddie."

"Split it!" my voice got away from me.

"Who's with you out there?" the man asked as he stepped

out onto the platform. At that moment the moon slipped from behind a cloud, bathing the figure of Tom Biggard, a sword in his hand. He started out for us, his weapon held treacherously in front of him.

"So you're back, Mr. Oaks. Well, that makes it all the better. It will be a simple case of you two killing each other over the loot."

He started for us and I grabbed the Lott boy and put him on the other side of me to protect him from the first thrust of the blade. He was at the center of the platform now, and ready to strike, when I saw it move. The jacamart came rushing forward and ran Biggard through with its steel.

"Well, don't stand there, Oaks," the jacamart said to me. "Hold this fiend up. I don't want him splattered all over the Reverend's quad."

Tom Biggard was badly wounded but alive when the Justice of the Peace came and had his men take him away. We were all in the common room, where Cork was holding forth with gusto in front of a slateboard.

"Oh, the shame of it," Reverend Travistock was saying. "One of our own graduates."

"And who else, sir? He had been a student here, he well knew the legend, and was probably once a member of a secret club which shall remain mercifully nameless."

"But I don't understand all this nonsense about Lott putting that do-re-me gibberish in his copybook," Crisp was yawning, but not bored.

"To fully appreciate the affair, let me say you were all suspects when I arrived here, and then the pieces began to fall in place. Let me put Chad Hull's September 19 notation on the slate." He wrote:

EF/FG/GA/AB/BC/CD/DE/EF ?

"As a mathematics teacher, does that suggest anything to you, Mr. Crisp?"

"It's a progression. The second letter of the first set becomes the first letter of the next set, and so on. But it doesn't make any sense to me."

"As well it shouldn't, unless you knew that Chad was

attempting to find the jacamart's treasure. The letters in
progression are the notes of the musical scale. I believe
Chad felt the uniqueness of the Roman strike, and tried
to find some clue in the notes of the scale, since he runs
from E, a low note, to F, a high note. But he gets nowhere
with it. He is truly embrangled. It is almost the same on
October 10, but he starts to get closer to the mark in a
small way.

"He shifts from the musical scale to the frugality of the
Roman strike system." Cork wrote the October 10 notation on the board:

$$78-34=44=GB?$$
$$78-32=46=GA?$$

"Now, this is nothing more than finding the stroke differences between the regular strike system and the Roman
strike system, and transferring the numbers into his progression scale of notes. Pure rot. But the second line of
the notation shows us that a glimmer of light has come
through, for Chad now calculates the difference between
the regular strike and deJoonge's Roman system minus two
strokes for the missing six o'clock sounding. Chad is still
at sea, but at least he is thinking like old deJoonge. If a
man were hiding a treasure, he would not mark a path
for a confederate with such complexities. He would make
it decidedly simple. I have reason to believe Chad had no
real ear for music."

He knew very well, for so Chad's father had informed
us. Miss Travistock, however, confirmed it again, thus
protecting our previous association with the Hull family.

"Hark," Cork said, "the clock is striking eleven."

We all listened to the two low gongs and the one high.
"What notes in the scale would you say those bell sounds
are?"

She smiled. "I have known that since I was a girl. They
are E and G, the first and third letters of the scale."

"And since the Reverend has told us that there are only
two bells in the system, the scale notes are always the
same in one E or G combination or another. So the missing six o'clock strike, VI, or one low and one high, would

be EG. Of course, Chad Hull's tin ear at first saw it as
EF, the first and second notes in the scale. But that would
make the low and high rings almost indiscernible, and
deJoonge widened the bell tone scale to EG, and thus told
us where the treasure is by leaving six o'clock silent."

"I can't see where EG gets us," Crisp, the mathematics
teacher, said.

"No, not as EG, but suppose they were sung in the
so-fa syllables such as children do."

"Do and mi," Miss Travistock said.

"Or do and *me*, as it is often expressed in the tonic
scale, so-fa."

"Do . . . me, dome," I said. "The dome of the clock is
where the treasure is hidden. That's why you had young
Lott put the do-re-me's into his notebook."

"Since all the instructors would see it and believe that
Chad's work had been decoded, his killer would watch
Lott like a hawk, and he did."

The Reverend looked dumbly at the slate. "You mean
there really is a treasure up there in the tower? When I
was a child, I remember some tough fellows showed up
just after deJoonge died, looking for him. It was the only
lie my father ever told. He informed them that the Dutchman had gone south to the Carolinas, and they left in
pursuit. My father never talked about it again, although
I heard talk during my student days."

"A headmaster's son is hardly a schoolboy's confidant,
Reverend."

I was overcome with glee. After all, if Cork had solved
the riddle, then the treasure was rightly his. "Well, shall
we start a thorough search of the dome?" I suggested.

"I'm afraid you would search in vain, Oaks."

"Then there is no treasure?"

"Oh yes, my old friend. I believe there is. But think, the
tower does not have a dome. It has a spire. No, deJoonge
was a sly old fox, but he gave himself away. You'll remember that our watchmaker in New Haven told us of the
crudity of the Fenway clock. It doesn't even keep proper
time. And yet, the same man constructs the beautiful
piece of precision hanging now from Miss Travistock's
chatelaine."

"This old thing?" she said holding it up. "I always correct it to match the tower clock."

"And thus fall for the Dutchman's deception. May I have it again, please? I'm afraid you weren't paying much attention, Oaks, when the New Haven man was cleaning your watch. He told you that your timepiece had been worked on by several people over the years. Do you know how he knew that? No, because you, like most people, are hesitant to open a precision instrument that you might harm." He put his thumbnail along the back of the catch and flipped the cover open.

"Do you see this inner cover? It's called a dome, is it not, and if we open that we find . . . ah yes, an inscription in the same place watchmakers carve their initials or mark when they work on a timepiece. Does 'the foot of the westward oak' mean anything to you, Reverend? I think you will find your treasure buried there."

Mr. Goselow, the professor of Greek and Latin, looked at Cork with unabashed admiration. "How perfectly Socratic, sir. My compliments."

"My compliments" indeed, for that's all our reward was to be. We were back at the Oar and Eagle the next evening, and I sat at the accounts dais glaring at him. "At least we could have claimed half of the jewels," I said. "Poor boys scholarship, indeed."

"And why not? Old deJoonge's evil has done some good at last. Besides, possibly one of the indigent lads who will benefit from an education will become a doctor or lawyer and save you from sickness or me from the gallows. Come in, Tedderhorn. Good, you've brought the Knock. I've missed it."

I half-heartedly took my mug and sipped.

"Well, Oaks, have you figured it out yet?" Cork chaffed.

"Cloves," I said. "I'm sure of it."

"Good. Tedderhorn, hand the paper I gave you the other day to Oaks."

I read it and fumed:

Tedderhorn:
Add nothing to the Knock, but don't tell Oaks.

                                              Cork

"This is . . . ah . . . dishonesty, foul play," I cried.

"Nonsense, my old son, it is deception, no more."

"And do you not consider deception dishonest?"

"Not when all the facts are in front of you. You had your sense of taste. I just misdirected you. Come, man, as Shakespeare says, 'would you pluck out the heart of my mystery?'"

I persevere.

life from contamination, are we not?"

"Yes my old world and they will and so do, they and headlong."

"You know? I've not to remember this. It is to be done a moment. I repeat all those years, don't think of their agony over the years to come. We may saving

THIRTEEN

The Pennsylvania Thimblerig

THE OPPRESSIVE BLANKET of heat that plagued the colonial seaboard in the summer of 1776 well matched the revolutionary fever in the body politic, and Captain Jeremy Cork's own seething indignation.

His choler arose from his failure to be elected a Connecticut delegate to the Second Continental Congress, despite the fact that he had given his ship, *The Hawkers*, to the rebel navy. It seemed the past events of Lexington and Concord had unleashed a civic unrest from which my employer was not immune. *The Hawkers* is, or was, the mainbrace of the financial empire I had constructed for him with patient yeomanry.

Ostensibly, his reason for coming to Philadelphia in late June was to oversee the ship's transfer to Commodore Hopkins, but I was not taken in by that ruse. Cork wanted a place of importance in these revolutionary doings, and, finding no opening, had decided to be as close to the hive as possible.

Thus, in addition to the swelter and recurring thunderstorms, I had to sustain the brooding and silent Cork. My evenings were made bearable by his absence from our rooms at Morby's in Spring Garden Street. He would spend the dark hours at the City Tavern with the various delegates and would come home cheered. But by daylight he became morose again.

It was mid-morning of 4 July when the first breeze in days rose up from the bay and wafted through the windows of our sitting room. I looked up from my reading of the *Gazette* to enjoy the zephyrs.

"The wind's up. It's a shame we don't have a ship to take advantage of it," I chided him.

"Consider her on loan," he said, dishing up another helping of oysters from the sea bucket in the corner. It was his third plateful of the day; since our arrival, shell-fish had been the mainstay of his diet.

"A loan without collateral is often uncollectable," I said. This was our first interchange since dawn, and I feared I had now ended all conversation for the rest of the day.

"Oaks," he said, shucking a shell and sprinkling the oyster meat with Madeira and a pinch of dillweed, "you always manage to sound dangerously like a Tory."

Now there you have it! The main difference between us was this damnable war. I well realised the injustices of the King, and the possible need to rectify them with arms, but I am a man of commerce, a man who must protect an investment. Reconciliation on better terms was my thinking, not revolution and separation, which could destroy us all.

You will mark well I said the war was our *main* difference. There is another that has plagued me for years, and that is his excursions into the solutions of crime and skulduggery, which he calls "social puzzles." Yet, despite my previous misgivings about these puzzles, I found myself wishing that one would turn up, if only to occupy that fertile mind that was now so fallow.

Not wanting to sit in silence, I said, "I see your friend Dr. Franklin has lost his dog, and from the reward in this advertisement, he seems to value the animal highly."

"Are you suggesting that I become a dogcatcher?" He glared at me.

"Just making conversation, Captain. Might I ask, how long are we going to sit here doing nothing?"

He didn't answer, for a knock came at our door, and Morby himself entered. The portly innkeeper had a military man with him. The officer's blue coat, criss-crossed at the breast with white belting, and his bucktailed, cockaded hat bespoke him to be a Major of the Philadelphia Associators, a militia company of tradesmen. Yet the part-time soldier did not have the demeanour of a tradesman any more than he did of a military man. He was pale and thin, and his hands were milky white like those of a gentleman. Morby's introduction clarified the matter.

"Beg pardon, Cappin, sor, but Dr. Church would like a word with ye."

"Yes, Captain," the middle-aged soldier said, stepping forward. "I was at drill with the company at the State House Yard when Morby summoned me. I know of your reputation in such cases and would appreciate your help with Mr. Custis."

"By all means, Doctor. What seems to be Mr. Custis's problem?"

"He's dead, Captain. Dead by foul means, if I know arsenic poisoning when I see it."

I looked at Cork, who, for the first time in days, had a glint in his eye.

Morby clutched his pudgy hands. "I would sorely like ye help, Cappin. A man dying of pie-son makes the house look bad."

"Ah, then he's a guest here at the inn. Well, where away, man. What room?"

We followed our callers down the hall and up a landing to the third-floor attic.

"Came in two days ago, he did," Morby said, opening the door and showing us into a simple bedchamber. "Paid a week's advance."

It was a typical second-class room with a writing table, chair, and small cot upon which lay the corpse. The Captain examined the body and smelled the mouth.

"Arsenic, to be sure, Doctor," he said, testing the flexibility of the dead man's hand and arm. "Would you say he died not more than an hour ago?"

"Undoubtedly. I was about to summon the sheriff when Morby here mentioned your name."

"He should be summoned in any case. Have you been through his effects?"

"We thought it best to have other witnesses," Dr. Church said.

"Yes," Cork said, walking to the writing table. "Did he take breakfast this morning, Morby?"

"No, sor, just asked for hot water, he did."

"To make himself some tea, no doubt." The Captain picked up a travelling cup and smelled it. "A deadly cup at that." He handed the container to the doctor, who sniffed it.

"Arsenic, Doctor. Look here. A box of green tea on the table, along with some orange peels. I think our Mr. Custis would have been better off to have availed himself of the pleasures of Morby's dining room below this morning. Well, who is he? Where is he from? And why was he poisoned? Morby!"

"Lor's be, Cappin, all I know, he was a gentleman in travel of some kind. From New York, I think he said."

"Yes," Cork said, returning to the bed, "a gentleman by clothing, but with the hands of a workman, and living in second-class accommodations. It is certainly strange."

I had been too busy watching Cork to fully take in the body. Cork was, as always, quick to observe minute points. The man's linen was expensive, yet somehow it did not go with the sunburnt face and rough hands, or the queue tied back with a fine silk ribbon.

"A bit incongruous," I said.

"Incongruity is often the nub of a puzzle, Oaks," Cork said, opening a travelling case he had drawn from under the cot. He dumped the contents onto the bare floor.

"Incongruity, indeed," he frowned. "Our Mr. Custis lies in death in a fine brocade suit, yet his satchel yields raw buckskin breeches and vest, worn boots, and rather despicable hose." The box also contained a quill, a small slate, an hourglass, a book of Common Prayers, and a sharp dagger.

Dr. Church, who had been going through the table

drawer, held up some strips of paper. "Could this have any meaning, I wonder?"

Cork came across the room, took the seven strips, and examined them. They were white, thin, and no more than a quarter of an inch in width by about twelve inches in length. He mused over them for a few moments and then took them to the window, where he held each one up to the sunlight.

"Most interesting," he said, after a careful study. "Doctor, I trust that you can handle the details here as far as the corpse is concerned, and Morby, I leave you to deal with the sheriff."

"But, sor, sor," the innkeeper pleaded, "the suspicion on the house!"

"As likely not, Morby. He brought his death in with him in the tea. You only supplied the water. Come, Oaks."

We started to leave when the good doctor called after us. "Begging your pardon, Captain, but you are taking those strips with you. If they are important, and you seem to think they are, shouldn't you leave them here for the sheriff?"

"Under the rules of evidence in the Commonwealth of Pennsylvania I would agree, Doctor, but this transcends boundaries. Pay my respects to the sheriff and tell him I will be in touch with him."

"Well, this leaves me in a rather precarious position. After all, I am only a physician. Where can you be reached?"

"On Bristol Road at the home of Dr. Benjamin Franklin," he said, turning towards the door with myself in tow and, as usual, in the dark.

The haste with which Cork moved bespoke the pent-up energy that had been building within him the past fortnight. He no sooner had left the death chamber when he entered our rooms, slipped into a coat, and was off down the stairwell to the common rooms below. He paused to send Josh, the boy of all work, to tell Tyngs to have the calash ready.

The calash, driven by its owner, Falcor Tyngs, is one of the many luxuries Cork allows himself in Philadelphia. It galls me to pay out good monies for the carriage, horse, and driver when we rarely use them, but the Captain insists. Within minutes all was ready and we were away.

"If you don't mind my asking," I said as we clattered over the scorching cobbles into Broad Street, "why all this rush to Dr. Franklin's?"

"We have here a perplexity of no mean proportions, Oaks." He leaned back into the breeze that our locomotion created. "Consider the facts at hand. A workman disguised as a gentleman is poisoned. In his possession are curious strips of paper. Who, then, is the best paper expert in Philadelphia to confront them with than Poor Richard, the master printer himself?"

"You think the paper had some bearing on Custis's death then?"

"Of course. Put all the points together. How did this poor devil die? By poison, mixed with tea. When was the last time you ate an orange, Oaks? Don't you see?"

"Tea and oranges," I mused aloud. Then it struck me. "He's British. The only oranges are on the Redcoat's tables."

"And tea, too, for that matter. Then there is the sun-parched skin to be considered. West Indies, if I make it right."

"That is reasonable. But the paper? That confounds me."

He reached into his pocket and drew out the seven strips. "Note that they are similar in shape and size. But there the similarities end. The quality of each piece of paper is different. All are of top grade, but different."

"Samples of some kind," I said.

"Yes, that could be, but the oblong shapes suggest another function. Paper samples are usually square or triangular. Paper is too expensive to waste so much on a sample. Well, let us see what Dr. Franklin has to say."

The appointments of the house on Bristol Road mirrored its owner's eclectic taste. Amid the sturdy native furniture were beautifully shaped pieces from Europe, as well as lush draperies and fine oil paintings.

He sat in an armchair of red brocade, his foot resting gingerly on a low stool. Here was a man who had met three kings and had visited with numerous lesser royalty, and yet he chose the brown frock of the Quakers as his garb. His grey hair was cut to the length of his collar, and his face was remarkably unlined for a man of 70. He looked up from a sheaf of documents in his lap as we entered, his blue-grey eyes peeping over his eyeglasses.

"Forgive me for remaining seated, gentlemen. The gout again, my dear Jeremy," he said, offering some port from the table beside him. I was surprised to hear Dr. Franklin call the Captain "Jeremy." Few people ever do.

After Cork had explained the Custis affair, he turned over the paper strips, and the venerable doctor examined them closely.

"You are right about all the pieces being of good quality, Jeremy," he said, holding them up to the light.

"Three of them have a portion of a watermark, Doctor."

"Yes, I see that. Now this one with the cloverleaf is from the Rittenhouse Shop here in Philadelphia. And if I read the bead and chain lines correctly in this one, it is from DeWees's Shop in Virginia. I have sold Gerald DeWees rags in the past for use in his papermaking process.

"Excellent," Cork said, picking one of the strips. "The watermark here appears to be a C and an L, which I immediately recognized as the product of Chris Leffingwell of Connecticut. Now we have something more to go on. Three different papers from three different colonies, and if I guess right, the remaining four are from still other colonies."

"Jeremy," the doctor laughed, "you will have to erase the word 'colony' from your speech, my boy."

Cork dropped the paper strip he was holding. "Then it's done," he said, the surprise showing in his voice.

"This very afternoon. The Declaration of Independence was approved by the Congress, so you will have to start calling these colonies states."

"But I've had no word of it. Do you have a copy?"

"The document is at Dunlap's, the printer. Our courier took it there this afternoon. Copies will be struck off and carried by post-riders to all the states to-night."

I sank back into my chair. So it was done. These shores were now independent and vulnerable.

"Well, well," Cork beamed, "that is good news, but I'm afraid it will do Mr. Custis no good. Have you any notions about this, Dr. Franklin?"

The old man heaved a sigh. "Jeremy, I would like to be of more assistance, but at the moment I am heavily involved in Congressional work. I have to find factories for flint and gun production, and there's food to be raised for the army. I'm afraid I haven't time to spend on trifles."

I truly felt sorry for Cork. The word "trifles" went through him like a rusty blade. But I could sympathise with Franklin, an aged, overburdened man being pestered with a minor crime. Yet he was sensitive enough to see that he had hurt the Captain.

"Trifle was a poor choice of word, Jeremy. A person's death is no trifle. You'll have to forgive me. I am a bit out of sorts to-day. My gout is acting up, my son has decided to remain with the Royalists, and some scoundrel has slain my dog."

"Slain?" Cork asked. "I thought it was merely lost?"

"And so it seemed when I placed a notice for his return, but the old fellow was found just two hours ago out in the brush with its throat cut."

"Perhaps he attacked someone," I suggested. "In this heat, dogs often become angry at the slightest agitation."

"The cur, like his master, was old and beyond agitation, Mr. Oaks. No, it was an act of malice—probably by a Tory seeking some petty revenge against me. I fear this division between Tory and Whig will be a greater problem than General Howe's army. Perhaps the Declaration of Separation will change some minds. Ah!" he said to a visitor who had just been shown into the room, "here's its author now."

The caller was strikingly handsome and straight as a gun barrel. He was over six-foot-three and in his mid-thirties. Despite the heat of the day, his high forehead was dry, his reddish brown hair unrumpled.

"After eighty-six changes by others, I could hardly call it original authorship," the man said. He was introduced as Thomas Jefferson.

"I warned you that is the hazard of preparing a document that must be approved by a body of men. It is a risk

I have always avoided," Dr. Franklin said impishly, but Jefferson didn't appreciate the jest.

Cork must have felt we were intruding, and got ready to leave, when Dr. Franklin stopped him.

"You might explain your problem to Tom while you're here, Jeremy. He enjoys solving problems as much as you do."

Cork obliged and gave him all the details, as well as the paper strips.

"So," Jefferson said after examining the strips, "you believe these samples are from seven different places, yet they are all exactly the same length and width. The measurements intrigue me. Have you a measuring stick about, Ben?"

One was forthcoming and Jefferson measured the pieces of paper with great care.

"Twelve and three-quarters by one-quarter." The Virginian stroked his jaw. "Ben, you are familiar with such matters. What is the usual size of a paper mould?"

"These strips are from American wooden moulds. You can tell by the deckle. They are usually, if not always, twelve and three-quarter inches by sixteen and three-eighths inches."

"So these were trimmed from the lengths of single sheets. But why always in quarter-inch widths?" Cork asked.

"Trimmed—that's your answer, Jeremy," Dr. Franklin said with a wince as he moved his painful foot. "The quarter-inch width is a trimming, and if the trimming is the same in seven different parts of the country, it has to be a universal item."

"Like shinbucks! Money!" Cork cried, getting to his feet. "Now it all makes sense. Our Mr. Custis has somehow obtained samples of bank-note stock used in the printing of money in seven colonies—I mean, states. He was English, or pro-English, which means only one thing."

"A counterfeit scheme, of course," I said.

"To be sure, Oaks," Cork said, turning to Franklin. "With the proper stock and copper plates, the British could flood the land with worthless money, further compounding our troubles."

"Jeremy," Dr. Franklin smiled, "you have my deepest apology for calling this case a trifle."

"Think nothing of it. If it weren't for an alert medical officer, the plot would have worked. We will have to find out who this mysterious Mr. Custis really is, and how he planned to execute his foul deed."

Dr. Franklin got to his feet with another wince of pain and leaned gingerly on his cane. "I leave Custis to you, Jeremy. I have a more urgent task. Tom, we must send a message to Hancock to convene the Congress in emergency session. Details will have to be forwarded to all the state committees for safety and a countermine developed to block the British plot. If we work through the night, we can use the same post-riders who carry the Declaration."

The place was astir like a toppled nest of yellowjackets, with servants being called, notes being written and dispatched. Having no place in it, Cork motioned me with his head and we left.

"Captain, you have my congratulations," I said, as the carriage headed back to the city. "You not only have uncovered a plot, but you have protected your own estate. You realise how much of your cash is in Continental banknotes?"

He grunted and took on his brooding again.

"Good Lord, man," I said. "You are not offended because you weren't invited to the emergency meeting, are you? As I understand it, they are held in secret session."

"No, I doubt that I could do much there, Oaks," he said. "What does concern me is our new country's naivete in political subterfuge. We are helplessly new at what the Italians call *spione*. It is not in our nature to be deft in the double-deal, but I fear we will have to develop the black arts of Europe quickly and effectively. Well, now to Mr. Custis."

Dusk had fallen when we alighted at Morby's door to find Dr. Church waiting for us. We repaired to the taproom and took a table. The doctor was still in his Major's militia uniform, and was greatly agitated.

"Captain Cork," he said, looking furtively around the room, "I have made a very disturbing discovery. For my own curiosity I performed a necropsy on Custis's body after the sheriff had released it. In the victim's gullet I found this."

From his pocket he withdrew a piece of white linen and carefully unfolded it to reveal a small metallic ball about the size of a pea or rifle pellet. He also produced small bits of felt which, he said, he found under Custis's fingernails.

"I didn't notice any neck wound," I said, thinking the doctor was implying that Custis had been shot.

"I don't think that's the doctor's inference, Oaks." Cork rolled the ball in his palm and then smelled it. "It looks like silver, but it could be antimony."

"Aha, so it wasn't arsenic, then," I said. "And it wasn't murder, either. Custis committed suicide by swallowing a poisonous metal ball." I was quite proud of myself, for, though I have been against our involvement in crime, I had been around it long enough to learn something.

"I'm sorry, Mr. Oaks." The doctor gave me a weak, almost painful, smile. "The ball is of silver, which would have no effect on the body chemistry. Death was by arsenic, and it was in the tea. My tests proved that beyond question."

"I see what you are aiming at," Cork said, still playing with the ball. "You found it in the gullet . . ."

The doctor looked embarrassed. "Forgive my rude speech, Captain. My old masters at Edinburgh would be appalled. It was lodged in the esophagus, to be exact, midway in the *pars thoracica* area."

"Gullet will do me fine, Doctor," Cork went on. "Then if he was unconscious within minutes from arsenic, the ball had to be swallowed before his death trance."

"Precisely." The doctor knocked the table with his knuckles for emphasis. "But why would a man, with the clutch of death on him, try to swallow a silver bullet?"

Cork thought for a moment, then said matter-of-factly, "To conceal it, of course."

"Well, I see no rhyme or reason to it." Dr. Church rubbed his chin. "Any more than I can understand the bits of felt under his fingernails. At first I thought he might have grabbed at a material made of felt in his death agony, but I re-examined his room just before you returned, and can find nothing made of felt in the place."

"Well done, Doctor. You have proved a first-class investigator. The felt ties it all together, although the silver ball is still a mystery." Cork went on and explained the counterfeiting conspiracy and the significance of the paper samples. "Custis was posing as a coucher in various paper shops throughout the country. A coucher, gentlemen, is the worker who takes the wet sheets of paper from the mould and places them between pieces of felt to absorb the water. What better role could you adopt to gain inside knowledge of which paper was to be used for money printing? A man's occupation often clings to him unnoticed. Now, perhaps this little ball will unlock some more information."

"My, oh, my." Dr. Church's eyebrows went up. "Little did I know when I summoned you this morning that I would be involved in a matter of such magnitude. The Congress in secret evening session, a plot abroad in the states—my, oh, my."

"The smallest of us may have to make large contributions, Doctor. Is there a good jeweller in the neighbourhood?"

Church said yes, that a Martin Whitlow kept a shop in the next street.

"Well, Doctor, since he is probably closed for the day, might I rely on your official uniform as a Major of the militia company to fetch him here? Ask him to bring a jeweller's glass, a scale, and the sharpest cutting tool he has."

The doctor left, and Cork pushed his chair back to the wall and stretched out his long legs. For the first time in days he had a relaxed, if not a jubilant, look on his face.

"Well," he said, signalling to Morby, "we might as well enjoy our free moments. Morby, bring some Apple Knock, and send over the thimblerig for a few games."

Thimblerigging is something he never gets to play in our Connecticut homeport, gambling being frowned on there. But in the larger cities he indulges himself, and, I must say, he is rather lucky at it. But, considering the import of the problem at hand, I considered it frivolous to bet on which of the three shells hid the pea.

The thimblerig, a jaunty stout fellow, came up to the table and tipped his hat. His wide grin was catlike as he greeted what he assumed to be another pigeon.

"Evening, sirs," he said, spreading out the tools of his trade—a soft cloth, a hard pea, and the three shells. "Name your limit, but I only deal in gold or silver. No paper, thank you."

Cork threw his head back and laughed deeply. "Perhaps our efforts *are* futile, Oaks. Play on for a half-joe, my man."

The pea was placed under the center shell and the thimblerig's hands flew in a whirl, moving the shells in a complex choreography. When he stopped, Cork tapped the center shell, and the gambler looked annoyed. The pea was under it, and Cork collected his coin.

They were in the middle of the sixth game when the doctor-Major returned with an elderly, disgruntled man at his elbow. "I never saw such luck," the thimblerig said in disgust, paying off for the sixth time and leaving us.

"These fellows tickle me," the Captain said, pointing to a chair for the jeweller. "They use their clever hands to misdirect you, but the trick is to keep your eye on the pea. Well, sir, Mr. Whitlow, is it? We seem to have gotten you out of bed."

The old man had dressed hurriedly, and had not combed his hair, which fell over his eyes in a white thatch. "I retire at sunset, as God intended all His creatures to do. This bluejay came slamming at my door like the thunder of hell itself. What's this land coming to, I'd like to know? Toy soldiers disturbing a man's sleep, goods in short supply, and annihilation riding to us in British men-of-war. I tell you, sir, we are being cajoled by madmen—"

Cork cut off his tirade with an upraised hand. "We will take only a few minutes of your time, Mr. Whitlow, and then you can return to the safety of your bed. Would you examine this article?"

The jeweller took the silver ball, hefted it in his hand, and looked as if something were wrong. He took a glass instrument from his pocket and studied the ball's surface, then placed the ball on the scale.

"Just as I thought," he grumbled, "it's hollow. Its size doesn't match its weight. If it's a bullet, it's not heavy enough to kill anyone. Good Lord"—a sudden thought occurred to him—"these Continentals aren't going to use silver bullets, are they?"

Cork ignored the question and asked if there were any markings on the surface.

"Just the seam where it was sealed. It's very good work, no doubt about that."

"Very good," Cork said. "Now can you cut it open very carefully?"

The only man looked deeply insulted and picked up a small blade with a fine sawtooth edge. "Been doing delicate work for over fifty years," he muttered as he cut slowly through the metal. "The hands and the eyes are as good now as they ever were. Here you are. Is that all?"

"Yes, Mr. Whitlow," Cork said, pushing his thimblerig winnings across to the man. "Thank you. And my best to Mrs. Whitlow and your large brood."

The jeweller shot him a quizzical look. "Now how did you know I have many children?"

The Captain smiled and bid him good evening. "It seems that Dr. Franklin's advice about early to bed and early to rise produces more than wealth and wisdom." He chuckled.

"Isn't there something inside this?" The doctor pointed to the now split ball. Stuffed into one of the hemispheres was a white object. Cork probed it delicately with a knife point until it came loose. It was a tiny wad of material which, when unrolled, proved to be a square of the finest silk, of incredible thinness. Cork spread it out on the table and smoothed its surface.

"Why, yes, there is a message of some kind written on it," I said.

Cork read it through twice and then made room at the table for me to read over his shoulder.

King H has approved. Plates ready 1 August. Will deliver after word from B. that payment made.

                                                    Dor. Q.

I could make no sense of it, and the doctor-Major said, "What is it, Captain?"

"I'm afraid I will have to ask you to refrain from reading this," Cork said, folding the silk material. "I hope you won't be insulted, but this is a highly confidential matter."

"Of course," Church said with a hurt smile, "I am sure that the Congress can vouch for my trustworthiness since I serve as their courier."

He bid us good night and left, and I said to Cork, "You may have hurt his feelings, Captain. After all, he has helped us quite a bit. What's so secret, anyway? Is it a code of some sort?"

"That's what bothers me most, my boy. It is not a code, as I expected. Fetch me Falcor Tyngs, will you?"

"We are going out again?"

"Not at the moment. I will have to study this a bit further. Send Tyngs to our rooms and then have the ostler prepare two mounts."

When I returned from the stable to our rooms, Cork had finished giving Tyngs instructions of some sort, and sent him off.

"You're acting rather curiously, Captain," I said, sitting down opposite him at the table. He had taken out the silk material and was reading it anew. He knitted his brows for a long minute and then blinked his eyes wide open in surprise. "Of course!" he cried.

"You have decoded it, then."

"I told you it wasn't a code. It is just that I don't keep up with the social notes. Weren't you telling me that John Hancock has a new bride?"

"Yes, a Miss Dorothy Quincy. Quite a piece of frippery, I gather. Wait, Dorothy Quincy, Dor Q. Do you mean that the wife of the president of the Congress wrote that message?"

"The reference to King H would make it appear so. He is called 'King Hancock' by his detractors, is he not?"

"Well," I chuckled, "you can hardly blame people, the way he parades through the streets with all sorts of liveried servants in his train. Could we have intercepted a Congressional message?"

"Hardly, under the circumstances. We suspect the late Mr. Custis of having been a counterfeiter."

"And the message mentions payment for plates." I cried. "Bank-note plates! My God, I can hardly believe it. Hancock is one of the richest men in America. He's reportedly a snob—"

"And a smuggler," Cork added.

"I see your point, Captain. But King George has put a £500 reward on Hancock's head. But then a young new bride can turn a man's direction. Shouldn't we report this?"

"Yes, and as quickly as you can."

"As I can?"

"Oaks, I am depending on you, for I have other matters to attend to. Take this to Dr. Franklin at the State House and tell him all you know."

I started to protest, but he would have none of it, and rushed me to the stable and had me ahorse in minutes. My last objection was met with a slap of Cork's hand on my mount's hindquarters, and I found myself flying towards Chestnut Street.

I entered the courtyard and, while dismounting, could hear voices from the centre rooms of the first floor— the Congress was in heated argument. The doorkeeper's lodgings were in the west wing, and when I pounded on his entry, I was greeted by a gentlewoman. My frantic pounding had alarmed her.

"Sir, you scared me out of my wits. I thought the Indians in the upper east wing had finally burned us down."

I looked at her. "Indians?"

"Visitors. They are very careless with fire. What do you want, sir?"

I told her of the urgency of my talking to Dr. Franklin, and she took me to the centre hall, where I repeated my need to the doorkeeper of the Congressional chamber. It took me about ten minutes to persuade him to take my message to Dr. Franklin. I was surprised when Thomas Jefferson, and not the doctor, returned with him.

"Mr. Oaks," he said in an irritated tone, "Dr. Franklin's gout prevents him from coming out. He suggests that you talk to me."

Well, Cork had specifically said Dr. Franklin and no one else, but I took it upon myself to explain how we had come by the message and handed him the silk cloth. He read it slowly, as all lawyers do, and said nothing for several seconds.

"This is either preposterous or else the most dangerous charge ever. Wait here."

Jefferson was gone for quite a while, and I could hear the room within fall silent. Then Jefferson reappeared and beckoned me in.

All eyes were on me as I entered the large chamber. My heart was pounding with anxiety. Why, I asked myself, had Cork left this unpleasant task to me? The delegates' chairs were comfortably arranged in an informal manner, and I noticed the familiar, but not friendly, face of Roger Sherman from Connecticut, a man I admired for he had risen from a shoemaker to a prosperous land dealer. Sherman's glare told me that great gravity had settled over the body of men.

I walked forward towards the double brass-fitted fireplaces that faced the door. They were, of course, unlit, but the unbearable heat of the room made it seem as if they were both ablaze. The closeness of the room was further abetted by the pungent wafting that came through the narrow openings of the window tops from the stable across the street. I turned towards the back wall, where there was a panoply consisting of a drum, swords and banners. They were the trophies of the capture of Fort Ticonderoga, a place to which I wished I could be transported that instant.

Below the panoply was the President's desk, with the official mace on it. Behind it sat John Hancock, a look of black anger on his face. I found myself appealing to Jehovah.

"Sir," Hancock's voice roared at me, "you have brought a charge into this chamber that is both absurd and treasonous!"

"Mr. President," a shortish delegate began.

Hancock looked his way, still angry. "The chair recognizes Mr. Samuel Adams of Massachusetts."

"I move that we become a committee of the whole while we hear this man."

Someone seconded the proposal. Hancock called for a voice vote and all said "Aye." Hancock then rose from his chair and stepped down to sit with the other delegates. I have long heard of Samuel Adams's parliamentary ability, and this was a shrewd example of it. By moving for a committee of the whole, he had automatically made anything said unofficial.

"Mr. Oaks," Dr. Franklin said from his chair, "this is most disturbing. Can you give us all the details of the affair?"

My throat was parched as if from sand, my arms wouldn't move. I opened my mouth to speak and found salvation. I heard Cork's voice boom from the doorway.

"Gentlemen," he said, "forgive my intrusion, but I don't think Mr. Oaks's recitation will be necessary. The case has been solved to your advantage, Mr. Hancock."

Well, by jing, there he was, strutting into this august assembly like a peacock, a smile of self-satisfaction on his face. Dr. Franklin asked him to explain, and Cork raised the curtain on the most important performance of his life.

"Good sirs," he said, "and particularly you, Mr. President, have my heartfelt apology for being a jackanapes. Here I have been following false trails when the real problem lay under my nose. A traveller's mysterious death set off a chain of circumstances that led me to a counterfeit plot. And that, ironically, is what it was. A counterfeit, a fake. There was no plot—not against our money, at least. The plot was deeper and infinitely more dangerous."

Every man in the room leaned forward in anticipation.

"Mr. Thompson," Cork said to the secretary of the Congress, "is this the document you sent to Dunlap the printer late this afternoon?" He handed him a paper and the man looked at it quickly. From my vantage point I could only see that it was in holograph with many corrections on it.

The man looked at it quickly. "Yes," he said, returning it to Cork, "I recognise it as such."

"Good. Now, I give it to Mr. Jefferson, its original author."

Jefferson took the paper and read it with the same slow exactness he had used on the silk material. He looked puzzled and then reached down and took another paper from the lawyer's bag at his feet and compared the two papers.

"Why, the copy sent to the printer has been changed! I have here my own fair copy, which incorporates all the additions and deletions passed on this afternoon. The printer's copy has been altered. Here, where we originally said 'life, liberty, and the pursuit of happiness,' this copy deletes 'happiness' and says 'property.' And there are other changes. We took out the mention of slaves to appease the Southern delegation, and here it is back in again. This is dreadful. If printed copies have left for the states—"

"Take your ease, sir," Cork said. "But if that document had gone out to the people, you would have crushed any faith in this Congress, and possibly in the revolution effort as well. Just a few simple changes and a few additions would have pointed up the differences in regional attitudes, and set the northern states against the southern, the townsman against the farmer, the landed against the poor. Thus the document meant to unite would have served to divide. It was a simple thing to do. The copy sent to Dunlap's is indeed a calligraphic mess. Eighty-six changes and deletions. Words crossed over. A few more would not have been noticed."

"But unless it were one of *us*—" Hancock began. "I don't see how any outsider could have done it."

"And why not, Mr. President?" Cork shook a finger. "I would suggest better security measures in the future. There are troops in the State House yard each day. Perhaps not everything can be heard through the window, but the gist of things can be. Besides, our culprit didn't need to eavesdrop. He had seen the document after Mr. Jefferson wrote it."

"Why, no one saw it prior to submission but John Adams, Dr. Franklin, and myself," Jefferson said.

"Precisely. Did you leave it with them?"

"With Dr. Franklin, yes."

"And Dr. Franklin's dog was destroyed and the body hidden. Doesn't that suggest that someone broke into the house on Bristol Road, silenced the dog so his entry would not be discovered, and then read the document?"

"But why all this nonsense about counterfeiting," Dr. Franklin grumbled, "and this secret-message business?"

"The first was to create a crisis, which would bring you into session on the night the Declaration of Independence was to be dispatched. The second was to make sure you stayed in session until the post-riders had left. The next time you use your courier to take things to a printer, don't trust him simply because he is a medical man and a Major in the Associators."

It was after midnight when we reached Morby's and, as usual after a triumph, Cork was famished. Despite the late hour, the hearths were relit and a feast was in preparation. Cork eschewed fish since it had been his main diet, and ordered roast kid, ducklings in bing sauce, and a huge bowl of broccola laced with lemon butter.

"How did you get on to Dr. Church?" I asked him as we ate our snapper stew. "He certainly was convincing."

"Not really," he said. "Just up to a point. When he conveniently gave us the silver bullet with the message inside, I became suspicious. You will recall I was annoyed that it wasn't in code. Why would anyone go to such trouble to conceal a message and then write it out in plain language? That is bad *spione*."

"Then why didn't he encode it?"

"Because he could not be sure that I would be able to decode it in time to warn the Congress. But his telling us that he had found felt under Custis's fingernails was sheer poppycock. He wanted to strengthen the evidence that Custis had worked as a coucher in paper shops. A coucher works with his hands in water all day, and certainly would not have the callused and tanned hands that our corpse did."

"And what of Custis? Who was he?"

"We'll never know. Probably a seaman whom Dr. Church had duped into playing the role of a traveller. A little poison in his tea, and he became the perfect player."

"But, Captain, how could this lead you to the Declaration plot?"

"I had Tyngs check on Church, and he found that Church had been away from the city on trips at frequent intervals. Once my suspicions were aroused, I asked myself why he was doing this. It came to me when I thought of the thimblerig. Of course he was doing one thing to cover another, and the Declaration was the most important thing in Philadelphia this day. I went to Dunlap's and learned that it was Church, as an official courier, who had delivered the document from the State House, and there you have it."

We were just slicing into the ducklings when John Hancock entered the room with Mr. Jefferson and a third man.

"May I present Mr. John Jay," Hancock said. We shook hands and they sat down.

"Captain Cork," Mr. Jay said, "we were all very impressed by your ingenuity in solving this problem, and the Congress would not like to lose such a talent. At the moment I am in charge of covert activities against the enemy, but I would like you to take over my operational branch."

Well, that explained it. Now I knew why I was sent to the State House to give Dr. Franklin the silk cloth and bear John Hancock's ire. Captain Cork's gall is unspeakably enormous. Having detected the plot, he could have quickly reported it—but not Cork. He had to involve the entire Congress in his victory. And this new appointment told me he had worked a smart bit of thimblerig himself.

Later that night in our rooms I noticed that Cork had kept the copy of the Declaration that Dr. Church had changed.

"Isn't that the property of the government?"

"A gift from Mr. Hancock," he said.

Well, at least for once, we received something for our services, even if it was only a scrap of paper.

AUTHOR'S NOTE: The original Declaration that was sent to Dunlap's was, in reality, lost and never recovered. The document on view in Washington, D.C. is an engrossed copy on parchment, which was signed by the members of Congress on August 2, 1776. There were no signatures on the Dunlap copy.

"C.I.A., Mister Fletcher."

"Um. Would you mind spelling that?"

"Enough of your bull, Fletcher."

"Okay, guys. What's the big deal?"

"You are going to tape the most private bedroom conversations of the most important people in American journalism."

"You're crazy. What have you got on me?"

"Taxes, Mister Fletcher."

"What about 'em?"

"You haven't paid any."

Fletch's Fortune

Snatched from bliss on the Riviera, Fletch was flown to the journalism convention with a suitcase full of bugging devices and a bizarre assignment: dig up some juicy scandals on Walter March, the ruthless newspaper tycoon . . . Then Walter March was found lying face up with a long pair of scissors stuck in his back. It was the crime of the century. And a hell of a story.

A blockbuster of suspense by
GREGORY McDONALD

". . . the toughest, leanest horse to hit the literary racetrack since James M. Cain."—PETE HAMILL

 Avon/37978/$1.95

FF 7-78

THE BIG BESTSELLERS
ARE AVON BOOKS

☐	The Human Factor Graham Greene	41491	$2.50
☐	Oliver's Story Erich Segal	42564	$2.25
☐	The Thorn Birds Colleen McCullough	35741	$2.50
☐	The Insiders Rosemary Rogers	40576	$2.50
☐	Kingfisher Gerald Seymour	40592	$2.25
☐	The Trail of the Fox David Irving	40022	$2.50
☐	The Queen of the Night Marc Behm	39958	$1.95
☐	The Bermuda Triangle Charles Berlitz	38315	$2.25
☐	The Real Jesus Garner Ted Armstrong	40055	$2.25
☐	Lancelot Walker Percy	36582	$2.25
☐	Snowblind Robert Sabbag	36947	$1.95
☐	Catch Me: Kill Me William H. Hallahan	37986	$1.95
☐	A Capitol Crime Lawrence Meyer	37150	$1.95
☐	Fletch's Fortune Gregory Mcdonald	37978	$1.95
☐	Voyage Sterling Hayden	37200	$2.50
☐	Humboldt's Gift Saul Bellow	38810	$2.25
☐	Mindbridge Joe Haldeman	33605	$1.95
☐	Polonaise Piers Paul Read	33894	$1.95
☐	The Surface of Earth Reynolds Price	29306	$1.95
☐	The Monkey Wrench Gang Edward Abbey	30114	$1.95
☐	Jonathan Livingston Seagull Richard Bach	34777	$1.75
☐	Working Studs Terkel	34660	$2.50
☐	Shardik Richard Adams	43752	$2.75
☐	Anya Susan Fromberg Schaeffer	25262	$1.95
☐	Watership Down Richard Adams	19810	$1.25

Available at better bookstores everywhere, or order direct from the publisher.